2/02

CRIMINAL ELEMENT

Forge Books by Hugh Holton

Chicago Blues
Criminal Element
The Devil's Shadow
The Left Hand of God
Presumed Dead
Red Lightning
Time of the Assassins
Violent Crimes
Windy City

HUGH HOLTON

CRIMINAL ELEMENT

A TOM DOHERTY ASSOCIATES BOOK

NEW YORK

CRIMINAL ELEMENT

Copyright © 2002 by Hugh Holton

This book is printed on acid-free paper.

A Forge Book
Published by Tom Doherty Associates, LLC
175 Fifth Avenue
New York, NY 10010

www.tor.com

Forge® is a registered trademark of Tom Doherty Associates, LLC.

ISBN 0-312-87787-0

First Edition: February 2002

Printed in the United States of America

0 9 8 7 6 5 4 3 2 1

For Hannah Amiyah Cook

PROLOGUE

Alderman Phillip "Skip" Murphy, Jr. was drunk. He hadn't set out to get himself in this condition when he left City Hall at eight o'clock the previous evening. He'd merely wanted a quiet drink before he headed home to his South Lake Shore Drive bachelor apartment. But circumstances had arisen to not only thwart his plans for the evening, but also place his feet on a very dangerous path.

Skip Murphy was serving his second term in the Chicago City Council. He was a black man with short medium-brown hair and a light brown complexion. In his mid-thirties, he could have been considered handsome had it not been for a weak chin and a tendency to carry twenty extra pounds on his five-foot-nine-inch frame.

Skip had been born in a middle-class neighborhood on the South Side of the city. His father had owned and operated a successful dry cleaning business with Skip's two uncles. The Murphy family business produced a sufficient profit to enable all of the brothers to purchase homes and provide a decent standard of living for their families. Skip's mother was a house-wife, who raised her brood of four—Skip being the oldest—from birth until they left home to go out on their own. Skip had worked in the dry cleaners during summer vacations and discovered before the beginning of his freshman year in high school that he had no intention of following in Phillip Murphy, Sr.'s footsteps. In the future alderman's estimation, the hours were too long, the physical conditions oppressively hot, and the work much too hard. So the younger Murphy began looking around for an easier way to make a living, which led him into the world of politics.

Skip attended Hirsh High School and became deeply involved with student activities, including the school newspaper and annual yearbook publication. However, he wasn't much of a writer and was averse to the extra hours the school's volunteer journalism staff had to put in. So he threw himself headlong into politics and found that he was a natural at the game. He was elected class president in his junior and senior years and voted the "Boy Most Likely To Succeed" by his classmates. Also, along the way, he got three coeds pregnant before one of his uncles took him aside and explained the value of contraception.

After high school, Skip was educated by way of the Chicago city college system and earned a bachelor's degree in sociology. Then he went into professional politics, a career that had led to his two-time election as the alderman of a near southside ward with a population of 72,000 citizens. Now, he sat in a downtown saloon with a full glass of bourbon and water in front of him. This was his sixth drink.

The reason that Skip Murphy was drinking into the early hours of this June morning was cocktail waitress Sophia Novak. She had served him each of the drinks he had consumed. Sophie, as she was called, was a tall, big-boned, twenty-six-year-old woman with shoulder-length blond hair. She wasn't what could be considered pretty, but in Skip Murphy's eyes, she was very sexy.

The Lake Shore Drive Tap was located on Ohio Street, a half block west of Lake Shore Drive. It was a popular bar, which catered to a clientele consisting mostly of the nouveau-riche yuppies living in the area. As an African-American professional politician, Skip Murphy fit right in.

The citywide restaurant chain that owned the Lake Shore Drive Tap operated all of its properties by certain rules. Among them was the installation of dim indirect interior lighting to shroud the cheap chrome and vinyl furnishings, which were usually liberally patched with black duct tape. At one time the profit-conscious proprietors had even watered down the liquor until a complaint to the City of Chicago's Consumer Services Department had resulted in a temporary suspension of their licenses until the violation was rectified. But the owners found other ways to cut costs. Among them was the hiring of service personnel, particularly cocktail waitresses—like Sophia Novak—who had recently arrived in America, spoke passable, but hardly fluent English, and would work for minimum wage, as long as they received decent tips.

Alderman Skip Murphy had watched Sophia Novak, clad in a skimpy bunny costume, walk on long, muscular legs from the bar to the tables in her assigned section a number of times. And each time that she gave him a fresh drink, she had provided him with a little-left-to-the-imagination view of her cleavage. When she had delivered his last drink, she had even blown him a kiss. Now Skip Murphy was not only drunk, but also extremely turned on.

As midnight passed, the number of patrons in the bar dwindled, leaving Skip and a lone couple huddled together in one of the darkened booths as the only drinkers left in Sophie's section. It was then that the alderman decided to make his move. He summoned her to his table.

He got right to the point. "What time do you get off?" Skip had worked to develop a deep, authoritative baritone voice during his political career. Amazingly, it came out virtually devoid of any signs of his growing intoxication.

She gave him a shy smile. "One-thirty, if it's busy." Her accent was quite evident, but her English was good. "The way things are tonight, the other barmaid can handle the whole place by herself."

"Why don't you let me buy you a late supper at the Cape Cod Room in the Drake Hotel?"

Something about the simple immigrant barmaid changed. It was not only in her expression, but also in the way she carried herself. The only way that Skip Murphy could characterize this transformation was to say that she had become blatantly sexual. Suddenly, the usually confident city councilman felt that he was at a disadvantage with this woman.

"Sure, Sophie come with you." Skip wondered if her broken English was part of an act. "But is dinner all you want, mister?"

He fought off bourbon's grip on his brain to say, "Why don't we discuss that over dinner?"

"Okay," she said, turning around and walking away. "I be right back."

The alderman took a long pull of his drink and said, "Things are looking up for the Skipper."

In the narrow storeroom where the bar supplies were kept, a small area had been set up for the barmaids to change into their bunny costumes. Besides a metal wash tub, there was a rack with wire hangers for the workers' street clothes. After convincing the unconcerned bartender, who also served as night manager, to give her permission to take off early, Sophie had gone there to change. As she began stripping off her costume, the other barmaid, Grace Lepkowksi, a middle-aged woman with the figure of a twenty-one year old, also came in.

"What are you up to?" Gracie asked in Polish.

"I've got a live one," Sophie responded in the same language, while stripping naked and turning on the taps in the metal sink. She picked up a well used bar of Dial soap and began to lather herself from head to toe. "I've seen him on the television. He's some kind of official over at City Hall."

Gracie arched one of her thin eyebrows. "You've got to be careful with that type, Sophie. Men like him can make a lot of trouble for people like us."

Sophie began rinsing off the soap. The floor was wet and slippery as she began drying herself with a coarse towel. "He won't want to cause me any problems by the time I'm through with him. Give me a stick of gum."

Gracie handed her a package of Big Red. Sophie popped a piece in her mouth and began to dress. Finally, she stood before Gracie Lepkowski. The blond barmaid was clad in a black skirt, sleeveless white blouse—which was tight enough to accentuate her generous bosom—and a pair of recently purchased medium-heel black shoes. With her hair neatly combed, Gracie was struck by her native countrywoman's beauty.

As she headed for the door Sophie said, "Call Stella and tell her I'll be home late."

"Be careful, Sophie," Gracie cautioned.

"Don't be such an old grandmother, Gracie."

Then Sophie Novak was gone.

Joe Donegan had been a cop for nine years and a detective assigned to Area Six Violent Crimes for the last three years. His supervisors considered him a fair to mediocre investigator, because he expended a minimal amount of effort in getting the job done and was usually late with his reports. However, despite his bosses' opinions, Joe Donegan was a very hard-working man. A very hard-working man indeed.

Detective Donegan was a singularly unspectacular individual in appearance. He was of average height, standing five-feet-eight-inches tall, and of medium weight at 175 pounds. His hair was sandy-colored, but at the age of thirty-seven it was beginning to thin on top and going gray rapidly. He dressed in the conservative business attire of the Chicago police detective, which consisted of suits, sport coats, and slacks that usually came off the rack at JC Penney's or Sears. But there were two things about Joe Donegan that were different from the norm. One was that he had unusual eyes with irises of such a dark brown hue as to make them appear black. More than one of the people he came into contact with remarked that Donegan had dead, lifeless eyes like those of a shark. And the nondescript detective was capable of producing a stare that could chill even the most hearty to the very core of their being. The other thing that set Joe Donegan apart from his colleagues was his choice of on- and off-duty weapons.

Donegan carried a number of very formidable firearms on his person. Strapped to his waist on a Sam Browne belt, which was usually only worn by officers in uniform, was a four-inch-barrel .44 magnum revolver. Also on the belt were three speed loaders containing twelve rounds of magnum ammunition. In a shoulder holster he carried a 9mm Centennial-model Browning semiautomatic pistol with a fourteen-round magazine. Due to the bulk of these weapons he wore oversized suit jackets. He also carried a .38 Colt Detective Special in a holster strapped to his right ankle. To his fellow detectives, Donegan's excessive weaponry was something of a joke, and behind his back he was called the Demented Cabbie after Travis Bickel. In the popular film *Taxi Driver*, Travis Bickel, portrayed by Robert De Niro, also carried a large number of firearms. Donegan was an expert marksman with each of the guns he carried and would not hesitate to use them, although he had never been involved in an "official" shooting incident.

Detective Joe Donegan was off duty when he walked into the Lake Shore Tap, but he was definitely working. The bartender, a swarthy man with curly black hair, recognized the detective and reached beneath the bar for a white envelope. Inside this envelope were ten fifty-dollar bills. This was the Lake Shore Tap's price for staying in business. Detective Donegan was what was known as a "necessary business expense" on the unofficial accounting ledgers of the chain that owned the Lake Shore Tap.

When the detective walked over to him, the bartender placed the white envelope on the bar. Affixing the man with his dead stare, Donegan said, "What's that?"

"Your payoff from the main office."

Joe Donegan became very still. "Tell me something. How long have you been a bartender?"

The man frowned in confusion. "About three, maybe four years."

"Now I've heard it said that a good bartender is a fairly good judge of character. Is that true?"

The bartender shrugged. "I guess so." Then, after thinking for a moment, he added, "Yeah, I guess you could say that I'm pretty good at sizing guys up."

"Then why, my libation-dispensing friend, do you think that I am a complete and utter fool?"

The bartender stammered, "I . . . uh . . . don't . . ."

The detective's stare cut right through the man. "Of course you don't. How could you with the birth defect rate being so high?" Donegan took a seat on one of the bar stools. "Now this is how we're going to play this. You are to pick up that envelope and, after making sure there are no prying eyes to observe you, remove whatever is inside. Then you will take my drink order."

The bartender listened in dumbfounded silence.

"Now ask me what I want to drink."

"Okay. What'll it be?"

"A club soda on the rocks with a wedge of lime."

The bartender started to turn away.

"Wait a minute," Donegan said. "I'm not finished. After you pour my drink, you will collect this." The cop placed a twenty dollar bill on the bar. "When you return my change, you will add the contents of the envelope to it. Have you got all of that?"

"I think so," the bartender said.

While he waited Joe Donegan went over the reason behind his collection of tonight's payoff. It had been a simple shakedown. He was assigned by the Area Six case management sergeant to conduct a follow-up investigation into a robbery that had been reported at the St. Joseph's Hospital emergency room.

The victim had reported that he had been drinking in the Lake Shore Tap. When he left, two black men wearing dark clothing had robbed him out on the street. The middle-aged victim had a blood-alcohol level of .34 and couldn't provide much additional information about his assailants. But the fact that the victim had been in the Lake Shore Tap and had gotten drunk there before he got mugged was of primary importance to Detective Donegan. A report to the Consumer Services Department, after the problems the Lake Shore Tap had had with watered-down liquor, could result in a permanent license revocation. A revocation that would cost the owners a lot more than the five hundred dollars Donegan demanded for his silence. After he had skillfully presented his proposition to the general manager of the chain that operated the bar, the deal had been made.

The bartender returned with the club soda and the change. He'd even had enough sense to mix the fifties in with ten singles. Although Donegan gave him credit for that, the cop still considered the bartender an idiot.

Joe Donegan was about to polish off his club soda and vacate this dump when he recognized Alderman Skip Murphy sitting in one of the booths. One look at Murphy was all it took for the detective to detect that the aldermam was drunk. Then the well-built blond woman walked out of a room behind the bar and went over to join Murphy. Donegan watched as they left the bar together. Finishing his drink, the cop followed them out of the Lake Shore Tap.

Skip Murphy was astounded at the amount of food Sophie Novak put away. When they arrived at the Cape Cod Room of the Drake Hotel, the alderman was recognized by the maitre'd, who at Murphy's request, seated them in a secluded alcove. The barmaid had proceeded to order a fifty-dollar bottle of champagne, which she proceeded to drink like it was water. Although he didn't need it, Skip managed to down one glass before Sophie finished the bottle. When the dinner menus came, she ordered the most expensive items on it, including Beluga caviar served on a bed of frozen vodka crystals. For her entrée she ordered a whole lobster. Displaying atrocious table manners, she ate everything, finishing with apple pie topped with a scoop of vanilla ice cream. The steak sandwich Skip consumed and the size of the bill sobered him considerably. But during dinner, the couple had come to an arrangement. In fact, Skip Murphy was shocked at the blunt manner with which Sophie accepted his sexual proposition. She had told him, "Giving you a roll in the hay is the least I can do to repay you for such a nice dinner."

When they left the restaurant, Skip Murphy was feeling better than he had in a long time and Sophie was hanging on his arm.

Joe Donegan's car was a five-year-old dark blue Ford with black-wall tires. It looked like a plainclothes' cop car, which was easily identifiable on city streets. This was not a drawback for the crooked cop, because he could go virtually anywhere and park indefinitely without being hassled. The car also allowed him to blend in with the urban landscape.

With a cup of Dunkin' Donuts coffee in the dash-mounted cup holder, Donegan was parked directly across the street from the south entrance of the Drake Hotel. He waited patiently for the alderman and the blond woman to emerge. It was almost

3:00 A.M. when the couple came out and the valet parking attendant delivered the alderman's late-model Camaro.

Donegan always carried a Nikon camera with a long-range lens in the glove compartment of the Ford. Using it now he snapped a number of photographs of the alderman and his date. Right now the pictures had no value, but the night, or rather the morning, Donegan mused, was young.

When the alderman, who was legally intoxicated, got behind the wheel and drove off, the detective followed.

Although his mind was fuzzy, Skip Murphy was still smart enough to take the barmaid to a motel for their sexual interlude, instead of to his apartment. He picked a no-questions-asked establishment called the South Michigan Avenue Motel in a ward that adjoined his own. Skip Murphy got out of the car and went into the motel office to register. A black woman sporting a short Afro had him fill out a card and collected the thirty-five-dollar room fee. He was not required to present any identification or give her his license plate number. The female clerk read the name, "Mr. and Mrs. James Smith," and the phony address on the card. Then she said, "Have a good time, Alderman Murphy."

But Skip was so preoccupied with what he and Sophie were about to do that he didn't care about being recognized. He returned to his car with the key to Room 1C.

Detective Donegan drove into the motel parking lot just as the alderman and the barmaid entered the room, which was located three doors from the motel office. Donegan parked the Ford on the opposite side of the parking lot and again settled in to wait.

His only regret was that he hadn't been able to snap a picture of them entering the room. However, he planned to be there when they came out.

The sky began brightening when the sounds of violence erupted from inside Room 1C. Donegan had remained wide awake during the hours he had been tailing Alderman Skip Murphy. Briefly the detective wrestled with the problem of how he could get a picture of the alderman and the blonde in the act. He had checked the front windows, which were covered with tightly closed blinds. He had even walked around to examine the bathroom window, which was off a filthy, garbage-strewn alley. But the opaque glass frame, which was painted shut, sent him back to his car. All he could do now was get a picture of them on the way out.

Now Donegan could hear the sounds of a fight coming from inside 1C. Maybe things would turn out better than he had anticipated.

Since the alderman had checked into the motel, no additional guests had arrived. Other than Murphy's Camaro and Donegan's Ford, there were only three other cars in the lot. This indicated that there were few guests in residence. So there would be few, if any, witnesses to what was going on in Room 1C.

The detective got out of his car and crossed to the alderman's hotel room. The sounds of the fight had stopped and all was now silent. He banged hard on the door with his fist and yelled, "Police! Open up!"

The black woman from the office stuck her head out of the door and said, "What's going on?"

Donegan turned away, so that she couldn't see his face, and lifted his badge. All she would be able to see was the flash of metal. She was too far away to read the numbers on the badge or see the name or photograph on his identification card. "I'm a police officer," he called to her. "I'll check this out."

Then the door to 1C opened a crack and the bleeding and bruised Alderman Skip Murphy appeared. Donegan shoved his way inside and shut the door behind him.

The interior of the room consisted of basic cheap motel décor. Donegan remarked silently that the place was clean. At least it had been before the alderman and his blond lover arrived. Room 1C was now a wreck. Glasses had been smashed, the mirror over the dresser was broken, and the bedclothes were twisted into sweat-stained ropes. Then there was the blood.

Bright red stains dotted the bed, the headboard, and the floor. It took only a glance for Donegan to see that all of this blood came from the naked alderman's nose and mouth. The detective looked around for the woman. From the door all that he could see was one of her feet up on the bed. The rest of her was on the floor.

"What happened here?" Donegan demanded of Murphy.

The alderman staggered over to the bed, slumped down on its side, and cradled his bleeding head in his hands. Quickly, Donegan crossed to the nude man and handcuffed him to the headboard. The alderman's head came up briefly and he looked through bleary eyes at the steel bracelet now adorning his wrist. However, he made no comment.

Donegan then went to check on the woman. She lay motionless on her back with her legs splayed open. Her nudity transmitted to Donegan that she was a natural blonde. A massive bruise, that was beginning to swell, was visible above her right temple. Although she was unconscious, her eyes were partially open and her breathing labored.

"I'm going to be sick," Murphy said.

Donegan came around the bed, removed the headboard handcuff and led the alderman into the small bathroom. Murphy dropped to his knees and lowered his head into the toilet bowl. He became violently ill and Donegan was forced to hold his breath against the stench of regurgitated booze. The detective handcuffed his prisoner to a pipe beneath the face bowl and left the alderman alone, closing the door behind him.

Back in the bedroom, Donegan checked the woman once more. She had not moved and was quite obviously in a bad way. An egg-shaped knot was forming on her forehead and the temple bruise was growing darker. The detective knew she needed emergency first aid right now or she would probably die. Then Alderman Skip Murphy would really be in trouble.

The idea came to Detective Joe Donegan so suddenly and with such impact that he didn't have to go over the details. Right now the equation only included this woman and Skip Murphy. Now he decided to become a factor. Donegan removed a blood- and sweat-stained pillow from the bed and straddled the unconscious woman's upper body. Placing the pillow over her face, he held it down with all of his weight for several minutes until he was certain that she was dead.

Skip Murphy was unaware of how long he had been kneeling on the cold tile floor. He had flushed the toilet to get rid of his stomach's contents, but the smell remained. He tried to get to his feet, but the encumbering handcuff and his weakened condition made this impossible. Then the policeman returned.

Pushing the shower curtain aside, Donegan sat on the edge of the tub and looked down at the wretched, nude man. Then he removed a camera from his baggy suit jacket and took a picture of the alderman.

"What was that for?" Murphy asked, weakly.

"Call it a souvenir," Donegan said, returning the camera to his pocket. "You want to tell me what happened?"

Murphy looked at the closed bathroom door. "That broad is crazy. She comes in here with me and screws like she can't get enough. Then I want to vary the action a bit and . . ."

"Alderman Murphy," Donegan said with surprise tinged with sarcasm, "are you into kinky sex?"

Murphy frowned, as if he was suddenly in excruciating pain. Taking a deep breath, he whispered, "Who did you say you were again?"

Donegan removed the black leather badge case from his pocket and extended it at arm's length. Squinting, Murphy read the identification card and compared the photograph to that of the man seated across from him. Murphy attempted to adjust his body on the cold floor, which made the handcuff bracelet cut into his skin. "Is this necessary?"

"Sure it is," Donegan taunted. "After all, you are under arrest."

For a brief instant, Alderman Skip Murphy looked as if he was going to be ill again. Then, despite his being naked and handcuffed to a sink in the bathroom of a cheap motel room, he managed to summon some of his large stores of pride and arrogance and say, "That's the most ridiculous thing I've ever heard, Detective Donegan. In fact, she hit me first."

The emotionless black pools that were Joe Donegan's eyes bore into Skip Murphy. The detective said, "But she's dead, Alderman."

This time Murphy's reaction was decidedly more pronounced. His eyes widened in shock and his mouth opened as he attempted to speak, but no sound came out. Then he started to tremble violently. Silently, Joe Donegan waited.

Finally, the alderman found his voice. "This can't be happening."

The detective shrugged. "Oh, it happened, Alderman, and you did it."

"But it was an accident. I didn't mean to do it. I was defending myself," Murphy pleaded.

"I'm quite sure that you were." Now was the time for Donegan to bait the hook. "She was a big girl and you were in something of a depleted condition physically." However, he didn't want to overdo it. "But you understand the reality of such things, Alderman. You're a black man engaged in an immoral act with a white woman. Maybe with the right lawyer you can get off with a voluntary manslaughter charge. That'll net you a few years in the joint, but you won't do time in one of those country club prisons. You're going to Stateville. Now that won't be very nice, Alderman. Not very nice at all."

Although he was experiencing intense distress, Skip Murphy was still a political animal and capable of detecting the underlying message in the policeman's words. Slowly, he began bringing his emotions under control so that he could think better. Despite Sophie being dead, this might work out for him.

"Perhaps . . ." Murphy paused to search carefully for the right words, ". . . perhaps we can come to some type of accommodation?"

Donegan's stare intensified to the point that it made the nude man uneasy. When the policeman spoke, his tone was angry and mocking. "I always figured that you politicians over at City Hall were crooked enough to begin with, but trying to get away with murder is really too much."

Not to be denied, Murphy pressed, "I will make it well worth your while, if we can make this problem go away."

Donegan raised an eyebrow. "We?"

"There are a number of things that will have to be . . ."

Donegan held up his hand, silencing the alderman. "I know exactly what to do to make this thing, as you say 'go away,' but the price is going to be high. Very high."

Murphy scrambled onto his knees. "I can pay you. My father left me a fortune from his dry cleaning business. I'm also an influential member of the city council." He would have added more, but there was something in the detective's gaze that frightened him to such an extent that goose bumps erupted on his exposed flesh.

The leer Joe Donegan cast on the murderer was that of a madman. Donegan had never looked at anyone like this before, because there had been no reason to reveal his psychotic personality. Now he could do so with Murphy, because they were about to become partners in crime. The alderman had no way of knowing it, but he had just made a deal with the devil.

The first item of business was to remove every trace of the alderman's presence in the motel. The sky was brightening rapidly, but the sun was not yet up when Detective Donegan exited Room 1C into the silent motel parking lot. The same number of cars were in the lot and there were no signs of life anywhere in the area. The policeman proceeded to the motel office. The clerk, who had checked Murphy in, was still on duty. She was obviously nervous when Donegan entered.

"What happened down there?" she said. "I don't need no trouble on my shift, especially when it involves an alderman."

Donegan's dead eyes scanned her from head to toe. "So you know who he is."

She nodded.

"That is very unfortunate."

It took the two of them to carry Sophie Novak's body from the motel room. They put it in the trunk of Donegan's car.

When they were finished the detective turned to the alderman and said, "Make yourself scarce for at least a week so that you can heal up. Do you have someplace you can hole up outside the city?"

Murphy, disheveled with blood still on his face, was dazed as he said, "I can go to my uncle's cabin in Union Pier, Michigan."

"Is there a telephone there?"

Murphy was staring at the trunk of the Ford.

"Is there a telephone there?" the policeman repeated more insistently.

The alderman managed to nod.

"Give me the address and the number."

A few minutes later, they drove from the lot in their separate cars.

The sun was spreading its rays across the Windy City when an explosion ripped through the South Michigan Avenue Motel. The resulting fire consumed most of the structure, which was constructed of substandard materials and had a faulty sprinkler system. The explosion was later found to originate in a gas stove in the motel office. The motel clerk and three of the six guests renting rooms in the establishment were killed. The three survivors received third-degree burns over 50 percent of their bodies. No one saw or heard anything suspicious before the motel became engulfed in flames. Room 1C was completely destroyed in the fire, which would later be classified as an arson, making the deaths that occurred there homicides.

PART

I

"It ain't on the legit."
—Detective Joe Donegan

1

Detectives Lou Bronson and Manny Sherlock were directed to investigate the homicides by arson at the South Michigan Avenue Motel. They were assigned to the Area One Detective Division under the command of Commander Larry Cole. Their case-management sergeant was Blackie Silvestri. Bronson and Sherlock were considered two of the best detectives in one of the highest crime areas in one of the largest cities in the United States.

Bronson, a stocky, balding African-American with gray hair and a wise manner, was the senior detective. He was a sharp dresser, who wore custom-tailored suits and stylish hats. He always stood out when he arrived at crime scenes, but this was not just because he looked good. Lou Bronson was the type of officer who other cops went to when they needed answers. Of course they could always go to their supervisors, but most of those seeking Bronson's aid had discovered long ago that the black detective was not only always right, but gave his advice willingly and without reservation.

Manny Sherlock was white, six-feet-four-inches tall and beginning to put on a little weight after being a gangly beanpole with an Abe Lincoln lean figure for his first few years on the department. He purchased his clothes from the same tailor as Lou Bronson and had also begun imitating some of the black detective's mannerisms and figures of speech. Lou Bronson had been raised on the South Side of Chicago in the predominantly African-American Washington Park Boulevard enclave. So when Manny uttered such phrases as, "Look, my man," or "Right on, brother," or "Get righteous, fool, before I bust a cap in your behind," he had generally been looked at with varying degrees of shock and amusement.

But one thing was indisputable: When Bronson and Sherlock were assigned to investigate a homicide, it was usually safe to say that someone would soon be going to jail.

Sherlock parked the unmarked black Chevrolet police car behind the Bomb and Arson Unit van on Michigan Avenue and the two detectives got out. Bronson was wearing a tan suit with a yellow shirt and dark brown shoes, socks and a yellow-and-brown patterned tie. On his head was a flat-topped straw hat with a brown hatband. Sherlock was dressed in a natty dark brown blazer; however, all of his accessories, at least color-wise, were exactly the same as Bronson's. Sherlock was hatless and despite his obvious efforts with a comb and brush to bring order to his dark brown hair, it was still standing up in odd places. Once, when Sherlock had complained about his unruly mop, Bronson had told him, "Don't sweat it, my man, it gives you character." This comment had made Sherlock feel marginally better about his appearance.

The uniformed sergeant from the Second Police District, who was in charge at the burned-out motel crime scene, was the superbly muscular, dark-complexioned Clarence McKinnis. Mack, as the sergeant was called, had been a high-school classmate of Commander Cole. Seeing the detectives approach, he disengaged himself from a group of uniformed cops and walked over to brief them.

The sergeant possessed a deep baritone voice with a near melodious quality. "Bomb and Arson just finished up, guys, and the fire was definitely set intentionally. The point of origin was the manager's office located on the south end of the parking lot driveway. There was a gas stove in a small room behind the counter. Even with all of the debris from the explosion and fire, the arson investigators found a full book of matches inside the stove. Apparently our perpetrator blew out the pilot light, rigged the matchbook for all of the matches to ignite at once by either using a lit cigarette or a single match as a fuse, and turned on all of the gas jets. When a sufficient volume of gas built up and the matches ignited, there was an explosion."

"Crime lab people through with the scene yet, sarge?" Bronson asked.

"Everything's wrapped up, Lou. We were just waiting for you."

"Let's go, Manny."

As they walked away, McKinnis called to them, "How is Commander Cole doing?"

Bronson said, "Just great, Sarge. We'll tell him you said hello when we get back to the station."

The second floor of the motel had collapsed and pancaked onto the first-floor ceiling making the complex appear to have consisted of only a single story. Of the thirty rooms on the first level of the former motel, all of the windows and doors were gone and in order to effectively fight the fire, the Chicago Fire Department was forced to ventilate the individual units by knocking holes in the rear walls. The surviving injured had

been removed to the Burn Unit of Cook County Hospital. The
dead were left on the scene in the exact positions in which they
were found to make it easier for the homicide detectives to
discover who had caused their deaths and why.

Despite it being the origin of the fire, the motel office was
in fairly good shape, although every surface had been charred
to a crisp. Yellow barrier tape bearing the admonition in bold
black lettering, "Police Line—Do Not Cross," was stretched
completely around the property. Water dripped from the ceiling
and walls, which forced Bronson and Sherlock to return to their
police car. There they removed their jackets and donned rubber
raincoats and knee boots. Then they entered the burned-out
structure.

Bronson and Sherlock were inside for forty-five minutes.
Once, during that period, Sherlock came out and asked a crime
lab technician to go back inside with them to photograph an
area of the crime scene from a particular angle. When they
finally did exit the burned-out building, their faces and hands
were streaked with soot, but, when they removed the rubber
coats and boots, their clothing was still immaculate.

Sergeant McKinnis and four officers were waiting for them.
It was only after the detectives gave the word could they remove the bodies to the morgue and cease protection of the
crime scene. The sergeant stood by as they packed their gear,
including kelite flashlights and a metal case containing mag-
nifying glasses, a metal tape measure, and miscellaneous investigative tools, into the trunk of their squad car. Beneath the
dirt on the detectives' faces, Mack could tell that they were far
from happy.

"Is it that bad, guys?" the sergeant asked.

Bronson was lost in thought, so Sherlock responded,

"We've got a textbook arson here, Sarge. It doesn't look like the work of a professional torch, because there was no attempt to make the fire look like it started accidentally."

Bronson came out of his mood of deep concentration. "That fire was set to cover something up. I'd also be willing to bet that when the woman inside the office is autopsied, the M.E. will discover that she was killed before the fire started."

"Where are you guys going to go from here?" Sergeant McKinnis asked.

"After we get cleaned up, we've going to interview the owners of this place. But I've got the feeling that it won't lead us anywhere."

Detective Bronson was absolutely right.

Detective Joe Donegan got to his desk early at the Area Six Police Center located at Western and Belmont on the North Side. He had been up all night, but didn't feel the slightest bit tired. Last night had been the most important of his life. The five hundred dollars he had collected from the Lake Shore Tap was now, in the vernacular of the Chicago streets, nothing but chump change.

Donegan now had a Chicago alderman in his pocket, which was a powerful bargaining chip for a cop of Donegan's ilk. And the criminal-minded cop planned to suck everything he could out of Alderman Phillip "Skip" Murphy, Jr.

The majority of the cops who go bad do so after they've been on the job awhile. Then due to greed, deteriorating moral character, and, in some cases, peer pressure, they surrender to negative influences and become part of the criminal element they are sworn to combat. Donegan was an exception to this rule, because he had joined the Chicago Police Department with the specific intention in mind of using his badge to steal.

Joseph Patrick Terrence Donegan had been born in the same year and in the same city as Alderman Skip Murphy. However, they were raised in completely different worlds. Donegan came up in the Marquette Park neighborhood, which was known for the high number of city employees who resided there, the good quality of its parochial and public schools, and its virulent racism. Racism that had been known to erupt into open violence against innocent blacks and Hispanics who happened to wander into the area.

In 1966 Dr. Martin Luther King, Jr. led an open housing march into the all-white neighborhood, which resulted in the residents coming out en masse to pelt the peaceful marchers with bottles and rocks. Joe Donegan was raised in this environment.

Donegan's father, Robert "Bob" Donegan, Sr. was a Chicago fireman, who was capable of single-handedly consuming an entire case of Budweiser at one sitting. The future cop couldn't remember much about his father and had no recollection at all of him without a beer can in his hand. Lieutenant Bob Donegan of the CFD perished in a warehouse fire when young Joe was seven. The family managed to get by on his line-of-duty-death insurance policy.

The Donegan clan consisted of four children: Bob Jr., the oldest, Ted, Joe, and their baby sister Megan. Their mother Barbara, who had been two years older than their martyred father, never remarried. As the years went by, she developed a fondness for vodka, which she drank by the fifth. She rapidly aged toward debilitation, forcing her children to care for her. This was a task that Joe hated. He also developed a pronounced aversion to liquor in any form, which he never touched. And although his father's pension was generous by middle-class standards, in Joe's estimation there was never enough money when he was growing up.

There was enough for the necessities of life, but little more. The oldest son, Bob Jr., kept a tight rein on the purse strings and, at an early age, all of the Donegan children were forced to get part-time jobs after school. Then, as each of them became old enough, they were given city jobs. Bob Jr. and Ted followed in their dead father's footsteps. Megan got a job as a clerk for the Water Department at City Hall and Joe joined the police department. Joe arrived at this decision after giving his choice of career a great deal of thought.

There was a saying about the internal workings of the government of the City of Chicago, as it applied to the all-white Marquette Park neighborhood, that went, "It ain't on the legit." This meant that anything could be taken care of in the Windy City if one had the right connections and the requisite amount of cash. All of the Donegan family's city jobs had been obtained through the local precinct captain's ward office and, although each of them was required to go through screening for their positions, there was no chance of them being rejected as "unqualified." This was because, "It ain't on the legit."

The first day he entered the police academy, Donegan began working toward his goal. This entailed learning as much as he could about not only the department, but also the officers who commanded it. Probationary Police Officer Joseph Patrick Terrence Donegan was an exceptional recruit in the estimation of his instructors at the Chicago Police Academy. In fact, on more than one of his monthly fitness reports, the word "obsessive" was used. And, despite the hours he spent in training, PPO Donegan went home and hit the books for an additional

four to six hours a night. On the pistol range, he was also
superior. The only area in which he did not excel was physical
training, because he simply didn't possess the physical gifts of
some of his classmates. However, he still finished first in his
class.

Donegan was initially assigned to the Sixteenth Police District near O'Hare International Airport. "Sixteen" was known
as a country-club station, because the volume of calls was very
low and there was little reported crime. Officers possessing limited ambition were known to spend their entire careers in the
Sixteenth District. Joe Donegan had no such intentions.

As soon as he was off probation, Donegan requested a
transfer to the Eleventh Police District, which was in the heart
of a high crime, ghetto area known as the "Wild Wild West
Side." There he jumped into high intensity police work with
both feet. To say that Donegan was "gung ho" would be a gross
understatement. He was so aggressive that he was often called
to the side by supervisors and veteran officers and told to slow
down before he got himself killed. But despite appearances, Joe
Donegan was being extremely cautious. Being a city martyr,
like his dead firefighter father, was not in his plans. His aggressive attitude toward police work enabled him to learn faster. And he was learning a great deal.

At this early stage of his career, Donegan had yet to engage
in any form of corruption. He was patiently awaiting the right
opportunity, which he was certain would eventually come.

Unlike the citizenry of the "country club" Sixteenth Police
District, the residents of the Eleventh District were all black
and poor, and the number of crimes in "Eleven" was substan-
tially higher than in more affluent neighborhoods in the city.
There were also certain societal elements present, which con-

tributed to particular types of law-breaking. These elements were blatant racism, lack of proper education for the majority of the residents, narcotics and alcohol abuse. The law-breaking these conditions bred was a high incidence of public drunkenness, a plethora of illegal firearms on the streets, and a large number of violations by vehicle operators.

At the beginning of his second year in the department, Donegan, working alone, conducted his first traffic shakedown. It was of a reputed drug dealer, who was driving drunk and carrying a pistol. Faced with a choice between going to jail and paying the cop off, the dealer paid. The price was two hundred dollars. Donegan did a few more of these traffic shakedowns; however, he realized that they were too high-risk for the return gained. As the third year of his police career began, he decided to take his plan to the next level, which was to seek an assignment out of uniform.

The Area Six squad room was filling up rapidly with day watch detectives. None of the men and women in civilian dress spoke to Detective Donegan and he ignored them as well. He was not very well liked by either his fellow officers or his supervisors. Also he was the only Area Six Detective, specializing in the follow-up investigations of violent crimes, who was allowed to work alone. This was by way of mutual agreement between Donegan and the other detectives.

The commander of Area Six Detectives was Richard Shelby, who was a nondescript type and who seemed out of his depth to command a detective area. In the cheap conservative business attire that most of the detectives in the room wore, and with his hair slicked back from a high forehead and held in place with hair tonic, Shelby stepped to the podium at the front of the room. The lieutenants in command of the Violent Crimes and Property Crimes sections stood behind him.

Donegan suppressed a sneer. Shelby was about to spout off about some big operation he wanted to initiate. This commander was a notorious grandstander, a shameless butt-kisser, and an unrepentant blowhard. Shelby didn't know it, but he had provided a single item about which Detective Joe Donegan and his fellow detectives were in complete agreement. That was that they all felt that Commander Dick Shelby was a total asshole.

"Could I have your attention please," the commander said. "I'll only take a few minutes of your time."

Shelby talked for half an hour.

Police Officer Joe Donegan realized, after only spending three years on the CPD that being assigned to uniform duty was an extreme drawback to his larcenous pursuits. Actually, everything about working "in the bag," as it was commonly called by police officers nationally, made undetected misconduct virtually impossible. This was due to the traditional police uniform being festooned with identifiers.

Every badge bore distinctive numerals and the cap shield bore a duplicate of these numbers, which were as individual to the officer as his social security number. Additional identifiers were their district or precinct numbers on their uniforms, and marked police vehicles bore not only license plate numbers, but also individual police vehicle numbers with oversized numerals. However, the simplest way to identify an officer wearing a police uniform was to read his name tag over the right breast of his outer garment. Because of this, most officers working in the bag conducted themselves in an appropriate manner.

This became even more intensely the case with the advent of civilians videotaping police actions.

But Joe Donegan was not about to let such encumbrances make him vulnerable to a system that was set up to elevate the privileged at the expense of the little guy. In addition to this philosophy, Donegan had also discovered that uniformed street work was dangerous. During the three years that he was assigned to the Eleventh Police District, four officers were killed in the line of duty.

With the help of his older brother Ted, Joe obtained a transfer to the Vice Control Section of the Organized Crime Division. Vice Control was responsible for spearheading investigations into organized narcotics, gambling, and prostitution operations. Most of the investigations conducted were undercover, which authorized the assigned officers to work in casual clothing and drive undercover cars. For Joe Donegan, working Vice Control was the equivalent of celebrating every Christmas and birthday of his life. And although the Chicago Police Department didn't know it, he had just been issued a license to steal.

Utilizing the same "obsessed" attention that had taken him to the top of his police academy class, Donegan studied every mission undertaken by his fellow cops in the Vice Control Section. Despite being assigned to the Prostitution Unit, which primarily kept an eye on the mob-operated call girl operations in the city and contiguous suburbs, he closely and carefully monitored the Gambling and Narcotics Units. Hacking into the Vice Control Section's central computer from his home computer was the "careful" part. The "closely" part was that during the three years that he was assigned to the Prostitution Unit, Donegan collected extensive files on every mob figure, major dope dealer, Mafia pimp, and high-stakes gambler that came to the attention of the Chicago Police Department. Along the way the crooked cop used the "careful" part of his illegal enterprise to make a great deal of money by engaging in simple, but anonymous "cash for information" exchanges. Officer Joe Donegan became so good at making anonymous contacts and setting up dead-letter money drops to collect cash bribes from the criminals he was helping, that he began considering himself invincible. This was a mistake.

The mental reference to him being "invincible" brought him back to the here and now in the Area Six squad room on the morning of June 13, 1992. Commander Shelby was still talking. As far as Donegan was concerned the commander was a complete idiot. Had it not been for Shelby using the same source of political influence that Donegan did, Shelby would still be on a beat car. Donegan also had a negative opinion of the majority of the department's command officers. However, there were a few whom he respected, because they were good cops. And good cops were a serious threat to all levels of the criminal element. One of these cops was Commander Larry Cole, Shelby's opposite number in Area One Detectives. Another cop that Donegan was wary of was a crazy undercover Narc he had known when he was in the Organized Crime Division. Her name was Judy Daniels and she went by the moniker, "The Mistress of Disguise/High Priestess of Mayhem." She had forced Donegan's hasty transfer to the Detective Division three years ago. He still owed her for that.

Finally, Shelby concluded his lengthy remarks by saying, "I want all of you to do your jobs and be careful out there."

As the Area Six Detective Commander stepped from the podium, he didn't see Detective Joe Donegan smiling at him. In the mind working behind those black pools that Donegan called eyes, the crooked cop was thinking, "I always do my job, Commander, and I'm also always extremely careful."

2

JUNE 13, 1992

NOON

Commander Larry Cole was working at his desk at the Area One Police Center located at 5101 South Wentworth. He had been at it since 8:30 and was so immersed in the crime reports he was reviewing that he had lost all track of time. The commander was conducting a review of unsolved felony cases from the past five years with an eye toward reassigning them for additional investigation. He had created two piles on top of his desk. One contained reports in which all possible leads had been exhausted; the other were reports he had attached stick-on message slips to. These message slips contained suggestions for the detectives assigned to these cases to go over certain aspects of the already completed investigations or to proceed in a completely new direction. Cole was quite adept at probing these old cases and finding that one insignificant or seemingly unimportant fact, which was missed at the time of the initial investigation. This had led to the arrests of surprised perpetrators who had thought they had gotten away scot-free.

Cole had just completed the review of the four-year-old

unsolved homicide of a twenty-six-year-old male who had been hacked to death with a machete in a Hyde Park garden apartment. Despite an exhaustive investigation conducted at the time, the case still remained open. During his review, Cole noticed that a number of fingerprints, which had not belonged to the victim or any of his acquaintances, were discovered at the scene. In due course they had been collected and run through the computerized Automated Fingerprint Identification System (AFIS) without obtaining a match. This was because whoever the prints belonged to was not in the system. Four years had passed, Cole mused, which could have altered that situation. The person, whose prints were all over the murder weapon, could now be on file. Cole wrote a note to the case management sergeant to have the prints run through AFIS again.

Had there been anyone in the office observing the detective commander, they would have seen a handsome black man with curly hair and the well-defined features of a matinee idol. He had a wiry, but tightly muscular body with broad shoulders and thick arm muscles tapering to a narrow waist. It was difficult to guess his age and he could pass for a man as young as thirty or as old as fifty. He was somewhere in between. Larry Cole also wore the conservative business attire of the Chicago police detective, although he dressed more along the polished lines of Lou Bronson and Manny Sherlock, as opposed to the off-the-rack drabness of Joe Donegan and Dick Shelby. Cole's weapon of choice, which was strapped to his waist in a hand-tooled black leather holster, was a 9mm Beretta 92FS semiautomatic pistol equipped with a nineteen round Ramline clip. Although he had been doing most of his work via computer or ballpoint pen since he had been promoted to the rank of commander, he tried to get to the range and practice with his firearm at least once a month.

There was a knock on the commander's office door followed by Sergeant Blackie Silvestri coming in. Blackie was Cole's best friend in the department, as they had been partners on the Nineteenth District tactical team fifteen years ago. The sergeant was a barrel-chested, powerfully built man with thinning black hair. A no-nonsense scowl that was usually wrapped around an unlit cigar seemed to be his perpetual expression and he was known as a man's man in the mold popularized by such movie personalities as Sean Connery and Anthony Quinn.

Blackie carried a folder stuffed with reports. He took a seat across from the commander and said, "Bronson and Sherlock just got back from interviewing the owners of the South Michigan Avenue Motel. The place was insured, but what the owners will get won't come anywhere near to covering the cost of rebuilding the joint. Lou Bronson doesn't think it was an arson for profit, but instead a fire set to cover up another crime."

"With four people dead," Cole said, "that means whoever did it was probably trying to hide a murder."

"Lou and Manny both agree, boss, and we just got a call from the medical examiner's office. The motel clerk, a . . ." he consulted the folder he carried, ". . . Anna Collins, died of multiple skull fractures. We took a look into her background and she had a sheet." Blackie pulled out her police record. "She had six prior arrests for everything from shoplifting to forgery. Her last bust was in 1979 and she did eighteen months in the women's reformatory in Joliet. Since then she's been clean. Had the job at the motel for the past two years. According to the owners, she was a reliable employee. She was single and had no known boyfriends. Lived with her sister, a Louise Johnson, a few blocks from the motel. Lou and Manny broke the bad news to the sister and she took it hard. When they were finally able to get some information from her, she pretty much said that our dead night clerk had no enemies that she knew of and, outside of her job, her only other interest was politics."

"Politics?" Cole said.

"Yeah, she was quite active in local politics," Blackie explained. "She worked as a volunteer in the ward office, was a block captain, and served as a poll watcher for the losing aldermanic candidate in the last election."

"I doubt if that got her killed," Cole said.

"Yeah," Blackie agreed. "Especially since her guy lost the election."

Cole glanced at his watch. "Tell Bronson and Sherlock to keep digging until they come up with something. I've got an appointment with my physical therapist."

Attempting to sneak into the resort town of Union Pier, Michigan, at the beginning of the summer vacation season was not the easiest task that the bruised and battered Alderman Skip Murphy had ever attempted, but he managed to pull it off. The drive from Chicago had been uneventful and he had made it to his uncle's beachfront home without drawing too much overt attention. The house itself, a one-story, eight-room ranch-style affair, was kept in excellent condition by a local retired couple. Skip paid them on a monthly basis, because he spent almost as much time at the cabin throughout the year as he did in Chicago. His uncle had died two years ago.

Murphy turned off the main highway onto a paved access road, which wound for two miles through a dense forest. There was a circular driveway in front of the house and a dirt road that ran around to the beach. He parked the Camaro behind the house in a spot that would make it difficult to be seen from the access road.

The house was clean, but hot and stuffy after being closed up since the maintenance people had last been in. From the condition of the furniture, Murphy guessed that they were here within the past week. That meant he wouldn't have to worry about them for a while.

He turned the air conditioner on high, but it would take time to cool the big house. Going into the kitchen, he checked the refrigerator. There were no perishables, but the freezer was well stocked. He checked the cabinets for canned goods and, satisfied that he had enough food to last him for a few days, headed for the bathroom.

Stripping off his wrinkled, blood-stained clothing, he turned on the shower. Before stepping under the spray, he checked his reflection in the mirror. Actually, his injuries weren't too bad. His nose had stopped bleeding; there was a small cut on his lower lip, and a slight discoloration below his left eye. He would heal up in a day or so. Then . . .

As he gazed at himself in the mirror, the events of last night flashed suddenly through his mind. For a moment, he thought that he was trapped in a bizarre nightmare and could not wake up. Then, with a rapidly rising panic, the reality of his situation descended on him with such force that he dropped to his knees, gasping for breath. For long minutes he remained there until his breathing returned to normal. Finally, he forced himself to stand up and get into the shower. He remained there for twenty minutes until the skin of his palms and the soles of his feet began to wrinkle. When he stepped out and began toweling himself dry, he was still haunted by what had occurred last night, but now he was capable of logical thought.

There were clean clothes in one of the bedrooms and, after donning shorts, a T-shirt, and sandals, he went into the kitchen to heat a can of corned beef hash. He ate the simple meal slowly, because his stomach was still queasy. When he finished, he felt better and his mind was racing through the alternatives for dealing with his current situation.

The barmaid was dead, which was an incontrovertible fact. Detective Donegan could have arrested him, but did not. The detective had also taken the body away, which made him not only an accessory after the fact, but also guilty of official misconduct, because he was a police officer. So at this point the cop was in it as deeply as Skip Murphy. This could eventually be worked to the Chicago city councilman's advantage.

Rising from the kitchen table to wash the dishes he had used, Murphy began developing a plan. Not once did he give even the slightest thought to the dead woman. To him she had been no more than an object for his sexual gratification. The only thing he was sorry about was that her death had complicated his life.

After drying the dishes, he went into the wood-paneled recreation room, which was outfitted with a pool table, a fifty-two-inch TV set, and a fully-stocked bar. Murphy went to the bar, but, as he was still hungover, ignored the booze in favor of a stomach-settling can of ginger ale. Utilizing a remote control device, he turned the television on. The WGN super station was broadcasting local news from Chicago. An in-studio newscaster was talking about an ordinance that was up for a vote in the City Council today. Skip Murphy listened carefully, because he was a co-sponsor of that ordinance. Had it not been for last night's events, he would have been in the council chambers right now.

The political piece ended and the update of an earlier story came on. "Area One Detectives have now informed WGN that the fire that destroyed the South Michigan Avenue Motel earlier today, resulting in the deaths of four people, was definitely an arson."

Skip Murphy didn't hear the rest of the newscast, because his mind was screaming, "Who are you, Detective Joe Donegan?!!!"

In April of 1991 a madman named Steven Zalkin had taken Commander Larry Cole and Detective Lou Bronson hostage. The policemen had been drugged and trapped in the basement chapel of the Our Lady of Peace rectory with the church pastor, Father Kenneth Smith, and Sister Mary Louise Stallings. To settle a fifteen-year-old score with Cole, Zalkin had nailed the policeman's left hand to the chapel floor.

To heal the damage, Cole was forced to endure three operations followed by weekly therapy sessions in order to repair the massive damage done to the ligaments and tendons of his hand. The results had been quite impressive, as he had regained over 90 percent of his strength. Now he was on the way to his weekly therapy session at University Hospital.

He parked his black Chevrolet command car with the white-wall tires, buggy-whip antenna, and red accent stripe, in the visitors' lot behind the hospital. A short time later he entered the physical therapy wing. The room he was ushered into by a white-coated attendant was equipped with the usual physician's examination area to include a paper-covered table, a sink, and

an anatomy chart taped to the wall. Cole removed his suit
jacket, shirt, and tie before sitting down in a chair next to the
sink.

The therapy sessions that the detective commander had
gone through so far had been very beneficial, but at times they
had also been quite painful. The objective was to break down
the scar tissue in the area of the puncture wound and at the
same time increase the flow of blood to enhance the healing
process. In some cases patients going through this form of rehabilitation dreaded these sessions. Cole actually looked forward to his. This was because of Stella Novak.

Cole had been waiting for five minutes when the door
opened and the therapist came in. Stella Novak was twenty-
three years old, stood five-foot-four-inches tall, and had a slender build. She had short brown hair and features that could be
termed "wholesomely pretty." But Stella was not a woman who
relied on her looks. Instead she used her formidable intelligence
to forge her way in this world.

Stella had been born in Lodz, Poland in 1969. Her grandfather had been a highly decorated colonel in the Polish Home
Army, which had fought the Nazis during World War II and
her father was a distinguished professor of literature at the University of Lodz. There was only one other child in the Novak
family. That was Stella's older sister Sophia.

It was Sophia who first immigrated to America in the late
1970s. After she got settled in Chicago she sent for her younger
sister. Stella arrived in the United States at the age of fifteen.
Then, in record time, she had proceeded to master the English
language, complete high school, and commence a course of
study at the University of Chicago toward a medical degree.
To finance her education she had worked at a variety

of jobs including being a manicurist, a translator at the Polish Consulate in Chicago, and even did a brief stint as a barmaid at the Lake Shore Tap. Then she had completed enough medical courses to qualify to work as a licensed physical therapist.

"Good afternoon, Commander Cole," she said. She spoke very distinctly with barely any trace of an accent. "How are you today?"

"I'm fine, Stella. How have you been?"

She went to the sink and washed her hands, saying over her shoulder, "Oh, I guess I'm okay." She exhaled a deep sigh, which transmitted to the policeman that something was wrong with his usually cheerful therapist.

Stella dried off and turned to attend to her patient. Cole noticed the worry lines etched into her young face. She began by examining the healing wound, front and back. She had him make a fist, then relax it and make a fist again. With delicate-appearing, but exceptionally strong hands, she began to probe the injury. At times her actions hurt the patient, but when that happened, she quickly moved on to another area. Then, utilizing pressure on the muscles, the nerves, and the tendons, she relieved the pain and stimulated the healing process.

Stella was sitting on a stool in front of Cole and held his left hand in both of hers as she worked. "How is your wife and your little boy, Commander?"

"They're just fine, Stella, and I wish you'd call me, Larry."

She looked directly into his eyes and said in a mock scolding tone, "My grandfather was a colonel in the Armia Krajowa during the Second World War. When my sister and I were children, we always called him 'Colonel.' It is a matter of great respect, which I also confer on you, Commander."

Cole smiled. "Whatever you say, Stella. Oh, by the way,

my wife is enjoying the book of poetry you loaned her. I'll bring it back next week."

"*The Author's Evening* is Wislova Szymborska's most recent work. She is quite a famous poet in Poland. Someday she will win the Nobel Prize in Literature."

A period of silence ensued during which Cole remarked to himself that Physical Therapist, soon to be Doctor, Stella Novak was one of the most knowledgeable and exceptionally well-read people he had ever met. And her area of literary expertise was not confined to the poetry of her native land. On more than one occasion he had been amazed by the depth of her knowledge about not only literature, but also history, geography, and world politics.

Once he had jokingly asked her, "What do you do, Stella, go home at night and read the encyclopedia?"

She had looked at him with her guileless expression and replied, "Sometimes I do, Commander."

Now, as the therapy session was ending, she said, "Could I ask you a question about your work?"

"Shoot."

She stopped massaging his palm. " 'Shoot?' I don't understand what you mean?"

Cole laughed. "I'm sorry, Stella. It's just a saying that means you can go ahead and ask me about my work."

"Oh, the word 'shoot' in that context is a colloquialism."

"Exactly."

"Okay, I will 'shoot.' When someone is missing is it true that the police will not take a formal report until they have been gone for at least twenty-four hours?"

"That depends on who the person is and the circumstances under which they went missing."

"Say it is a thirty-two-year-old adult female."

Cole decided to cut right to the heart of the matter. "Who is missing, Stella?"

She hesitated a moment, looked away from him vacantly off into space while she weighed what she should do, and came to a decision. She liked and trusted this policeman, and she definitely needed help.

"My sister Sophia did not come home last night and I have a bad feeling that something terrible has happened to her."

3

JUNE 13, 1992

3:55 P.M.

Detective Joe Donegan had not been to sleep in over thirty hours, but except for some slight eye irritation, he was feeling no ill effects. He had worked a full tour of duty for the police department and had even expended a bit more than his usual minimal effort. However, Donegan had a secret agenda. He was covering his tracks as thoroughly as was humanly possible. And he was doing so to such an extent that even if suspicions were raised about what had occurred at the South Michigan Avenue Motel this morning, there would be no evidence to support them.

As his tour of duty came to an end, he turned in the four supplementary case reports he had completed that day and left the police station at Belmont and Western. He drove his dark blue Ford two miles to a service station near the Kennedy Expressway. There he filled up his tank at the self-serve pump and poured an additional gallon of gasoline into a metal can he carried in the backseat. Walking around his car, he noticed that a sour odor emanated from the trunk, where the body of the dead waitress was concealed. She was starting to decompose, making it imperative that he get rid of the body soon. But he had to take care of another pressing matter first.

Donegan pulled his car away from the gas pumps over to a bank of pay telephones at the edge of the station lot. From memory, he dialed the Michigan number Alderman Skip Murphy had given him. The phone was snatched up after only one ring.

"Hello." There was evident panic in the politician's voice.

"Good afternoon, Skip. How's it going?"

"Who is this?"

"Don't you recognize my voice after all that we've been through together in such a short period of time? Oh, and by the way, before you get too vocal on this open line, I suggest you be careful about what you say."

A long pause ensued from the Michigan end of the connection.

"Are you still there, Skip?"

In a hoarse voice, he responded, "I'm here."

"Now the reason I'm calling is to make sure you haven't developed any second thoughts about the arrangement we made earlier. As you are probably already aware, there have been complications with the deal."

"How did . . . ?" The words caught in the alderman's throat.

"Let's just call it a fortuitous accident. But I wanted to reassure you that everything will remain under control as long as you keep your head."

"I don't understand what you mean."

Donegan's voice held an icy threat. "Let me say that for you to reconsider our arrangement at this stage of the game would be extremely disastrous for you."

"What about you?" A challenging tone had crept into Murphy's voice.

"I'm in the clear, Alderman, because everything points to you, including a set of very nice photographs, which are in my possession. Now you keep your legendary politician's cool and I'll be in touch."

Donegan hung up the phone and returned to his car. He got on the Kennedy Expressway and fought rush hour traffic all the way to the Indiana Toll Road, where he was able to pick up speed. He made it to Union Pier, Michigan, before dark.

The detective located the summer home where Skip Murphy was staying. He drove by it slowly; checking the position of the alderman's Camaro parked behind the house. There were lights on inside the expensive ranch-style summer home, although Donegan was unable to see any movement inside. But he knew that Murphy was in there. However, this was merely a secondary consideration. He didn't expect the alderman to be going anywhere for quite a while. Instead the detective was more interested in seeing if there were any official-type vehicles in the area. This would indicate that the politician's conscience had gotten the better of him and he had called the local cops. So far everything looked pretty good. With the passage of the first day, Murphy was being locked tightly into the murder of Sophia Novak.

Part of Detective Joe Donegan's day had been spent finding out all that he could about the dead barmaid. She had no police record and was listed only once in CPD files as a witness to the mugging outside of the Lake Shore Tap that Donegan had personally investigated a few weeks ago. He didn't want to get too deep into the woman's background right now, because to do so would leave a paper trail that could lead right back to him. But he now had an address and a telephone number for her, which might come in handy later.

He cruised the back roads around Union Pier for over an hour before he found what he was looking for. Darkness had fallen, but there was still a lot of activity in the area, most of which was centered on the main drag of the town, the beach, and the occupied cabins. Then, down a gravel road half a mile from Murphy's cabin, Donegan found a garbage dumpster in a deserted clearing. Parking his car on the side of the gravel road, he got out and examined the area on foot. Beer cans, the leavings from a score of early summer barbecues, and even a few condoms littered the ground around the metal trash receptacle.

After making absolutely certain that he was alone, he returned to his car and removed the dead woman's body from the trunk. That morning they had wrapped her in a motel sheet. Since then the corpse had leaked body fluids due to loss of bladder and bowel control. Holding his breath, while fighting a spasming gag reflex, he pulled her from the car and dragged the body across the clearing. With an effort, he hefted the sheet-shrouded corpse into the dumpster. He went back to the car and returned with the gasoline can. He spread the accelerant liberally over the corpse and in the dumpster. Then he lit the gasoline with a disposable cigarette lighter.

The fire erupted with a loud thump and flames leaped skyward. Donegan stood by with a fire extinguisher in case the blaze spread to the surrounding woodland. He also kept an eye out for anyone who might be attracted by the flames. If such an eventuality did occur, he was prepared to get the hell out of there and let the chips fall where they may as far as Skip Murphy was concerned.

But the site he had selected was indeed remote and, as the body and garbage inside the dumpster were consumed, Donegan remained unseen. It took almost an hour for the fire to burn down to ash. Then, using a snow shovel, which had also been in the trunk of his car, he poked through the charred remains until he located what was left of the corpse.

The flames had reduced the body to a black mass that no longer appeared to be of human origin. But the veteran policeman knew that the remains could be found and traced back to Chicago. This, Donegan was not going to permit.

He placed the blackened remnants of the corpse in an old fireman's raincoat that had once belonged to his brother, Bob Jr., and returned it to the trunk of his car. He burned his hand on the side of the dumpster, but it wasn't bad and he ignored the pain. After all, he came from a family of firemen.

Driving back to Chicago, Donegan began adding up the down payment that Alderman Skip Murphy owed for his services. It would cost the Chicago city councilman a minimum of ten thousand dollars. And that was only for starters. It would take Alderman Murphy a long time to pay off the entire debt. A very long time indeed.

Now Joe Donegan was on his way back to Chicago to implement the next phase of the cover-up.

Gracie Lepkowski's feet were starting to hurt, but she couldn't slow down. For a weekday night the Lake Shore Tap was unusually busy and she was forced to serve all of the tables and booths alone. Sophie hadn't shown up for work. So far Gracie had managed and was even making some good tips. But it was now past midnight and the bar wouldn't close until 2:00 A.M.

Last night, after Sophie left, there was a surge in business. It had been the same since Gracie had come on at seven o'clock. She had even forgotten to call Sophie's sister Stella and tell her that her fellow barmaid had left with the bigshot.

As 1:00 A.M. approached, the number of bar patrons dropped off to the point that Gracie was able to take a short break. She went back to the changing area and lit a cigarette. She wanted to take her shoes off, but she was afraid that if she did so her feet would swell and she'd never get them back on. She noticed Sophie's bunny costume hanging on the clothing rack. For a moment Gracie unfocused and remembered their last conversation.

"Men like him can make a lot of trouble for people like us."

Sophie had told her not to be such an old grandmother.

Sophie Novak had gone out with bar patrons before and Gracie knew that she had gone to bed with some of them. One in particular, an older gentleman who couldn't have been a day under seventy-five, had even started coming in every night and nursing a glass of sherry while he watched Sophie work. Finally, the evil-tempered bartender had gotten angry and ordered Sophie to get rid of her aging suitor. Gracie didn't know what she said to him, but he never came back to the bar again. And Sophie had taken money from these men in exchange for her sexual favors. Gracie refused to think of what this made her friend.

Stubbing out her cigarette, she was heading back to the bar when she made a promise to herself that when she got off work tonight she would call Sophie and find out why she hadn't come to work.

Gracie Lepkowski didn't notice that anything was amiss until she walked back into the bar. When she saw the bartender with his hands over his head and all of the patrons lined up at the bar, she knew that something was wrong. The robber had on one of those masks that skiers wear and carried a large gun.

"Get over here," he ordered Gracie, motioning with the barrel of the gun.

She did as he told her, because she hated firearms. When she was a child in Poland she had seen Russian soldiers shoot people. The noise those weapons made was terrifying enough. Then there were the horrifying things that they did to the human body.

"Empty the cash drawer," the robber said to the bartender. "And if you get cute, you'll get very dead."

Quickly, the bartender did as he was told, holding up a fistful of bills. Coming forward, the robber snatched the money from his hand and shoved it into his suit jacket pocket. Gracie was doing all that she could to avoid looking at the robber, but she did notice that the jacket he wore was not only wrinkled and soiled, but also too big for him. She recalled someone with a jacket like that who had been in the bar last night. He had even talked to the bartender.

There were six people in the Lake Shore Tap at the time of the robbery. They were all shocked by what happened next. The robber shouted, "I told you not to get cute!" and shot the bartender right in the center of his forehead. The bartender hadn't done anything before he was killed.

One of the female patrons, a black woman in a short red

dress, screamed. Most of the others dropped to the floor and a silver-haired man, who had consumed three double scotches on the rocks in the last hour, passed out. Gracie Lepkowski began trembling, but remained in place as if her body had somehow sunk roots through the scarred black tile floor. Then the robber turned his gun on her.

In the scant seconds before she died, the second barmaid working in the Lake Shore Tap to be murdered in less than twenty-four hours, Gracie came to the realization that she knew the man whose face was hidden behind the ski mask. Somehow the memory of the police detective who had questioned her after one of the patrons had been mugged a couple of weeks ago, merged with that of the man who had been in the bar last night and that of the armed robber in the ski mask standing a few feet away from her right now. A man who she remembered leaving the bar right after Sophie and the politician left last night.

At that instant she looked into the black pools visible through the eyeholes of the mask and an understanding passed between victim and offender. He pulled the trigger again, firing a bullet into her head at almost the exact same spot as the one that had killed the bartender.

Then, as the others present waited to die, the robber ran out of the bar. His take was $685. None of the survivors gave even the briefest thought to following him. The deaths of the bartender and barmaid were classified as homicides occurring during the commission of an armed robbery.

The coverup was now complete.

4

Larry Cole would have looked into the mysterious disappearance of Stella Novak's sister as soon as he returned to the station after his therapy session had he not been forced to kill Jeffery Pender. Before leaving University Hospital, Cole had written down all of Sophia Novak's vital statistics and planned to call Area Six Detective Commander Dick Shelby, whom he didn't know very well, to ask for his assistance. But Blackie was waiting for Cole in his office when he returned.

"Boss, those prints you had re-run earlier on that four-year-old Hyde Park homicide," Blackie said, "belong to none other than *the* Jeffery Pender."

The shock of what Blackie had just told him erased Sophia Novak from Cole's mind. At least temporarily.

"Are you sure?" the detective commander asked.

Blackie handed over the AFIS printout. The results of the match were listed as having a "ninety-six percent reliability factor." No Cook County State's Attorney would refuse to approve a homicide charge in the face of such unimpeachable scientific evidence. But that was not the most pressing problem facing the detectives. Jeffery Pender was.

The Pender name had been prominent throughout the history of Chicago, dating back to the days of Fort Dearborn. The early Penders had made a fortune selling everything from whiskey to guns on the early northern Illinois frontier. After Chicago was incorporated as a municipality on March 4, 1834, the Penders became marginally more respectable by going into the real estate business. The patriarch of the family in the mid–nineteenth century was Jeremiah Pender, who became one of the city's first multimillionaires and who purchased a mansion on South Grand Boulevard. The Penders seemed poised to take their place among the ranks of other tycoon families in the Windy City; however, a scandal intervened.

It began with Horace Ignatius (H. I.) Pender, Jeremiah's son, who was known by the nickname "Hi." In 1867, after he flunked out of a number of East Coast universities, he was given an assistant vice president's job in the family's real estate firm. Hi Pender's job was meaningless, because he was totally incapable of performing even the most simple of business tasks. He spent most of his time drinking and patronizing brothels. During one of his alcoholic binges in the summer of 1869, Hi was approached by a uniformed city police officer, who ordered him and his confederates to move along. Pulling a Derringer from a vest pocket, Hi Pender killed the cop. Following a sensational trial, Pender was found guilty and sentenced to be hanged. That sentence was carried out on Christmas Eve 1870.

The Pender family managed to put the scandal behind them and continued to prosper in various lucrative business pursuits until after World War I. That's when the criminal "ministrations" of Dorothy Teresa Pender blazed across the front pages of Chicago tabloids.

Dorothy T. Pender was the granddaughter of Horace Ignatius Pender. She had been haunted by the tale of his hanging when she was growing up in the massive South Grand Boulevard mansion. She became a big, homely woman who never married, and, at an early age began collecting small animals, which she kept in cages in the coach house behind the mansion. The fate of the many squirrels, rabbits, and white mice that made up the young woman's menagerie was never made public, but they were replaced on a monthly basis.

When the Depression devastated the national economy in 1929, Dorothy Pender became a volunteer worker in the Windy City's shelters and soup kitchens. Along with working for free, she also donated food and clothing for the homeless and hungry, which were paid for out of her generous family allowance. She was dubbed a genuine "Angel of Mercy" by the press. That is, until a number of the people she aided came up missing.

It took nearly a year for an enterprising black police officer named Joe Warren to establish a connection between the heiress and the poor people who had mysteriously vanished. Even then it was difficult for the policeman to get his superiors interested in the fate of a few disenfranchised people out of an impoverished society numbering in the millions. But Joe Warren persisted and with some difficulty managed to obtain a warrant to dig up the garden on the grassy lot next to the Pender family's South Grand Boulevard mansion. All of the flowers had been planted by Dorothy and were quite beautiful. This was due to the careful attention the young woman gave them and the unique fertilizer that she employed.

The remains of a number of small animals, along with the decomposing corpses of ten of the poor people who disappeared from the soup kitchen where Dorothy Teresa Pender had worked, were found there.

The story caused quite a sensation in the newspapers of the day and resulted in a very violent backlash. The poor, hungry people of Chicago, who were unable to get jobs, were whipped into a vengeful fury by the city's daily newspapers. As the murderess awaited trial in the Cook County Jail, a torch-carrying mob stormed the Pender Mansion. Before the police could intervene, the mob first looted the place and then set it on fire. Miraculously, the surviving members of the Pender clan managed to escape without injury. They stayed away from Chicago for twenty years, living in opulent exile in another state, while a LaSalle Street law firm looked after their business interests. In due course, Dorothy Teresa Pender followed Horace Ignatius Pender to the gallows.

For the next forty years nothing was heard from the Penders. Some of them moved quietly back to Chicago; however, the remains of the South Grand Boulevard mansion had been demolished long ago. Except for a few local history buffs, the crimes of Horace and Dorothy Pender were forgotten. Then the Pender family once more stepped onto infamy's center stage.

It began with something called J. Pender and Company attempting to acquire an interest in the Chicago Cubs baseball team, the majority of the stock in the Zumboldt and Payton Real Estate Consortium, and a 42 percent share of the *Chicago Times-Herald* daily newspaper. Close to a billion dollars in property and negotiable bonds was pledged for these transactions, which drew the attention of the Windy City's financial community.

Then it was discovered that the "J. Pender" of J. Pender and Company was none other than Jeffery Pender, a descendant of the notorious Pender family.

The local newspapers, with the exception of the *Times-Herald*, ran articles on the history of the Penders. Jeffery Pender was interviewed and a current photograph of him run with each piece, which revealed a thick-featured, broad-shouldered man with flaming red hair. Pender was quoted as saying that his ancestors' transgressions were ancient history and had nothing to do with him. A short time later, the Chicago Cubs deal was disapproved at the winter meeting of the major league baseball owners in Sarasota, Florida. The Zumboldt and Payton Real Estate Consortium followed this by withdrawing from its deal and the board of directors of the *Times-Herald* voted to postpone its stock sale. Jeffery Pender sued.

A lawsuit was filed on behalf of J. Pender and Company against the Tribune Company, which owned the Cubs, the Zumboldt and Payton Real Estate Consortium, and the *Chicago Times-Herald*. The plaintiff, Jeffery Pender, alleged breach of contract by all of the defending parties and demanded $250 million in damages. At the same time that the lawsuit was filed, a massive public relations campaign was launched. In the press Jeffery Pender was portrayed as the victim of elitist business factions in a city that had produced such notorious criminal figures as Al Capone, Frank Nitti, and a long list of crooked politicians. *The New York Times, Washington Post,* and *Time* magazine all ran lengthy stories about Pender and his ancestors. And in each article the question was raised, from the hindsight stemming from close to a century having passed, if the charges against the executed Penders had been legitimate.

The controversy was still raging when Jeffery Pender's fingerprints were linked to the scene of a four-year-old homicide.

"How did Pender's prints get into AFIS?" First Deputy Superintendent William Riseman asked Cole.

The detective commander had called Riseman when the complications had been discovered that could shake up the dated murder investigation. The current first deputy superintendent was a former chief of detectives and currently the second-highest ranking officer in the Chicago Police Department.

In response to the question, Cole said, "Pender applied for an Illinois Firearms Ownership Identification card about a year ago and his prints were put into the system."

"Do we have anything to link Pender to the victim?"

"Right now nothing at all, but we haven't talked to him yet."

"I want you to handle this personally, Larry," Riseman said. "Take Silvestri with you and see if you can somehow finesse Mister Pender into implicating himself without turning this into a media circus."

"You got it, boss."

The offices of J. Pender and Company were located on the twenty-first floor of the Warling Building, which was located on Wacker Drive half a block west of Michigan Avenue. Cole and Blackie followed the hallway directory around to the suite and rang a bell outside the frosted glass doors into which the words were etched in gold leaf, "J. Pender and Company."

A male voice came over the intercom speaker located above the bell, "May I help you?"

"I am Commander Larry Cole and this is Sergeant Blackie Silvestri. We're with the Chicago Police Department and would like to speak with Mr. Jeffery Pender."

"May I ask what this is pertaining to?"

Cole could feel Blackie tense angrily. "This is a highly personal matter that I don't think should be discussed from out here in the corridor," the commander responded.

"Just a moment." The intercom went dead.

A short time later the instrument again crackled to life.

"Please come in." This was followed by a buzzer sounding, which opened the corridor door with an audible click. Cole and Blackie entered the offices of J. Pender and Company.

The suite that J. Pender and Company occupied consisted of a reception area and three offices. A dark-haired young man with broad shoulders and a deep tan sat behind a desk in the reception area. He rose, giving them an impressive display of his size, and said with an incongruously high-pitched voice, "I need to see some identification."

Both Cole and Blackie displayed their badges. "Yours is prettier than his," he said of the commander's gold badge. Neither of the cops commented.

Satisfied of their legitimacy, the receptionist said a more somber, "Right this way, gentlemen."

The receptionist led them down a carpeted corridor to a door, which bore the legend, "Jeffery Pender—CEO."

The receptionist knocked before opening the door and admitting the policemen. Pender's private office faced north with large windows providing an impressive view of the Wrigley Building, the Chicago River, and Navy Pier. The room itself was quite spacious and had been designed by a professional decorator. Along the west wall there was a sophisticated entertainment center and a bar, which was fully stocked with bottles displaying very expensive liquor labels. Cole remarked silently that this place had not been set up for work, but rather for play. This impression was reinforced by the fact that there were no computers, file cabinets, or other business paraphernalia in evidence. The lone desk on the opposite side of the room had nothing on top of it other than a single telephone. Seated in a high-backed leather armchair behind this desk was Jeffery Pender.

The CEO of J. Pender and Company possessed a formidable physical presence. Seated casually behind his desk, he exuded the passive menace of a dangerous wild animal, such as would be the case if one were to accidentally encounter a sleeping cobra or a hibernating grizzly bear. Jeffery Pender had a big square head that possessed various shades of red from the bright color of his hair to the deep suntan of his face. His shoulders were fifty-two inches in circumference and his neck vanished into his eighteen-inch collar. However, the hands resting on top of the barren desktop surface were small to the point of being almost delicate in comparison to the rest of his body.

"Please be seated, gentlemen," the CEO said in a voice that rumbled up from deep inside of his chest. "Can we offer you any refreshments, such as soda, coffee, or perhaps something stronger?"

"No thank you," Cole responded as they sat down across from Pender.

The receptionist waited until the guests were settled before he turned and left the office.

The cops noticed two things instantly. One was that their chairs were bolted to the floor to keep them from being moved. The other item was that Pender's desk and desk chair were placed in such a position in relation to the windows behind him, so as to cast his upper body in shadow. This made it difficult for Cole and Blackie to see his features, particularly the eyes. This gave the CEO the advantage. At least temporarily.

"Commander Larry Cole and Sergeant Blackie Silvestri," Pender said. "I am honored to have officers of your distinction pay a visit to my humble office. I have followed your exploits since your well-publicized run-in with the Mafia some years ago. And it seems that the two of you make the front pages quite frequently. Among your peers, you must be legends."

"Thank you," Cole responded, concentrating on the square block of flesh and bone that was Jeffery Pender's head. "We appreciate your taking the time to see us without an appointment."

"I'm sure you are quite busy with all of the things you are involved in," Blackie added.

Pender's only response was to raise his hands slightly off the surface of the desk and then lower them to their previous position. This transmitted to the cops that maybe this particular CEO wasn't so busy.

"So what can I do for you today?" Pender asked.

"Could you tell us where you were on April twenty-ninth, 1988?" Cole said. By concentrating on the shadows, the commander was able to make out a portion of Pender's face; however, he still couldn't see the eyes.

"That was over four years ago," Pender said with that kettle drum voice. "I can barely remember where I was last week."

"Do you think you could give it a try?" Blackie said, with the slightest "bad cop" edge in his voice. This was aimed at needling Pender and possibly forging a crack in that icy facade. At this point there was no indication that he had been affected at all.

"Let me see," Pender said. "In April 1988 I was in Chicago. I was taking care of some business for my family. You know I am a licensed attorney. I'm sure that if my staff looks through the files, they will find records of my legal activities at the time."

Playing the "good cop," Cole said, "I know how difficult this must be, but please bear with us."

Pender's right hand came off the desk and then was quickly returned to its former position, which indicated that they had his permission to continue.

"In your legal work did you ever encounter a lawyer named Edward Anderson?" Cole asked. "He generally went by the first name of 'Ted.' "

The response came too quickly. "I never heard of him."

Despite Pender's unmoving silhouette, both Cole and Blackie were able to detect a slight increase in the CEO's breathing rate. He was frightened, which they had anticipated.

"Begging your pardon, counselor," Blackie said, moving forward to perch on the edge of his chair, "but wasn't Ted Anderson the plaintiff's attorney in a lawsuit against your family's acquisition of a certain parcel of lakefront land in the upper peninsula of Michigan?"

Again, virtually without hesitation, Pender responded, "But I was not the attorney of record during that litigation, Sergeant Silvestri."

Cole noticed that the placid hands on the desktop were now clenched into fists. Not tightly, but definitely exuding tension. "Have you ever been to Ted Anderson's apartment here in the city?" Cole asked.

"As I've already told you, I didn't even know him." Now Pender's voice trembled and his right hand was no longer in sight.

"But you were aware that he opposed your family's interests in the Michigan lawsuit?" Blackie said in a tone that came out sounding like an accusation.

"Do you two want to tell me what this is all about?"

Cole dropped his own hand from the arm of his chair into

his lap, as he responded, "Four years ago, Ted Anderson was murdered."

For the first time since Cole and Blackie had entered the office, Pender laughed. But it was a sound that held no mirth. "And it took you guys four years to investigate the crime? I thought that the Chicago Police Department was more efficient than that."

"Oh, we're efficient enough," Blackie snapped. "So we saved all of the fingerprints we found at the murder scene. And guess what, we found a set of your prints on the murder weapon."

"That's ridiculous," Pender said, starting to move around in his chair, which enabled them to see his eyes. The irises were blue and bulging slightly, because Jeffery Pender was deeply frightened. "I've never been in Hyde Park, so there's no way that I could have killed Ted Anderson."

A moment of protracted silence ensued among the three men in the corner office on the twenty-first floor of the Warling Building on the south bank of the Chicago River. Each of them, including murder suspect Jeffery Pender, realized that a damning admission had just been made. Neither Cole nor Silvestri had made any mention of the victim having lived in the Hyde Park neighborhood.

Now Jeffery Pender began rising from the chair behind his desk. Besides possessing door-width wide shoulders, he was also tall, standing six feet seven inches in height. As Pender stood upright, he raised a .38 caliber stainless steel, four-inch barrel Colt Trooper revolver to point at Cole and Blackie. The suspect was extending his arm, as he had done on the pistol range, and preparing to line up the front and rear sights on his targets. On the pistol range Pender had scored thirty-five hits out of fifty rounds fired. The 70 percent score would net him a barely passing grade on the Chicago Police Department range. In addition to this, Jeffery Pender had done all of his shooting at stationary targets.

For his first target, Pender selected the sharp-tongued Sergeant Blackie Silvestri. Then, after firing a bullet into the cop's torso, he planned to turn his gun on Cole. But the two policemen were not stationary, unarmed targets.

The current superintendent of the Chicago Police Department had been in office for three troubled years. On a nearly continuous basis, since the day he'd been appointed to the post by the mayor, there had been either a scandal involving department officers, media criticism for poorly handled cases, or one public relations gaffe or another caused by his own actions.

He had been a police officer for twenty-nine years and had never been known as a "street cop." From the moment he came out of the police academy, he had worked in administrative positions within the relatively safe confines of district stations. He developed into a fairly decent report writer and became conversant with the reams of forms and reports required to keep the fifteen-hundred-member bureaucracy functioning. With these attributes and the right political backing he had risen rapidly, but quietly through the ranks to the top cop's job.

The superintendent had been having dinner at a Rush Street restaurant with his wife when he was notified by an aide that Jeffery Pender had been shot to death in his office by two Chicago cops. When he heard who those cops were, his ulcer began acting up. Larry Cole and Blackie Silvestri were supposed to be good detectives, but they were controversial and the superintendent avoided controversy as much as possible. The superintendent had also followed the sordid history of the Pender family, which had been carried in recent news reports. And despite the Jeffery Pender shooting being classified as legitimate by the investigating officers, the superintendent was afraid there would be a great deal of negative publicity. He was absolutely right.

JEFFERY PENDER SHOT TO DEATH BY COPS, was the headline blasted across the front page of the *Chicago Tribune*.

The Sun-Times had a similar front page headline and lead story on the incident; however, a related article on page three bore the black highlighted charge, PENDER AND COMPANY EMPLOYEES ALLEGE COPS EXECUTED BOSS.

Now the superintendent arrived at his office with his stomach in an uproar and a headache beginning to take hold. A large contingent of print and electronic reporters were camped out in the lobby of police headquarters. His attempt to forge his way through them without making any comment was impossible. He stopped in front of the elevator bank on the east end of the lobby and turned to face them.

"Superintendent, are you aware of the allegation by J. Pender and Company employees that Commander Cole and Sergeant Silvestri shot Jeffery Pender down in cold blood?" a reporter shouted, as three banks of bright lights from minicams engulfed the top cop.

"I am unaware that a formal complaint has been filed against the officers involved, but I will be looking into it immediately."

"Superintendent, isn't it unusual for a detective commander to go out in the field to investigate a routine crime?" another reporter asked.

"My understanding is that there were special circumstances involved that required the expertise of an officer of Commander Cole's rank."

The next question held a decidedly hostile tone. "Cole and Silvestri have a long history of shooting first and asking questions later, Superintendent. Do you have any idea how many people they have killed during their careers?"

The superintendent was caught off guard and it showed by the surprise on his face. An elevator door opened behind him and he quickly retreated into the car without answering the last question. This action succeeded in adding further fuel to the controversy surrounding the shooting of Jeffery Pender.

Blackie Silvestri was waiting behind the wheel of a police car outside the headquarters building when Larry Cole, wading through the same phalanx of reporters that had stopped the police superintendent a short time before, finally came out. Even from across the street, the sergeant could tell that things had not gone well inside for the commander.

Cole had been ordered to meet First Deputy Superintendent Riseman at the 1121 South State Street police headquarters building at 8:30 A.M. Then the commander and the first deputy were to have a meeting with the superintendent at 9:00. Blackie wasn't worried about Cole's meeting with Riseman, because the first deputy was a real cop. In the sergeant's estimation, the current superintendent was an empty-holstered, politically minded bureaucrat. In Blackie's estimation, this was not good.

One look at Cole's face transmitted that things had not gone well.

Getting into the car, Cole slammed the door behind him. Blackie put the car in gear and cruised south on State Street.

"What happened?" Blackie said, after they'd traveled a few blocks.

Cole managed a smile. "Our esteemed leader wanted to know how many shootings you and I have been in since we've been working together."

"What's that got to do with Pender?"

"Nothing. Some reporter asked him when he came in the building earlier."

"You're kidding."

"I wish I was," Cole said, showing signs of relaxing. "He actually didn't spend much time talking about Pender at all. Instead he lectured Riseman and me about the use of deadly force. Told us how he'd never had to draw his weapon in the line of duty. He even said something about officers, to include you and me, who become involved in a number of deadly force incidents, should look in the mirror and probe their consciences to see if they are doing police work in a proper manner."

"Why doesn't he just take all of our guns away and let us throw rocks at perps like Pender?"

"I wouldn't give him any ideas, Blackie, but Riseman ended up setting our 'Top Cop' straight. He did it in a nice respectful way, but was still able to show the superintendent how Pender's fingerprints on that murder weapon justified not only what we did yesterday, but also put to rest the allegations that the city has been harassing his family over the years. By the time Riseman finished, the superintendent came close to complimenting us for a job well done."

"But there was no compliment?" Blackie asked.

"Nope." Cole changed the subject. "What have we got on for this morning?"

Blackie turned the police car onto the Chinatown feeder ramp to the Dan Ryan Expressway. "Bronson and Sherlock are still working on that motel fire, but they haven't come up with any new leads. Last night there were the usual murders and mayhem in our area, but nothing demanding our ham-handed touch."

"Turn around and head up to Area Six at Belmont and Western," Cole said. "I'm going to pay a social call on Commander Richard Shelby."

5

JUNE 14, 1992
10:12 A.M.

Commander Richard "Dick" Shelby was in his office with the Area Six Case Management Sergeant Mark Lewis. As commanders were doing all over the city this morning, they were going over the crime reports for the previous twenty-four hours. There was emphasis placed on certain crimes, which were either high profile or what were known as "heater" cases. The double murder during the robbery of the Lake Shore Tap was such a case. However, the majority of the attention being directed at the Chicago Police Department today centered on the shooting of Jeffery Pender.

The relationship between Commander Shelby and Sergeant Lewis was nearly as special as the one between Larry Cole and Blackie Silvestri. The major difference was that Cole and Blackie were fast friends. Shelby and Lewis had known each other for twenty years, but they had never worked together as partners. Mark Lewis, a balding, white-haired black man, was fifty-nine and had been a supervisor in the Detective Division for most of his career. He had been around long enough to remember when Cole and Blackie were tactical officers in the Nineteenth District. Lewis had once recommended to a previous Area Six detective commander that the star tactical cops be recruited into the Detective Division. During his time at Area Six Lewis had also made a number of other recommendations. Among them was the strong suggestion that then-Detective Dick Shelby be demoted back to the uniformed patrol officer ranks due to gross incompetence.

Now Shelby was the boss, which made Sergeant Lewis very uncomfortable. But Lewis was two years away from a full pension and didn't want to transfer at this late stage of his career. For his part Shelby did all that he could to constantly remind the sergeant of their earlier at-odds relationship.

As his job required, Sergeant Lewis was briefing the commander on last night's crimes. "The witnesses were pretty shook up, but there's one thing they all agree on. The bartender and the barmaid at the Lake Shore Tap didn't do anything to provoke the gunman. He killed them for no apparent reason."

Shelby was seated behind his desk with his feet, clad in worn unshined loafers, propped up on an open desk drawer. He was leaning back with his hands clasped behind his head. His eyes were half-closed as if he were either sleepy or bored.

"He had a reason, Sarge," Shelby said. "Our stick-up man was in the act of committing an armed robbery and something spooked him."

The sergeant flipped through the file folder on his lap and quickly scanned portions of the most detailed witness statements. Actually, Mark Lewis was aware of what the witnesses had said, but he didn't want to reveal this to Shelby.

"A couple of the more observant witnesses stated that he was extremely calm and calculating before he pulled the trigger, Commander. And he was also one helluva shot. He put both bullets right in the center of the victims' foreheads."

Shelby yawned. "That's nothing more than pure, frigging coincidence, Lewis."

The sergeant was about to say something else, but Shelby interrupted him by snapping, "Next case!"

Resigned to do as he was told, the sergeant closed the file on the Lake Shore Tap homicides. He simply didn't have the energy to buck Shelby.

The commander's intercom buzzed. Shelby made no move to answer it. After a moment, Sergeant Lewis put his files down on the floor and reached over to pick up the telephone receiver. Pressing the button over the blinking light, he said, "Commander's office."

Lewis listened for a moment and then said, "I'll tell him."

Shelby hadn't moved from his lounging position. That is, until Sergeant Lewis informed him that Commander Larry Cole was waiting outside to see him.

Jerking himself upright, Shelby said a nervous, "What does Cole want up here on the North Side?"

Sergeant Lewis was enjoying Shelby's distress immensely. Although the Area Six commander was an arrogant fool, he was also prone to become nervous around other command officers. The sergeant believed that the reason behind this was because Dick Shelby was incompetent and he knew it.

"Shall I have them send Commander Cole in?" Lewis asked.

"No, uh . . . yes," Shelby stammered, running a hand nervously through his oily hair and straightening his tie. "Send him in."

Collecting his case files, the sergeant was leaving the office just as Cole was coming in. They met in the doorway.

"Mark," Cole said, shaking the sergeant's hand. "How's it going, you old war horse?"

"I'm good, Larry. How's Blackie?"

"See for yourself." Cole pointed at a desk on the other side of the outer office bay. There Blackie Silvestri was renewing acquaintance with a number of the cops he had known when he worked the Nineteenth District with Cole.

Seeing his friends brightened the sergeant's spirits considerably. After the reaction that Shelby had to Cole's arrival, Mark Lewis could actually say that he was having a very good day.

Detective Joe Donegan had been working at his desk since eight o'clock that morning. After making his escape from the Lake Shore Tap, he had disposed of the gun, the ski mask, and the flesh-colored latex gloves he had worn to eliminate the bartender and barmaid. He had placed everything into a brick weighted sack, which he had dropped in the Chicago River near the Merchandise Mart. When he worked Vice, Donegan had stolen the gun from a pimp's weapons stash. Now it had served its purpose.

Donegan still lived in the Marquette Park house he was raised in. His sister Megan also lived there and, to a certain extent, took care of him. The other Donegans, Bob Jr. and Ted, had married and moved into their own homes. However, they still lived in Marquette Park. Their mother died in 1990.

Donegan had not seen his sister for three days. The water department clerk was a frail, shy woman, who was soft spoken and kept pretty much to herself. She suspected that Joe was engaged in some form of misconduct, but she had been terrified of her brothers all of her life and had learned to hold her tongue. Had it not been an economic necessity to stay, she would have gone out on her own a long time ago.

When Joe Donegan finally did get to the house on West Sixty-eighth Street, it was 3:00 A.M. Megan was asleep, but he discovered that she had cleaned up his bedroom and washed his clothes. The den, where their dead father had once watched ball games and drank beer, was off limits to her. To be on the safe side, he had padlocked the door to insure his privacy.

Inside the study were Donegan's computer and a cast-iron safe in which he kept the proceeds of his larcenous activities. He worked the combination and added the money he had collected in the last two days to the pile of bills already there. He estimated that he had about twenty-nine thousand dollars in his unofficial retirement account, which he never touched.

After securing the safe and locking the study door, he had showered and gotten a couple of hours sleep before it was time for him to go back to work. At his Area Six desk, he was expeditiously updating all of his cases. He didn't need his jerk commander or the case management sergeant on his back right now. He was formulating his next move, which was to arrange a face-to-face meeting with Skip Murphy. The cop had revised the price for his services to the alderman upward to the twenty-five thousand dollars in cash range. Utilizing the Chicago Police Department computer, he had tapped into the municipal Government program, which contained background information about all elected city officials. It revealed that Murphy was indeed rich, as he was listed as one of the wealthiest politicians in Illinois. A monetary figure was not provided, but the cop estimated that the alderman was worth at least four or five million dollars. Detective Joe Donegan had struck the mother lode.

He was attempting to come up with a secure location for his meeting with Murphy when Commander Larry Cole and Sergeant Blackie Silvestri walked into the office. The crooked cop felt a chill pass through him at the same time that he broke out in a cold sweat. Donegan knew the reputation of the two cops and also that they were from Area One, where the South Michigan Avenue Motel was located. In the initial moment of panic, Donegan was certain that he had been discovered. His mind raced in an attempt to come up with how he could have slipped up. Then he forced himself to calm down and think logically. He had carefully covered his tracks, so there was nothing that the great Larry Cole and Blackie Silvestri could have on him. At least nothing that they could prove. Joe Donegan managed to relax and wait for them to make the first move. From his desk, he watched Cole go into Shelby's office, while Silvestri went over to talk to some of the other detectives, whom the sergeant seemed to know well. Maybe, Donegan hoped, they weren't here about him at all. But he kept his eyes and ears open.

"All I'm asking from you, Commander," Cole was saying to Dick Shelby, "is for you to have one of your detectives look into this woman's disappearance." The Area One commander couldn't understand why his opposite number in Area Six was so nervous.

"Shouldn't you get authorization from downtown to do

this?" Shelby said, frowning as if he had developed a severe case of anal pain. "I mean the Missing Persons Section is responsible for those types of investigations."

Cole affixed Shelby with a cold stare. "Look, Dick. You don't mind if I call you Dick, do you?"

"Sure. That's okay."

"And you can call me Larry."

"Larry it is," Shelby said, relaxing a bit.

"I don't want to make a big deal out of this investigation. This woman worked at the Lake Shore Tap as a barmaid and her sister, who is a personal friend of mine, hasn't heard from her in a couple of days."

Shelby suffered a relapse of his anal pain. "There was a double homicide at the Lake Shore Tap last night. The bartender and a barmaid were shot to death by a stickup man."

This shocked Cole. "There was nothing about it on the news this morning."

Shelby sneered. "I have a rule that my people are not to talk to reporters under any circumstances. The press is always out to embarrass the department anyway."

Now Cole was able to see quite clearly that Commander Richard Shelby was not only an incompetent fool, but also a dangerous incompetent fool. Yes, the Fourth Estate was at times at odds with the police department. However, in a democratic society this was not only desired, but necessary. Throughout history the operations of secret police forces have contributed to some of the most horrendous crimes against humanity. It was true that the press is often critical of police operations and at times viciously so. Frequently such criticism is justified. However, keeping the press uninformed was the same as shutting out the public and the police department was a service organization set up for the public good.

Recovering quickly, Cole asked. "What were the names of the victims?"

"Just a minute, Larry," Shelby said, reaching for the telephone to summon Sergeant Lewis.

Now Cole wished that he had never told Shelby his first name.

"Jeff Pender was a really huge guy," Blackie was saying to the group of Area Six detectives who had come over to renew acquaintances. Sergeant Mark Lewis had also joined them. The only detective present in the squad room not there was Joe Donegan. The strange cop remained at his desk with his head bent over his typewriter.

Blackie continued the story. "So Pender decides to resist arrest by pulling this stainless steel thirty-eight and actually attempting to aim it at us. But he was far from being Quick Draw McGraw. In fact, it was almost like he was moving in slow motion."

"What'd you say to him, Blackie?" Detective Ronnie Davenport, a round-faced, portly man, asked. " 'Freeze, police!?' "

"Hey," Blackie said, spreading his palms in a distinctively Italian gesture, "he's got a loaded firearm in his hand and he's aiming it at me and the boss. Now, in keeping with the deadly force policy of this esteemed law enforcement organization we work for, me and Commander Cole said something like, 'Drop it,' 'You're under arrest,' or, as you said, Joe, 'Freeze, police!' Of course, Jeffery Pender was so caught up in the moment that I don't think he heard us."

"Then what did you do, Blackie?" Mark Lewis asked.

With a totally deadpan expression, Blackie Silvestri re-

sponded, "We used only the force necessary to protect ourselves in the face of such life-threatening danger and . . ." he
paused momentarily, ". . . blew his ass away."

For a long moment there was silence from the circle of
detectives standing around Blackie Silvestri. Finally, Sergeant
Lewis cleared his throat and said, "So what else is new down
in Area One?"

This succeeded in drawing laughter from all of the cops.

"Sergeant Lewis," Donegan called from his desk, "the commander wants to see you."

With each passing minute, Donegan was becoming less and less
worried about any threat posed by the presence of Cole and
Silvestri. The detective had monitored the group around the
visiting cop. All that Silvestri had done was tell war stories.
Big deal, Donegan thought. He felt that he was smarter than
either of these so-called hero cops. Of one thing he was certain;
he was making a lot more money than the two of them combined.

"Donegan." Sergeant Lewis had come out of Shelby's office and was now standing next to the detective. "The commander has an assignment for you."

The detective grabbed his notebook and got to his feet.
"Did Shelby say what he wanted me to do, Sarge?"

Sergeant Mark Lewis didn't like Joe Donegan. Although the
balding detective, who always wore a-size-too-large suit jackets, managed to get the job done, he expended only a minimal
effort and most of his work was often either incomplete or
haphazard. Donegan also didn't get along well with the other

detectives, making it necessary for him to work alone. This was dangerous. But Shelby seemed to like the strange, withdrawn detective and kept him in the unit. Sergeant Lewis, who had been around for a long time, believed that this was because the Area Six commander saw something of himself in the inept Joe Donegan.

In response to the detective's question, the sergeant said, "You're supposed to check on a missing person for Commander Cole. The assignment shouldn't be too difficult. Oh, Donegan, you need to get more sleep. You look like hell."

A short time later Detective Joe Donegan left the Area Six commander's office with the assignment to investigate Sophia Novak as a missing person. And although he was a lapsed Catholic, who no longer believed in the existence of a Supreme Being, he took the job that Dick Shelby had given him as a good omen.

6

JUNE 14, 1992
4:08 P.M.

Physical Therapist Stella Novak went off-duty at University Hospital at 3:00 P.M. It was an unseasonably warm ninety-two degrees and by the time she got to her used four-year-old Pontiac Bonneville, she was hot and uncomfortable. She had purchased the secondhand car from a doctor and it was in excellent condition with low mileage. The air conditioner worked perfectly and she flipped it on high. The car's interior cooled off quickly.

For a moment she leaned back against the headrest and closed her eyes. For the past two days she'd been worrying about her sister. Commander Cole had told her that he would have someone look into Sophie's disappearance, but she hadn't heard from him since his last therapy session. Of course, as was the case with everything else, she realized that it took time to get results. Finally, Stella sat up, put the car in gear, and headed home.

The drive to her Lake View apartment building usually took half an hour, but today the traffic was heavy, making the journey twice as long. Not once along the way did her thoughts waver from her sister.

The Novak sisters had always been quite different in their separate tastes, temperaments, likes, and dislikes. As much as Stella was quiet and studious, Sophie was gregarious and fun loving. Back in Lodz, Poland when they were growing up, Sophie had liked boys. One of the reasons the older girl had come to America was due to the constant arguments she had with their very proper college professor father about her staying out late. Stella decided to join her simply because it would be easier to become a doctor in America as opposed to Poland. But when the younger Novak sister arrived in the Windy City, she had been shocked by her sister's lifestyle.

Besides working in a bar, Sophie was dating three men simultaneously and one of them was married. She was also quite loose in sexual matters and contracted a curable venereal disease from one of her lovers. Stella succeeded in obtaining private treatment for her at University Hospital. But this only slowed Sophie down a step or two. She now saw only one man at a time, but changed them so frequently Stella couldn't keep them straight. But one thing Sophie never did was bring any of these men home to their second-floor walkup apartment. She wouldn't even allow them to pick her up outside the building. Sophie had stayed out all night before and had even taken a week's vacation with one of her boyfriends. But she always called to let Stella know that she wouldn't be home. Now Sophie had been gone for two days without a word.

The Lake View neighborhood on the north side of the city was populated predominantly by Eastern European immigrants. In neighborhood stores foreign languages were spoken nearly as often as English. The janitor in Stella's building was Lithuanian and her elderly next-door neighbor was Hungarian. All of the buildings in the neighborhood were clean and well maintained. The street she lived on was tree-lined and there was always ample parking because few of the neighbors owned cars.

Stella got out of the Pontiac and was walking toward the building entrance when a man got out of a dark blue Ford down the block. She glanced at him briefly, but at that moment didn't give him more than a second thought. Then he called to her.

"Miss Novak?"

She stopped. Her initial impression was that he was very average with a suit jacket that was too large for him. But Stella Novak was an exceptionally intelligent and observant woman. This enabled her to detect two things about the approaching man. One was that he was a policeman; the other was that he had the gaze of a borderline psychotic.

He came up to her and said, "I'm Joe Donegan from Area Six Detectives. My commander assigned me to look into your sister's disappearance."

"Do you work for Commander Cole?"

"Not a chance," he said, derisively. "Cole works down in the ghetto with the black folks."

Stella began developing a huge dislike for this man. "Well, Detective Donegan, my sister hasn't been . . ."

"Why don't we go inside and talk about it, Miss Novak? It will be more private that way."

He was starting to make her skin crawl. However, he was right about the need for this discussion to be private. She led him into the building.

The second floor apartment was small, but had been re-modeled the year that the Novak sisters had moved in. The living room furniture consisted of a sectional sofa covered with a floral brocade pattern and a pair of matching armchairs. There was a heavy wooden cocktail table with a marble top in the center of the room, the windows were covered with lace cur-tains, and there were a great many plants. To keep the five-room flat cool on such a hot day, fans were installed in all of the windows.

She offered the detective a seat on the couch, but he stepped to the center of the living room and performed a slow inspection of the place. This forced Stella to remain standing as well.

"This is a nice apartment you have here, Stella, but it's a tad warm for me."

He removed his suit jacket, revealing the numerous weap-ons he carried. Under other circumstances, Stella Novak might have laughed at him, because he reminded her of the Yosemite Sam cartoon character with all of those guns strapped to his body. The fact that she was alone with him in her living room was far from funny.

"How much do you pay for rent on this apartment anyway?" he asked. "Three, four hundred dollars a month?"

She refused to answer such a personal question. "How do you plan to go about finding my sister?"

He tossed his jacket on one of the armchairs and turned to face her. Sweat stains were visible under his arms and down the back of his shirt. She was standing too far away from him to detect any odor, but he didn't look clean. Then there were those dark eyes that seemed capable of looking right through the sleeveless cotton dress she was wearing.

"I'm a trained investigator, Stella. Do you think that your friend Larry Cole would have sent me if I couldn't do the job?"

He had her there. She did trust the commander, but this strange-looking man was far different from her patient.

She looked down at the carpet and said, "How can I help you?"

"Show me your sister's bedroom."

The request startled Stella, because she couldn't understand how seeing Sophie's room would help him find her. However, he was the detective. As she led him out of the living room to the back of the apartment, she corrected her former thought; he was Commander Cole's detective.

Sophie's bedroom was across the hall from Stella's. The doors to both rooms were left open because for most of their lives, back in Poland, the sisters had shared the same bed. The rooms were neat and the furnishings nearly identical, due to the dressers, chests of drawers, and night stands having been purchased at the same store on the same day. The color schemes were also very similar with pale pastels favored for the curtains and bedspreads.

"This is Sophie's room," Stella said.

He stopped and glanced into the other room. "And that, I assume, is yours."

"That's right."

"Just you and your sister share this place?" he said walking into Sophie's room.

"Yes."

"Do you have many visitors?"

"No."

He was examining a picture of their mother and father, which was on top of Sophie's dresser. "No male gentlemen callers?"

Stella was forced to compare this intrusion to a physical examination. Medical personnel were at times forced to ask extremely intimate questions in order to effectively treat their patients. She rationalized that if she wanted her sister back she would have to cooperate with this man.

She explained about Sophie having a number of male friends; however, she did so in an understated manner, leaving out any mention of her sister's bout with venereal disease.

He continued to examine the room as he listened. She noticed that he kept his hands clasped firmly behind his back and didn't touch anything.

"What type of men did your sister like?"

The question confused her. "I don't understand what you mean?"

Detective Donegan completed his inspection of Sophia Novak's bedroom. He returned to the entrance and stopped so close to Stella that she was forced to take a step back. Now his voice came out with a harsh, near scolding, tone. "Well, you're friends with Cole. Maybe your sister has a thing for black guys too."

Stella straightened her spine and looked Detective Joe Donegan directly in the eye. "Commander Cole is my patient. Our relationship is completely professional. As far as my sister goes, she never revealed either a preference or a prejudice for people in any way. Now is there anything else that you need to know?"

Donegan smiled. "Naw, Stella, I guess I've got it all." He walked past her and headed back to the living room. She followed.

Snatching his jacket from the chair, he let himself out of the apartment, calling over his shoulder as he went down the stairs, "Take it easy, Stella. I'll be in touch."

Closing and locking the door, she sat down on her living room sofa and buried her face in her hands.

It was eight o'clock that evening when the phone rang in Skip Murphy's Union Pier summer home.

"Hello." Murphy's voice bore no trace of the panic it had held the previous day.

"We need to talk, Alderman," Donegan said.

"Go ahead and talk," Murphy said.

The arrogant tone in the politician's voice surprised the detective. However, Donegan figured he had the means to take the wind out of his sails.

"I want to see you."

"Where?" Murphy asked.

"The Sports Challenge Bar down on Grant Street right here in Union Pier."

"When?"

"Right now. I'm waiting for you."

* * *

The Sports Challenge Bar was a popular tavern on Route 12 in Union Pier, Michigan. It consisted of a one-thousand-square-foot room with a thirty-foot-long bar manned by three full-time bartenders wearing referee-striped shirts. A coterie of barmaids served the tables and booths around the room. The principal beverage was beer and there was food available from the kitchen consisting primarily of hamburgers, hot dogs, french fries, popcorn, and pizza. In keeping with the bar's name, twelve monitors were strategically placed making at least two visible from any seat in the house. On these monitors reruns of previously played professional football, basketball, baseball, and hockey games were constantly telecast.

From late spring until mid-winter, the Sports Challenge was packed every night of the week until closing time. The crowds could at times be quite raucous and occasionally things got out of hand and the local cops were called. However, on this week-day night, although most of the tables were occupied, the bar had been fairly quiet.

Detective Joe Donegan was seated in a back booth with a glass of club soda and a basket of popcorn on the table in front of him. He was watching a replay of Super Bowl III between the New York Jets and the Baltimore Colts on a nearby monitor. The cop wasn't paying much attention to the game. Instead he was concentrating on what he was going to say to Skip Murphy. Ten minutes after he had placed the call to the Union Pier summer home, the Chicago city councilman walked into the bar.

Donegan timed Murphy. It took the alderman seven minutes to get to the back booth. The politician shook hands and exchanged greetings with at least a dozen people and kissed three women as he made his way across the room. The detective saw Murphy whisper something in the ear of one of the females, which made her turn crimson. Obviously the alderman was quite the Don Juan.

Finally, Murphy took a seat in the booth across from Donegan. Immediately, one of the barmaids came over to take his order.

"Jack Daniel's on the rocks, Jennie."

"You want a water back, Skip?" she asked, writing it down.

"Sure thing," he responded before turning to Donegan. "How's it going, Joe?"

The alderman's confident arrogance angered the detective. "Having a nice vacation?" he asked, sarcastically.

"As a matter of fact, it has been very restful. I even caught a few rays this afternoon. Do I look more tanned than the last time you saw me?"

"I'm not the one to ask."

The barmaid brought Murphy's drink and another basket of popcorn to the table.

"Thanks, Jennie."

"No problem, Skip," she said. "Call me if you need anything else."

Donegan had been forced to ask for popcorn before she would bring any to the table. "You seem to have a real way with barmaids. Someday it will be the death of you."

Murphy took a pull of his drink, chased it with water, and then popped a handful of popcorn into his mouth. Swallowing, he said, "You sound a bit truculent, Joe, and you look exhausted. Maybe you should consider taking some time off from the department and coming up here yourself for a few days."

Donegan's gaze bore into the politician and through clenched teeth he said, "I wouldn't worry about my off-duty time. You should be more concerned about your outstanding debts."

Munching more popcorn, Murphy said, "Then let's get down to business."

Donegan's gaze didn't waver. "As we agreed to yesterday morning, I have taken care of your problem with the barmaid to the extent that no one, except me, will ever be able to connect you to the Lake Shore Tap, the South Michigan Avenue Motel, or the dead barmaid. You are completely in the clear and for that there is a price."

Casually, Murphy asked, "How much?"

"Twenty-five thousand dollars in cash."

Murphy laughed. "Where am I supposed to get that kind of money?"

"You're rich, Alderman," Donegan said, angrily. "I checked you out. You've got to be worth four or five million dollars."

"On my last city ethics statement I listed my net worth at six-point-two million," the alderman said with smug arrogance. "But that doesn't mean that I can simply go out and put my hands on twenty-five thousand dollars. Most of my assets are tied up in long-term investments and real estate."

The cop was becoming increasingly agitated. He actually began considering a strategy he could utilize to kill Murphy and dispose of his body, as he had done with the barmaid. "All that means is that you'll have to liquidate a few of your financial resources. I suggest that you do so quickly."

Murphy took a sip of his bourbon and placed the glass back on the table. "And if I don't get the money, Detective Donegan, do you plan to turn me in?"

"I think you've got the picture." Donegan patted his suit jacket pocket.

"Oh, yes," Murphy said. "You have the photographs you took of me yesterday morning. Very incriminating evidence." Now the alderman removed a photo envelope from his sportshirt pocket and tossed it on the table in front of the detective. "Maybe you should take a look at those."

Donegan hesitated before touching the envelope. There were six photographs inside. All were of him removing the sheet-shrouded corpse from the trunk of his car in the Michigan forest last night and then burning it in that garbage Dumpster.

"I particularly like the one of you standing beside the flames with that fire extinguisher in your hand," Murphy quipped.

Donegan looked up from the pictures across at Murphy. There was murder in the cop's gaze.

The alderman explained. "I saw you drive by my cabin last night. That road isn't used much, and I'll never forget your blue Ford. I figured that you were up to something, so I tailed you. I could tell you didn't know your way around up here very well, and it was also obvious that you were looking for something in particular. When you pulled into that clearing, I hid the Camaro on a side road and returned on foot with my own camera."

Donegan returned the photos to the envelope and slid it back across the table. "That doesn't change anything. I still want my money."

Murphy leaned toward Donegan and lowered his voice. "You need to look at this from a different angle, Joe. Twenty-five grand is peanuts. How much is that to you? Half a year's salary? You'll blow it in no time."

"It's none of your business what I do with it, Murphy."

"Listen to me, man. You and me can form a mutually lucrative partnership instead of fighting over a few bucks."

"I like working alone," Donegan countered.

"I can understand that. But there are ways that we can help each other. In fact, there is a lot we can accomplish from our respective positions if we put our minds to it."

"How is that?" In spite of himself, Donegan was interested.

"Obviously you are a man who gets things done. In my business I can always use someone who can be depended on to make certain difficulties go away like you did last night."

"So now I work for you?"

Murphy removed another envelope from his pants pocket and tossed it on the table. "That's for you. Call it expense money for the services you've performed for me so far."

Donegan looked inside. "What's this?"

"Ten thousand dollars."

"I thought you couldn't get your hands on this kind of money?"

"That is every cent of disposable cash I have in the world. I'll be living on credit cards for a long time."

Donegan pocketed the money. "Okay, Skip, we're in business, but I want to get something straight right now. If you ever try to doublecross me or figure that you can give me up for an immunity deal, I'll kill you. I don't care if they lock me up in solitary confinement in a prison on the moon; I will find a way to get you. Do we understand each other?"

Murphy forced himself to maintain eye contact with Donegan. There was no doubt in the politician's mind that this man was not only in deadly earnest, but also dangerously insane. The alderman extended his hand. "Shall we shake on it?"

Joe Donegan stuffed the cash envelope into his jacket pocket and, ignoring the proffered hand, stood up.

"I'll be seeing you around, partner. You can take care of the bill."

After the detective left, Skip Murphy finished his drink and ordered another. Before Jennie could serve him, one of the young women he'd kissed on the way in came over to his table. A short time later they left together and went back to his summer home.

7

JUNE 15, 1992
1:52 P.M.

It began with an emergency call from a Chicago Housing Authority police unit. "Four-five-one-two, emergency! We're under fire!"

The radio zone the CHA cops operated on went dead silent. In a calm voice, the police dispatcher, who was stationed on the second floor of Chicago police headquarters, said, "Give us your location, four-five-one-two."

"Oh, God, give us some help! My partner's been shot!"

"Where is he?" shouted an unidentified male voice.

The dispatcher remained calm. "All cars clear this frequency. Four-five-one-two, it is imperative that you give us your location."

When the distressed officer came back on the air, he was gasping for breath due to a combination of exertion and terror.

"We're . . . this is . . . I think we're on State Street." The five second pause before the next transmission seemed to last an eternity. "We're at Forty-fourth and State!"

The initial reaction by the responding units was pronounced in intensity and scope. Emergency equipment was activated in every available police car—both marked and unmarked—within a square mile of Forty-fourth and State. The sound of numerous sirens could be heard converging on the area. Flashing Mars lights were visible a mile away approaching from every direction.

The Chicago Housing Authority police force was a separate law enforcement agency from the Chicago Police Department. CHA officers were charged with patrolling the extensive public housing properties in the Windy City. They were given the same powers of arrest as CPD cops and their uniforms and vehicles were nearly identical. At times, in the brief three-year history of the CHA police, there had been conflict between them and city cops. However, whenever a police officer needed help, all differences were forgotten and every able-bodied cop rushed to render assistance.

The first unit to arrive at Forty-fourth and State approximately thirty seconds after the location was given, was a female Chicago police sergeant. She saw a black and white CHA police car in the center of a barren lot between two sixteen-story high-rise buildings. Driving across the sidewalk, she entered the lot. One of the CHA squad car doors was open and an officer was visible sitting behind the wheel. As she got closer, the sergeant could see blood on the officer's blue shirt. A great deal of blood. She began searching for the wounded cop's partner when a high velocity bullet shattered the front windshield of her squad car. The safety glass became a spider-web mosaic, but remained in one piece. The bullet penetrated the front seat, missed the driver, and passed through the rear seat cushions. It was later found in the trunk.

The sergeant jerked the steering wheel hard to the left and floored the accelerator. The car fish-tailed wildly and the rear tires lost purchase in the soft ground. Then a second and third bullet struck the car. She was still miraculously unhurt and struggling to right the car when additional units arrived on the scene. More bullets began raining down from the sniper's perch.

Word was transmitted from the scene that the police were pinned down by sniper fire coming from the upper floors of a public housing building at Forty-fourth and State. It was reported that there was at least one officer injured and three police cars had been damaged by gunfire. The incident was three minutes old and the sniper continued firing, but had not been located. A greater police response was initiated.

Uniformed police officers and detectives rushed from the Area One Police Center a mile away from Forty-fourth and State. Larry Cole, Blackie Silvestri, Lou Bronson, and Manny Sherlock ran to their cars in the parking lot. Opening the trunks, they removed their bulletproof vests, which they donned before heading for the shooting scene. But unlike the first wave of officers responding to Forty-fourth and State, the detectives began formulating a plan to deal with the sniper.

The siren in Cole's car made it necessary for him to shout to be heard. The commander was driving, with the sergeant riding shotgun.

"We need to have the responding units establish inner and

outer perimeters," Cole said. "Get on the radio and establish communication with the patrol division supervisor on the scene. We've got to start bringing some order out there."

There was no need for Blackie to ask for a clarification. They had been working together too long for that. Using the car radio in the glove compartment, Blackie switched to a city-wide frequency and in due course got in touch with the ranking officer at the scene. It was discovered immediately that the sniper was in the 4412 South State Street building, which was to the north of the vacant lot. Also, some degree of order was being imposed at the scene.

Now they had to neutralize the sniper.

"Forty-fifth and Wabash," Cole yelled over the siren's wail.

"What was that?" Blackie shouted back.

They were traveling north on State Street rapidly approaching the 4400 block. Cole reached beneath the dashboard and shut off the siren. Now Blackie could hear him.

"Have Bronson and Sherlock go over to Forty-fifth and Wabash. Bronson carries binoculars in the trunk of their car. It will enable him to see the south face of the four-four-one-two building. Bronson will be out of range and can locate the sniper."

"Ten-four," Blackie acknowledged before calling Bronson and Sherlock on the radio. The sniper incident was approaching the five-minute mark.

The unmarked car, bearing Lou Bronson with Manny Sherlock driving, skidded to a stop in mid-block at Forty-fifth and Wabash. From the east side of the street, looking in a northeastern direction, the high-rise project building was visible. Bronson raised the binoculars and scanned the building. It took less than thirty seconds to locate the sniper. The incident was now in its sixth minute.

As the sniper siege reached the nine-minute thirty-second mark, Larry Cole, Blackie Silvestri, and Manny Sherlock, backed up by six uniformed officers, exited the stairwell onto the four-teenth floor corridor of the 4412 South State Street building. At Cole's direction, the officers fanned out to begin covering the exposed gallery in the event that they encountered hostile fire. They were also planning to remove the occupants from all of the apartments on the floor. The evacuation proved to be easy, because only half of the ten apartments were occupied.

Lou Bronson had identified apartment 1406 as the location from which the sniper fire originated. This apartment was va-cant and the windows boarded up. The lock on the front door had been punched out. As the incident entered its tenth minute, eight armed police officers entered the sniper's reported posi-tion.

They could hear the report of a high-powered rifle coming from the rear of the apartment, as the sniper continued to fire on the police cars below. All of the cops on the fourteenth floor were aware that the sniper had prevented any attempts to rescue the wounded, possibly dead, CHA officer. The units had been forced to retreat out of the line of fire commanded from the vacant apartment 140 feet above the ground. But the cops ac-companying Larry Cole had expected the sniper to cease fire and attempt to escape prior to their arrival or to put up fierce resistance. Now they had the shooter trapped.

Apartment 1406 at 4412 South State Street consisted of six rooms and a bathroom. The sniper was shooting from a rear bedroom, which overlooked the barren lot. The door to this room was closed. Moving rapidly, but carefully, Cole's raiding party checked each room for hostile action. Finally, they reached the sniper's location.

Cole kicked the door open and rushed in with Blackie and Manny close behind him. The sniper was on the other side of the room next to an open window. The plywood boards that had secured the window of this vacant apartment had been pulled away and were on the floor beside a metal military-issue ammunition case. The sniper's weapon and the ammo case revealed that he had been firing 30.06 rounds. This type of ordnance was designed to do only one thing; kill human beings. Then there was the sniper.

As the eleventh and final minute of this incident began, the police officers and the person who had victimized them and their colleagues faced each other for the first time. For their part, the cops were prepared to kill the sniper. That is until he dropped his weapon and began to cry. The shooter was eleven years old.

The CHA police officer was dead. The 30.06 round had penetrated the area just above his bulletproof vest and tore through his throat. There was speculation, among the detectives investigating the sniping incident, that an expert military-trained sniper could not have made an identical shot on the initial attempt under similar circumstances. The dead officer's partner was found beneath the police vehicle, where he had crawled in order to get out of the line of fire. It was from this position that he had transmitted his terrifying call for help. And despite the juvenile sniper having fired over twenty high-powered rounds at the police, the dead officer was the only casualty.

The eleven-year-old was interrogated at the Area One Police Center in the presence of his parents, a youth officer, and Detective Lou Bronson. The questioning was done solely by Bronson and recorded with the permission of the boy's stunned parents. And what this process revealed only resulted in deepening the tragedy that this day had so far produced.

The juvenile lived on the eighth floor of the 4412 South State Street public housing building with his mother and father. There were two other children in the household, also boys who were younger than the shooter. Both parents worked and were saving money to enable the family to move out of public housing. They had attempted to closely supervise the activities of their children and none of them had ever had any problems with the law. The parents were at a complete loss to explain how their son had come into possession of a gun.

The sniper told them and Detective Bronson. "I found it in a vacant apartment."

The odyssey of the 30.06 rifle was as notorious as the incident in which it was finally used. The Remington-model weapon was shipped via rail from an East Coast arms factory with a scheduled destination of Fort Riley, Kansas in February 1989. On a layover in St. Louis, Missouri, the train car was broken into and the rifle, along with six hundred other assorted firearms, was stolen. The 30.06 Remington surfaced in Los Angeles, California, two years later. It was used in a well-publicized robbery in which three armed masked men entered a bank and took fifty people hostage. A silent alarm summoned the LAPD and a gun battle ensued in which all of the robbers and five hostages were killed. The Remington-model 30.06 rifle was recovered from one of the dead robbers. It was inventoried by the Los Angeles Police Department and, following a coroner's inquest, the gun was ordered destroyed. But a year later an eleven-year-old boy used it to kill a Chicago Housing Authority police officer.

The vacant apartment was in the 4444 South Federal public housing building a block from the scene of the shooting. The apartment was on the sixteenth floor and, like its companion building, half of the units were vacant. And what the detectives discovered in a garbage-littered back bedroom astounded them.

Back in his office in the Area One Police Center some hours later, Larry Cole examined the list of weapons recovered from the vacant apartment. There were three high-powered rifles, five Tech Nine machine guns, and eighteen assorted handguns.

"This had to be the Black Gangster Cobras arsenal," Cole said. "The Gang Crimes Unit has been looking for these guns since all of the gang's leaders were jailed last month."

Blackie, who was seated across from the commander, laughed. "That doesn't make the Gang Crimes people look too good. An eleven-year-old accomplished something that they couldn't."

"Did Bronson find out why the kid shot the CHA officer?" Cole asked.

Blackie's face became set in grim lines. "The boy didn't fully understand what he was doing. Shooting at the police car with a high-powered rifle was no different for him than playing one of those arcade video games."

Cole looked at the photograph of his own wife and son on his desk. He wondered if the child sniper had any concept of how much pain he had inflicted on his family.

"Now that we've got the sniper out of the way, your pal Commander Shelby forwarded the report on the missing person you requested." Blackie handed over a single sheet of paper. "This Detective J. Donegan didn't come up with much."

Cole opened the envelope and scanned the single page report. There wasn't much there, but the one thing that Cole did notice was that this Donegan stated that the complaining witness, Stella Novak, had not cooperated with the investigation. The Area One detective commander knew his physical therapist much too well to believe that.

"You don't look happy, boss," Blackie said.

"I'm not," Cole responded, reaching for the telephone.

8

JUNE 16, 1992

10:02 A.M.

Alderman Phillip "Skip" Murphy, Jr. returned to City Hall with a flourish. After parking his Z-28 black Camaro in the municipal parking lot across the street from the famed 121 North LaSalle Street address, the city councilman strode confidently into the seat of municipal government. He was dressed in a white cotton suit, black shirt, white silk tie, and white shoes. A white straw hat, cocked to one side, topped off his ensemble.

On the way to the council chambers, he played the game of glad-handing politician with masterful skill. He shook hands with any number of men from the lowliest building custodian to the esteemed chairman of the clout-heavy Finance Committee. Occasionally, with a few of his more influential colleagues, Murphy would guide them into a relatively se-cluded corner and engage in whispered conversations. Then there was the way that the alderman treated the women he came into contact with.

Skip Murphy came on to every woman he encountered whether she be young or old, short or tall, fat or skinny, black, white, Hispanic, Asian, or of other racial or ethnic description. He possessed what he liked to call "bedroom" eyes and this, along with something of a perpetual leer, he flashed on each female while speaking to her softly in that baritone voice he was so proud of. And he would never shake hands with a woman unless he was absolutely forced to do so by her. In Alderman Murphy's opinion, the fairer sex was meant to be greeted with a hug and a kiss.

To many of those who observed him, Skip Murphy was a shameless, incorrigible womanizer. Many also thought of him as an amoral idiot. But the alderman considered himself on a par with such great lovers of romantic fiction as Romeo, Ca-sanova, and Don Juan. By the time he made it to his seat in the council chamber, after an unexplained absence of three days, the mayor was calling the session to order. Doffing his straw hat, Murphy took his seat and assumed his serious leg-islator's face.

This morning's City Council meeting dealt with fairly in-consequential items from zoning restrictions to the passage of minor ordinances. For the most part, Murphy was bored and spent his time doodling on a scratch pad. The session was an hour and ten minutes old when he happened to glance up into the VIP section at the south end of the chamber and noticed two men seated there. Initially, he couldn't remember their names, but he was aware that they were cops. He began searching his memory to identify them when the black man looked directly at him. The cop's gaze frightened Murphy and he quickly looked away. It was then that the cop's name came to him. It was Larry Cole, the Area One Police detective commander. About a year or so ago, Cole had become involved in a case with some guy named Zalkin, who was worth twenty million dollars. While he was in Union Pier, Murphy had also monitored the news report about Cole and some other cop killing Jeffery Pender.

The alderman chanced another look in the cop's direction. Now both Cole and the white guy, who looked like a *Godfather* movie extra, were looking at him. A tremendously uneasy feeling gripped Skip Murphy and he involuntarily flashed back to that morning in the motel room with the barmaid. But Donegan told him he had taken care of everything. Then a terrifying thought frightened the white-suited politician into rigidity. Maybe they had somehow gotten to the strange policeman?

The City Council meeting concluded just before noon and the aldermen broke for lunch. Murphy hung around his desk for a while making small talk with fellow aldermen. Then, when he chanced to look back at the VIP section, the cops were gone.

Now Murphy felt silly. "What am I going to do," he quipped to himself, as he placed his white straw hat back on and cocked it at a rakish angle, "get the shakes every time some dumb flatfoot looks at me?"

The alderman decided to stop by the pressroom on the way out to lunch. It was always a good thing to keep in touch with the reporters assigned to the City Hall beat. They could always be counted on for some free publicity around election time.

He left the chambers by way of the same VIP section where the cops had been seated. This section was now vacant. He entered a small conference room, which could be accessed by passing a security checkpoint manned by a white-haired uniformed cop, who looked as if he was having trouble staying awake. The conference room was deserted and Murphy was crossing it en route to the pressroom when someone behind him called out, "Excuse me, Alderman Murphy, but could we have a few minutes of your time?"

Skip Murphy turned around to see Larry Cole and Blackie Silvestri approaching him.

The missing person's investigation that Detective Joe Donegan had submitted on the disappearance of Sophia Novak had been carelessly done. When Cole saw it he had seriously considered registering a formal complaint with the Internal Affairs Division charging Donegan with gross dereliction of duty. But that wouldn't find Stella Novak's sister any faster. So Cole decided to have his own people conduct the investigation, which was a violation of established department procedure.

At Cole's direction, Blackie gave the assignment to Lou Bronson and Manny Sherlock.

"I know you guys have a full case load, but this is a favor for the commander's therapist. And you're going to have to be careful, because you'll be operating in Area Six."

However, Bronson had been around long enough to know exactly how to handle this situation. Within less than two hours after receiving the assignment, they had a lead on Sophia Novak. A woman fitting her description had been seen in the early morning hours of June 13th having dinner at the Cape Cod

Room of the Drake Hotel with a black man. A check with the hotel's valet parking attendant uncovered that only one car had been parked after 1 A.M. This car was picked up at 3:32 A.M. The car was described as a late-model black Camaro bearing Illinois license plate number TR-9161. The Area One detectives ran this plate and discovered that it was registered to Phillip Murphy, Jr., the Chicago city councilman.

Detective Joe Donegan had not done a thorough job of covering up the barmaid's death.

When Skip Murphy's name came up in connection with Sophia Novak's disappearance, Larry Cole was surprised. The police commander didn't know much about the alderman, but what he did know wasn't good. Murphy had the reputation of being something of a player and his name had been mentioned in newspaper gossip columns on a number of occasions since his election. There had also been some hints of scandal surrounding him and some of his associates. However, bribery and malfeasance in politics were as much a part of the city of Chicago as the Sears Tower and Lake Michigan. But Skip Murphy's political background was secondary at this point. Cole was primarily interested in what had happened to Sophia Novak.

People go missing for a number of reasons. Some do so in order to escape from their lives and the complications in those lives. Such people don't want to be found. There are others who become missing persons against their will. A number of these cases end up becoming homicides. Cole realized that the longer Stella's sister remained missing, the greater the chances were that she was dead. That meant that the last person she was seen with was a possible murder suspect.

As was the case with the high profile Jeffery Pender, Cole and Blackie handled the interview with Skip Murphy personally. However, this time they did not let anyone at police headquarters know what they were doing. In a political town like Chicago this could end up compromising the investigation before it got started.

Cole and Blackie had waited for the council session to end before they approached the alderman. They were aware that Murphy had been absent from the City Council for three days, which would have placed his last showing at City Hall the day before Sophia Novak's disappearance.

Now, the cops approached the white-suited politician in the conference room. With an outwardly cool detachment, Murphy waited for them to come to him. After examining their identification, he said, "And what can I do for Chicago's finest today?"

"Have you ever been in a north side bar called the Lake Shore Tap?" Cole began the questioning.

"Occasionally."

"Did you happen to know any of the personnel who worked there?" Blackie said, slipping easily into the bad cop role.

"Before we go any further here," the alderman said with open irritation, "I demand to know why you're questioning me like some common criminal."

"We're looking into the mysterious disappearance of a young woman, Alderman," Cole said.

Now Skip Murphy was virtually bristling with outrage. "You mean to tell me that the Chicago Police Department has nothing better to do than send a commander around to investigate the disappearance of a barmaid?"

"How did you know that the young woman we're looking for is a barmaid?" Blackie said.

"Why you yourself said that this woman worked in a bar." Murphy was still indignant, but Cole and Blackie noticed that he had become a bit apprehensive.

"Perhaps it would be best if we told you exactly what we're looking for," Cole said.

"I think that would be the least you could do," Murphy snapped.

"A woman named Sophia Novak, who worked at the Lake Shore Tap as a barmaid, disappeared without a trace a few nights ago."

"And what has that got to do with me?"

"You were seen having a late supper at about two A.M. on the morning of June thirteenth with a woman who fit Ms. Novak's description," Cole said.

Now Murphy made no comment.

The cops waited.

Finally, Murphy said, "I never heard of anyone named Sophia Novak."

"Could you tell us the name of the blond woman that you were with at the Cape Cod Room of the Drake Hotel that night?" Cole asked.

"That's a personal matter, Commander Cole, and, as this is not a criminal investigation, I do not feel compelled to respond at this time. Now I have a busy schedule today, so if you don't mind." He turned to leave.

"There's just one more thing," Cole said to Murphy's back.

The alderman stopped, but did not turn around.

"This is not a criminal investigation, yet."

With that Skip Murphy walked out.

After he was gone, Blackie said, "So what do you think, boss?"

"He knows what happened to Stella's sister, Blackie. Now all we've got to do is prove it."

9

JUNE 16, 1992

3:25 P.M.

Megan Donegan pulled up in front of the Marquette Park bungalow she shared with her brother and was surprised to see Joe's car parked in the driveway. He hadn't been home this early in the day for months. The frail Water Department clerk let herself into the house and was crossing the neat, but gloomy, living room when she noticed that the message light on the answering machine was blinking. The telephone equipment was on a metal stand next to the wood-encased hi-fi set that their father had purchased on the installment plan twenty-two years ago. The answering machine call counter listed five recorded messages since the device had last been cleared. This was a very unusual number, as she and her brother seldom received any calls at all. However, when Megan ran the tape, there was nothing on it.

"How odd," she said to herself when the machine completed the replay. But Megan Donegan was a basically simple woman, who did not spend much time pondering the unexplainable.

She found her brother in his bedroom. Joe was stretched

out across the bed sound asleep. He was fully clothed, including his guns. She was a bit annoyed when she saw those filthy soft-soled black shoes he always wore on her nice clean bedspread, but she was not about to wake him up with all of those guns he carried. So she quietly closed the door and left him alone.

She went into the private bathroom off her bedroom, which had once belonged to their parents, and washed her hands and face. Studying her pale complexion and lank dark hair in the mirror above the sink, she wondered if she was going to spend the rest of her life in this house with her brother. She was not an unattractive woman; she was simply plain and, as one of her high school classmates had called her, totally lifeless. She had even consulted a doctor once and submitted to a blood test to determine if she had leukemia or some other form of exotic blood disease. This was because she always moved slowly and had little zest for anything in life. And even in this day of low personal morals, at the age of thirty-four, she was still a virgin.

She left the bedroom and went into the kitchen to fix a cup of tea, which she would drink while she watched the four o'clock news. Then she planned to take a short nap before it was time to start dinner, which she would probably eat alone. Tomorrow was a full workday at the Water Department.

There was a white envelope on the kitchen table. Her first name was scrawled across the front of it in Joe's nearly illegible handwriting. She picked up the envelope and tore open the flap. There was a note inside that read, "Buy a couple of things for the house and the rest is yours, Joe." There was a thousand dollars in cash inside the envelope.

"How in the world?" she said out loud, staring at the money. Then the phone rang.

Still clutching the envelope, she reached over and picked up the kitchen extension. "Hello?"

"May I speak to Joe Donegan?"

"Who is calling?" Her father had taught all of the Donegan children to make this request of callers.

"Tell him Skip and that it's important."

"Hold on."

She placed the phone down on the kitchen counter and, carrying the money with her, went to wake her brother.

It took five minutes of standing safely out in the hall, while knocking on the door frame and softly calling her brother's name, for her to wake him up. Because Joe was asleep in the middle of the day, which was highly unusual for him, she was beginning to worry if he was sick. When he finally did wake up and heard the name of the caller, he developed a ferocity that frightened her as he ran for the telephone.

"Yeah," she overheard him say into the living room extension. She remained in the hallway outside of his bedroom watching him. His shirt was a wrinkled mess with a dirt-encrusted collar and his cotton trousers looked as if he'd been wearing them for a month. Joe's nickname as a kid had been Pigpen after a "Peanuts" cartoon strip character. At least Bob Jr. and Ted, their older brothers, had called him that. After Joe became a cop the nickname was forgotten: however, he was still a slob.

Stuffing the envelope containing the money into her house-dress pocket, she went into his room and laid out clean clothes on the bed. She would also suggest politely that he take a shower and eat something before he went back out. Of course, her brother always did whatever he wanted to do.

*   *   *

The telephone call from Alderman Skip Murphy had been placed from a telephone booth in the lobby of a Loop office building. For each of the five calls he had placed to Joe Donegan's house, he had moved to a booth at a different location. He had also placed two calls to the Area Six Detective squad room. The second time Sergeant Mark Lewis had informed the unidentified caller that the detective was gone for the day.

When Murphy had finally made contact with Donegan, the alderman had given the detective a secure line and told him to call back from a pay phone. Joe Donegan, who had taken off early so he could catch up on his rest, was far from happy over this development. But he could tell by the tone of the politician's voice that something was wrong.

A late spring thunderstorm lashed the Windy City from late afternoon until dark. Torrential rains dropped two inches of water on the streets, flooding viaducts and clogging traffic arteries. The only public telephone Donegan could find was exposed on the edge of a self-service gas station two miles from his house. The clean clothing his sister had laid out for him became thoroughly soaked before he could get in touch with Murphy.

With his hair plastered to his skull and water running down his face, the cop shouted to be heard over the rumbling skies, "What's the problem?"

Murphy was indeed in a panic. "I thought you said you took care of everything?"

"I did."

"Well, earlier today a detective commander named Cole questioned me down at City Hall about the barmaid. He asked me if I'd ever been in the Lake Shore Tap before and for the identity of the woman I had dinner with at the Drake Hotel."

The part about the dinner surprised Donegan. "How did he find out that you were with her at the Drake?"

"How in the hell am I supposed to know, Donegan? But I paid you to make this thing go away and now it's right in my damned face, man!"

"Wait a minute, Murphy," Donegan responded, angrily. "You did no more than give me some expense money as a down payment on our partnership. You do remember that, don't you, partner?"

The alderman went silent for a moment before responding with a subdued, "I remember. But what about Cole?"

"Don't worry about Cole, Murphy. All he's got is a missing bimbo barmaid, who might or might not have been seen with you. There is no longer a murder scene nor a dead body, which even Cole needs to bring a murder charge. He's just pissing in the wind by questioning you. Do you follow me, Skip?"

Donegan was soaked to the skin; however, the discomfort was secondary, as he was beginning to feel a shift in his relationship with the philandering politician.

"What am I supposed to do now?" Murphy asked.

"If I were you, I'd make a complaint to the department about Cole harassing you. He probably had that thug sidekick of his Blackie Silvestri with him."

"Silvestri was there," Murphy admitted.

"Now you shouldn't make a big thing out of this complaint, Skip. Maybe it would be best if you handled it from the Hall. You could talk to the mayor or maybe the director of Public Safety, who's over the police department. What's that guy's name?"

"Edward Graham Luckett. He's a former alderman."

"There you go. A word in his ear should put enough heat on Cole to keep him and Silvestri off your back until this thing blows over."

There was a long sigh from Murphy's end of the line. "Okay, I'll play it your way, Joe, but I have one question to ask you."

"Go ahcad, partncr."

"What did you do with the barmaid's body? I saw you remove the charred remains from the Dumpster and place them back in the trunk of your car."

Donegan managed to laugh despite the horrible weather. "You need something called Plausible Deniability on that one, Skip. If you don't know, you can't ever tell anyone."

"There's just one more thing, Joe."

"Go ahead, but make it quick before I catch pneumonia."

"Burning that body so close to my Michigan cabin looked like an attempt to incriminate me."

The detective responded honestly. "It was then, but it's not now. Just do what I told you and everything will be just fine. Goodnight, Alderman."

With that, Joe Donegan hung up the public phone and ran back to his car.

10

Salvatore Scalise was a made Chicago mob wise guy. He was a member of the Antonio "Tuxedo Tony" DeLisa organization and had spent fifteen of his forty-four years of life in prison for everything from manslaughter to armed robbery. In his younger years he had been an amateur boxer before he graduated to mob enforcer. After his last stint in prison, Sal began putting on a great deal of weight and now topped the scales at three hundred pounds. He kept his curly hair dyed black and his features bore the scars from his earlier fight career. In a word, Sal Scalise was a brute.

He was still a mob enforcer, whose specialty was collecting overdue loan-sharking debts. But he also had a criminal sideline of hijacking trucks. And he was very good at it. With a crew of six mob soldiers, Sal had stolen over $18 million in merchandise from trucks delivering goods in and around the Chicago area. The Scalise crew went after only high-ticket items, such as computers, television sets, guns, and electronic components. Utilizing mob connections within the truckers' union, Scalise was alerted to the routes taken by certain shipments, so that he could select the location where they could be intercepted. In the majority of the hijackings the drivers put up little or no resistance and it was strongly suspected that a few vehicle operators gave passive cooperation in return for cash kickbacks.

However, in mid-May a truck hijacking went bad and a driver was shot to death. Sal Scalise's crew was suspected, but until they could be caught in the act, it would be difficult to mount a prosecution. The Chicago Police Department stepped up its efforts to apprehend the hijackers.

Blackie Silvestri had been raised on the west side of the city around mob types. He still had contacts over in the Taylor Street area who were not directly involved with the mob but were in positions to know things.

After their meeting with Alderman Skip Murphy at City Hall, the sergeant had dropped Larry Cole off at the Area One Police Center and drove down to Mama DeLeo's Pizzeria in the old neighborhood. The lunch crowd was beginning to slacken when Blackie walked in. There were a few mob types enjoying pizza and pasta dishes at the tables, which were covered with red-and-white checkered cloths. A number of the old-timers spoke to the cop. An equal number ignored him.

Blackie walked into the bar where Jimmy DeLeo, the grandson of the restaurant's owner, Grace DeLeo, was tending bar.

"Hey, Blackie," Jimmy said with a grin, "where in the hell have you been, paisan?"

"Working, Jimmy," he said, taking a seat at the bar.

"What'll it be?" Jimmy DeLeo was a good-natured, rotund man, who wore his hair in a slick-back ducktail.

"Make it a Coke and a slice of pepperoni."

"You got it," he said, pouring soda into a glass and shouting to a passing waitress, "Give me a slice of pepperoni thin crust at the bar."

Blackie had selected a seat, which placed him out of earshot of the other diners. DeLeo checked on the other bar patrons and filled a couple of orders for the waitresses before returning to the cop. Jimmy lowered his voice, as he said, "I've had my ear to the rail for you about Sal Scalise's crew and there's supposed to be something going down in a couple of days."

The waitress serving Blackie's pizza forced a pause. When she was gone, Blackie asked, "You got any particulars?"

DeLeo smiled. "I got everything for you including the truck registration and the description of the cargo."

"What about an invoice number?"

For a moment DeLeo thought Blackie was serious. Then he shot back, "Give me a day or so and I'll come up with it for you."

Three days later on the morning of June 19, a silver tractor-trailer pulled out of the loading yard on West Thirty-ninth Street. It contained VCRs valued at a wholesale price of fifty-thousand dollars. The truck proceeded westbound until a red light halted it before it could make the turn onto the Dan Ryan Expressway. The hijackers approached from both sides. One of them, a short bald man, jumped on the running board on the driver's side; the other, a broad-shouldered blond with a droopy mustache, yanked the passenger door open and pointed a gun at the driver.

"Let's make this easy," the blond said, "and nobody gets hurt. In fact, if you play this thing right, there might be a few bucks in it for you."

The driver was a dark-complexioned, extremely muscular black man wearing a trucker's union ball cap. He responded with a docile, "No problem, fellas," and slid into the center of the trunk cab bench seat to give the hijackers room.

The bald man got in behind the wheel, put the Mack truck in gear and turned south onto the Dan Ryan Expressway.

A red Cadillac Coupe De Ville was parked in a vacant lot a quarter of a block away from the scene of the hijacking. There were two men in the car, who were quite similar in appearance. The passenger was Sal Scalise and the driver was his first cousin Joey Scalise. They were supervising the robbery. A gray panel truck, which had transported the two hijackers, who were now in the cab with the driver, followed the truck down onto the expressway. The red Cadillac joined in the procession.

Keeping just below the posted speed limit, the caravan proceeded south to 104th Street and exited into an industrial area in the South Chicago neighborhood. Without incident they reached a warehouse on a tree-lined street. While Joey Scalise parked the car on the street, Sal got out and went to unlock a side door. He vanished inside and a moment later an overhead door opened and the hijacked tractor-trailer was driven inside with the panel truck close behind.

The warehouse was a block long and vacant except for two other trucks, which were half the size of the hijacked vehicle. The driver was ordered out of the truck and Sal Scalise and the other hijackers came over to join them.

The ex-boxer noticed that the truck driver possessed world class bodybuilder dimensions. "Look, my friend," Scalise said, "we're going to unload your cargo, but you can keep the truck. You can tell the cops what happened, but if you're smart . . ." He turned to look at the other hijackers, "Does he look smart to you guys?"

"Yeah, boss, he looks smart enough," one of them responded.

"So, my friend, if you're smart, you'll get real hazy about

what we look like and totally forget about this place. Tell the cops that we blindfolded you or some such. Am I making myself understood?"

"You sure are, Mr. Scalise. I'm reading you loud and clear," the driver said.

"What did you call me?" Sal said. The mobster was well known in Chicago.

The big black guy snapped his fingers. "You know, I forgot the name already."

"Good boy. Now why don't you give us a hand unloading the truck and you'll walk away from this with a few extra dollars in your pocket."

"Thanks a lot," the driver said with a grin.

They walked to the back of the trailer, where one of the hijackers used bolt cutters to snap the lock. As they began opening the rear door, the driver said, "There's just one more thing, Sal."

"I thought we had an understanding about you using my name," the mobster snarled.

"I think I'll be calling your name quite a bit from now on, Sal," Sergeant Clarence McKinnis said. "You're under arrest."

At first the hijackers thought it was a joke. Then the back doors of the truck flew open to reveal that there were no VCRs inside, but there were four shotgun-wielding cops: Larry Cole, Blackie Silvestri, Lou Bronson, and Manny Sherlock.

While they were booking Sal Scalise and his hijacking crew, First Deputy Superintendent William Riseman paid a visit to the Area One Police Center. Having the city's number two cop drop in on them unannounced was something that happened very rarely.

Blackie Silvestri was processing Scalise in an interview room. The defiant mobster was handcuffed to a metal ring embedded in the wall. The sergeant sat at a desk a few feet away typing up an arrest report. Blackie was almost able to fill out the document from memory. He was unaware that Riseman had entered the room until the first deputy was standing right next to him.

"How's it going, Blackie?"

"Hey, boss. What brings you out this way?"

"Just a social call." Riseman looked across at the handcuffed prisoner. "Still up to your old tricks, Sal?"

"Drop dead, Riseman," Scalise snarled. "I'm still waiting to make my phone call so my lawyer can come down here and spring me and my boys."

"I wouldn't worry about a lawyer, Sal," Blackie said. "You're facing multiple armed robbery counts. Only a judge can set your bond and it's going to be high."

"As soon as they do set the bail, Silvestri, I'll be out of here so fast you won't have time to say 'donut break.' Then I'll see you and Cole in court."

"Where is Larry?" Riseman asked.

"I think he's in his office," Blackie said.

As the first deputy left the interview room, he said to the prisoner, "I hope you enjoy your vacation in Joliet, Sal."

The mobster snorted in reply.

"That was good work bagging the Scalise gang, Larry," Riseman was saying over a cup of coffee in Cole's office. "You have any idea what they did with the proceeds from the other robberies?"

"From what Blackie has been able to find out from his

informants, they've fenced most of the stuff through organized crime families all across the country. I don't think we're going to recover any of it. One thing is certain; Scalise and his people aren't going to talk."

"The old Mafia oath of Omerta," Riseman said. "That means the insurance companies will have to absorb the loss, which will make all of our premiums go up."

Cole had known Bill Riseman for a long time and was aware that a man who was as busy as the first deputy hadn't simply dropped by to discuss a routine arrest. The detective commander decided to bait the hook. "How are things at headquarters?"

"The superintendent is attending an international law enforcement conference in London. He won't be back until next week."

"So you're running the show," Cole said.

"Yeah, but it's a real pain in the ass job. The main problem is dealing with the politicians."

Cole saw it coming. "Like a certain South Side alderman named Murphy?"

Riseman set his coffee cup down on Cole's desk. "I didn't hear directly from Skip Murphy, but I did get a call from Edward Graham Luckett."

"What did our esteemed director of Public Safety have to say?"

"Quite a bit. He accused you of mounting a scandal campaign against the alderman."

"You know me better than that, boss. But Murphy is involved in the case I am looking into. I'm certain of it."

"Maybe you'd better fill me in."

Cole told Riseman everything. But there was a new angle

to Sophia Novak's disappearance. He shared this with the first deputy. "The night after Sophia Novak went missing, there was an armed robbery at the Lake Shore Tap where she worked. The bartender and a barmaid were shot to death in what could be considered execution-style. None of the patrons were hurt. With a bit of imagination thrown in, we could have someone killing them as part of a coverup to protect Murphy. The alderman was seen with a woman fitting Sophia Novak's description in the Cape Cod Room on the morning of the thirteenth. He could have picked her up at the bar, taken her out to dinner, and then gone someplace else with her. There something happened. To cover up the connection between Murphy and the missing woman, the bartender and barmaid at the Lake Shore Tap were killed."

Riseman was openly skeptical. "I don't know much about Skip Murphy, Larry, but we're talking about a serious homicidal maniac here. I don't think the alderman's into killing people."

"Suppose he hired someone to do the dirty work for him?"

"Like who?"

"If I keep looking into this thing, I'll find out," Cole said.

"That's the problem," Riseman said with an edge in his voice. "You're mounting a completely improper investigation against a Chicago city councilman without a great deal, if any, probable cause. An investigation that is bringing heat on the department, on me, and on you. You're lucky that the superintendent is in Europe or you'd be on the carpet down in his office about this right now. For chrissakes, Cole, Sophia Novak is nothing but a missing person. Don't you have enough crime in your own backyard without going up to Area Six looking for more?"

Cole took the tongue lashing in stride. "I didn't mean to embarrass anyone with this investigation, especially you, boss. If you want me to lay off of Murphy, I will."

Riseman, who was considered something of a soft-spoken academic within the department, felt guilty for having become so emotional with Cole. "I'm not ever going to tell you to look the other way if you have evidence that Murphy or anyone else has committed a crime. But I want you to have hard evidence before the politicians start shouting 'foul.' "

"I understand you completely, boss."

The first deputy got to his feet. "That was good work nabbing Sal Scalise. In fact, you're having a pretty good week with nailing Jeffery Pender and that juvenile sniper." He reached the door. "Larry, you're the best field commander in the city. Let's keep LaSalle Street happy. Okay?"

"Whatever you say, boss," Cole said. "Let me walk you out."

After booking Sal Scalise, Blackie went to Cole's office. The sergeant took one look at the commander's face and realized that Riseman's visit had not been a strictly social call. "Our political friends causing problems?"

"Murphy went all the way up to the director of Public Safety. Riseman's afraid that the superintendent will react badly to the pressure, so he's ordered me off of the Sophia Novak investigation."

Blackie took a seat across from Cole. "This whole thing stinks, Larry. Murphy killed that woman and hid her body. Once we find the corpse we can build a case against the alderman and to hell with City Hall."

Cole didn't respond right away, but Blackie could tell that

the commander was as adamant as he was. Finally Cole said, "Since we can't go after Murphy directly, we'll just have to go about it a different way."

"I'm not following you."

"Maybe it's better that you don't, Blackie," Cole said. "I promised Stella Novak that I'd find her sister and I intend to do just that, one way or another. Only now I'll have to do it alone."

11

OCTOBER 14, 1993
2:45 P.M.

The municipal elections were scheduled for the first week in February. The offices of mayor, city clerk, city treasurer and all fifty aldermanic seats were at stake. On every street in the city, posters advertising the candidates were attached to light poles, billboards, and the walls of buildings. For certain offices, the major political parties opened their coffers and poured millions into the various races. However, most of the money expended came from the individual candidates.

In twentieth-century America, elections were decided in the majority of cases on the basis of which candidate had the largest war chest. The funds in these war chests were subject to IRS and Federal Election Commission oversight and generally came from fund-raisers sponsored by the candidates. Skip Murphy had amassed a sizeable campaign chest and he spent this money freely on everything from campaign ads to election posters. Yet, with the election less than a month away, the incumbent alderman was lagging behind his opponent by ten percentage points in all of the polls.

Murphy's challenger was the Reverend Harrison Jones, who had completed divinity college by going to night school. He was a sixty-year-old, overweight, white-haired black man with an impoverished congregation of three thousand devout followers. To supplement the small salary he was paid by the church, he was forced to keep his job with the U.S. Post Office. But despite his having the equivalent of two full-time jobs, Reverend Jones was a very dedicated man, who took his commitment to the community seriously.

During the eight years that Skip Murphy had been the alderman of the depressed ward in which Reverend Jones's church was located, all city services were allowed to slip to a nearly nonexistent level. Streets were seldom cleaned, sidewalks deteriorated into a state of such disrepair as to become dangerous to pedestrians, and garbage collection was sporadic. Complaints to the alderman's office went unheeded and complaining constituents were often treated rudely by Murphy's staff. Reverend Jones was one of the playboy alderman's most vocal critics and decided to take him on in the next election. With only a handful of volunteers and no money, Harrison Jones launched his campaign.

Instead of slick ads and posters, Jones took his campaign to the people, visiting churches, community meetings, and walking the ghetto streets to meet people. At the beginning of the campaign, Murphy had considered his opponent little more than a minor nuisance. Then, despite all of his money and the mayor's endorsement, he began to slip badly in the polls.

Skip Murphy didn't believe in going out to "press the flesh" so to speak. Instead he convened mass gatherings, which were packed with his supporters. All in attendance were plied with free beer and food as they cheered him wildly. Usually, again due to his huge campaign war chest, Murphy paid to have a freelance video photographer standing by to record the events. The footage was provided free of charge to the alderman's contacts in the news media, which he had cultivated at City Hall. By early fall of this election year, Skip Murphy had run a well-financed, slick reelection campaign. A campaign that he was losing.

In his ward office, a worried alderman listened to the report of one of his unofficial staffers, whom he had dispatched to spy on a Harrison Jones rally. The staffer was a thin young black man with corn-rowed hair, who had a record as a drug dealer and street gang member. And although Murphy paid well for the information, what he heard wasn't good.

"Jones is really putting you down, Skip," the spy told him. "He called you 'morally bankrupt.' Says that instead of looking after the people in the ward, you spend all of your time chasing women and drinking in taverns."

"Nobody is going to pay attention to that kind of garbage," Murphy said.

"There were about four hundred people at the rally and they all seemed to be eating it up. In fact, there was a camera crew there and they interviewed Jones. I listened in and this chick from the TV station compared the reverend's campaign to a religious movement."

The alderman didn't like the sound of this at all. Politics was one thing, but fighting some type of holy quest for justice was another matter.

Murphy brooded alone in his office for a long time after

the spy left. There were two alternatives facing the politician. He could risk losing the election and retire from public life. He definitely had enough money to live very comfortably. But he was neither ready nor willing to relinquish the power and prestige that came with being a member of the Chicago city council. Then his vanity took over. He was prepared to do whatever was necessary to win the election even if it meant killing the troublesome Reverend Harrison Jones.

Skip Murphy reached for the telephone and dialed a number from memory.

"Area Four Detective Division, Detective Parker."

"I would like to speak to Sergeant Donegan."

"Please hold."

In the fall of 1992, promotions to the ranks of sergeant, lieutenant, and captain within the Chicago Police Department were given based on three criteria: the applicant's score on a multiple choice examination, the applicant's job performance rating, and the applicant's seniority. Factoring in all elements, a final numerical grade was arrived at and the candidates ranked on a list. This list was compiled in secret at City Hall and often, after the final list was posted, allegations of political tampering were made. And there had been no CPD promotional list in recent memory that was not challenged by a lawsuit.

On the promotional list for the rank of sergeant posted in January 1993, Detective Joe Donegan, with the assistance of Alderman Skip Murphy, finished number seventy-five out of a field of six thousand candidates. Through the alderman's political connection to Edward Graham Luckett, the director of Public Safety, Sergeant Donegan's first assignment in his new rank was back in the detective division. His former colleagues in

Area Six, to include Sergeant Mark Lewis, were not surprised that an incompetent like Donegan had been promoted, because, after all, "It ain't on the legit."

Murphy had let the new sergeant know in no uncertain terms, exactly what he had done on Donegan's behalf. To an extent, the cop was grateful. The promotion was simply an act, which further solidified the partnership between the two men.

The Area Four Detective Unit was headquartered in the police center at Harrison and Kedzie on the west side of the city. The office that Joe Donegan now worked out of was on the second floor above the Eleventh Police District, where he had worked as a uniformed patrol officer. As far as Donegan was concerned nothing had changed for him with the exception that he now made more money and carried a sergeant's badge in his pocket. His duties entailed the supervision of eight detectives assigned to the Property Crimes Section. Most of his subordinates had more seniority than Donegan and didn't think very much of the strange disheveled supervisor who carried all of those guns. But as time passed the detectives became indifferent toward their new sergeant, because he never bothered them and, in fact, they seldom even saw him. The detectives on the squad were good cops and didn't need to be closely monitored. So Donegan was free to do what he wanted.

Now the cop was about to take care of another problem for Alderman Skip Murphy.

"Donegan." The sergeant answered the telephone in the same gruff manner that he had employed when he was a detective.

"It's Skip. I need to discuss something with you."

Donegan was aware of Murphy's position in the election polls. "Are you going to have me standing out in the rain at a public phone booth or are you going to invite me over for coffee?"

There was a pause from the other end that Donegan could only classify as nervous. Then, "I don't think that it would be a good idea to have a meeting at my apartment. But there is a place that is safe from prying eyes."

"Give me the address and the time," Donegan said.

Randy's Roost was a tavern in Skip Murphy's ward that catered to an older jazz-loving crowd. For a depressed area on the south side of the city, the Roost, as it was called, was clean, nicely furnished, and always had a muscular, tough-looking bouncer stationed at the front door to discourage trouble. The drinks were more expensive per shot than was the case in other bars in the neighborhood and the disc jockey played only easy listening music or soft jazz, which had a tendency to keep the riffraff out. This kept the number of patrons at a manageable level even during peak hours on the weekend.

It would seem to the careful observer that Randy's Roost couldn't do enough business to keep the doors open. Actually, the business lost money, but the proprietor did very well, due to a few secret, highly illegal enterprises.

Randy's Roost was actually owned by William S. "Dollar Bill" Randolph, who was a professional gambler with an extensive criminal record. The liquor license was in his estranged wife's name. Although Sharon Powell Randolph hated her husband, she received five thousand dollars a month in cash and a 20 percent share of all legitimate bar profits. Dollar Bill Randolph made a great deal more money than what it cost him to keep the Roost in business.

Dollar Bill was a thin, gray-haired black man, who wore

horn-rimmed glasses and sported a pencil-thin mustache over his upper lip. It had been remarked on more than one occasion by those who came in contact with him, that the gambler looked like a bank clerk. This was an apt description, because the little man definitely had a way with money.

Although his criminal specialty was listed as "gambler," he didn't participate directly in games of chance. Instead he operated "floating" dice, poker, and roulette games, which changed locations on a constant basis to keep a step ahead of the cops. All of Randolph's games of chance were held in Skip Murphy's ward because of an arrangement the gambler had made with the politician. However, this was only one of Dollar Bill's criminal sidelines.

The introduction of cheap crack cocaine into the illegal narcotics market in the United States had resulted in an increased need for 100-proof grain alcohol, which was an ingredient required to cook pure cocaine down into instantly addicting crack rocks. Dollar Bill Randolph purchased gallons of grain alcohol from a local wholesale distributor, which he in turn sold out of the back door of Randy's Roost to a narcotics connection. And although William S. "Dollar Bill" Randolph was a smart man, getting into the narcotics business was the biggest mistake he had ever made during his long criminal career.

Randolph was in his office at the back of the Roost. He was wearing a gray silk leisure suit that cost over a thousand dollars and wore only two pieces of jewelry: a jewel-encrusted horseshoe-shaped pinky ring and a gold Rolex wristwatch. The total value of the jewelry was ten grand. Despite being a career criminal, Dollar Bill was a very intelligent man, who laundered most of his illegal income through a mob-controlled investment company and paid his federal and state taxes on time. He possessed a high I.Q. and was well read, but had a limited formal education. Had he been born at a different place and time, he might have been able to make more of himself. But the black ghetto of Chicago had left him few opportunities to succeed in the legitimate world, so he had done what he felt he had to do. The gambler swore that his only son would do better.

His private office was constructed so that Dollar Bill could look out through a one-way pane of glass and see the entire bar and the tables below. It was a quiet afternoon and the Roost was virtually deserted. The gambler had a full range of illegal activities planned for tonight. The delivery of twenty-four gallons of grain alcohol to the Gangster Disciples street gang, a crap game being held in a vacant building (which had once housed a funeral home), and a high-stakes poker game in the basement of the Roost itself were all on the agenda. The gambler anticipated a profit from the alcohol sale and a 10 percent cut of the gambling games of over one hundred thousand dollars.

Then Alderman Skip Murphy walked in the front door.

Concealed in his office, the bar owner frowned. He didn't like politicians. In fact, he had a marked aversion to government officials of any ilk. Dollar Bill Randolph was a businessman, who made money whenever and wherever he could. In his opinion, the government had been set up to make success as difficult as possible for him. Especially because he was black. And there was always some politician or cop with their hands out for a bribe. Dollar Bill realized that he needed them to stay in business, and now Murphy was here and the bar owner was forced to play a role that he hated.

The owner of Randy's Roost left his office and descended

a short flight of wooden steps to a secret door hidden at the back of a broom closet behind the bar. Unseen by the bartender and the bouncer stationed at the front door, Dollar Bill slipped out of the closet just as the alderman took a seat in one of the back booths. Besides Murphy, there were only two other patrons in the Roost at this time of the day.

"What's happening, Skip?" the bar owner said with a broad smile, which effectively masked his true feelings.

"Dollar Bill," Murphy responded, remaining seated and extending an upraised palm. "Are you still raking in tons of cash every day?"

Randolph slapped the upraised palm. "If I had your hand, I'd throw mine in, Alderman. You drinking the usual?"

"Just give me a beer right now. I'm expecting company."

"A good-looking woman?"

"No. It's business."

Randolph didn't like the sound of this. "Political business?"

Ignoring the question, Murphy said, "I'll have a glass of Budweiser from the tap."

Angered at having been dismissed like a menial, but continuing to conceal it behind a smile, Dollar Bill Randolph went behind the bar and filled a stein of beer for the alderman. He was just about to deliver it to the table when Sergeant Joe Donegan walked in.

Randolph had been around too long not to be aware of a number of things about the newcomer. First and foremost was that the odd-looking white man was mentally unstable. He was also a cop and carried a couple of good-sized firearms beneath that cheap, oversized, off-the-rack sports jacket he was wearing. And although the newcomer wasn't Vice, or at least any vice cop that Dollar Bill knew, he took a long, slow, thorough look around the place before he approached Murphy's table. In a word, this particular cop was trouble.

Randolph waited until the cop was seated before he approached the table. He considered the presence of the politician and the cop in his bar on this day a bad omen for things to come.

The bag lady was bundled up against the forty-degree temperature of this mid-October afternoon. A stiff breeze was blowing leaves and other debris, making the woman's eyes tear as she struggled under the weight of the two shopping bags she carried, which contained all of her belongings. She had been on the street in front of Randy's Roost for most of the day attempting to panhandle some spare change from passersby. She had taken in a total of $72.35.

To the casual observer, she would appear to be quite unremarkable and was hardly an unusual sight in the 1990s. Actually, she had become virtually invisible. On his way in to Randy's Roost, Skip Murphy had given her two dollars. When Joe Donegan arrived a few minutes later he had totally ignored the homeless woman. In fact, she had photographed both of them utilizing a camera concealed in the left lapel of her seedy overcoat. And she was not an aged crone, even though she looked like one. Officer Judy Daniels, known in the Narcotics Section of the Chicago Police Department as the Mistress of Disguise/High Priestess of Mayhem, was actually an attractive young woman in her twenties.

The Narcotics Section of the Vice Control Division had mounted a mission in an attempt to stem the ocean of crack cocaine flooding the Windy City. The street dealers were so numerous that it would take a police force ten times the size of the entire CPD to affect even a small segment of the problem. So they went after the source of the illegal drug, which led them to Randy's Roost.

Employing three undercover vehicles on a rolling surveillance and the formidable talents of Judy Daniels, a team of Narcotics officers had kept Randy's Roost under surveillance for three days. The delivery of twenty-four gallons of 100-proof grain alcohol had been recorded on videotape the day before. Now the Narcotics cops were waiting for the shipment to be picked up so that they could follow it to the next step up the pipeline.

Out on the street in the cold, Undercover Officer Judy Daniels had been surprised for the first time since the surveillance began when Joe Donegan arrived at Randy's Roost. After the strange cop had entered the tavern, the bag lady shuffled down the street to an alley. At the mouth of this alley she stopped and took in an additional $1.25 before carefully checking the street in front of the tavern to make sure that she was not being observed. Then she vanished.

A few minutes later Judy was slipping out of her bulky outer garments and peeling off the latex mask she had worn all day. She was in the back of a gray panel truck crammed with surveillance equipment, which was manned by a portly technician named Mike Thompson. The technician had a serious crush on the Mistress of Disguise/High Priestess of Mayhem.

Judy was wiping her face with an alcohol-based astringent when Mike turned from the monitors, which were connected to cameras covering every angle of the exterior of Randy's Roost.

"I've got some coffee and turkey sandwiches," he said, handing her a brown paper sack.

She smiled. "Are the sandwiches on onion rolls with mayo?"

He blushed. "I got them from that deli you like up on Diversey."

"You are too sweet, Mike," she said, thoroughly rinsing the dirt off of her hands with more alcohol before unwrapping a sandwich. After chasing a bite with a swallow of black coffee, she asked the technician, "Do you remember a cop who used to work the Prostitution Unit named Joe Donegan?"

"The Lone Stranger. Yeah, I remember him."

"The Lone Stranger?" she questioned.

"Yeah, that's what they used to call him. I heard he got promoted to sergeant."

"He did," Judy said. "I worked a joint Narcotics/Prostitution Unit operation with him a few years back. I was brand new and scared to death. Five female junkies ended up dead and there was a rumor that a gangster pimp on the west side was getting them hooked before sending them out on the street and then killing them with hot shot overdoses. I went undercover and managed to get a lead on the pimp.

"We got a warrant and raided his apartment. Discovered six kilos of heroin, a couple of strung-out teenage runaways, a small arsenal, and a pile of cash. Donegan was assigned as the inventory officer for the contraband and a sergeant from Prostitution told me to assist him." Judy paused to take a bite of her sandwich.

Mike was listening intently.

"Like I said, it was one of my first undercover jobs and I didn't completely understand the procedure. Donegan kept trying to get me out of the room so he could be alone with the money and the guns. I strongly suspected that he helped himself to some of the cash. But I couldn't prove it."

Mike Thompson was wide-eyed with shock. "What did you do, Judy?"

She finished her sandwich. "I hate crooked cops, Mike. Especially when the day might come when my life could depend on one of them backing me up. So I made a complaint to the commander of the Narcotics Section about Donegan. A short time later he was transferred to the Detective Division, but I'm pretty sure nothing happened to him. The IAD never even took a statement from me."

The young technician became uncomfortable. He hadn't been in the Chicago Police Department much longer than Judy and he was ideologically opposed to dishonest cops. But he had also been taught that you never turn in another cop. This was a serious contradiction, which had destroyed a number of good cops' careers in the past. Finally, Mike asked her, "What made you think of the Lone Stranger anyway?"

She pointed at the monitor displaying the front of Randy's Roost. "He's in there right now with a Chicago city councilman named Skip Murphy."

12

OCTOBER 14, 1993
4:35 P.M.

Skip Murphy was a master of misdirection and the double meaning. Joe Donegan listened to the alderman patiently as he explained the problem he faced with Reverend Harrison Jones leading him in the election polls. Murphy was asking for

Donegan's help, but he wouldn't come out and actually say what he wanted the cop to do.

Finally, Donegan said, bluntly, "So you want me to kill your opponent in the February election, isn't that right, Skip?"

Nervously, Murphy looked around to make sure no one had overheard him. "I just want to make sure that I get reelected. That's all."

"From what I've been hearing on the news, there's a strong possibility that you'll lose even if something does happen to the black preacher." There was a sarcastic tone in Donegan's voice.

Murphy glared at him. "That's not funny."

"Sorry, Skip, but I thought it was time to lighten things up a bit. I'll take care of this problem for you just like I've handled things in the past. Now let's talk terms."

"Terms?" Murphy said with a raised eyebrow.

"Compensation, brother," Donegan said, flashing a rare grin. "And I don't work cheap anymore."

"I got you promoted."

"Did you? I thought it was because I'm a pretty smart guy, despite what some of my colleagues think."

"Okay, Joe," Murphy said with a sigh. "What do you want? Another promotion? Money?"

"I'll let you figure it out, Skip. How much is your aldermanic seat worth to you?"

Murphy thought for a moment. "Twenty-five thousand in cash and a promotion to lieutenant on the next list."

"Make it fifty grand and you can keep the lieutenant's badge. I don't need that kind of rank. I'm happy right where I am."

"Done," Murphy said. "Now I need this taken care of . . ."

Abruptly, Donegan changed the subject. "This is a nice place. Kind of out of the way; off the beaten path, so to speak. Good music too. That is, if you like jazz."

"It's just a front," Murphy said. "The owner's named Dollar Bill Randolph. He's a professional gambler. Nothing you'd be interested in."

Donegan affixed the alderman with one of his chilling stares. "Why don't you let me be the judge of what does or doesn't interest me?"

In the sixteen-month period since the mysterious disappearance of Sophia Novak, Larry Cole had conducted an ongoing, very discreet investigation of Alderman Skip Murphy. Finding out what the politician had done with the Polish-born woman became an obsession for Cole and was not something that he was going to give up on. Perhaps the moment when he became irrevocably committed to the search for Stella's sister was at Sophie's memorial service.

It was held the day after Christmas at Saint Stanislaus Catholic Church, which was Stella's parish. Cole and Blackie were invited to attend what ended up being a funeral without a casket. Following the service, the mourners were invited back to the Novak apartment where Stella now lived alone. The surviving sister, with help from some of her neighbors, served lunch from a buffet table adorned with red and green candles. There was also a beautifully decorated Christmas tree in the living room. Despite the cheerful surroundings, everyone present was painfully aware that they were attending a wake.

Cole managed to speak privately with Stella. "I'm not going to stop looking for Sophie."

The therapist's eyes were red, but she was in control of herself. "I appreciate everything that you have done, Commander, but I don't think there is any hope that my sister is still alive."

Cole's jaw muscles rippled. "Then I will make whoever is responsible for what happened to her pay." At that moment the detective commander swore a blood oath.

The background information that Cole collected on Skip Murphy was extensive, but of little consequence. The dossier the policeman compiled was gleaned primarily from public records and news accounts. As the months went by, all Cole had was a vague sketch of the man. If Cole was ever going to discover what Murphy had done to Sophie, he would have to learn a great deal more. It would be necessary to see the dark hidden side of Phillip "Skip" Murphy, Jr.

It was at that point that Cole moved into a very precarious area. Because of politically motivated secret investigations, which the Chicago Police Department had previously engaged in, spying on private citizens was strictly prohibited. Larry Cole was not examining the life of Skip Murphy for political reasons, but to obtain enough information to charge him with murder someday.

To find out the bad about a man, go to his enemies. Cole started with the alderman's former political opponents. Posing as a freelance journalist, he telephoned Curtis Ramey, the seventy-four-year-old former senior statesman of the Chicago city council, whom Skip Murphy had beaten in a heated election eight years ago. After his defeat, Ramey had accused Murphy of running a dirty tricks campaign, which included the intimidation of campaign workers and voters by a street gang.

Ramey's reputation preceded him as he was known for being somewhat long-winded. When Cole stated that he was doing an article on Chicago politics, the former alderman, who had languished in obscurity since his defeat, was eager to cooperate. And it didn't take long for him to get around to Skip Murphy.

"Murphy represents everything that is wrong with our current municipal system of government. He has no interest in serving the people, but is simply hungry for the power that comes with elected office. And you can quote me on that, sir. What was that name again?"

"Just call me Larry," the cop said, hoping that he wouldn't delve too deeply into his phony journalist's background.

Ramey didn't. "Well, Larry, if the truth be known, Skip Murphy has more skeletons rattling around in his closet than a graveyard after the levee breaks."

Cole was eager to ask what kind of skeletons, but restrained himself. The former alderman came through for him.

"The boy is into real kinky sex. He'll screw a snake if he could get it to stay still long enough. He picks women up in bars and wines and dines them before taking them to some cheap motel for an assignation. And between you and me, Murphy should have owned a part interest in that motel that burned down some months ago, after all the rooms that he rented there under phony names."

Cole felt a chill go through him. "The South Michigan Avenue Motel?"

"That's the one, Larry. Well, it's my understanding that he would take his dates to that place and had even been known to get a bit rough with them. If I remember correctly, a few years ago he barely escaped a major scandal when he slapped a woman around so severely that she was forced to go to a hospital. This was maybe five years ago and Murphy paid off some people big-time to keep it quiet. I heard the girl got a bundle out of him."

"You wouldn't happen to remember the woman's name?"

"Theresa Anne Forrest. Lives out in the South Side. But I doubt if she'll talk to you. Murphy's money saw to that."

She wouldn't talk to a freelance journalist, but she might to Commander Larry Cole of the Chicago Police Department.

Joe Donegan left Randy's Roost a few minutes before Skip Murphy. Darkness had fallen on the city and the temperature had dropped into the thirties. Sitting in his battered Ford down the street from the tavern, Donegan turned the heater on and sat behind the wheel waiting. A short time later Murphy came out, got into his new metallic blue Corvette, and drove away. Still Donegan remained.

The crooked cop was thinking about what the alderman had told him about the goings on at Randy's Roost. Apparently a lot of cash passed through Dollar Bill Randolph's hands. Money that was the proceeds from criminal enterprises. Donegan realized that he had a more pressing matter to take care of for Skip Murphy. However, once that was done he planned to return to Randy's Roost.

Cole looked up Theresa Forrest's name in the department's computerized victim file. He found that she had reported a simple battery to a uniformed officer in the emergency room of University Hospital at 3:45 A.M. on February 11, 1988. The offender was listed as "unknown." The location of the crime was the South Michigan Avenue Motel. The file also contained a copy of the emergency room admittance sheet, with a photo of the victim's injuries, and a copy of the detective's follow-up report. The picture, which was somewhat grainy, was clear enough for Cole to see an attractive young woman with the left side of her face swollen to twice its normal size. But none of the police reports identified the person responsible for her injuries.

Cole read the narrative of the police report taken at the hospital: "The victim stated that she was struck in the face by an unknown person. At the time of the incident, the victim also related that she was highly intoxicated and had used marijuana."

The detective's follow-up report was even shorter: "After numerous attempts to contact the complainant have failed, the reporting detective requests that this case be closed due to the victim's failure to cooperate."

Cole didn't recognize the name of the officer who had taken the report, but he did know the detective who had done the follow-up. He had retired the year Cole had taken over as the Area One Detective Commander. The detective's phone number was still on file.

He was unable to tell Cole much more than what was contained in the report. Despite a number of personal visits to her apartment and at least ten phone calls to Theresa Anne Forrest five years ago, she had failed to respond. Cole decided to attempt to make direct contact with her now. The address listed for her was in the Park Manor neighborhood. Cole went there alone.

There was no "Forrest" listed on the mailboxes in the vestibule of the three-flat building. He rang the first-floor bell, which was answered by a heavyset black woman with rollers in her hair. She started to flirt the instant she saw the handsome cop.

"I'm sorry to bother you, ma'am, but I was looking for Theresa Anne Forrest," Cole explained, displaying his badge and ID card.

"Honey," she said, expansively, "you're about five years too late. That child moved out of the second-floor apartment back in 1988. She got beat up by her boyfriend and to shut her up, he gave her a lot of money. She moved to California and hasn't been seen or heard from around here since."

"You wouldn't know who that boyfriend was by any chance?"

She dropped her voice to a whisper. "It was Skip Murphy, the alderman. Now he never come by here to see Terry. We called her Terry. But she used to tell me that he was into weird sex, if you know what I mean."

Cole didn't see any need to go into particulars at this point. "Did he beat her up often?"

"No. Just that one time. But her face looked like he'd used it for a football. Her eye was swollen out to here." She cupped one of her hands over the left side of her face. "But she got paid off and then some. She moved out of here in style."

Reverend Harrison Jones had never worked harder in his life, but he felt that he was on a divine mission. When he began the campaign to unseat Skip Murphy, he had no expectation of winning. Primarily, Reverend Jones wanted to call the alderman's shortcomings to the attention of the ward's residents.

Then the campaign developed a momentum of its own, which was almost frightening in intensity.

Harrison Jones's church was in the middle of the block on a ghetto side street. A white and red stucco edifice, it had been built in the thirties and was so poorly maintained over the years that in 1979 the structure was condemned as a hazard. It was then that Harrison Jones's predecessor, the Reverend Edward McCann, mounted a movement to save the building and restore it. But money was in short supply from a congregation existing on poverty-level incomes and the repairs were sporadic and often haphazardly done. The church managed to remain open by what could only be considered the Will of God.

Now Harrison Jones sat in his office off the front vestibule. The noise made by the wind blowing through cracks in the old walls made a whistling sound, which some of the older parishioners claimed was caused by ghosts chanting religious hymns. Jones didn't believe in ghosts, but one thing that the old walls and poor insulation made him painfully aware of was that they made the old church an ice box when it was cold outside.

To keep from freezing, the pastor had a space heater going full blast beneath his desk. Jones had been working on a schedule of his appearances for the next week of the campaign. All of the pre-election polls reported that he would sweep to an easy victory in February. The prospect of what it would be like for the simple ghetto preacher to take a seat on the Chicago city council terrified him. Then he remembered that hot Sunday this past August when his supporters had organized a mass rally for his aldermanic campaign.

The interior of the old church had been stifling hot on that summer day, but not one pew was empty and the walls were lined with standing-room-only supporters. It was an amazing sight to behold for the postal worker turned preacher. After giving a rousing speech, which was part sermon, Jones had called for Skip Murphy's resignation. The cheers of the assemblage rocked the building and could be heard as far as four blocks away. Then they began chanting, "Harrison . . . Harrison . . . Harrison!" With tears running down his face, Reverend Jones felt himself borne up as if angels had lifted him.

Now a noise coming from the rear of the church snatched Reverend Harrison Jones from his memories. He was alone in the church and his deacon, who also served as his campaign manager, had gone home an hour ago. Although the church was decrepit, volunteers kept the building clean and there was a licensed exterminator in the congregation who kept unwanted vermin under control. So Reverend Jones could only conclude that an unauthorized penitent was inside the church. He refused to use the word "intruder" for anyone entering God's House.

In this ghetto ward, drugs, crime, and poverty had gone unchecked for so long that nothing was sacred, including the church. Picking up an eighteen-inch iron pipe that he kept beside his desk, Reverend Jones went to investigate.

Despite his age, Jones was still a strong man, who had been raised in a pretty tough neighborhood and knew how to take care of himself. However, he had sworn to "turn the other cheek," when he became an ordained minister and the pipe was merely for show.

When he entered the church proper, finding no signs of an intruder, he heard another noise coming from the back of the church. Unlike the previous sound that had alerted him, this one was repeated at regular intervals. Going around the altar and crossing the choir loft, Reverend Jones entered the narrow sacristy where he changed into vestments before services. This room was ten degrees colder than the rest of the church, because the rear door leading into the alley stood open, flapping back and forth in the wind.

Turning on the single overhead light bulb, which partially illuminated the sacristy, he moved across the narrow space to the alley door. Now frightened, he raised the metal pipe in a defensive gesture. The alley was deserted, but it was obvious that the door, which had been secured with a sturdy padlock from the inside, had been pried open. This puzzled Harrison Jones. There was nothing in the church worth stealing for even the most desperate narcotics addict.

Jones turned, planning to return to his office and call the police, when his foot struck an object on the floor. He looked down to see a device that succeeded in totally confusing him.

There was a blue metal tank with the words: "Propane Gas—Contents under Pressure," printed on its exterior. This tank was connected to what initially appeared to be four flares and a cheap clock. The hands on the clock were moving rapidly toward twelve. Then, in a final damning moment of revelation, the Reverend Harrison Jones realized that the oblong, circular tubes attached to the propane tank were not flares, but instead sticks of dynamite. That was the last thought that Skip Murphy's political opponent ever had in life, as he and his church were completely destroyed by a massive explosion.

13

William S. "Dollar Bill" Randolph left Randy's Roost by way of a rear exit into a private garage where he kept his black-and-gold Rolls Royce Silver Cloud. He had the car washed daily come rain or shine, in good weather or bad. He had it waxed once a month. The car was readily identifiable because of the "Dollar Bill" vanity license plate it bore. The gambler had spent his entire life struggling to escape from the confines of mediocrity. He had succeeded.

Utilizing a remote control device inside the Rolls, Dollar Bill opened the garage door and drove into a paved alley that ran behind the Roost. Later tonight emissaries from the Gangster Disciples street gang would enter this alley to pick up the grain alcohol, which Dollar Bill would sell them, making a hefty profit. At midnight the high-stakes gamblers would park their cars in the alley, while they played poker in a private room of Randy's Roost. The game would go on until dawn and off-duty cops from the Cook County Sheriff's Department would provide security. A neat arrangement; a very neat arrangement indeed.

As he drove across the South Side, Dollar Bill's car was noticed by a number of people. Many gazes held admiration for the self-made millionaire; however, an equal number were envious. But no one messed with Dollar Bill Randolph, because he was as connected as anyone in his line of work could possibly be.

The gambler had been born in the Ida B. Wells public housing development in 1943. He was one of six children, who were abandoned by their father to be raised on welfare by their mother. Bill Randolph learned at an early age to do whatever was necessary in order to survive whether it be legal or illegal. By the time he completed his freshman year in high school, he realized that formal education was a waste of time. At least it was for him. In the late 1950s and early 1960s, advancement was severely limited for a man of color in any occupation in America. That was with one exception: crime. And despite a limited formal education, Bill Randolph was an exceptionally intelligent man. As such, he was aware that the political and social structure in the United States kept the black man down. So, in order to succeed, he would have to manipulate that system to his advantage.

Before getting started, he obtained a firm grasp of the rules he would be forced to play by. He could never be perceived as threatening to the status quo, nor could he become too openly powerful. This meant that he had to appear to be so small time as to be virtually nonexistent. He would also have to provide a service, so to speak, that would benefit the establishment. Finally, he would have to put enough money into the right pockets to keep that same powerful establishment on his side.

Randolph decided that gambling was the enterprise he would pursue to make his fortune. There was also prostitution and narcotics sales available, which also flourished in the depressed neighborhoods of the city. But they came with more built-in dangers than illegal games of chance. Randolph knew that he didn't possess the temperament to be a pimp, and dope, despite the huge profit potential, was frowned upon by the powers that Randolph was attempting to enlist as his allies. And although he saw no need to waste time with formal education, Randolph did realize that he would have to learn his craft thoroughly before he could ever become successful at it.

At the age of fifteen Bill Randolph became a runner for a Policy wheel. The game of Policy, which was an illegal precursor of the state lottery system, was considered nothing more than a nickel-and-dime ghetto game. When the Mafia discovered the millions of dollars being raked in, the mob stepped in and took over. The Policy wheel Randolph originally worked for was protected. Keeping his eyes open and his mouth shut, he learned to whom the payoffs went and how much was paid to each official up the ladder all the way to City Hall. Then slowly, employing tenacious cunning, the man who would become Dollar Bill Randolph began developing separate gambling operations, making sure to grease the palms of the right people in and outside of the criminal element. It took him years to get established, but due to a sharp understanding of business and the right connections, Dollar Bill Randolph became a tremendous success.

The black-and-gold Rolls Royce entered an exclusive residential area of the city. The streets of this neighborhood were lined with mansions protected by cul-de-sacs and private security guards. He pulled into the driveway of a twenty-two-room house that had once belonged to a former president of United States Steel. Although Dollar Bill didn't live here, the mansion belonged to him. His wife Sharon, whose name was on Randy's Roost liquor license, and his son William Jr., lived in the house attended by a staff of servants, which included a full-time housekeeper, two maids, a chauffeur/butler, and a cook. All were provided by the largesse of Dollar Bill Randolph, yet he was considered no more than a visitor in this place.

Locking the Rolls, he walked up to the front door. Against the chill of the fall night, he was bundled in a vicuna overcoat and matching wide brim hat, which were as expensive as every other item of apparel and the jewelry he wore. He did not have a key, so he was forced to ring the bell. This was another minor humiliation that his estranged wife had inflicted on him as part of the agreement they had reached to keep her from divorcing him and taking custody of his only child.

Jamison, a very proper Southern black man with snow-white hair, answered the door. Dollar Bill's wife had hired the butler and, after having him thoroughly checked out, the gambler had been satisfied with his genteel domestic-service pedigree. Jamison, who gave no other name on the job application that Dollar Bill had forced him to fill out, could have walked right off the pages of *Gone with the Wind* or *Uncle Tom's Cabin*. Dollar Bill knew that Jamison's last name was Mosley and considered him simply another prop that Sharon Powell Randolph used to maintain this mink-lined fantasy she lived in.

"Good evening, Mister Randolph," Jamison said with a deep voice that made him sound like James Earl Jones. "Master William is in the study." Maintaining a solicitously compliant manner, Jamison took Dollar Bill's hat and coat.

"And Mrs. Randolph?" Dollar Bill asked.

Without missing a beat, Jamison replied, "Madam is not available, sir."

The gambler became angry, but managed to conceal it from the servant. This was Dollar Bill's house and was maintained with his money. He had come here tonight to give Sharon the agreed-upon sum in cash to keep up this charade. However, as a gambler he knew when he was betting into a stacked deck. And Sharon Powell Randolph held all of the cards.

Forty-five minutes later, Dollar Bill Randolph left the mansion and got back in his car. There was a grim look on his face and he gripped the Rolls's steering wheel tightly as he drove back across town to Randy's Roost. The thing that enraged him most of all was that his wife had known who and what he was when she married him. At the time she had been a beautiful college graduate, whose family was only a generation removed from picking cotton in the fields of Mississippi. Raised as a staunch Catholic, Sharon Powell was working as a receptionist in a law office when Dollar Bill met her. Initially, she had been flattered that a man as obviously wealthy as he was would want to court her. For his part Randolph was drawn to the pretty young black woman with the long lashes and hazel eyes. He was fifteen years her senior and there had been other women in his life, but none that he ever considered marrying. For her part, Sharon told her family her future husband owned a bar and had a number of other lucrative sideline business ventures going. And even though he sat her down before the wedding and told her exactly what he did for a living, she simply failed to understand that gambling was illegal.

For the next eleven years they had lived a fairly idyllic life. The Randolphs were churchgoers and Sharon became quite prominent in religious affairs. She was even given an award for her charitable activities by the archbishop of Chicago. William Solomon Randolph, Jr. was born in the second year of their marriage and, due to complications with the pregnancy, she was unable to have any more children. But this was hardly a problem for the Randolph family, as the three of them lived the good life of the wealthy.

In retrospect, Dollar Bill Randolph thought that he had given Sharon too much, because as their marriage progressed through the years he noticed her developing a marked arrogance. She wore an air of superiority like a queen's coronation gown. Then, shortly after their twelfth anniversary, disaster struck. One of Dollar Bill's gambling games was raided and his name, as the husband of the prominent Catholic layperson Sharon Powell Randolph, was blasted across the pages of all of the newspapers in Chicago. That was when his relationship with his wife ended.

Dollar Bill drove the Rolls down the street in front of Randy's Roost. It was approaching nine o'clock and the temperature had dropped below freezing. The sight of the battered blue Ford parked down the block interrupted his memories of what his marriage had been like in happier days. The car looked like a police vehicle, but he realized instantly that it was much too old and dilapidated, as the city replaced their cars more frequently than was the case with this piece of junk. Dollar Bill also noticed that there was someone seated behind the steering wheel. A white male who was casing the Roost.

Sergeant Joe Donegan was watching the comings and goings at Randy's Roost in an attempt to come up with a plan to rob the poker game that Skip Murphy had told him would be taking place at midnight. A number of high rollers would be attending and Murphy estimated that as much as twenty-five thousand dollars in cash would change hands before dawn. A sum that Donegan planned to steal.

He checked his guns. He had a ski mask and a pair of latex

gloves in the glove compartment. His plan was to wait until the gamblers began arriving, then wearing the ski mask and with a gun to a gambler's head, he would force his way inside. Of course, he wouldn't leave any witnesses behind.

Donegan had seen Dollar Bill Randolph's Rolls Royce leave earlier and had also observed its return. The cop wondered how much money a guy would have to have to drive a Silver Cloud. The cop looked around the shabby interior of his old Ford. Perhaps it was time to get rid of this old buggy and buy something better. Maybe not a new car, but one along the same lines as the Ford, which could pass for a police car.

He waited another hour, while Randy's Roost remained quiet. Since Dollar Bill's return no one had gone into or come out of the tavern. Donegan checked his watch. The game was supposed to begin in another couple of hours. The crooked cop had already had a busy enough night with the planting of the explosive that had taken care of Skip Murphy's political problems. But Donegan wasn't about to give up on Randy's Roost.

Approaching headlights made him look up in his rearview mirror. He could make out a fairly large vehicle, maybe a big van or a truck, coming toward him. And it was moving fast. Too fast and it was aimed straight at his car.

Before he could react, a stolen three-quarter-ton truck slammed into the trunk of the Ford with such force that the cop was hurled against the dashboard. He was dazed and while attempting to figure out what had happened, the driver's-side door of his destroyed car was yanked open and he was pulled out of the car to land hard on the ground. There was a sharp pain shooting from the base of his skull down to the small of his back. His arms and legs had gone numb. Then someone kicked him hard in the ribs.

Through the fog of pain that was enveloping him, Donegan managed to look up to see four men standing over him. They were all black and they were all big. It took no great feat of the crooked cop's imagination for him to recognize them as gang members. Frantically, he clawed for his guns, but another kick immobilized him and he was easily disarmed. Then they pulled him up onto his feet and forced him across the street into Randy's Roost.

14

OCTOBER 14, 1993
7:27 P.M.

Larry Cole was reading an adventure story from a picture book to his son. They were in the living room of their South Side home. Lisa Cole was in the kitchen and the policeman and his son had gone to the living room after dinner to engage in this nightly ritual. Larry "Butch" Cole, Jr. was five and in kindergarten; however, his teachers had reported that he possessed the reading and math skills of a child twice his age. This was due to the younger Cole being born with an above-average learning ability. But a major contributing factor to Butch's academic success was that his parents had taken a personal interest in his education from almost the moment of his birth.

"Then the handsome prince and his new bride entered the golden carriage and rode off into the sunset as all the residents of the tiny kingdom cheered. The End."

Butch could have read the picture book himself, but he preferred having his mother or particularly his father read to him.

Lisa Cole was a tall, exquisitely built black woman with long hair. She had the features of a movie star or fashion model framed by a heart-shaped face and could be classified by anyone's standards as a "knockout." Now she stepped to the kitchen entrance and took a moment to silently observe the two men in her life.

From the instant that she set eyes on her child, Lisa had been startled by the resemblance between her husband and her son. As the boy got older he grew into a smaller version of his father to the point that at times it became frighteningly eerie. Their individual mannerisms, gestures, and facial expressions were exactly the same. She had initially thought this was because the boy was imitating his father. And although the two males spent a great deal of time together, Butch was with Lisa much more. Yet at times she couldn't see anything of her in this little man, whom she had named after his father. She was forced to suppress a building resentment over not only their sameness in appearance, but that she seemed to have so little impact on her son's life. But watching them at this moment she felt an affection sweep over her that warmed every fiber of her being.

Cole closed the book and looked at his watch. "With that, Butch, I think it's time for bed."

Obediently, the child, who had been seated next to his father on the couch, got up and headed for the stairs.

"Don't forget to brush your teeth, Butch," Lisa called.

"Yes, Mom," he responded without turning around.

"I'll be up to tuck you in, Butch," Cole said.

"Okay, Dad."

Lisa came over and took the seat next to her husband that their son had just vacated. Kissing him on the cheek, she said, "Can I fix you a drink, honey?"

"Sounds good."

Going to the bar in the den off the living room, she poured him a shot of bourbon on the rocks with water and herself a glass of sherry.

This was also a ritual with them before they turned in for the night. They would spend this time together checking up on the events of the day. She filled him in on what she had done, from a meeting with the volunteer parents' group at Butch's school to the next novel that her fiction book club would be reading. Lisa was aware that she was rushing just a bit, because she wanted to get to what he had done today. She was aware of his ongoing investigation of Alderman Skip Murphy.

Finally, she said, "What did you find out?"

He took a sip of his bourbon and placed the glass down on a coaster on the cocktail table. Then he told her.

After narrating what he had learned from former Alderman Ramey and Terry Forrest's neighbor, Cole told Lisa his conclusions. "We know that Skip Murphy is not only a womanizer, but also a woman beater, but we can't prove it without his former girlfriend coming forward. Then there was something that Ramey said that I found very interesting."

Lisa Cole waited with barely controlled anticipation.

"Supposedly, Murphy would wine and dine the women he picked up and then take them to a motel. According to Ramey, Murphy frequented the South Michigan Avenue Motel. On the morning Sophie Novak disappeared, the South Michigan Avenue Motel was completely destroyed by a fire, which was intentionally set. An arson that could have concealed a homicide."

Now Lisa jumped in. "That would jibe with the barmaid and the bartender at the Lake Shore Tap being mysteriously shot to death during that robbery back in June."

"Exactly," Cole said, picking up his drink. "And I'm getting closer, Lisa. I can feel it."

"Dad," Butch called down to his father. "I'm ready for bed."

"I'll be right up."

While her husband was gone, Lisa pondered what he had just told her. She didn't know Skip Murphy personally, but he individually stood for everything she hated about politics Chicago-style. Graft, corruption, and malfeasance in office were all part of the game played by the elected officials at City Hall. However, of one thing Lisa Cole was certain: if Skip Murphy was responsible for whatever happened to Stella Novak's sister, Larry Cole, Sr. would eventually prove it.

While he was upstairs tucking Butch in she turned on the living room television set to catch the evening news. The top story made her call out urgently to him. The tone in her voice brought him immediately. He carried Butch in his arms. Then the Coles stood together in the living room staring at the news story being broadcast about the raging fire that was rapidly consuming a two-square-block area of the inner city. The fire was believed to have originated in the Baptist Church pastored by the Reverend Harrison Jones. The candidate who was leading Alderman Phillip "Skip" Murphy, Jr. in all pre-election polls.

*   *   *

When Joe Donegan came to, he found himself handcuffed to a chair in a room outfitted with a felt card table and a fully stocked bar running along one wall. Then he became aware of his various injuries. The most pain originated in the small of his back and pulsed up his spine to his neck and down the backs of both of his legs. His ribs ached where he had been kicked, blood trickled from his nose down into his mouth, and his left eye was swollen. Then he became aware that he was not alone. William S. "Dollar Bill" Randolph was sitting across the table from him. Donegan's guns were arranged on the flat surface in front of the gambler. The cop looked around for the gang members, but they were not in sight. This gave him some degree of relief. At least temporarily.

All of Donegan's personal belongings were on the table next to the weapons. Now Dollar Bill Randolph picked up the badge case and flipped it open. "Sergeant Joseph P. Donegan," the gambler read the CPD ID card. "Obviously you're not from the Narcotics Unit."

"What makes you say that?" Donegan's voice came out a weak croak.

"Because I made sure that all of the narco cops were pulled off my place at six o'clock."

"Sure you did." Donegan managed a modicum of defiance. "You're not that heavy."

Randolph smiled. "I'm heavy enough to turn you over to the Disciples, who will make you disappear without a trace. By the way, Sergeant Donegan, before they get rid of you they're going to play baseball. They're going to have the bats and you're going to be the ball."

Donegan had heard of the way that the Disciples disposed

of rivals and it wasn't pretty. But if Dollar Bill Randolph had wanted him dead, they wouldn't be sitting here making idle chit chat. "What do you want, Randolph?"

"I want everything, Sergeant Donegan."

"I don't understand what you mean," the sergeant said, licking blood from his upper lip.

"What you are going to do, my nosey cop friend, is tell me everything starting with what you were doing in my place earlier today with Alderman Skip Murphy."

"And if I don't?"

"Then I'm going to turn you over to the Disciples," Randolph said. "And I'm certain that you won't last nine innings."

The flames from the fire that had consumed Reverend Harrison Jones's church and every structure within a two-square-block area could be seen for miles. The extra-alarm blaze had brought fourteen pieces of fire equipment to the scene to battle the conflagration. The fire had spread quickly to the ghetto tenements and ragged storefronts in the area and was in danger of getting completely out of control. Then, gradually, the flames began to subside.

First Deputy Superintendent Riseman stood behind the barrier tape at the edge of the outer perimeter. Smoke and ash were so thick in the cold air that his eyes became irritated. He was waiting for the CFD battalion chief and the Chicago Police Department's arson investigators at the scene to brief him on the suspected cause of the fire. Right now all they could do was provide the number two Chicago cop with an estimated guess. But this case was going to draw a great deal of scrutiny from the media, the public, and City Hall.

Finally, the battalion chief and a Bomb and Arson detective

approached him. In hushed tones the fireman, whose helmet and turnout coat were blackened with soot, said, "We found fragments from a propane tank and what was left of a cheap clock in the ashes of the church where the fire started."

"We're pretty sure that stuff was part of a bomb," a thin black detective named Stanley added. "We'll know more when we get the evidence to the crime lab, boss."

"I want this expedited with a report on my desk by midnight if not sooner," Riseman ordered.

"Yes, sir," they responded together.

Turning away from the scene, Riseman walked half a block to his chauffeur-driven department car. Getting in the front seat next to his driver, a muscular young Hispanic patrolman named Martinez, the first deputy said, "I want to reach out for Larry Cole. I think he's going to find what happened here quite interesting."

15

OCTOBER 14, 1993
9:27 P.M.

Alderman Sherman Ellison Edwards was hosting a fundraiser in support of his own campaign for reelection. Edwards was the chairman of the Chicago City Council Police and Fire Committee and was completing his third term in office. He was a former Cook County sheriff's deputy who had been indicted for bribery and official misconduct in the early eighties. But the grand jury had failed to return a true bill. Sherman

Edwards had trembled in the cold shadow of the state penitentiary for six months and then all charges were dropped. Taking
his freedom as a good omen, he decided to run for local elective
office. And the former cop won.

Sherman Ellison Edwards was a thick waisted, gray-haired
black man, who had been born and raised in Chicago. However,
when he made his initial run for office he had adopted a phony
"down home" drawl to cater to the transplanted senior citizen
Southerners, who made up the majority of the citizens living
in his ward. Because he had never traveled farther south than
St. Louis, Missouri, before his election, his Confederate colonel
accent came out sounding like a poor imitation of the cartoon
character Foghorn Leghorn. He was actually given the nickname behind his back of Alderman Foghorn Leghorn.

The fund-raiser was held in a public meeting hall on South
Chicago Avenue and was well attended. As the posturing alderman was the chairman of one of the most powerful City
Council committees, present at the affair were the movers and
shakers of Chicago politics to include the mayor, the president
of the Cook County Board, a trio of United States Representatives, a smattering of judges, a few cops looking to pick up
some political clout, thirty-five of Edwards's forty-nine council
colleagues, and six hundred supporters of the politician known
as Alderman Foghorn Leghorn.

A five-piece band played on a stage at one end of the meeting hall and the entire overheated room was decorated with
colorful balloons and paper streamers. Everyone present, from
the elite to the lowly, was jammed in shoulder-to-shoulder attempting to see as much as be seen. So far this had been a
slow news night and the political event was covered by a number of print and electronic media types.

Sweating profusely, which forced him to frequently mop his face with a white handkerchief, Alderman Edwards stood at the center of the meeting hall and received his colleagues and supporters who had lined up to shake his hand. There were two bars serving the crowd and the lines for alcohol were almost as long as the one to greet the alderman even though only wine and beer were served. The minimum donation to get into the hall was twenty-five dollars and many of those attending gave as much as one hundred to two hundred and fifty dollars. The highest donation of the night was five hundred dollars and came from a supporter of the alderman who was not in attendance. That supporter was William S. "Dollar Bill" Randolph, who was otherwise occupied on this fall evening. Also present at this political soirée was Alderman Skip Murphy.

A busty young black woman, who stood a head taller than her escort, accompanied the playboy councilman. Answering to the name Storm, she was a part-time exotic dancer and a full-time sales clerk in a Loop women's boutique. That was where she had met Skip Murphy when he had purchased a negligee for one of his other girlfriends.

When Murphy left Joe Donegan at Randy's Roost earlier that day, the cop had assured him that he would soon be taking care of Harrison Jones. So the playboy would have to maintain an alibi until the deed was done. This had brought Storm to mind. Besides her obvious physical attributes, she was an unsophisticated woman, whose main goal in life was to get her dancing career started in Chicago, which she hoped would provide her with an entrée to Hollywood. With his usual élan, Skip had made enough promises to keep her right by his side, night and day, until his political problems went away courtesy of Joe Donegan.

Murphy and Storm had arrived at Sherman Edwards's fundraiser early and made sure that they were not only seen but also photographed by a photographer for the gossip column in the *Chicago Times-Herald*. Skip had also talked to a number of politically prominent people, but he was having a hard time concentrating and he was drinking.

In the inside jacket pocket of his tailored blue pinstriped suit was a silver flask, which had been filled with Remy Martin cognac before he and Storm had arrived at the meeting hall. Now two hours later, he had consumed half of the flask's contents and three glasses of wine. He was more than a bit tipsy when he introduced Storm to Sherman Edwards. This prompted Alderman Foghorn Leghorn to quip, "You'd better lay off the booze, Skipper boy, or you'll be too drunk to take care of this lady's needs later tonight."

So Skip eased off on his alcohol consumption and even forced down a couple of hot dogs and a bag of potato chips, which was the only food being served. His head was still spinning, but he was more or less sober. Then a heavy depression dropped over him.

Despite being in the midst of a raucous political party surrounded by the movers and shakers of his elite world, Murphy began to brood about his relationship with the insane, crooked cop Joe Donegan. Donegan knew too much about Murphy, which was dangerous. Now with the fate of Harrison Jones hanging in the balance, there would be no way that Murphy could ever rid himself of the policeman. That is, short of death.

Suddenly, the idea of killing the cop became very appealing to Skip Murphy.

"Let's get out of here and go someplace where we can have

some fun, Skip." Storm was forced to shout to be heard over the din emanating from the crowd.

"In a minute," he grumbled. "I still got some people to see."

"You've talked to everybody here," she argued. "They know who you are, so I don't see the point of hanging around this stupid place."

He was about to tell her to shut up when there was a stirring in the crowd surrounding them. Suddenly, the wall of bodies parted and Sherman Edwards rushed toward them. Grabbing Murphy by the arm, he whispered urgently in his ear, "There was an explosion at your opponent's church a little while ago. He's dead and some reporters are looking for you to make a statement. This can help your sagging numbers in the polls. Pull yourself together and get ready to give the interview of your life."

The exotic dancer didn't know much about politics, she had never voted, and she'd only met Skip Murphy a month ago. However, in her entire life she had never seen anyone make as dramatic a transformation as he did at that exact moment. It was as if he had become plugged into an enormous energy source. To say the least, she was impressed.

Cole met Riseman at the first deputy's office on the sixth floor of Chicago Police Department headquarters at 1121 South State Street. It was a few minutes before ten o'clock and Riseman had the television in his office turned to a local news station. A fresh pot of coffee was brewing on a table beside the first deputy's desk. When it was ready he offered Cole a cup, which was declined. The detective commander didn't want to be awake all night.

"I got a preliminary report back from the crime lab on the church fire," Riseman said, handing over a typewritten report.

Cole scanned the narrative portion of the formset. "This isn't saying much, boss. At this point the lab people can't determine if the remnants of the propane tank and the clock had been part of a bomb. If we can't prove arson, we can't make a murder charge stick."

"That does complicate matters, Larry," Riseman said. "But one thing that the Reverend Harrison Jones's death did was convince me that you're right about Skip Murphy. Now I don't know how he did it, but he's responsible for not only what happened to his political opponent, but also your missing barmaid. The problem facing us now is proving it."

Cole placed the lab analysis report back on Riseman's desk. "Don't worry. I'll prove it sooner or later."

The first deputy superintendent was certain that his Area One Detective Commander was in deadly earnest.

The newscast began. The top story was about the fire in which Reverend Jones had died. Riseman and Cole sat back to watch.

Alderman Sherman Ellison Edwards had commandeered the administrator's office at the meeting hall where his fund-raiser was still in progress. The office itself was a spacious but fairly spartan affair with enough room to accommodate a mini–press conference. Edwards had put together this haphazard extravaganza and prepared Skip Murphy to face the cameras with the careful attention of a Hollywood motion picture director. He ordered Murphy to wash his face in the closet-sized bathroom off the office. There was a full bottle of mint mouthwash on the sink and Edwards forced Murphy to gargle three times.

Storm was waiting out in the office and when he first set eyes on her, Alderman Foghorn Leghorn viewed her physical attributes from a completely lascivious standpoint. He now saw her as a political liability for Murphy. Although she was far from happy about it, she agreed to wait for them outside. Then Edwards positioned his client behind the meeting hall administrator's desk.

"Sit up straight, Skip," he said, pulling up a chair behind Murphy close enough so that the cameras couldn't miss him. The primary stated purpose of Edwards's presence was to provide support for his colleague; however, getting his face on television wouldn't hurt his reelection chances either.

Then, when all was in readiness, he signaled to the reporters that they could begin. The press conference would commence just in time to provide a live feed for the ten o'clock news.

Joe Donegan shuffled into the University Hospital emergency room. He walked bent over at the waist due to the intense back pain he was experiencing. There was a tall, thin uniformed police officer filling out a report at a desk in the small police room off the main entrance. When the disheveled, bruised man stepped into the room and collapsed on one of the straight-back chairs, the annoyed uniformed policeman said, "You have to check in with the emergency room nurse, pal."

"I'm a cop," Donegan said, managing to pull his badge case from his pocket.

Alarmed at the sergeant's appearance, the officer said, "What happened to you?"

"I got run over by a truck," Donegan snapped. "Now get me some help, dammit!"

The officer jumped up and ran out of the room. Left alone, Donegan took stock of his situation. Despite the intense pain he was experiencing, he was actually glad to still be alive and in one piece. Now he had a new partner: Dollar Bill Randolph. The crooked cop would play as long as he was forced to. But someday he would get even for what happened to him tonight.

A few minutes later he was placed on a stretcher and hustled into a treatment area. Sergeant Joe Donegan would be admitted that night and would spend three days in the hospital.

Skip Murphy had been on television many times in the past, but never had there been so much at stake. As Sherman Edwards had explained to him when they were getting ready in the meeting-hall administrator's office, this impromptu press conference was not simply about denying that he had anything to do with his election opponent's death. It was also an opportunity for Murphy to gain some heavy points with the electorate. It would be necessary for the playboy politician to make a pledge to continue the quest for justice that Harrison Jones had begun. Yes, Edwards understood that the objective of that quest was Murphy's defeat. But this was what politics Chicago-style was all about. Basically what Skip Murphy would have to do was lie through his teeth and do it in such a convincing fashion as to fool the voters, or at least a large number of them, and make them vote for him.

As Sherman Edwards saw it, Murphy had a lock on the election, because his opponent was dead. But if the playboy failed to carry the election convincingly, then Harrison Jones's former constituents could make enough noise to force the Board of Election Commissioners to hold a special election. This would place Murphy right back where he started. So there was quite a bit riding on the press conference.

Before they left the washroom to face the cameras, Murphy asked Edwards, "You don't believe that I actually had anything to do with what happened to Jones, do you, Sherman?" Lying came easily to the playboy/politician.

Alderman Foghorn Leghorn reverted to his exaggerated Southern drawl. "Skipper boy, that don't really matter right now. What you got to do is go out there and win yourself this here election."

Sitting before the banks of lights waiting for the clock to strike ten, the usually confident Skip Murphy was frightened. He felt that his life had gone into an out of control tailspin, which had begun in that cheap motel room with the Polish barmaid. Now, because of Joe Donegan, Murphy had become involved in two murders. In his current state, Murphy refused to acknowledge any culpability on his part for the deaths of Sophia Novak or Harrison Jones. Then there was the cop Larry Cole. His words still echoed through the politician's head, "This is not a murder investigation, yet."

The image of the dogged policeman caused a rapid change to begin taking place inside Skip Murphy. A spark of anger flared, igniting a fire that burned inside of him with a white-hot intensity. His fear evaporated and suddenly he felt stronger and more potent than ever before in his life.

"We've got five seconds, Alderman," one of the TV newsmen said.

Murphy looked up into the cameras. He was supposed to wait for a question from a reporter who was a friend of Sherman Edwards. But now all of Alderman Foghorn Leghorn's elaborate preparations and advice became trivial.

"We're on, sir," the reporter said. Then, "Have you any comment . . ."

Skip Murphy got to his feet and stared unflinchingly into the sea of reporters. The move surprised even the calculating Sherman Edwards. The politician felt very much in control to the point of invincibility. Cutting the reporter off, Murphy said, "Reverend Harrison Jones died tonight. His church burned to the ground with him in it. He was my formidable opponent in the next election. But he was not my mortal enemy. He was a man that I admired and, under other circumstances, could have called a friend. His death saddens me, but we all must go on together."

Skip Murphy spoke with a passion and an eloquence that impressed Alderman Sherman Ellison Edwards, the media members covering the event, and the voting audience it was targeted for. On television in Chicago and all across the country, viewers watched what would later be called the rebirth of Phillip "Skip" Murphy, Jr.

On the sixth floor of Chicago Police Headquarters, First Deputy Superintendent Riseman and Commander Larry Cole were also impressed by the alderman's oratory. However, he was still a suspected murderer.

PART 2

"Because he's Larry Cole, Mr. Randolph.
Who do you think we are dealing with?"
—Sergeant Joe Donegan

16

The congressional subcommittee hearings into allegations that the Central Intelligence Agency had been actively involved in drug smuggling in the United States lasted for nine months. The proceedings were conducted behind closed doors and all of the witnesses ordered to refrain from discussing their testimony outside of the committee rooms. Of course there were leaks.

The series of events that had led to convening the closed hearings began in Chicago in 1999. There a mass-production drug plant was discovered by Larry Cole and Blackie Silvestri on the South Side. A prominent Chicago attorney named Cleveland Emmett Barksdale III had been convicted and sent to prison as the principal owner and operator of the drug plant. However, the story did not end there.

In December of 2002, a Russian-made tactical nuclear weapon had been smuggled into the United States via a C.I.A. network. By the time the package reached its final destination in Chicago, the bomb was replaced with a large quantity of cocaine. Again, through the efforts of Cole and his crew, the shipment was traced back and a C.I.A. connection discovered. The bomb was accidentally detonated in Colombia, South

America, becoming only the third non-test nuclear detonation in history.

The hearings began in January 2003. When they concluded in September a sealed report was sent to the Justice Department. Within a week federal indictments were returned against a current C.I.A. agent and a former agency deputy director. The official story was that the C.I.A. itself was blameless in what had become known as the Chicago Affair and that the indicted operatives had used their positions to engage in international drug smuggling.

The controversy surrounding the allegations of criminal activity within the American intelligence community was horrendous. Mass citizen rallies were held all over the country, which featured antigovernment rhetoric of such a violent nature as to verge on open anarchy. Despite assurances from the White House and Congress that the intelligence community had been purged of all corruption, there were still calls for a complete overhaul of all federal law enforcement and intelligence gathering agencies along with a demand that the C.I.A. be disbanded. The world watched what could possibly become a second American Revolution.

Damage control became a continuous process at all levels of government and the war for popular public support was waged on a special interest, bipartisan basis. For the media this was the most spectacular news event since the Watergate scandal or the Clinton impeachment trial. Weekly news magazine programs used their time to showcase the problems taking place in Washington, D.C. As such, the *Eye of the Public* news magazine program scheduled an interview with Larry Cole.

Now Cole had risen to the rank of chief of detectives and was considered one of the most outstanding law enforcement officers in the country. The Barksdale drug manufacturing plant represented the largest drug confiscation in history. It was also Cole who had uncovered the alleged C.I.A. connection to the smuggling of drugs into the United States. This was discovered to be of even greater importance when it was learned that a defunct C.I.A. network had been used by an international assassin in an attempt to smuggle the atomic bomb into Chicago. A nuclear device which the assassin planned to use to destroy the city.

The interview was taped in the *Eye of the Public* TV studio on the twenty-third floor of the John Hancock Building on Michigan Avenue. The interviewer was Greg King, who had a reputation for being a good investigative journalist and who would indeed ask probing questions while at the same time maintaining a friendly rapport with his subject. This was rare in electronic journalism, but it had served King well, as he was the host of one of the most popular news magazine programs on the air. A tall, slender man with a receding hairline, King wore metal frame bifocals, which had a tendency to give him a slightly owlish look. He waited for Chief Larry Cole in the reception area of the *Eye of the Public* studio. Cole was accompanied by Blackie Silvestri.

A few minutes later Cole and King were seated in the studio, as the sound technician busied herself around them attaching small microphones to their suit jackets. In the moments before the taping began, the reporter briefed the cop on the direction he planned to take with the interview. "As I mentioned on the telephone last week, I'd like to run through the events surrounding the initial discovery of the narcotics plant back in 1999. Then we can proceed from there."

"That would be fine, Greg," Cole said, adjusting his suit

coat and making sure that he was sitting up straight. Then the
cameras were ready and the interview began.

The *Eye of the Public* news program had perennially won the
ratings war in its time slot since it premiered six years earlier.
On the night that the interview aired with Chicago Police Department Chief of Detectives Larry Cole, the ratings jumped a
phenomenal fifteen points. This was primarily due to fallout
from the recently completed congressional subcommittee hearings. Also the American public had become a great deal more
interested in the drug problem in the United States. Especially
when it was alleged that taxpayer resources were being used to
smuggle illegal substances into the country.

With King asking the questions, Cole narrated the events
of an overcast afternoon in 1999 when he, Blackie Silvestri,
and two Gang Crimes officers named Becker and Castigliano
had accidentally stumbled upon the largest narcotics processing
plant in the world. An operation run out of a factory that was
secured like a fortress and owned by a prominent Chicago attorney. An attorney who was suspected of having C.I.A. connections.

"Were you shocked by the volume of narcotics inside the
plant, Chief Cole?" Greg King asked.

"Definitely," Cole responded. "It was actually far beyond
anything that we believed was out there on the streets. But it
did explain something that has been puzzling law enforcement
professionals for years."

"And what would that be?"

"How the amount of narcotics out on the streets in this
country are distributed in such continuously high amounts. Up
to that point we were focusing most of our resources on com-

bating the problem at street level. By discovering the Barksdale operation, we were able to take the war on drugs to a higher level."

The camera switched back to Greg King. "But you never got the opportunity to inventory the contents of the factory, because the building and everything in it was mysteriously destroyed."

With a solemn expression, Cole nodded. "That's right, Greg. The night following the discovery of the drug processing operation, the plant was destroyed in a massive explosion. The building and surrounding grounds were being guarded by a pair of uniformed police officers, when what could only be classified as a commando operation was mounted by a group of heavily armed men wearing black outfits. The officers were restrained with their own handcuffs and left unharmed a safe distance from the plant. Then an explosive was detonated that had enough force to completely pulverize the building and everything contained inside of it."

"That sounds like a well-organized commando raid to me, Chief," King said.

"I agree," was Cole's only comment.

Skip Murphy watched Cole's taped interview. The alderman was in his new Central Station townhouse west of Grant Park. The view from his first-floor living room and second-floor master bedroom windows was of Museum Park at 1200 South Lake Shore Drive. The townhouse was a stylish residence that Murphy had furnished with the aid of a very expensive interior decorator. He felt his new residence mirrored his status as a senior member of the Chicago city council.

Since the problems he'd experienced back in 1992 and

1993, Murphy had led a relatively sedate life. He was still a womanizer, but age and his prominent position in public life forced him to stay away from what could be called "at risk" females. So he had eliminated barmaids and exotic dancers from his life. Now he attempted to deal only with women who had professional pedigrees. Lawyers, accountants, bankers, and the like, which he generally came in contact with in connection with his city council duties. He'd had a minor fling with a school principal, but the only really dangerous situation that he had placed himself in over the past ten years was a one-night-stand with a married woman after a raucous City Council Christmas party.

Occasionally, over the decade that had passed since the last "job" Joe Donegan had done for him, the alderman had been in touch with the crooked cop. Donegan was still a sergeant; however, when Larry Cole became the chief of detectives back in 1997, Donegan had asked for Murphy's assistance in obtaining a transfer to the CPD's Intelligence Unit. This had taken some doing on Murphy's part, as Donegan had a less than stellar reputation with his former and present commanding officers.

The Intelligence Unit handled highly confidential criminal investigations into the activities of organized crime members, street gangs, and subversive groups. It was necessary for the officers selected to work in such a prestigious unit to be not only extremely dedicated, but also scrupulously honest. Although Sergeant Joe Donegan possessed no formal disciplinary history, not one of his previous commanders would provide him with a written recommendation to the Intelligence Unit C.O. Donegan ended up being transferred to Intelligence, because, after all, "It ain't on the legit."

But Donegan had long ago ceased to be a problem for Skip

Murphy. Actually, the alderman's life had become routine to the point of boredom. There had been a few highlights during the ten-year period since he, with the help of Joe Donegan, had secured an election victory by the murder of the Reverend Harrison Jones. On that night when he faced the cameras to proclaim his false innocence, Murphy had discovered that he could be quite the orator. In his prior political career, his speeches had been of the drab, read-from-a-prepared-text variety. He had observed many a hell and brimstone speaker who could bring an audience to its feet, but that had simply not been Murphy's style. This was because he had always attempted to maintain a façade of unflappable cool in keeping with his "player" image. Somehow, when he had faced the media on that October night in 1993, something had stirred inside of him and he had indeed delivered an impressive oration.

Over the years, following his reelections to four more terms in office, he had been invited to be the keynote speaker at a number of engagements. And with each speech he became better and better to the point that he was being compared to such great historical orators as William Jennings Bryan and Dr. Martin Luther King, Jr. Impressive company, the alderman was forced to admit, yet he was still just another Chicago politician with a questionable past.

On the fifty-six-inch television set in the living room of his Central Station townhouse, Larry Cole was making a point about the drug trade in the United States.

"There are certain similarities between the Prohibition Era and our current crime problems with the drug trade," the chief of detectives was saying. "When alcohol was illegal and the police smashed one section of the liquor pipeline, another would go into operation immediately to take its place. The destruction of the narcotics processing plant caused a drying up of illegal drugs all across the country, but this was only for a very short period of time. Within a few weeks, cocaine, heroin, and crack were once more being sold on our streets and at the same illegal levels as before."

"Then what can we do to permanently stop this illegal drug flow, Chief Cole?" Greg King asked.

"A number of strategies are being explored at all levels of the criminal justice system," Cole responded. "From increased enforcement to the point of a full scale war employing the same resources as was the case in the world wars, Korea, Vietnam, and the Persian Gulf, all the way to decriminalizing narcotics and taking the illegal profits out of street sales."

The *Eye of the Public* host frowned. "Wouldn't legalizing drugs be a somewhat radical step?"

Cole nodded. "Definitely, but I don't think that we can afford to ignore any possible solution to solve this very serious problem."

Skip Murphy had aged well. His hair was graying at the temples and he had grown a seaman's style beard to hide his weak chin. The modification of his playboy lifestyle had taken him out of the saloons where he had swilled large amounts of high calorie liquor. This and a moderate three-times-a-week exercise program had shed thirty pounds from his frame. He had stopped wearing the garish gangster suits and wide-brimmed hats and his clothes closet contained only conservative black, blue, and gray suits with tastefully subdued matching accessories. In a word, the six-term city councilman sought to present a "stately" image to the public. That image didn't mean much if he couldn't rise above his current position.

Murphy realized that the options open to him were limited. He couldn't muster the support to run for mayor and he had no interest in capturing any of the county offices. And in Murphy's estimation, being a Chicago city councilman was a more prestigious position than that of a state legislator. The only political avenue left open to him was in Washington, D.C. But he would have to be slated by his party for a seat in the House of Representatives. At this stage of the political game, running for the U.S. Senate was as far-fetched for Skip Murphy as would be a bid for the presidency.

In order to make a legitimate run at the House, two things would be necessary: Murphy would need a valid issue that would attract voters and a great deal of cash. Money had never been a problem for him because of his inheritance. In the past ten years his personal fortune had tripled and he was currently worth close to $20 million. But what about an issue?

Greg King was concluding the *Eye of the Public* program interview with Larry Cole. "Well," the reporter was saying, "Chief Cole has provided us with an insider's viewpoint into the ongoing problem our society faces with illegal narcotics in America. Thank you very much for taking the time out of your busy schedule to be with us, Chief."

The camera switched to Cole. "Thanks for having me, Greg."

King's image once more filled the screen. "*Eye of the Public* will be right back after these announcements."

* * *

As had been the case the night of Sherman Ellison Edwards's fund-raiser at the South Chicago meeting hall ten years ago, Skip Murphy found that he was becoming inspired by Larry Cole. The politician had followed the policeman's career since their first run-in over the disappearance of Sophia Novak. Murphy had watched with grudging awe as the cop defeated attempts to derail his career by two successive City of Chicago directors of public safety—Edward Graham Luckett and Tommy Kingsley. Down at City Hall, Cole had assumed an aura of invincibility and even the mayor treated the chief of detectives with a marked degree of respect.

Murphy still despised the policeman because he stood for everything that could be considered threatening to someone of the politician's ilk. Skip Murphy was pathologically dishonest, a backslider, and a blatant prevaricator; Cole was scrupulously honest, relentless, and dedicated. All of his life, Murphy had looked for the easy way out; Cole had always gone the extra mile to get the job done. They were indeed opposites, but, Murphy mused, wasn't that what politics was all about, the art of compromise? Of course he realized that Cole would never voluntarily go along with anything that someone like Murphy might propose. But Cole might not have a choice.

An expression displaying amusement and contemplation rested on Skip Murphy's face, as the next segment of the *Eye of the Public* news magazine program began.

17

William S. "Dollar Bill" Randolph had also seen Larry Cole's interview on the *Eye of the Public* TV program. The owner of Randy's Roost had been very interested in the narcotics plant's mysterious destruction back in 1999. For a brief period, Randolph had provided financial backing to certain gang factions, so that the drug void on city streets could be filled. But narcotics had proven to be a very messy business for Dollar Bill, which he was forced to learn the hard way.

Despite his connections, which reached high into the city, state, and federal governmental structure, Dollar Bill was still vulnerable to that which was anathema to members of the criminal element. That was the honest cop. When he was indicted on thirteen counts of conspiracy to deliver controlled substances there was nothing that he could do but hire a good lawyer and hope that he wouldn't receive a lengthy sentence. He didn't. After a six-month trial, he was sentenced to five years in the Joliet State Penitentiary. He only served eighteen months and was paroled early because he had developed colon cancer. The cancer went into remission by the time he returned to Chicago, but the prognosis was not good. With little time left to him, Dollar Bill Randolph began preparing his only son to succeed him. That was not to say that Randolph wanted his son to follow in his footsteps. The professional criminal had enough money to insure that this would not happen.

After the news magazine program ended, Randolph turned his set off and devoted his total attention to business. He was in his office above the bar in Randy's Roost. The place had remained pretty much the same over the years and it was still his base of operations; however, he no longer ran any poker games or narcotics ingredient sales on the premises. But he wasn't about to go completely legit. He had simply entered into more sophisticated criminal activities.

A recent acquisition to his office was a Dell PC. Utilizing this computer, a printing press, and a high-resolution color copy machine in the basement where poker games had once been held, Dollar Bill made more money per week than he ever had before during his long criminal career. Money that he knew he would never live to spend. The cancer had taken hold again and was spreading. The prognosis was that he had less than a year left.

Now Dollar Bill Randolph turned on the computer and called up a program, which was encrypted and that he had personally labeled "P.I.D." He was aware that a number of federal, state, and local law enforcement agencies were working overtime to bust this operation. But Dollar Bill was always a step ahead of them, because he had a high-placed spy in the law enforcement camp. That spy was Sergeant Joe Donegan, who was assigned to the Chicago Police Department Intelligence Unit.

Dollar Bill Randolph was now a dealer in counterfeit documents. He was not interested in manufacturing phony cash, although he could have been just as competent at it as he was with every other illegal enterprise he had ever attempted. What he did produce made more real money for him than any cash currency counterfeit operation could. And with a great deal less risk. With a few innovations thrown in, the documents that Randolph's operation made could often hold up under the most intense official scrutiny. This was due to the efforts of Joe Donegan.

When the "Lone Stranger" or "Demented Cabby," as he had been derisively nicknamed by the cops in his former units, reported for duty at the Intelligence Unit, his new commander was waiting for him. The commander had done his homework on Donegan and knew that he had never fit in anywhere within the department in the past. The commander was also aware that the new sergeant had political clout. So, being an innovative individual, the Intelligence Unit boss had come up with a plan.

"What do you know about computers, Sergeant Donegan?" the commander asked on that spring morning in 1997 when the new guy had reported for duty.

The crooked cop wasn't about to tip his hand. "Not much, sir. I've never been very mechanically minded."

"Well, let me tell you what I have in mind."

For Donegan it was the same as had been the case earlier in his police career. He was being issued a license to steal. The offices of the Intelligence Unit were located in the basement of a West Side factory only a few blocks from the Area Four Police Center, where Donegan had been assigned to the Detective Division for four years. Although the location was supposed to be a secret, every cop and bad guy in the city knew where this particular cop unit was housed. In fact, the *Eye of the Public* news magazine program had once done a story on what was called, "The Chicago Police Department's Secret Spy Operation." Pictures and the address of the factory were included in the piece. But the Intel cops stayed, because the city got free rent on the basement facility.

There were eight large rooms occupied by the CPD. Four were offices, one was a temporary detention facility with a heavy metal door to secure it, another was a property room where the unit's special equipment and extra weapons were kept, there was a photo lab, and, finally, a computer room. The computer room became the sole domain of Sergeant Joe Donegan.

After a brief period of training from a fat cop who was supposed to be an expert, Donegan was left to run the facility by himself. There were other computers in the Intel Unit complex, but everything was run through the computer room. If any special computer projects were necessary, Sergeant Donegan was the man. If a search for special data became necessary, Donegan was it. His efficiency at the post became phenomenal to the point that as the years passed, he became an indispensable member of the unit, although a strange one. This was because when he was on duty, which seemed to be all the time, he stayed locked in the computer room. A room paid for by taxpayers' money, which remained locked when the sergeant wasn't around. Except for the commander, Donegan discouraged visitors to his domain.

Over the years, the crooked cop had done a great deal with what had once been no more than a couple of desk computers, a single notebook computer, and a few telephones. Now all of the computers were hooked to the City of Chicago mainframe, which, with the proper access, could provide entry into state and federal systems. From the original setup, there were now four fairly new, state-of-the-art, desktop models; a pair of notebook computers—one of which was the duplicate of the Dell model in Dollar Bill Randolph's office; a multiple secured telephone system equipped with three phone lines possessing tracing ability; portable and desk model radio scanners; and equipment capable of tracking devices placed in aircraft, in vehicles, or on people. This equipment also possessed the sophistication to track cellular phones by turning them on and pinpointing their location on a wall-mounted tracking map inside the computer room. There were also a number of cellular phones with secured lines, which the sergeant would personally issue to any Intel officers who required them.

At times Donegan's control of the computer room caused friction with the other cops in the unit, but as the sergeant had become so indispensable to the operation, the commander ignored the complaints. He even had a sign made up to display his support of the strange cop, which was placed on the computer room door. It read, "Donegan's Domain—Access by Invitation Only." The commander signed it.

Now Donegan had a wealth of riches from the CPD, which he could use to steal. It was from this room in a basement on the West Side that he had provided Dollar Bill Randolph with the information that was used to effectively and flawlessly counterfeit driver's licenses, State of Illinois I.D. cards, social security cards, birth certificates, credit cards, and even car titles and phony auto insurance cards. Everything was done in total secrecy right under the noses of the police officers assigned to discover such illegality in Chicago, which made the operation twice as interesting and enjoyable to its operators.

But computers, cellular phones, printing presses, and copy machines were only a part of this elaborate criminal enterprise.

Certain types of official cooperation were also required, which Donegan was also required to provide. This the cop did grudgingly.

While the *Eye of the Public* news magazine program was being telecast, Donegan was parked outside of a far southwest high school. He was waiting for the part-time varsity wrestling coach to exit the gym. The wrestling team was in contention for the Class 5A Illinois State Championship and the coach was working his charges very hard to reach this goal. The coach was also the general operating manager of a State of Illinois Department of Motor Vehicles facility in a western suburb of Chicago.

The wrestling coach was a rotund, middle-aged man who walked with a limp due to a knee he had torn up when he was a backup linebacker at Ohio State thirty years earlier. Following his college career, he had moved to the West Coast and gone to work as a gym teacher and football coach at a small high school in Oregon. He was away from the Midwest for twenty-three years. When he returned he went to work as a driver's license tester for the Illinois Department of Motor Vehicles. It took him seven years to be promoted to the general operating manager's position. Then he had taken the part-time wrestling coach's position.

He was a very hard-working, industrious man, who had a wife and two grammar-school-aged children—a boy and a girl. He had a twenty-five-year fixed-interest mortgage on his suburban home, owed ten remaining payments on his two-year-old Chevy Blazer, and he and his wife owned her late model Toyota Tercel outright. The Illinois Department of Motor Vehicles general operating manager also owned something else: a past.

Sergeant Joe Donegan now drove a 1996 dark brown Chevrolet with black-wall tires. There was a buggy-whip antenna attached to an AM/FM radio that didn't work. But Donegan never listened to the radio anyway, and for communications purposes he had a CPD cellular phone and a laptop computer in the car. The cop's physical appearance hadn't changed significantly over the years and, in fact, he still wore some of the same clothing that he had on the night that he first encountered Skip Murphy. Now he was almost completely bald and possessed a pale, gaunt appearance. But his dark, psychotic eyes were the same lifeless pools they had always been. Due to the damage that had been done to his lower back during his encounter with the Gangster Disciples outside of Randy's Roost, he suffered periodic bouts of incapacitation due to damaged disks. However, he was still working as hard at being a crooked cop as he ever had before in his career.

Donegan watched the wrestling coach exit the gym and begin making his way slowly down the steps. Before he could reach his car in the parking lot, the cop intercepted him.

Rolling his window down, the cop said, "How's the team look this year, coach?"

The coach stopped, but did not turn around. His shoulders slumped at the sound of Donegan's voice. Then he said, "The new password is 'Warlock.' "

"I'm impressed," Donegan said. "You guys over at Motor Vehicles are becoming real poets."

The coach didn't comment. With his limp more pronounced, he continued to his car, got in, and drove from the parking lot.

Donegan watched him go through the dirt-streaked wind-shield of his most recent dilapidated auto. Then the cop smiled. The "Warlock" password was required for entry into the State of Illinois Department of Motor Vehicle's computer system. Access to this network was a key element of the counterfeit identification scam that Donegan was involved in with Dollar Bill Randolph.

Through his CPD Intelligence computer, Joe Donegan had thoroughly checked the backgrounds of every Motor Vehicle facility operations manager in the state. It was very convenient when Donegan discovered that the part-time wrestling coach had been arrested in Oregon fifteen years ago for child moles-tation. Although he was cleared of all charges, the coach had failed to mention the arrest on either his job application for a position with the State of Illinois or when he was hired by the high school. The disclosure of that arrest in his past life would ruin him, which was a fact that Donegan had made quite ap-parent to the coach. Although he hated what the crooked cop was forcing him to do, the coach went along.

The State of Illinois Department of Motor Vehicles changed its computer passwords every sixty days. And on the first day of each of these periods, Donegan contacted the coach to obtain the new password.

The sergeant drove from the high school parking lot and headed back to the Intelligence Unit computer room. He had to transmit the new password to Dollar Bill Randolph. But Don-egan had grown very tired of the arrangement he'd been forced into on that night ten years ago. A night during which Randolph had not only learned everything about Sergeant Joe Donegan, but also everything about what Donegan had done for Alderman Skip Murphy. The relationship between the crooked cop and the professional criminal had been quite profitable for them both over the years, but now Donegan was again ready to go it alone.

18

SEPTEMBER 26, 2003
1:35 P.M.

Sergeant Judy Daniels, who was assigned to the staff of Chief of Detectives Larry Cole, parked her car a block from the Oceanside Restaurant on Rush Street. Then she hurried down the sidewalk, because she was late for her lunch appointment. She had been a cop for fifteen years, but didn't appear to be a day over thirty. For almost her entire career she had worked in undercover assignments. As such, she prided herself on her ability to don disguises with such skill that virtually no one could recognize her. And the day was coming, the woman known as the Mistress of Disguise/High Priestess of Mayhem swore, when no one would be able to recognize her no matter how skilled an observer they were.

Today she had on another of her numerous disguises. This one made her look like your basic stereotypical librarian. Her dark hair was worn in a short pageboy style, she wore a pair of black horn-rimmed glasses, a black pants suit with a ruffled white blouse, and plain-toed black flat shoes. To complete the impersonation she walked with a stoop-shouldered bouncy walk, which gave the impression that she was indeed a nerd. The effect she had sought had been achieved. No one she encountered would see her to be in the least bit threatening and her police officer persona was effectively masked.

The Oceanside Restaurant specialized in the preparation of seafood. The prices were moderate and it was a very popular eating place located right in the center of the Windy City's principal nightclub district. The restaurant was housed in a brownstone that had once belonged to a famous madam who operated one of the most notorious brothels in nineteenth-century Chicago. Now the three-story house had been restored to its original elegant splendor and the rooms where expensive courtesans had once practiced their sexual arts had now been turned into elegant dining rooms.

A muscular young man in blue jeans escorted Judy to a table in a secluded alcove on the second floor. Seated at this table waiting for her was Sergeant Elaine Anderson.

"I'm sorry I'm late," the Mistress of Disguise/High Priestess of Mayhem said, taking a seat across from her friend. "Things at headquarters have been a bit crazy today."

Her lunch companion managed a smile. "I thought that you were at least three of the women who came in here after I sat down. I even started to wave to one of them. She probably thought I was either crazy or on the make."

Judy laughed.

Elaine Anderson was a pretty young woman with red hair and eyes of such an exotic emerald green color as to appear artificial. She had a shy manner and a quiet smile that made her very attractive; however, Judy had seen the young police sergeant turn from a cute Barbie doll–type into a raging maniac when she was crossed. More than one lawbreaker had made the incredibly bad mistake of underestimating her.

Elaine was dressed in a denim suit and red blouse. Her hair was pulled back off her forehead into a ponytail and she wasn't wearing makeup. Judy noticed that her friend was very pale and didn't look well. There was a glass of white wine in front of Elaine and she nervously fingered the stem. She managed another smile for Judy and said, "I saw your boss on television the other night. I was quite impressed with his presentation."

"Yeah, he is something," Judy said. "But he's still the same regular guy he's always been. And there's not a smarter cop anywhere in the world."

A waiter came to the table and Judy also ordered a glass of wine. Elaine asked for a refill.

Judy Daniels and Elaine Anderson had been in the same Chicago Police Department's pre-service promotional class. When the two-week course concluded, Judy had gone back to the chief of detectives' office and Elaine had been assigned to the Intelligence Unit. The two women hadn't seen each other in three years and Judy was pleasantly surprised when her former classmate had called and invited her to lunch.

After they exchanged small talk for a time, Judy was able to tell that her friend was deeply troubled. "How are things going in the intelligence business?"

The waiter selected that moment to serve Judy's shrimp salad and Elaine's perch. The Intelligence sergeant took a moment to spread tartar sauce on her fish. Then she pushed the plate away and took another sip of wine.

"Is something wrong with the food?" Judy asked.

Elaine shook her head. "I haven't got much of an appetite. I'll probably have them wrap this up and I'll take it home."

She paused a moment. "I need some advice, Judy."

"Sure," Judy said, feeling guilty for continuing to eat. But she was hungry.

Finally, Elaine began. "Since I've been assigned to Intelligence I've been working phony identification scams. You know, fake driver's licenses, social security cards, green cards, and the like. You'd be surprised what kind of market there is for that kind of stuff out on the street."

Judy really didn't know anything about counterfeiting, but she continued to listen attentively.

"I've got a crew of four officers that I supervise and they are really good kids." Elaine misted up a bit, but quickly brought herself back under control. "Two guys—Warren and Mark—and two girls—Janet and Connie, which is short for Consuela. They're out on the streets working damn near around the clock to get a handle on these counterfeiters.

"We managed to bust a few minor operations, which are turning out an obviously flawed product. But we're aware of a major outfit, which is so good that they can produce an undetectable phony state driver's license or I.D. card."

Judy was confused. "You mean it's so good that it takes an expert to tell it's a phony, don't you, Elaine?"

The sergeant leaned toward the disguise artist and lowered her voice. "No, Judy, I'm talking about a document that is so good not even the F.B.I. lab can tell it from the real thing. That is right down to the holographic logo and registration in the state computer."

"How can . . . ?" Judy began, but Elaine held her hand up.

"Let me fill you in on all of it and you can judge for yourself. Connie and Warren developed information through an informant that a counterfeit driver's license was available on the street that was an exact duplicate of a real one and would even appear legit if run on our computer system."

"That's impossible," Judy said, unable to contain herself.

"I thought so too, but my guys are very thorough. They discovered the identity of a convicted drunk driver whose license was revoked. He was supposedly in possession of one of these bogus licenses. They ran him on our computers and verified the revocation before they set up a surveillance on him. They caught him drunk as a lord coming out of a North Side tavern. They let him get behind the wheel before they stopped him. He produced a driver's license, which was in his own name, but with a couple of minor discrepancies. His last name was spelled in a different way and his address was a post office box. But the license was one hundred percent authentic.

"Initially we figured that we were onto a scandal in the Department of Motor Vehicles like the one uncovered a few years ago. Then the drunk driver sobered up and decided to cooperate. He said he knew that the license was a fake, but he didn't know where it came from. He went on to say that after his revocation went into effect he was contacted on the telephone by a man who he said sounded like a cop."

Judy had finished her lunch and was now listening with tremendous interest.

"Now get this," Elaine said. "The drunk driver said that the voice on the phone told him that he was not only aware of the driver's license revocation, but also of the driver's financial situation. The price for the service was five thousand dollars and the drunk paid by leaving the money in a paper bag under the front seat of his unlocked car, which was parked in the Grant Park Underground Garage. The fake license was hidden under a trash can on the lower level of the garage. By the time the drunk returned to his car, the money was gone."

"Your revoked driver was certainly a trusting soul," Judy said.

Elaine shrugged. "He's a drunk, Judy. People like him get ripped off all the time. But that was all he was able to tell us about the counterfeiter, so we started looking at the Department of Motor Vehicles and hit a dead end. Then I decided to become a bit more inventive with the investigation."

"That's my girl," Judy said.

"I developed phony identities for Connie and Warren and put them in the Department of Motor Vehicle's system with revoked licenses. But nothing happened. In the interim, we got leads on another fake license, a green card, and a birth certificate, which were all counterfeit masterpieces. We later found out that the people who had the documents obtained them in a similar fashion to our drunk driver by way of what they call in espionage fiction a dead letter drop."

"Somebody with a very sophisticated computer system is out there setting up these phony I.D.s to appear legit," Judy said, flagging the waiter with the intention of ordering desert.

Before he could come over to the table, Elaine Anderson said urgently, "I don't believe that the computer system we're talking about is 'out there,' Judy." To emphasize her words she pointed at the restaurant windows. "I think that it's right inside the office complex where I work. The Intelligence Unit computers are among the most sophisticated in law enforcement and are capable of interfacing with any mainframe in the state and all of the federal law enforcement systems."

The waiter finally came over and Judy ordered a dish of mint ice cream. When they were once more alone, she said,

"So you suspect that your counterfeiter is someone in Intelligence?"

Now the strain on Elaine Anderson's face revealed the terrible pressure she was under. "It's not a 'someone' I suspect, Judy. It's the supervisor of the computer room itself, Sergeant Joe Donegan."

"The Lone Stranger," Judy said, shocking her luncheon companion.

Joe Donegan was sitting in his brown Chevy down the street from the Oceanside Restaurant. There was a great deal of foot and vehicular traffic in the Rush Street area, which made his presence virtually undetectable. He had tailed Sergeant Anderson to the restaurant after he'd overheard her making a luncheon date with his old nemesis Judy Daniels. From his computer room in the Intelligence Unit's basement complex, he had bugged all of the land lines and cell phones operating in the complex. The conversations were monitored, recorded, and stored in an encrypted computer program, which only he could enter. The crooked cop had returned to the computer room just in time to play back the conversation between the two women. There was no mistaking the obvious strain in Anderson's voice.

Donegan didn't recognize the Mistress of Disguise/High Priestess of Mayhem when she entered the restaurant. He had anticipated the fact that he wouldn't be able to identify her. That wasn't necessary, as after he'd been watching the exterior of the restaurant for an hour and fifteen minutes, Sergeant Anderson emerged accompanied by a mousy-looking woman who reminded Donegan of his sister Megan.

"I don't believe it," he said, examining the two women

through a pair of palm-sized binoculars that had been developed by the U.S. Army and had the range of a high-powered telescope. Figuring that the librarian type was Daniels, the Lone Stranger quipped, "This broad must have a screw loose."

Donegan picked up an omnidirectional antenna from the front seat, rolled the front passenger window down, and pointed it at the women. The device was attached to a pocket-sized computerized amplifier developed for police operations by the F.B.I. for use in court-ordered eavesdropping. Court orders, or the lack of them, had never bothered Joe Donegan in the past.

Their voices came through with crystal clarity.

Judy Daniels was saying, "When I get back to headquarters, I'll run this by Chief Cole and Blackie. I'm certain that they'll come up with a strategy to discover what's up with this Sergeant Donegan."

That was all that he had to hear. He couldn't risk exposure, which meant that Sergeant Elaine Anderson would have to meet with an unfortunate accident. Donegan was sorry about this, because he was very fond of the pretty young woman. But he had no interest in her sexually, because the crooked cop was asexual and possessed no sex drive at all. This was a form of handicap, which he actually viewed as an asset, because it gave him more time to contemplate scams and steal.

Donegan put his rust-bucket Chevy in gear and headed back to the Intelligence Unit.

19

D r. Stella Novak had her patient take deep breaths while she pressed a stethoscope against the flesh of his bare back.

"Do you keep that thing in the refrigerator before you use it?" Larry Cole said, flinching at the instrument's touch.

"Be still, Commander," the doctor scolded, "or I'll use a thorned glove to examine your prostate gland." Despite Cole having been promoted to the rank of chief of detectives, they had both decided it would be easier if she continued to refer to him by the title "Commander."

Cole turned and looked at her with alarm. "I thought you were going to have your male associate perform that part of the physical?"

The doctor patted his shoulder and laughed. "Don't worry. I won't jeopardize your modesty. Doctor Ramone will indeed do that part of the physical, but I reserve the right to draw your blood."

"Great," Cole said with a pronounced lack of enthusiasm.

A short time later doctor and patient were seated in her office. The unseasonably warm, bright autumn day had turned cold and overcast with a menacing gray sky sporting low ceiling clouds. Cole, who was now fully clothed, waited while the doctor studied his file.

With the exception that her blond hair was now completely silver, Stella looked exactly the same as she had when she was a physical therapist at University Hospital ten years earlier. While she had been giving Cole his semiannual physical she had not worn eyeglasses. Now in her office, she wore a pair of enormous horn-rimmed glasses with what looked to Cole like windowpane lenses. The cop suspected that the thin young woman's eyewear and even her hair color were intended to make her look older than her thirty-two years. This alteration in appearance was intended to overcome the prejudice that some people have against young doctors. However, Cole had complete confidence in Dr. Stella Novak.

"Your blood pressure is lower than it was when you were here back in April, Commander, but it is still too high," she scolded. "And I don't like your pulse rate. Have you been exercising regularly?"

"I work out five days a week and run three to five miles at least four times a week."

She looked up at him and the huge glasses were almost ludicrous sitting on her thin face. "I am impressed. How much sleep do you get?"

The guilty look gave him away. "Maybe four to six hours a night. It's usually enough, because I seldom feel tired."

"With your occupation you are probably operating on so much adrenaline you don't have the time to actually notice fatigue. What about your coffee consumption?"

"It's moderate."

"Define 'moderate,' Commander."

He shrugged. "Five to six cups a day."

"Which probably means that you're actually consuming a great deal more." Before he could respond, she added, "But I can understand that. I have a tendency to drink nine or ten cups a day myself. That means that we both must cut down on caffeine and, in your case, working out like a man in training for the Olympics or a professional sports team is no substitute for adequate rest."

"Yes, doctor," Cole said, obediently.

But Larry Cole was in good health and excellent physical shape. Dr. Stella Novak admitted this as she wrote him a prescription for a mild diuretic to ease his blood pressure down a bit more. This was only the second time that he had been in his doctor's office, because she had only occupied this suite in the North State Parkway Medical Building for one year. Prior to that she had been an intern at University Hospital, where she had once served as a physical therapist. Since her graduation from medical school, Larry Cole had been her patient. In fact, he had become her first regular patient.

Dr. Novak's office was nicely furnished and the examining rooms were state-of-the art equipped. There were a few personal items in her office: some plants, a smattering of first edition books—a number of which were in her native tongue, and two framed photographs. One was of her parents and the other was of her sister Sophia.

Cole stared at Sophie's photo. Her decade-old disappearance was still a mystery, but the cop had developed a couple of theories over the years. Theories that all led back to Alderman Skip Murphy.

"But seriously, Commander," Dr. Novak was saying, as she handed him the prescription, "if any more of my patients keep themselves in the same shape that you do then there will be no more need for doctors."

The policeman's manner became a bit more formal. "In the

world that we live in, Stella, there will always be a need for doctors, because of the murder and mayhem we have out there on our streets."

For a moment Dr. Novak stared across at her patient. Finally, she said, "I guess you've got a point, Commander."

The battered gray Ford van was parked across the street from the Gold Coast Liquor Store and Delicatessen on North Clark Street. The engine of the van was running and the defective muffler beat out a steady loud drumbeat as excessive exhaust fumes polluted the air. Seated behind the wheel of the offending vehicle was a painfully thin, bloodlessly pale, red-eyed woman, whose hands trembled uncontrollably due to her need to obtain a heroin fix as soon as possible. Primarily, the emaciated woman was a streetwalker, who at the age of twenty-five had a record of twenty-seven arrests for prostitution. But the illegal drugs she had forced into her veins over the years had taken a toll and now, along with being infected with an untreated case of AIDS; she was no longer capable of plying her trade on the street. So she had joined an armed robbery gang made up of fellow addicts.

The sounds of gunshots came from inside the closed door of the Gold Coast Liquor Store and Delicatessen. This was followed by two armed men—a white and a black, who possessed a similar physical profile to the gray Ford van's driver—running out the front door. The white man brandished a Tech Nine machine pistol and the black a 9mm semiautomatic handgun. While they were in the process of robbing the combination package liquor store, bar, and deli, an off-duty Chicago police officer had entered the establishment to purchase a six-pack of beer, a half pound of chicken salad, and half a loaf of pumpernickel bread. When the thirty-four-year old Hispanic cop walked in the door he was wearing a nylon windbreaker with a distinctive Eighteenth Police District logo over the left breast. The windbreaker was open, making his five-pointed CPD star and off-duty stainless steel, holstered pistol visible. For a long moment the robbers, who were forcing the cashier to empty the register, and the cop stared at each other from a distance of ten feet. Then the cop reacted.

Forgetting the money that the young, long-haired male cashier had shoved into a brown paper bag, the junkies turned their guns on the policeman and opened fire. He never got his own gun out of its holster and, as he was off-duty, he was not wearing a bulletproof vest. The robbers had never fired the Beretta or the Tech Nine before, yet they exhibited tremendous accuracy striking their target repeatedly in the chest and abdomen. In all, the policeman suffered ten gunshot wounds. An autopsy would later reveal that any one of his wounds could have resulted in death.

After the shooting, the junkies panicked and ran out onto the street leaving their loot behind. For what seemed an eternity none of the sixteen employees and customers present in the Gold Coast Liquor Store and Delicatessen at the time of the shooting were able to move. Then one of the male patrons, who was a retired Cook County Circuit Court bailiff, shouted to the stunned cashier, "Call the police!" The retired bailiff then ran over to lend assistance to the fallen cop. One look at the man transmitted that he was dead.

As if coming out of a deep trance and still holding the brown paper sack containing the cash, the cashier reached for the telephone on the wall behind the front counter. It took him three tries to connect with 911. When an emergency operator answered, the cashier found speech difficult.

"Something . . . uh . . . happened . . ."

Seeing his distress, the retired bailiff grabbed the phone. In a tone that was noticeably stressed he narrated what had occurred. The most important part of the conversation between the retired bailiff and the 911 operator was the description of not only the two gunmen, but also their escape vehicle.

Larry Cole was driving back to police headquarters after his physical. He realized that Dr. Novak was absolutely right about his sleeping habits. He tried to remember the last time that he had slept a solid eight hours. In fact, he couldn't recall the last time that he'd slept six hours at a stretch. It was simply the nature of his job as the top detective of one of the largest police departments in the world. And he wasn't a micromanager in any sense. He was instead what he liked to call "involved."

Cole considered the law enforcement profession the most fascinating line of work that anyone could choose. It was at once interesting, terrifying, and totally absorbing. It possessed the elements of drama, humor, and tragedy taken to the extremes of human experience. Larry Cole had made this occupation his way of life.

But if that life were going to continue into a ripe old age, he would have to follow his doctor's advice. He vowed to get eight hours of sleep tonight. Well, maybe not a full eight, but at least six. He suddenly realized how silly he was being, which forced him to laugh out loud. He'd worry about sleeping when he got home tonight.

Cole was driving eastbound on Fullerton from Clark Street.

Entering Lincoln Park he stopped for a red light. His black Mercury police car was the only vehicle at the intersection. The light changed and he was about to proceed when a gray Ford van sped southbound from the inner drive in Lincoln Park to run a red light in front of him and careen wildly onto Fullerton. Cole watched the van race toward Lake Shore Drive. He was about to activate his alternately flashing headlights and the emergency blue strobe lights concealed in the Mercury's grill when the police radio broadcast a description of the killers and the vehicle they had used to escape from the Gold Coast Liquor Store and Delicatessen.

Cole waited until the broadcast concluded before picking up the microphone and depressing the transmit key.

"Car Fifty, emergency," he said in a clear, controlled voice.

"Go, Car Fifty."

"I am following the suspect vehicle for the homicide of the police officer. That vehicle just turned southbound on Lake Shore Drive from Fullerton. I am operating as a ten-ninety-nine (one-officer) unit and will follow the suspects. Because they are heavily armed, we need to stop them in the most isolated location possible. Keep all marked police vehicles out of sight and this unit will keep you advised of the suspect vehicle's position. Do you copy?"

"Ten-Four, Car Fifty," the dispatcher acknowledged.

Cole turned onto southbound Lake Shore Drive and, maintaining a discreet interval, followed the gray Ford van.

After spying on Judy Daniels and Elaine Anderson, Sergeant Joe Donegan was on his way back to the Intelligence Unit. He was at the southwestern edge of Lincoln Park at North Avenue when he monitored Cole's transmission. He was less than a mile from Lake Shore Drive. The crooked cop's dark eyes glistened with anticipation, as he floored the accelerator and sped east to intercept Cole.

The armed drug addicts in the gray van were physically debilitated due to the substance abuse they had engaged in for such a long period of time. Each of them suffered from malnutrition, skin lesions, and the driver and the white stick-up man were infected with advanced cases of tuberculosis. The desperate trio appeared barely human, but now, after killing the off-duty policeman, they were extremely dangerous. Fear of incarceration was not the primary force driving them, but instead the fact that jail would cut them off from heroin. The drug was the most important part of their existence. This also contributed to their extraordinary cunning.

Within two minutes of entering Lake Shore Drive, which was a forty-five-mile-per-hour thoroughfare bisecting the western shore of Lake Michigan and the city, the van was approaching the downtown area of Chicago. The driver had been carefully watching the traffic in front of them as well as to the rear. There were no marked police cars in sight, but there was a new black sedan back there with a lone black guy behind the wheel. This car had followed them onto the Drive at Fullerton. But there was a lot of traffic at this time of the day, because the rush hour was beginning.

The female junkie spied the Lower Wacker Drive exit up ahead. The van's destination was a crash pad in a ghetto area of the west side. The fastest way to get there was via the Eisenhower Expressway. The van driver was aware that if the cops were on to them there could be a trap looming up ahead.

That is if whoever was back there in the black sedan was a cop. With her nerves scraped raw by the events of the past few minutes and her need to shoot up becoming critical, the driver twisted the steering wheel hard right and sideswiped a taxi cab traveling in the far right-hand lane. She managed to maintain control of the van after the collision and floored the accelerator to escape the scene of the accident by rocketing down the exit ramp on to Lower Wacker Drive. The cab driver jumped out of his damaged taxi and shook his fist at the hit-and-run vehicle. The black Mercury driven by Larry Cole pulled around the damaged taxi and followed the van down the ramp. Joe Donegan's rusty Chevy was right behind Cole.

Manny Sherlock ran into Blackie Silvestri's office at Detective Division headquarters. "Turn your radio to Frequency One."

Blackie, who had been working on a report for Chief Cole, looked up over the tops of his bifocals at the tall sergeant. He suppressed the urge to yell at Manny for interrupting his work and switched to Frequency One on the portable radio on top of his desk. Cole's voice came over the speaker.

". . . Lower Wacker Drive. Have responding units block eastbound traffic at LaSalle Street. I want to intercept the wanted van at State Street and Wacker. Advise all responding units that the occupants should be considered armed and dangerous."

Alarmed, Blackie looked at Manny. "What in the hell is going on? The boss went to take a physical. How did he get involved in this?"

The sergeant quickly explained about the off-duty officer being shot to death during the attempted robbery of the Gold

Coast Liquor Store and Delicatessen. When Manny was finished, Blackie still had questions, but they would have to wait until the emergency was over.

"Who do we have out there?" Blackie said.

"Judy."

After leaving Elaine Anderson outside of the Oceanside Restaurant, Judy had gotten into her car and traveled west toward the Kennedy Expressway. As Cole was leaving Dr. Novak's office and heading east to Lake Shore Drive and the junkie robbers were making their escape from the Gold Coast Liquor Store and Delicatessen, Judy was backed up in a construction zone on Chicago Avenue. She had just cleared the traffic tie-up when Cole broadcast that he was following the robbery suspects onto southbound Lake Shore Drive.

"Damn," she said, as a surge of adrenaline raced through her. The Mistress of Disguise/High Priestess of Mayhem estimated that she was over two miles away from Cole's last reported position. If he was going south on the Drive, she could plot an interception course through the streets on a south/southeast vector. Activating all of her emergency equipment, Judy Daniels executed a tire-screeching U-turn and sped off to rescue her boss.

"The black car is still behind us," the fugitive van driver said, as they raced westbound on Lower Wacker Drive. "There's also an old rust bucket that looks like a cop car behind him."

The robber checked his Tech Nine. He had fifteen rounds left in the magazine. He was also in dire need of a fix. The junkie had been a criminal for most of his life and had learned a great deal about police procedures due to his numerous arrests and stints in jail. Now he anticipated the cops behind them having arranged a trap somewhere up ahead.

"Turn around," he shouted to the driver.

"What?!" she responded in confusion.

"Turn this thing around!" he repeated, reaching over to yank the wheel.

The woman lost control of the van and struck the concrete median strip. The left front rim became bent and the tire rapidly deflated.

"Make the turn!" he screamed, pointing the Tech Nine at her.

She jerked the wheel and the van lurched up onto the median. The undercarriage scraped the cement surface causing sparks to fly. For a moment the van became hung up on the median. Finally, the remaining inflated tires gained purchase and the gray van, damaged from the collision with the taxi, completed the U-turn and began traveling in the opposite direction. The robbers' vehicle had temporarily eluded the police trap waiting for it at State and Wacker.

Larry Cole's black Mercury and Joe Donegan's rusty Chevrolet duplicated the gray van's maneuver.

Two one-man police cars and a sergeant arrived at the intersection of Lower Wacker Drive and State Street. Their first priority was halting the eastbound traffic and diverting it away from the intersection. As this was the middle of rush hour in downtown Chicago, it was not a simple task.

There were more police cars on the way and the sergeant in charge had spent twelve years in the detective division and knew Chief Cole. The sergeant had expeditiously deployed the officers and their vehicles to prevent the killers from proceeding beyond the State and Lower Wacker barricade. Then, just as two more police units arrived, Cole broadcast that the suspects' vehicle had changed direction back toward the lake. The sergeant ordered his cars to abandon the barricaded position and take up pursuit.

Judy Daniels was coming fast down Lake Street approaching Upper Wacker Drive from the west. When she heard the killers' course change, she snatched off the fake glasses she had worn as part of her disguise, tossed them on the seat beside her, and said, "Hold on, boss, I'm on the way."

Cole began overtaking the gray van, which was throwing up sparks and smoke from the blown tire rim scraping the asphalt. The suspects' vehicle was listing badly and wobbling precariously as it retraced the route back to Lake Shore Drive. Cole knew they couldn't go much farther, which meant that one of two things were about to occur: they would either surrender or abandon the van.

He was just about to alert the responding units of his current situation when he again noticed the old Chevy behind him. Something about the ragged, rusting car bothered Cole, but he was too preoccupied to worry about it at the moment.

Then the gray van came to a dead stop and the three junkie killers jumped out.

"We've got to split up," the Tech Nine–wielding junkie shouted.

The female driver panicked. "We'll never get away from that cop behind us!"

The junkie with the handgun said, "We will if he's dead."

She slammed on the brakes, grabbed a six-shot stainless steel .38 caliber Ruger revolver from beneath her seat and leaped out of the van with her companions.

At the point where they left the getaway van, Lower Wacker Drive ended under Lake Shore Drive. To the east of the intersecting thoroughfares was a grassy area, which led down to a cement walkway running along the Lake Michigan sea wall. The walkway would leave the fugitives exposed and did not provide them with much of an escape route. However, they were desperate.

Running from the van, the two male junkies turned and fired wildly back at the black Mercury. Of five rounds discharged—three from the Tech Nine and two from the Beretta—all but one bullet missed the black police command-car completely. That lone round ricocheted harmlessly off of Cole's driver's sideview mirror. But two of the Tech Nine rounds shattered Joe Donegan's windshield.

Without waiting to see the results of their marksmanship, the deadly junkies ran toward the lake.

"I've got shots fired by the robbery suspects at Lower Wacker Drive at Lake Shore," Cole said in a deadly calm tone of voice. To those who heard the chief of detectives' broadcast, he could have been discussing a routine police call, such as an illegally parked car or a non-functioning traffic signal. "They are described as . . ."

Joe Donegan's vehicle was stopped right behind Cole's. He was unable to see through his smashed windshield, but that didn't matter. For what Donegan planned to do, the chief of detectives would have to get out of the car. Cole was between him and the robbers, who had opened fire. Crossfires could be quite deadly. Finally, the great Larry Cole was going to meet his demise. Of course it would later be discovered that the bullet that killed the chief of detectives had come from one of Donegan's guns. Donegan had that figured out. It would be an unfortunate, but explainable, accident. This was due to one of the junkie robbers' bullets piercing the crooked cop's windshield and penetrating his shoulder. He was beginning to bleed heavily, but at this point there was a minimal amount of pain. Even with Cole dead by his hand, the department would have to give Donegan an award for the wound he suffered in the line of duty.

Pulling the .44 magnum revolver from its holster, Donegan opened the car door and put one foot out on the ground. The spot where the junkie's bullet had pierced his shoulder had gone numb; however, he knew that the pain would soon be upon him. He was forced to shift the gun from his right shooting hand to his left. He would lose little accuracy with the weapon at this range.

Donegan said an almost purring, "C'mon, Cole, get out of the car so I can blow you away."

At that instant, Cole opened the door and got out of the Mercury.

With all emergency equipment activated, Judy Daniels entered Lower Wacker Drive from upper-level Randolph Street a few blocks north of the Sears Tower. Down in the concrete corridor of Lower Wacker, the siren was amplified to an eardrum shattering level. This was exactly what she wanted as it succeeded in clearing a path through the dense traffic. The police car traveled the half-mile distance from the west Loop to Chief Cole's location in less than twenty seconds.

Exiting the Mercury, Cole was aware of the car behind him. Not knowing whether whoever was back there was friend or foe, he decided to first check out the old Chevy before he went after the fugitives. Cole could see the bullet holes in the car's windshield and that someone was seated upright behind the steering wheel. He was aware that the ragged car had followed him from Lake Shore Drive onto Lower Wacker. There was always the possibility that whoever was in the Chevy could be in league with the three, who had just run from the gray van. With gun raised, he walked toward the car.

Through the spider web glass mosaic of what was left of his windshield, Donegan watched Cole approach. The black cop had a gun in his hand, which did not overly concern the crooked cop. One shot from Donegan's .44 Magnum would be all that it would take. But Cole was now facing him, which would make the explanation of an accidental shooting impossible to sell convincingly. If the department applied enough heat, the Cook County States' Attorney could go for an indictment against Donegan. He would probably beat the charges, as there were no witnesses to Cole's shooting, but the crooked cop's CPD career would be over. And he still had a great deal he wanted to accomplish personally and financially before he gave up his badge.

All of this went through Donegan's mind as Cole advanced on the Chevy. Before the chief came up to the driver's side window, Donegan had de-cocked the .44 and returned it to its holster beneath his suit jacket. He then took out his Chicago Police I.D. case.

Slowly, he rolled the window down and said, "I'm on the job, Chief. I saw you chasing that van and I followed. They shot me."

Cole, keeping his Beretta down at his side, looked in the window of the dilapidated car. At the moment he saw the blood on Donegan, Judy Daniels and three marked police cars arrived on the scene.

The white female and the black male robbers attempted to make it to the Navy Pier recreational park, but were cut off by four police cars. They were trapped at the center of an empty parking lot and decided to surrender without firing a shot. The third fugitive proved more difficult to apprehend.

After summoning an ambulance for Sergeant Donegan and leaving one of the responding uniformed units with him, Cole, accompanied by Judy Daniels, led a search party for the final fugitive. Word had reached them by radio that the killer was last seen running north on Lower Lake Shore Drive toward the Lake Point Towers apartment complex. The police cordoned off all of the streets west of Lake Shore Drive, while Cole and Judy raced to the luxury high-rise building overlooking the lake.

The killer was sweating profusely and breathing heavily as he made his way through the shadows on the deserted lower level of Lake Shore Drive. He was frightened, desperate, sick, and extremely dangerous. He still had the Tech Nine, but he didn't know how many rounds were left in the magazine. He had separated from his accomplices, because he figured going it alone would increase his chances of effecting a successful escape.

Since killing the off-duty cop at the Gold Coast Liquor Store and Delicatessen, the junkie had begun deteriorating rapidly into a state that he had been descending into since the day he had injected that first shot of heroin into his arm. Any vestiges of humanity were now gone and he had become a vicious wild animal, who would kill without hesitation.

He was incapable of logical thought, but fear had enhanced his survival instinct. He realized that he would need transportation to make good his escape. He would have to commandeer a car. In fact, he decided that he would also need a hostage; perhaps two. In that way if the cops began closing in on him, he could graphically demonstrate his determination by killing one of the hostages.

The killer could hear the police sirens echoing off the walls of the skyscrapers towering over him. He began searching the streets for hostages.

He rounded the corner of the Lake Point Tower building and headed east. He was searching for a car with two, maybe three, occupants. He'd prefer a vehicle with a kid in it. The cops would be real careful before they made any funny moves against him if he had a child for a hostage. Then he spied a woman on the sidewalk up ahead. She was maybe two hundred feet away and approaching on foot with a funny little bouncy walk. He would have preferred more than one hostage, but this woman would serve until something better came along. He increased his pace to close the distance between them. He held the Tech Nine down at his side against his right leg. She wouldn't see it until he came within arm's reach of her. Then, using her as a shield, he would look for something better. She kept coming and he had closed the distance to eighty feet when he became aware of footsteps coming fast from behind him.

Frantically, he looked back to see a tall, broad-shouldered black guy walking toward him. Everything about the man screamed cop! Raising the Tech Nine, he spun around to locate his potential hostage. She was still there, now only thirty feet away; however, what he saw in her hands made his blood run cold. The slightly built woman with the funny walk was pointing a large semiautomatic blue steel pistol at him. The killer turned back to the black cop, who had closed to within twenty feet. He also had a pistol in his hand.

"I'm only going to say this once," the cop said. "Drop the gun right now and raise your hands above your head."

There was never any question in the junkie criminal's mind that he was not going to surrender. All that was left was for him to do was make the decision as to which of them he would take with him. He decided on the woman. Jerking the Tech Nine up, he fired from the hip. He got off three rounds, all of which missed the intended target. In return, the black cop and the female cop fired, but each of their eight bullets struck the fugitive in vital places. He lived for fifteen seconds after he hit the ground. The last thing that he saw in life was Larry Cole and Judy Daniels standing over him.

20

W. Solomon Randolph was the only son of William S. "Dollar Bill" Randolph and Sharon Powell Randolph. He was now twenty-seven years old and had earned a master's degree in business administration from the University of Chicago. Raised in an atmosphere of pious privilege, his estranged parents had competed aggressively for his affection. As far back as he could remember, he despised the idea of being a "junior," so when he was sixteen he began going by the name W. Solomon Randolph. Solomon had been his paternal great-grandfather's first name and when his father heard about the name change he was far from happy. This drove his mother to become openly supportive of her son's choice of name simply because it displeased her husband. Sharon Randolph was also fond of the name because it had a prominent biblical connection.

Solomon or "Solly," which was a nickname he hated as much as he disliked being referred to as a junior, had always been the center of attention and he grew into a self-centered, totally selfish adult. He had never wanted for anything and his mother and absentee father fulfilled his every wish. Somehow he managed to avoid being a stereotypical, tantrum-throwing spoiled brat and instead, at an early age, developed into a calculating sadist. By the time he reached manhood, he had become a sociopath.

Solomon Randolph was a clean-cut, marginally handsome young man with a slender build, medium-brown complexion, short cropped black hair, and a neatly trimmed goatee and mustache. He dressed in the expensively conservative attire of the successful business professional that he had studied to be in college. After graduating from the U. of C. he did not make any attempt to get a job, despite MBA graduates being in great demand. Due to his father's money, Solomon didn't have to punch a time clock on a nine-to-five job. However, he didn't plan to remain idle all of his life. He intended to build an empire on his father's fortune and, again contrary to Dollar Bill's wishes, he planned to pursue that career on the wrong side of the law.

He drove his late-model, fire-engine-red BMW south on Stony Island Avenue toward Saint Ailbe's Catholic Church. He was picking up his mother, who was attending an Altar and Rosary Society meeting. Outwardly, Solomon appeared to be the ever-dutiful son; however, chauffeuring his mother around was simply a way to continue his manipulation of her and his father.

Solomon parked his car in the lot next to the school building and entered through a rear door. Descending a flight of steps brought him to the closed doors of a meeting room. He could hear the strident tones of voices raised in an argument coming from inside. Having no compunctions about eavesdropping, he remained out in the hall and listened.

"But Mrs. Walton is a very devout Catholic," one of the Altar and Rosary Society members was saying. "She participates in all church and school activities, and is putting her three children through private high schools and college without any assistance at all from her ex-husband."

Solomon Randolph was fairly certain that the woman speaking was Mrs. Anna Hernandez—a white-haired portly woman who was fond of wearing baggy flower-print dresses and always had a rosary in her hands whenever she was on holy ground. Although he was unable to see her, the eavesdropper could tell that she was very close to tears.

Then he heard his mother's voice. Solomon could easily visualize Sharon Powell Randolph. She would be dressed to the nines in an outfit with accessories that had come out of only the most exclusive stores on the Magnificent Mile of North Michigan Avenue. None of the other members of the all-female Altar and Rosary Society could afford to spend the money on clothing that his mother spent on underwear alone. The esteemed Mrs. Randolph's hair was done weekly by a hairdresser who came to the southeast-side mansion at a cost of $250.00 per visit. Because she would be attending the Altar and Rosary Society meeting tonight, Solomon knew that her hair had been washed and set this afternoon along with a manicure and her makeup professionally applied. In the drab St. Ailbe's school hall, Sharon Powell Randolph would stand out like an empress in her throne room surrounded by peasants.

In the imperious tone of voice that she always used when addressing the less materially fortunate than herself, she said, "Mrs. Walton's church attendance and the sacrifices she makes to educate her children are not at issue, Anna. We simply cannot entertain her membership in this organization, because she is a divorced woman."

"Look who's calling the kettle black," Solomon mumbled to himself.

"This isn't right, Sharon." Anna Hernandez was sobbing openly.

Sharon Powell Randolph countered with, "Of course it is, or would you prefer that we take this up with the pastor?"

"A lot of good that is going to do," Solomon quipped. "You own that old fool, Mother, and everybody in there knows it."

There was little else said about the matter of Mrs. Walton's aborted membership in the Altar and Rosary Society and Solomon Randolph was becoming bored. He opened the door and entered the school hall.

All of the ladies turned to watch the son of their esteemed chairwoman walk across the room. Of the fifteen members present, only two were younger than forty; however, each of them had a crush in one way or another on the twenty-seven-year-old man. To them he was clean cut, extremely intelligent, and invariably polite. To the women who no longer had any romantic aspirations, he represented the type of ideal son that none of them had. But at least one or two of the members of the Altar and Rosary Society, which Sharon Powell Randolph ran so autocratically, had silently commented that their chairwoman's son was just a little too good to be true. And if any of those present in the St. Ailbe's school hall on this fall evening had been carefully studying their esteemed chairwoman when she set eyes on her prized son, they would have observed a flicker of pain or perhaps dislike pass momentarily across her still pretty, but aging, features.

"So how was your Altar and Rosary Society meeting, Mother?" Solomon asked as he turned the red BMW north on Stony Island Avenue and shifted through the gears.

Sharon Powell Randolph responded, "It went quite well and would you please slow down!"

"Certainly, Mother." He did not slow his car down at all.

"Tell me something," he said, as he sped through a yellow caution light at the intersection of Seventy-ninth Street and South Chicago Avenue. "This Mrs. Walton you denied membership to in the Altar and Rosary Society?"

His mother stiffened. "Solomon, it is very rude to listen in on the conversations of other people."

He laughed. "Spare me, Mother. I learned to do it from you." After a short pause, he said, "So Mrs. Walton's being divorced disqualified her for membership, isn't that right?"

"Isn't that what you overheard?"

"Yes, it was. But if being divorced eliminates this Mrs. Walton, what about you and Dad's estrangement?"

"Your father and I are still married," she said with glacial annoyance.

"Technicalities, Mother. Mere technicalities."

A short time later he pulled into the driveway of the mansion in which he had lived with his mother all of his life. Getting out of the car he came around to dutifully help her out of the car. He walked her to the front door, which was opened by Jamison, the butler, who had been with Sharon Powell Randolph and her son for years.

When Solomon saw the domestic, he said a sarcastic, "Good evening, Uncle Remus."

"Solomon, please," his mother moaned in exasperation.

Jamison appeared unaffected by the insult, as he said a very proper, "Good evening to you, Mrs. Randolph, as well as to you, Mr. Randolph. I've been keeping dinner warm."

"That was very thoughtful of you, Jamison," Sharon said.

"Leave mine in the microwave," Solomon said. "I've got to go back out."

"Where?" his mother demanded.

Knowing that it would irritate her, he said, "I'm going over to the Roost to see Dad."

Then he kissed her on the cheek and trotted back down the steps. As he got into his car and peeled rubber rocketing away, Sharon Powell Randolph and Jamison remained standing at the front door of the mansion.

When Solomon Randolph arrived at Randy's Roost, his father was in his office staring intensely at a television set. The son, who actually had a deep respect for his father, said, "What's going on, Dad?"

"Joe Donegan's been shot."

"Probably by another cop," Solomon said with a sarcastic sneer. He had a particular dislike for Donegan, because he was not only a cop, but also a crooked one. Such a man, as his father had taught him, could not be trusted. Dollar Bill had also told Solomon that the dishonest cop served an indispensable purpose in the operation that was bringing in a great deal of cash for them.

Dollar Bill explained, "Donegan was with the chief of detectives, attempting to capture some robbers who killed an off-duty cop."

Solomon was surprised. "Since when does a low-life like Donegan run around with a Dudley Do-Right type like Cole?"

"The news people aren't saying, because they probably don't know. I've got a connection in the police department who is going to let me know exactly what went down. Donegan getting next to Cole would be a definite coup for us."

Solomon pulled up a chair beside his father's desk. "Cole is too smart a cop to take Donegan into his confidence."

Suddenly, Dollar Bill Randolph was convulsed with pain. Alarmed, his son said, "Dad, what is it?"

He remained constricted for a moment longer with his face in a tight grimace and sweat streaming down his forehead. Then, as quickly as it began, the spasm subsided.

"Can I get you anything?" Solomon said, revealing an unusual depth of concern for another individual.

Dollar Bill shook his head. He had pills for the pain, which was caused by the reccurrence of the cancer he had developed in prison. But the drugs dulled his mind and, with the little time that he had left, he needed to give his son as much of his knowledge of the world as he possibly could. He couldn't do this effectively if he were doped up on painkillers.

Weakened, but lucid, Dollar Bill wiped his face with a handkerchief and said, "We need to talk about Donegan's connection to Alderman Skip Murphy. Cole figures in this as well."

Solomon Randolph gave Dollar Bill Randolph his total attention.

Following the wounding of Sergeant Joe Donegan and the fatal shooting of the junkie stick-up man, an automatic Chicago Police Department procedure kicked in. This required the response of a number of government officials to include the Assistant Deputy Superintendent on duty; an Assistant Cook County State's Attorney; an investigator from the Office of Professional Standards; the watch commander on duty in the Eighteenth Police District, where the shootings had occurred; and a shooting team from Area Three Detectives. As Chief Larry Cole and

Sergeant Judy Daniels were involved in the incident, there was a pronounced response from the news media. The names of the deceased Hispanic officer, who had accidentally stumbled into the robbery at the Gold Coast Liquor Store and Delicatessen, and the wounded Joe Donegan were withheld pending notification of their next of kin. Because of Cole's rank and the fact that Judy Daniels was on his staff, the investigation was conducted at police headquarters.

The procedure was routine, but fairly lengthy as the city of Chicago and the police department sought to insure that, when deadly force was employed, all procedures had been followed to the letter. Some hours later, the investigation was concluded with a finding that the shooting had indeed been justifiable.

Exhausted, Judy Daniels left the interview room and went back to her cubicle in the Detective Division headquarters complex. Actually, the personal space she was allotted in the CPD building, which had opened in 2000, was as large as Chief Cole's old office at 1121 South State Street had been. The floor was carpeted and the five-foot-tall panels covered with a padded blue fabric, which muffled sound, giving the area a relaxing atmosphere to work in. The cubicle was equipped with a department-issued computer, telephone system, desk, and desk chair. Judy had personalized the space with a couple of potted green plants and a few photographs from earlier in her career. There were no pictures of any family members or friends other than Larry Cole, his son—Butch Cole, Blackie and Maria Silvestri, and Manny and Lauren Sherlock. At once Judy considered her Chicago police department colleagues her family as well as her closest friends. There had been few other people that she had been close to in her life. At times such isolation haunted her, but she had discovered a long time ago that being alone did not necessarily mean that you were lonely.

The woman, who had developed the legendary reputation within the American law enforcement community as the Mistress of Disguise/High Priestess of Mayhem, attempted to never think about her life before that day when she had been sworn in as a Chicago police officer. In fact, even when she did revisit her past, it was with the detachment one would employ to view the life of a casual acquaintance or perhaps even a fictional character read about in a novel.

Her father and stepmother, who was a woman as cold and insensitive toward the child as she would have been with a total stranger, had raised Judy. Judy's natural mother had run off with a saloon piano player, abandoning her husband and then-four-year-old daughter. The child had never heard from her again. Her father, who was a supermarket manager for twenty-five years, provided Judy with as much love as he could, but it was simply not a substitute for her mother being there. At least it wasn't for Judy.

Perhaps, Judy mused, this was one of the reasons why she was so close to Larry Cole. He had also lost his parents at an early age and been forced to go it alone for most of his life.

Judy Daniels's childhood, adolescence, and young adulthood, prior to her joining the police department, had been lonely, awkward, and at times traumatic. The scars she had carried from that period of her life were contributing factors behind her constantly changing disguises. At times she experienced a great degree of comfort as she hid her true self from the world. Such anonymity became oddly soothing to the lonely little girl, who had cried herself to sleep on so many nights of her young life.

There was a noise in her cubicle. She looked around to find

the source. She was alone and it took her a moment to discover what the sound was that she had heard. Then, with a damning revelation, she realized that she had made the noise herself. She had sobbed out loud and now there were tears flowing down her cheeks.

"Dammit," she swore aloud through clenched teeth, "pull yourself together, woman!"

Slowly, she transformed her inner self back into the law enforcement professional that she was so proud of. The scared little girl crying herself to sleep was forgotten once again. Now she had more pressing matters to deal with. The Mistress of Disguise/High Priestess of Mayhem had a number of questions about Sergeant Joe Donegan of the Intelligence unit. Questions that she planned to take up with Chief Cole right now.

Getting to her feet, she snatched a tissue from a box with a floral pattern on her desk and used it to dry her eyes. After blowing her nose, she tossed the tissue into the wastebasket and headed for Cole's office.

Larry Cole was tired. It had been a long day and he remembered promising himself that he was going to go home tonight and get a good night's sleep. Whatever that was. However, it was past 9 P.M. and he was still in the office. Blackie and Manny were also there listening to Judy Daniels. She was talking about Sergeant Joe Donegan.

"Every time that Donegan becomes involved in something, there are questions raised about his integrity. Sergeant Elaine Anderson has some pretty strong suspicions that the Lone Stranger, as he has been called throughout his career, has something to do with this phony document scam she's been trying to bust. And he's in a perfect position to know the details of every investigation they mount in the Intelligence unit, because he's in charge of their computer room."

Manny, who was the resident computer expert in the Detective Division, said, "It's my understanding that the Intel computers are the most sophisticated in the department. In fact, if this Sergeant Donegan knows what he's doing, he can probably get into any law enforcement computer system in the world."

Blackie, whose computer skills were rudimentary at best, said, "I understand that you and Elaine Anderson are friends, Judy, but if she's got suspicions about this guy why didn't she take them to Internal Affairs?"

Judy sighed. "Elaine started out asking me for advice. Then, when she found out I had come in contact with Donegan a couple of times, she asked me for help. I told her I would run it by you and the boss, Blackie, and then who shows up and gets himself shot down on Wacker Drive, but the Lone Stranger himself."

"He was monitoring the police radio just like you were, Judy," Blackie said. "And he did get shot."

"I've got to admit one thing, Blackie," Cole said. "When Donegan was behind me during the pursuit of the robbers' van, I felt that he was primarily following me as opposed to being interested in apprehending our offenders. He was right on my tail all the way and that was his own car he was driving."

"So why has he got a police radio in his personal car?" Judy demanded.

"Oh, he had more than just a radio," Cole said. "After the junkies ran from the van and opened fire, I went back to make sure Donegan wasn't one of the bad guys. When I looked into his car, I noticed a department computer and an omni-directional listening device on the front seat."

Judy stiffened. "He was on the North Side at the same time that Elaine and I were having lunch. He could have been spying on us."

"That's a bit of a stretch, Judy," Manny said. "The North Side of Chicago is a mighty big place."

"We could always ask Donegan what he was doing," Blackie said.

"If he was spying on Judy and Sergeant Anderson I doubt if he's about to tell us," Cole said. "He wouldn't have recognized Judy anyway unless he's seen you in your present disguise."

She shook her head in the negative. "The last time I saw Donegan before today I was undercover as a bag lady on a narcotics surveillance outside of a South Side bar called Randy's Roost. That was about ten years ago. The Lone Stranger showed up and went inside the tavern, where grain alcohol was supposedly being sold to a street gang's crack cocaine operation. Alderman Skip Murphy was there too."

Cole and Blackie exchanged surprised glances. "Donegan and Murphy had a meeting at Randy's Roost?" Cole questioned.

"I don't know about a meeting, boss," Judy said, "but they both were in the bar together."

"Do you know when this was, Judy?" Cole pressed.

"I can look it up pretty quick. Can I use your computer?"

A few minutes later she had the ten-year-old surveillance logs from the Narcotics Unit on Cole's screen. "It was October fourteenth, 1993," she said, pointing at the entry. "The strange thing about the surveillance we conducted that day was that the operation was mysteriously terminated before we could make any arrests."

"October fourteenth, 1993," Cole repeated. "There's something about that day. Pull up the log of criminal incidents for that date."

Within seconds a listing appeared. The four cops were gathered around the computer, but it was Cole who had the most pronounced reaction.

In a deadly calm tone of voice, he said, "That was the night Skip Murphy's election opponent was killed in a mysterious explosion. And Joe Donegan was possibly meeting with Skip Murphy earlier that day. Donegan was also the detective from the old Area Six detective area, who investigated the disappearance of Sophie Novak, who was last seen with Skip Murphy. Now that is very interesting."

21

SEPTEMBER 26, 2003

9:20 P.M.

Megan Donegan had not aged well. Although she was in her forties, she didn't look a day younger than sixty. Her hair was a washed-out gray color, which received little care, and the flesh beneath her eyes and chin was sagging and wrinkled. Her thin figure had become bowed due to chronic fatigue and she moved about with a listless shuffle. She had qualified for an early retirement from the Water Department and now spent her days in front of the living room television set. She seldom left the house, where she planned to live with her brother Joe until the day that she died. Now she sat in the waiting room of University Hospital waiting to find out how he was doing after being shot in the line of duty.

Megan had been in hospitals before—in fact, exactly three times in her adult life. Those were on the occasions that her mother and father had passed away and once when Bob Jr. was injured fighting a fire. And she wasn't very good at this type of thing. In the past there had always been someone with her to take charge and show her what to do. Being alone terrified her, especially since her closest relative was being treated for a gunshot wound.

The other Donegans, Bob Jr. and Ted, had stopped briefly in the emergency room and spoken with the paramedics that had transported Joe to the hospital in a Chicago Fire Department ambulance. However, the brothers did not go back to visit with the wounded cop. They stopped briefly in the waiting room to say a brief hello to their sister and then they were gone. Over the years the surviving males of the Donegan clan had developed deep-seated differences of opinion. Megan had been unable to learn exactly what they were feuding about, but it had something to do with Joe's integrity.

Megan wanted to leave the hospital too, but she didn't think that would be right. After all, someone had to stay with Joe.

The waiting room wasn't crowded and Megan had a row of chairs all to herself. She was too anxious to read a magazine or even look at the television that was broadcasting a twenty-four-hour news station. Her eyes kept darting from the waiting room entrance back to the people sitting around her. Finally, after she'd been waiting for over three hours, her brother appeared. There was a distraught doctor following closely on Joe's heels.

Megan stood up and crossed the waiting room to the location where Joe had stopped and was arguing with the white-coated young doctor. She could see blood on her brother's threadbare sports jacket and wrinkled shirt. The shirt itself was open and white bandages were visible beneath it. She came within earshot of Joe and the doctor, who didn't look a day over twenty.

"Sergeant Donegan," the doctor was saying, "you need to remain in the hospital overnight for observation. You've lost a great deal of blood and have experienced a severe physical trauma. You could still go into shock or have some other form of adverse reaction."

Megan watched as her brother affixed the white-coated young man with a chilling stare. The doctor even took a step backward. "If I have a problem tonight, my sister will drive me back to the hospital. Now give me a prescription for some pills and don't give me anything that will knock me out."

The doctor shook his head in dismay. "As you are leaving the hospital against my advice, I think you can get by on an over-the-counter medication, such as Tylenol or simple aspirin."

Donegan turned his back on the doctor, spied his sister and said, "Where's your car?"

"In the parking lot," Megan responded. "I'll go get it and pick you up at the front entrance to the hospital."

"I can walk," the wounded cop snapped. "Let's go."

As they headed for the exit, the doctor called after them, "Would you at least make an appointment to come into the hospital tomorrow so that I can check your wound?"

"Don't worry," Donegan called over his shoulder, "I'll have my own doctor take a look at it."

As they went out through the revolving door, Megan said with dismay, "But, Joe, you don't have a doctor."

"Then I'll find one."

Sergeant Elaine Anderson entered the basement complex of the Intelligence Unit on the West Side. She went to the operations office where Officers Consuela Castenada and Warren Hitchcock were waiting for her. Other than these three, the facility was deserted.

"What's up, Sarge?" said Warren, a thin, square-jawed black man. He was dressed in jeans and a Chicago Bears sweatshirt. He had his feet, clad in worn cowboy boots, propped up on an open desk drawer. He was considered the free spirit of the Intelligence Unit.

Consuela "Connie" Castenada was an exceptionally pretty, dark-haired woman, who possessed a phenomenal memory. She had been working with Warren for three years and they were a good team. They were both officers that Sergeant Anderson trusted implicitly.

"Did you hear what happened to Donegan?" the sergeant asked.

"Yeah," Connie said, with the slightest hint of a Spanish accent. "I never thought of him as the hero type."

"I wonder what got him out of the computer room," Warren said. "I think the commander should charge him rent, because he just about lives in there."

"But he's not in there now," Sergeant Anderson said.

It took the two Intelligence Unit cops a moment to catch on. Then Warren said, "The commander has restricted access

to the computer lab to only those people that Donegan author-
izes."

"In fact," Connie interjected, "only Donegan and the boss
have the combination to get inside."

"Because the commander goes into the room so seldom, he
keeps the combination on a slip of paper beneath the desk blotter in his office," the sergeant explained.

"The boss keeps his office locked," Warren said, removing
a cloth pouch from his pants pocket. "But it has one of those
simple doorknob-type locks that isn't very secure." He removed
a pair of thin metal lock picks from the pouch. "Any amateur
burglar can get in there."

Elaine Anderson stopped them. "I want you guys to know
what you're getting into here. What we will be doing is vio-
lating a direct order from a superior officer."

"Something stinks to the high heavens about Joe Donegan,
Sarge," Connie said.

"And its about time somebody tried to nail him," Warren
added. "So what are we waiting for?"

It took them less than five minutes to obtain the combination from the commander's office. Then they went to the
computer room.

At the door Sergeant Anderson paused with Connie and
Warren by her side. Taking a deep breath, Elaine said, "Okay,
here goes," and punched in the combination. The sound of the
lock disengaging seemed as loud as a pistol shot in the deserted
basement complex. After a second longer hesitation, the three
cops entered "Donegan's Domain."

Donegan's car had been towed to the police impound garage
on Lower Wacker Drive a short distance from the location

where he was shot. He had received a mild anesthetic at the hospital while they removed the bullet from his shoulder and sewed him up. Despite the painkiller beginning to wear off, Donegan ordered Megan to drive to the impound garage. His explanation: there were some personal items in the raggedy old car that he had to retrieve tonight.

The officer on duty at the impound garage was a grizzled old veteran with an enormous beer belly. He wore a not-too-clean, dark blue police utility uniform and initially displayed open irritation when he was forced to abandon the situation comedy he was watching on a portable TV in the garage office. But when he found out that Donegan was a wounded cop, his attitude changed instantly.

The impound officer escorted Donegan down a row of cars that were in various states of extreme disrepair. In fact, when they finally did reach the rusty Chevrolet, it looked pretty good compared to the wrecks surrounding it.

Breathing heavily from the exertion of walking the short distance from his office, the fat cop said, "So you took a bullet in the line of duty. You're lucky to walk away from something like that, pal."

The pain had become a very real thing for Joe Donegan and, as he fumbled to get his car keys out of his pocket, he grumbled, "I'm not your pal, fatso."

Angrily the fat cop turned and walked away saying, "Too bad that bullet didn't hit you in the head, asshole."

Forgetting the garage attendant, Donegan retrieved his laptop computer and telephone from the front seat of his car. A few minutes later he was back in Megan's car.

"Find a drugstore where you can buy me some Tylenol," he said, turning the computer on.

Before she put the car in gear, Megan said, "You are as pale as a ghost, Joe. You should have taken the doctor's advice and remained in the hospital."

As the laptop's screen brightened, he said, "Do us both a favor and shut up."

Obediently, she drove off in search of a drug store. They had traveled a short distance when she heard him gasp.

"Are you in pain, Joe?"

"No," he said tightly. "I'm fine." He continued to stare intensely at the screen.

The reason that Joe Donegan had gasped was not his gunshot wound, but instead what he discovered when he turned his computer on. Someone had gained unauthorized entry to his computer room.

"Would you look at this?" Connie said in awe, as they looked around the interior of "Donegan's Domain."

"Welcome to the bridge of the Starship Enterprise," Warren added.

Indeed what Donegan had done to the computer lab was impressive. All of the equipment was state-of-the-art and a number of the units were continuously running programs. After getting over the initial shock, Sergeant Anderson led them further into the large room.

"Now we've got to figure out what to look for," the sergeant said.

Connie went over to one of the running programs. "Sarge," she called, "this computer is hooked up to the Secretary of State's office computer."

Elaine and Warren came over to examine the screen. "The program is in a search mode and going through the records of the Department of Motor Vehicles. If I don't miss my guess, this is a search in progress for revoked licenses."

The three cops were so absorbed with the evidence on the screen, they didn't notice the door slide shut silently.

Megan went to a Walgreen's drugstore in a shopping mall on Roosevelt Road near the Dan Ryan Expressway. Leaving her brother in the car, she went inside to purchase Extra Strength Tylenol. All the way from the impound garage to the shopping mall, Joe Donegan had remained hunched over his computer, cursing occasionally when the car hit a bump or pothole in the street.

As soon as Megan was out of the car, he began activating a program to eliminate the intruders in the Intelligence Unit's computer room. He interfaced with a computer in the basement complex by way of a remote cellular function. Then he began to rapidly feed information into the link that would start a fire. Of course, he didn't want anything to damage his prized computers.

"We need to make a copy of this information," Sergeant Anderson was saying about the Department of Motor Vehicles license revocation information.

"That should be simple enough," Connie said, punching keys to activate one of the printers.

As the printout began, Warren sniffed the air. "Do you smell something burning?"

The pungent odor was becoming increasingly more noticeable. Connie began coughing. Warren searched for the source of the combustion. It wasn't difficult to find, because it stood out against the high-tech equipment surrounding it.

The old radio was on the floor behind one of the consoles.

The housing was made of cheap plastic, which had been chipped and scratched by years of abuse. None of them had ever heard of the brand name Muntz on the front of the radio. A frayed cord led from the back of the radio to a wall outlet. There was also a cable leading to the radio from one of the computers. The frayed cord was burning with smoke becoming increasingly heavy. This was beginning to have an effect on all of them.

Warren reached down and grabbed the frayed cord with his bare hand. He jerked back quickly, as he had sustained a second-degree burn to the palm of his hand. The cord continued to burn and the smoke became thick. The printout wasn't completed, but Elaine Anderson was becoming concerned about her officers. Warren's hand was badly burned and Connie was starting to choke. They could come back for the information from the Department of Motor Vehicles later. Now was the time to vacate the premises.

"Come on, guys," the sergeant said. Her own eyes were starting to tear. "Let's get out of here."

She led them to the door, which she noticed was now closed. When she attempted to shove it open, the door wouldn't budge. She reached down and grasped the inside knob. It turned, but the door didn't open. She fought the panic that was attempting to seize her. Looking back she saw that the burning cord had erupted into open flames. The fire was licking up the cinder block wall and the air was becoming hotter. Warren and Connie had followed the sergeant across the room and were looking to her for guidance in this moment of peril. Turning back to the door, Elaine twisted the knob more violently and shoved forcibly against the unyielding surface.

Suddenly, there was a noticeable change in the atmosphere. The flames began to recede and the smoke was being sucked out of the air to be replaced by some type of fire-retarding gas. Initially, the three cops thought that this was their salvation. However, the gas being pumped into the computer room was called Halon, which was indeed a fire retardant. But the way that this particular substance fought combustion was to remove all of the oxygen from the air.

Sergeant Elaine Anderson, Officer Consuela Casteneda, and Officer Warren Hitchcock would not die of burns or smoke inhalation, but instead, suffocation.

Megan Donegan returned to her car in the Walgreen's drug store parking lot and handed a bottle of Extra Strength Tylenol capsules to her brother. He paused only momentarily from studying the screen of his laptop, to pop three capsules into his mouth and, with some difficulty, dry-swallow them. Then he checked his computer once more before shutting it off and closing the lid. Leaning his head back against the seat, he closed his eyes. Before Megan had driven a block from the parking lot, Joe was sound asleep.

22

NOVEMBER 1, 2003

8:50 A.M.

They knew that he did it, but they didn't know how he did it. After the bodies of Sergeant Elaine Anderson and Intelligence Unit Officers Consuela Castenada and Warren Hitchcock were found in the computer room, there had never been any doubts in the minds of Larry Cole, Blackie Silvestri, Manny Sherlock, and especially Judy Daniels that Joe Donegan had killed them. Proving it was another matter.

An officer arriving for duty at 7 A.M. found the bodies on the morning of September 27. He noticed that the door to the computer room was standing open, which was unusual. Then he saw the bodies inside and it was quite obvious that they had died horribly.

As the chief of detectives, Larry Cole was charged with the follow-up investigation into the deaths, which were initially classified as accidental. Area Four Detectives had the immediate investigative responsibility, but it soon became apparent that Cole and his people had more than a passing interest in what had occurred in the Intelligence Unit computer room. Although the Area Four Detectives were kept apprised of what was going on, Cole, Blackie, Manny, and Judy had taken over the case.

The computer lab was shut down and access restricted to only personnel authorized by the chief of detectives. The CPD crime lab went over every square inch of the room and all of the evidence, including the old Muntz radio with the frayed cord, was collected, catalogued, and shipped to police headquarters for careful analysis.

The cause of death was determined to be the flame-extinguishing Halon gas. The system, although fatal to humans, was not illegal. Due to the sensitivity of the equipment in the computer room, a nonliquid fire suppression system was recommended. The most commonly used element was the C245 odorless substance, which was not life-threatening. But the building, in which the Intelligence Unit was headquartered and received free office space, had employed the older, more dangerous substance in areas where delicate equipment was located.

The question the investigators were attempting to answer was: why didn't the three cops simply leave the area when the fire started? The fire had been localized to one area of the computer room and done a minimal amount of damage. So why hadn't they simply walked out before they suffocated? Undoubtedly, they couldn't, but Cole and his investigators would have to find out why.

This area of inquiry led to additional questions. The computer room had been off limits to personnel who did not have the authorization of the Intelligence Unit commander. Technically the dead officers were trespassing in a restricted area. Also, there had been no one else in the complex that night and Donegan, who had suffered a gunshot wound, had an alibi for the time Anderson, Castenada, and Hitchcock died. But somehow, Cole knew Donegan had managed to kill them. The motive? Donegan had found out that Elaine Anderson suspected him of being involved in the phony driver's license scam.

After the crime lab finished their tasks, Cole and his crew attacked the crime scene. They ran all of the programs and checked every square inch of wiring. The door-locking mechanism was taken apart and carefully studied. All of the interface operations with other computers were examined. Employing tremendous tenacity, they studied it all looking for the keys that would unlock the mystery of what had caused the computer-room deaths. They were also searching for evidence to prove that Joe Donegan had committed the murders. After over a month had gone by, they had come up empty.

Larry Cole had just come from a meeting with the superintendent of police. It had been a one-on-one session during which the CPD chief executive inquired as to when Cole would be finished with the computer room. After all, a month had passed, the deceased officers received full-honors funerals, and it was time for the Intelligence Unit to get back to work. Sergeant Donegan, along with the other members of the unit, had attended the funerals in uniform. His injured right arm had been encased in a sling. Now the sergeant, who had been cleared to return to duty by the department's medical director, was standing by waiting for the chief of detectives to release "Donegan's Domain" back to him.

After the meeting with the superintendent, Cole returned to his office. Blackie was there, but Manny and Judy were over at the Intelligence Unit computer room, where they had been spending from ten to twelve hours a day since the deaths of the officers.

Blackie poured Cole a cup of coffee and followed the chief into his private office. Setting the cup down on the Plexiglas desk cover and closing the door, the lieutenant said, "I guess they want us to release the computer room."

Cole nodded. "And we're going to."

Blackie shrugged. "We still don't know how Donegan pulled this off."

Cole took a sip of the hot coffee. "Keeping the computer lab impounded for another day or for that matter even another year won't get us any closer to finding the answers, Blackie. What we need to do is give Sergeant Donegan free reign to go back to his illegal pursuits. Eventually, he'll slip up and we'll have him."

"Do you think we'll be able to make anything more of the

connection he had to our favorite city councilman?"

Cole put his coffee cup back down on the desk. For a moment he was lost in thought. Then he responded, "Eventually we will get Donegan and Skip Murphy, Blackie. Just like we finally nailed Steven Zalkin and Baron Alain Marcus Casimir von Rianocek."

Over the weeks that had ensued, Joe Donegan monitored Cole's investigation with interest. Convalescing at home, he shadowed the movements and activities of not only Cole, but also Blackie Silvestri, Manny Sherlock, and the infamous Mistress of Disguise/High Priestess of Mayhem. On the night he had trapped Anderson, Castenada, and Hitchcock in the computer room, he also transferred all functions from the Intelligence Unit computers into Dollar Bill Randolph's computer at Randy's Roost. Donegan couldn't risk placing the data into his home computer, because Cole might convince some gullible judge to issue a search warrant for Donegan's personal files.

Then, after he'd had his dressing changed at University Hospital, he fought through the pain that the over-the-counter Tylenol could no longer suppress and placed homing devices on Cole and each of the cops assigned to his personal staff. To accomplish this, he had forced a bewildered Megan Donegan to drive him to within a block of the residences of Cole, Silvestri, Sherlock, and Daniels. When he finally managed to complete these tasks in the early hours of the morning of September 28, he realized that he was in dire need of a doctor. Now he was not only in intense pain, but running a high fever. He told his sister to contact Dr. Stella Novak.

*   *   *

On the morning of November 1, Joe Donegan had been Stella Novak's patient for five weeks shy of a day. When his sister had initially made the emergency appointment for him, the physician had recognized the name instantly. He was the detective who had botched her sister's missing person investigation. Stella recalled the frightening, dirty little man's visit to her apartment years ago. But that was before she had become a doctor. Then there was the trembling, frightened tone in Megan Donegan's voice.

That first appointment was for 9:00 A.M. on September 29. Stella always arrived at her office at least forty-five minutes before she was scheduled to see her first patient. Even at that early hour, she found the thin, nervous, hollow-eyed Megan Donegan waiting for her at the front door of the medical complex.

After identifying herself, Megan said, "My brother is in a very bad way, Doctor. He's unconscious and I can't get him out of the car."

"Where are you parked?"

Megan led Dr. Novak to her five-year-old, gray Ford Escort parked a short distance from the medical center. Following a cursory examination of the unconscious man, Stella ran back to her office to summon an ambulance. That morning she saved Joe Donegan's life.

The disregard he had given his injury and the exertion he had engaged in weakened him considerably. A massive infection set in with Donegan running a 103-degree fever and the wound festering close to gangrene setting in. When the crooked cop regained consciousness, he was flat on his back in a hospital room with an IV in his arm and Dr. Stella Novak standing

over him. When he discovered that the physician had saved his
life, Donegan was forced to smile at the irony of his situation.

After three days in the hospital he was released with the
strong admonition from Dr. Novak that he not only take it easy,
but also follow her instructions to the letter. To some extent
Donegan did slow down, because he retrieved the information
stored in Dollar Bill Randolph's computer and downloaded it
onto his home computer. From there he was able to monitor
the course of Cole's investigation inside the Intelligence Unit.

Once a week he had a standing appointment with Dr. Novak. He found his contacts with the young physician quite stim-
ulating. Especially since he had killed her sister years ago. He
felt a sense of power and control over her despite the relative
innocence of their relationship. By pure accident, he had
learned that Larry Cole was also a patient of Dr. Novak's from
a conversation he had overheard between Stella's receptionist
and her associate, a thin Latin-lover type named Dr. Ramone.
The crooked cop found this amusing. He and the great Larry
Cole, whom Donegan came very close to killing the night he
got shot, shared the same doctor. Someday, Donegan swore,
Cole would need the emergency services of Dr. Novak.

Donegan was always on his best behavior during his appointments with Dr. Novak. He showered, shaved, and put on
clean underwear and socks prior to each visit. A dab of cheap
drugstore aftershave, which he always thought made him smell
like a cheap hooker, and a couple of shots from a breath-spray
dispenser, made him almost acceptable in polite society. Megan
had observed the way her brother primped before going to the
doctor's office. She wrongly assumed that Joe had a romantic
interest in Stella Novak. But Joe Donegan's interest in his doctor was far from amorous.

The examination always began with Donegan signing in at the reception desk and taking a seat in the waiting room. In less than five minutes, a nurse would escort him back to an examining room, where he was instructed to strip to the waist. This took some doing because of all the guns he wore. By his first of November visit, the nurse had gotten used to Donegan's hardware.

After he stripped down, he took a seat on the examination table. There was a mirror over a wash basin set in the wall beside the door. He could see his reflection in this mirror. Even to Donegan the sight before him could only be termed "ugly." The flesh of his torso was pale and matted with dark hair. He didn't exercise and his muscle tone was poor. His arms were thin, his chest sunken, and his stomach sagged over his belt. The scar from the bullet wound in his shoulder was a red oval that stood out against the surrounding flesh.

"You're a sickly-looking bastard," Donegan said to his reflection.

Then the door opened and Dr. Novak came in.

Despite the dedication she possessed for the healing art of medicine, Stella Novak hated treating Sergeant Joe Donegan. She always viewed her patients as victims in need of protection, care, and nurturing. It never mattered to her how severely diseased or horribly scarred they were, because she was capable of looking beyond the physical to the inner beauty of the soul so that she could more effectively treat them. But she was unable to do this with Sergeant Donegan.

Stella made a conscious effort to erase from her mind the first meeting she had with Donegan when he was investigating Sophie's disappearance. The crass, racist comments he had made when he visited her apartment and examined Sophie's room still haunted Stella ten years later. She wasn't supposed to let the past interfere with her ability to give him the best medical treatment that she could in the present. But despite the Hippocratic Oath she had sworn and the serious manner with which she viewed her profession, she hated being anywhere near Sergeant Joe Donegan.

As she prepared to leave her office to go to the treatment room, she massaged her weary eyes. She was tired, because she had not slept very well the night before. She had been unable to sleep for more than an hour at a stretch without images of the policeman, with his evil eyes and the numerous weapons strapped to his body, invading her dreams.

Now she rose from the desk in her private office and headed resolutely for the examination room where he was waiting.

She knocked before opening the door and entering. With some difficulty she managed a smile for her patient. "And how do you feel today, Sergeant Donegan?"

"The shoulder gives me fits from time to time, Doc, but I'm managing."

She washed her hands in the sink above the mirror. She did not look up, but could feel his eyes on her. Pulling a paper towel from the wall dispenser, she took a deep breath and turned to face him.

"Let's have a look at you."

The wound was healing satisfactorily, but Donegan's range of motion and muscle rehabilitation around the scar were poor.

"You need to get more exercise," she said. "Perhaps some mild weight lifting. I can prescribe a regimen for you."

Donegan smirked. "You want to build my muscles up, Dr.

Novak? Perhaps make me look like one of your other patients?"

Dr. Novak stopped her examination to make a note on the patient's chart. "I'm not following you, Sergeant." However, she suspected that he was referring to Commander Cole.

"Just an idle thought, Doctor," he said. "Forget I mentioned it at all."

"You can dress now and I'll see you in my office."

"Yes, Doctor," he responded.

When he came into the office, Dr. Novak had put her glasses on and was seated behind her desk. He took the chair across from her.

"You seem to be progressing nicely, Sergeant Donegan. If you exercise your shoulder regularly and are careful not to reinjure it, you will make a complete recovery from your wound."

He sat there staring at her, which, as always, made her uneasy. "So you don't wish to see me again?"

Steeling herself against his gaze, she said, "If you develop future complications you can always make an appointment, but I don't foresee any problems right now."

"Suppose I simply want to come in for periodic checkups? Don't you have regular patients who do that?"

"If you want to have regular checkups you can also call and make an appointment to do so."

Joe Donegan smiled as he got to his feet. "Then I'll be seeing you around, Doc."

When he was gone she emitted an audible groan.

23

William S. "Dollar Bill" Randolph was buried in a private crypt in the Havenhurst Cemetery. He had died the day after Thanksgiving from cancer and over the vociferous objections of his mother, Sharon Powell Randolph, the gambler's son Solomon spent thousands of dollars laying his father to rest. A funeral mass was held at Saint Columbanus Catholic Church, which no member of the Randolph family had ever attended. The only reason that Solomon selected this particular church was because his father's tavern, Randy's Roost, was located within the geographic boundaries of the parish. Also, Solomon knew that if he had attempted to have the funeral at his mother's church, she would have done everything within her power to stop him from doing so.

The wake was held the night before the funeral at the A. A. Rayner and Son Funeral Home on East Seventy-first Street, which was right across the street from the main entrance to Saint Columbanus Church. Having been a very private man in life, Dollar Bill Randolph didn't have a great many personal friends, so his wake was a sparsely attended affair. The dead gambler's estranged wife, accompanied by the butler Jamison, put in an appearance. Sharon Powell Randolph prayed briefly in front of her husband's coffin before whispering a few words of comfort to her son, who was the lone mourner seated in the front row of the funeral home chapel. There was no one within earshot of the sole surviving son and his mother, but those who did observe them noticed a certain unease and rigid formality in their manner. Then, dry-eyed with Jamison following closely at her heels, she left the funeral home.

Solomon Randolph kept vigil over his father's body for two hours that night. Approximately twenty people came to pay their respects. Only a handful stayed for the services. At the one-hour-and-fifteen-minute mark of the wake, the Saint Columbanus Church pastor came in to say a few brief prayers, read a selection from the Bible, and deliver a short eulogy. Then the priest extended his condolences to the lone family member in evidence and was gone.

Finally, a funeral home representative approached Solomon and requested permission to close the casket. Agreeing to end the wake, Solomon watched as the casket was shut over his father's visage for the last time. Clad in a tailored black suit, black silk tie, white silk shirt, and brilliantly shined wing tips, Solomon Randolph stood up and turned to leave the chapel. That was when he saw one of the mourners seated alone in the last pew. It was Sergeant Joe Donegan. Solomon did not acknowledge the cop's presence.

The next morning, after the mass and internment at the Havenhurst Cemetery, Solomon Randolph drove over to Randy's Roost in his red BMW. He would miss his father, but Solomon was not emotionally distraught over Dollar Bill's passing. After all, the deceased man had been ill for quite some time. Also, Solomon was not the type of man who formed lasting attachments with anyone. Although he had a very active sexual life, none of his female bedmates had ever been able to achieve any type of emotional bond with him.

In the office above the bar, which now belonged to him, Solomon found a telegram that had been delivered earlier in the day. It was addressed to him:

TO W. SOLOMON RANDOLPH,

MY DEEPEST CONDOLENCES OVER THE LOSS OF

YOUR FATHER. HE WAS A GOOD MAN AND SOMEONE

WHOM I COULD CALL A FRIEND. HE WILL BE

GREATLY MISSED.

                              SKIP MURPHY

Angrily, Solomon crushed the yellow paper in his fist. Through clenched teeth he said, "If my father was such a great friend of yours, why didn't you come to his funeral?"

But the young man quickly got over his anger. He had a criminal organization to build and for what he planned to accomplish, he would need not only the talents of the crooked cop Joe Donegan, but also the connections of Chicago Alderman Phillip "Skip" Murphy.

Alderman Sherman Ellison Edwards was still the chairman of the Chicago city council's Police and Fire committee. As such he exerted a degree of political influence over affairs within the Chicago police and fire departments. So when he requested that the chief of detectives attend a press conference at City Hall, in regard to a new crime-fighting initiative, Cole, at the direction of the superintendent, was forced to attend.

Blackie accompanied Cole and when they arrived at the

second-floor press room at 121 North LaSalle Street, they were informed by the city council sergeant-at-arms that Edwards's press conference had been moved to the executive conference room on the fifth floor. Riding up in the elevator, Blackie asked, "Do you have any idea what this is about?"

Cole frowned. "I don't know, but you can bet Foghorn Leghorn is up to no good."

The executive conference room was located inside the suite of offices occupied by the mayor of Chicago. When Cole and Blackie walked into the room, which could comfortably accommodate two hundred print and electronic media representatives, it was about half full. This was an impressive accomplishment for an aldermanic press conference without a pre-stated agenda. A couple of the reporters approached the policemen to ask if they knew what Edwards had up his sleeve. Cole and Blackie were forced to admit that they were also in the dark.

A few minutes later, Edwards walked in. He was accompanied by Skip Murphy.

Edwards, who was wearing a pastel-blue double-breasted blazer with gold buttons, dark blue trousers, a fire-engine-red shirt, and white knit tie, stepped to the microphone on the podium in front of the room. Murphy, who was dressed in a custom-tailored charcoal gray suit, white shirt, and dark blue silk tie, looked like a male fashion model compared to his garishly dressed colleague, took up a position standing behind Edwards on the left. Murphy looked over at Cole and Silvestri and nodded. The policemen stared back at the politician without acknowledging the greeting.

"Good morning, ladies and gentlemen," Edwards said with his phony down-home drawl. "Thank you for responding so promptly. Before we begin, I'd like to ask Chief Cole and Lieutenant Silvestri to join me and Alderman Murphy up here at the podium."

The request surprised the cops. Slowly, they got to their feet and walked to the front of the conference room. They took up positions behind Edwards on the opposite side from Skip Murphy. It was obvious to everyone present that Cole and Silvestri were not happy over this development.

"Now I'd like to turn these here proceedings over to my esteemed fellow city councilman, Alderman Phillip 'Skip' Murphy."

Stepping to the microphone, Murphy paused for a dramatic moment before saying, "I would like to begin by commending the two officers that I have the honor of sharing this moment with. In the history of this great city on the shores of Lake Michigan, the names of Larry Cole and Cosimo 'Blackie' Silvestri have been in the past, are in the present, and will be in the future, synonymous with those of the most legendary in the field of law enforcement."

At the mention of his first name, Blackie emitted a soft groan. However, Cole was becoming increasingly intrigued by what was taking place here. There was obviously a rat lurking within the political agenda that was unfolding slowly, but it was one that neither Cole nor Blackie had ever encountered before.

Murphy expounded on the professional careers of the two officers that he had once accused of harassing him. Using his skillfully honed public speaking ability and deep baritone voice, he held the attention of the collective media for the next fifteen minutes, as he talked about the cases Cole and Blackie had solved over the years. The names of such high-profile criminals as Steven Zalkin, Antonio DeLisa, Margo DeWitt, and Jeffery

Pender rolled off the politician's tongue. Finally, he got down to the real reason why they were here.

"In a recent television interview on the *Eye of the Public* news magazine program, Chief Cole stated that a wide range of alternatives were being explored to deal with the out-of-control drug problem in this country. And, I might add, it was these two officers, Larry Cole and Blackie Silvestri, who were responsible for the largest drug confiscation in this nation's history. A drug confiscation that I might add led to the recently concluded congressional subcommittee hearings concerning misconduct within the American intelligence community. But the one thing I was most impressed with was that Chief Cole did not attempt to sugar-coat the difficulties, which the law enforcement community has in effectively enforcing the drug laws in America, but left all options open. Options ranging from increased enforcement efforts to decriminalization. This approach got me, in my capacity as an elected official in a democratic society, to thinking about the drug problem from a more analytical and thorough viewpoint. To force me to finally come to the realization that we can never win the war on drugs by enforcement, but must go to the opposite alternative, which Larry Cole proposed on the *Eye of the Public* program. That alternative is decriminalization of all currently illegal narcotics."

A collective gasp came from the media throng assembled in the executive conference room of Chicago's City Hall. Even Alderman Sherman Ellison Edwards appeared stunned beyond words, which was something no one had ever been able to accomplish in the past. Under his breath, Blackie mumbled, "Murphy must be out of his mind."

The only person present, other than Skip Murphy, who

didn't appear shocked by the decriminalization proposal, was Larry Cole.

At that moment the media erupted with a flurry of questions.

Sergeant Joe Donegan was back in his computer lab. He was alone and the door was shut and locked. Actually, there was no need for Donegan to worry about the security of his domain, because, since the deaths that had occurred here in September and the exhaustive investigation that the chief of detectives' office had conducted, all of his colleagues avoided the place. Even the commander stayed away. This could not have suited the crooked cop better.

On returning to duty, Donegan had gone over every square inch of the computer room. After all the time Cole's people had spent here, Donegan suspected there might be one or two nasty little surprises lurking within the equipment. But after a nearly forty-eight-hour examination, he came up with nothing. He was surprised. Had the situation been reversed, he would have bugged the place from floor to ceiling. Of course, that would have been illegal, but Donegan had never let the law stand in his way before.

But all was not well in Joe Donegan's criminal paradise. His partner in crime, Dollar Bill Randolph, was dead. This was truly unfortunate, because the gambler kept all of the document counterfeiting equipment in the basement of Randy's Roost. In order to continue the scam, Donegan would have to come up with a plan to get his hands on the printing press, high-resolution copier, and raw material used to produce the phony documents. However, before Donegan could come up with a plan, Solomon Randolph contacted him via e-mail.

DONEGAN,

I NEED TO SEE YOU AT THE ROOST, A.S.A.P.

—SOLOMON R.

The crooked cop's evil dark eyes glistened. Perhaps getting the equipment he wanted might be easier to obtain than he had thought it would be.

Donegan had replaced his rusty Chevy with a four-year-old Oldsmobile Cutlass, which he had purchased from another cop. The car was navy blue and in immaculate condition with an in-dash CD player. He was not very fond of this car, because it was too clean. He realized that time and abuse would alter that situation. He parked in front of Randy's Roost and went inside.

The interior of the tavern was much the same as it had been on the handful of occasions Donegan had been here in the past. There was only a single bartender on duty, soft jazz drifted from the speakers, and a couple of solitary drinkers were in evidence. As the bartender knew the cop, he was waved through to the private office. A moment later Donegan was seated across from Solomon Randolph.

The young man got right to the point. "I want to have the same business relationship with you that my father did."

Donegan was always careful. "What business relationship are you referring to?"

Solomon opened the center desk drawer and removed a brown envelope, which he tossed in Donegan's lap. The cop opened the envelope and looked inside to find the last batch of counterfeit identification cards that Dollar Bill Randolph had manufactured before his death.

"My father filled me in on the prices you charge for that

merchandise," Donegan's new partner said. "I tallied up the score and they should yield a cash return of seventy-seven thousand, two hundred fifty dollars. Of course, you are welcome to do your own math."

Donegan closed the envelope and stuffed it into his coat pocket. "You're the one with the fancy degrees, Solly. I don't think you would try to cheat me."

Randolph leaned forward and locked eyes with the cop. "My name is Solomon, Sergeant Donegan. Not Solly, Sol, or any other nickname you might decide to come up with."

After their stares remained locked for a full minute, Donegan smiled and, without lowering his eyes, said, "Maybe it would be best, due to the unique nature of our business, for us to maintain a certain degree of formality in our relationship. So I will call you Mister Randolph and you can continue to refer to me as Sergeant Donegan."

"That's just fine with me," Solomon said; however, the tension in the air remained high.

The cop started to get to his feet. "I'll distribute these and return your share to you after I make the collections. Oh, we do still have a seventy/thirty split on everything, don't we?"

Randolph waved him back to the chair. "That was seventy percent for my father and thirty percent for you, right, Sergeant Donegan?"

The crooked cop sneered. "That's right, Mister Randolph. For thirty percent; I take all of the risks."

"Suppose we change that arrangement to make it fifty/fifty?"

Donegan now stared at Solomon Randolph with disbelief tinged with suspicion. "What's the catch?"

"I've got an additional proposition for you."

*   *   *

"Of all the low-down, slimy political tricks," Blackie railed, as they walked across LaSalle Street to the parking garage to retrieve Cole's police car. "We should have known that something was up when we found out our old pal Alderman Foghorn Leghorn was involved."

Cole didn't say anything until they were in the car. "We've been blindsided by politicians before, Blackie." It was obvious that he was not as upset as the lieutenant was. "This time's no different."

"You're taking this better than me, boss," Blackie said. Exiting the garage, they became backed up in traffic on Washington Street in front of the Daley Center Plaza. In frustration, the lieutenant slammed his heel down on the horn.

"Calm down," Cole said. "You're going to work yourself up into a stroke."

Blackie took a couple of deep breaths, but his face remained flushed.

Cole waited until they reached Lake Shore Drive before he mentioned the press conference again. "All that we can do right now is wait to see where Murphy is going with this drug decriminalization plan of his. Obviously he's trying to use the drug issue to advance his political career."

"Begging your pardon, boss," Blackie argued, "then we should expose his crooked behind to the public and not let him go any further with this insanity."

"I wouldn't say that what he's proposing is insane," Cole said. "I did propose decriminalization as an alternative strategy to deal with the drug problem when I was on the *Eye of the Public* program."

"But you were serious about it. Murphy is just playing games."

"Yes, he is, but in order to advance his political agenda, he will need us."

Now Blackie looked as if he was indeed going to have a stroke. "You're not going to help that idiot, are you, Larry?"

Cole nodded. "I'm going to help him and then he's going to help me expose him as the killer of Dr. Stella Novak's sister ten years ago."

24

DECEMBER 9, 2003
2:51 P.M.

The career criminals arrived separately, as they had been instructed to do. They were not the types that took instructions easily from anyone, so it had been necessary for a monetary inducement to be tendered. Each of them had received five thousand dollars in cash in an envelope with an embossed invitation, which read:

If you are interested in making a
great deal more money than is
contained in this envelope, your
presence is requested in the McCall
Room on the twenty-third floor
of DeWitt Plaza at 1000 North
Michigan Avenue on December 9,
2003 at _____ P.M.

The instructions for entering DeWitt Plaza, proceeding to the McCall Room, and the times to arrive were different on each invitation. There was also the strict admonition that each of them come alone. The host of this meeting anticipated that each of the guests would come armed. Also, it went without saying that they were all dangerous.

The first to arrive was Carey "Homicide" Miller, the two-hundred-and-fifty-pound, ebony-skinned, shaved-headed leader of the Gangster Disciples. His street name came from the fifteen arrests and three convictions he had for murder. By rights, the last conviction should have gotten him a life sentence. But an exposé printed in the *Chicago Times-Herald,* concerning improprieties in the Cook County Felony Court system, had resulted in Homicide Miller's last conviction being overturned. Now he was back on the street in charge of one of the most dangerous criminal organizations in the Windy City.

At the age of fifty-one, Homicide was a bit old to be a gangbanger, but he was as vicious as any killer half his age. In fact, he was responsible for thirty-two murders, not the lesser eighteen he had been arrested for and the three he was convicted of. He was the most vicious of all of the career criminals invited today, but he was also the most intelligent. This could be attributed, in part, to the college degree he had obtained through the extension program provided by the Cook County Department of Corrections.

Homicide entered the complex through the multi-level parking garage at the west end of DeWitt Plaza. After parking his silver-gray Mercedes four-door sedan, he strode toward the elevators, keeping an eye out for any signs of trouble. There was always the possibility that one of his rivals had set up this appointment as an elaborate trap.

It was a cold, raw day with snow flurries blowing through the air. Against the elements, Homicide was dressed in a full-length mink coat, a wide-brim felt hat trimmed with mink, a black leather two-piece suit, leather knee boots, four ropes of twenty-four-carat gold chains around his neck, and assorted gold jewelry adorning his wrists and fingers. A pair of dark glasses and the goatee he sported gave him a marked resemblance to rhythm-and-blues singer Isaac Hayes. There were special pockets sewn into the lining of his coat. These pockets contained a pair of fully loaded, nickel-plated Uzi submachine guns with extra thirty-round magazines for each weapon. If he was crossed by anyone for any reason, he was prepared to live up to his street name by committing "Homicide."

Homicide Miller proceeded to the twenty-third level, where the McCall Room was located. He went to the entrance marked with the letter "A" and, after first checking to insure that his guns were in quick and easy reach, yanked open the door.

The McCall Room was in actuality a five-thousand-square-foot ballroom, which was now partitioned off into four smaller areas. The area Homicide entered, beyond the door marked "A," contained a refreshment table lined with unopened bottles of brand-name alcohol, a snack tray, soft drinks, and ice. There was also a television monitor on a stand with a lone straight-back chair in front of it. Although there was no one in evidence, Homicide could sense that he was being watched. But this did not alarm him. Had any of his numerous enemies sought to kill him, there were a great many more convenient places for them to do so than at DeWitt Plaza. It had also occurred to him that this mysterious invitation could be a government sting. While

Homicide was doing his last prison stint, he had learned that the local cops, posing as floating casino representatives, had sent a number of wanted criminals notifications by mail stating that they had won all-expense-paid gambling junkets. Being gullible, the criminals had shown up at a prearranged location with their significant others, and been wined and dined before the cops slapped handcuffs on them. Homicide Miller was not currently wanted by any federal, state, or local law enforcement agency. At least for the time being.

As he was here for business, Homicide shunned the refreshments and, still clad in his fur coat, hat, and dark glasses, took a seat on the lone chair to wait. He kept both hands on the handles of his guns.

Five minutes after Homicide Miller parked his car in the multi-tiered DeWitt Plaza parking garage, a souped-up, black, late-model Pontiac with tinted windows pulled up at the north entrance to DeWitt Plaza and a tall, gaunt, very pale Hispanic male emerged from the front passenger seat. His straight black hair was slicked back from a high forehead and he possessed penetrating eyes under sharply arched brows, giving him a pronounced demonic look. He wore a long black leather trench coat that extended below his knees. Beneath the coat all of his clothing was also black. He carried a smart black attaché case and strode into DeWitt Plaza roughly shoving aside a couple of tourists who got in his way. They started to protest the rude treatment, but one look at his cadaverous face made them reconsider.

The tall, thin man's name was Adolpho Dominico Campos. His street name was "Vampire." He held the official title of "war chieftain" in the Latin Lords street gang and, contrary to the specific instructions set forth in the mysterious host's invitation, he was attending in the place of the Latin Lords street gang's leader. In the attaché case Vampire Campos carried a number of items of mayhem including a .45 caliber Smith and Wesson semiautomatic pistol with two extra magazines, but the gun was only for long-range work. The remaining space in the case was taken up with various cutting instruments including a stiletto, a Bowie knife, and a scalpel. All of these instruments were razor sharp. Vampire was aptly nicknamed, because his favorite methods of executing rivals ranged from disemboweling to flaying his victims alive. And he not only loved the sight of blood, but had also been known to frequently drink it by the glass. Of all the members of the criminal element attending the meeting today, Adolpho Campos was the most certifiably psychotic. However, he also possessed a fairly high I.Q., which his prison test-scores verified.

Vampire Campos boarded an empty elevator on the ground floor of DeWitt Plaza for a ride to the twenty-third floor. The car stopped on the seventh floor and a woman, pushing a baby carriage, boarded. She took one look at the Latin Lords' war chieftain's face and would have fled had the doors not closed on her and her three-month-old infant. Frantically, she pushed the eighth-floor button, but she wasn't quick enough and the car continued to ascend. As if sensing the dangerous man's presence, the baby began to whimper and, with rising panic at being in the presence of this terrifying man, the mother froze.

Finally, the elevator doors opened on the twenty-third floor and Vampire Campos said a deep-voiced, but polite, "Have a nice day."

He stepped off the elevator and walked off toward the

McCall Room entrance marked with the letter "B." As the elevator doors shut once more, the terrified mother heard his insane, mocking laughter echoing back to her.

Vampire Campos paused outside the McCall Room, reached into his coat pocket, and removed an ivory-handled straight razor. Flicking the instrument open, he concealed it in the palm of his hand. Snatching open the door he charged into the room to find a partitioned-off area, which was a duplicate of the one Homicide Miller was waiting in a short distance away.

At the exact moment that Vampire Campos entered area "B" of the McCall Room, a large white man with a shaved head who appeared to be completely round from every angle, walked north on Michigan Avenue toward DeWitt Plaza. He weighed over four hundred pounds, which forced him to waddle from side to side and the exertion of moving his bulk caused him to wheeze noisily and sweat profusely. His features—eyes, nose, and mouth—were all oval-shaped and his waist measured eighty inches in circumference. He was dressed in a not-too-clean denim suit and unshined brogan shoes. He was an unusual figure, perhaps even a ludicrous one, to behold. In actuality, he was extremely dangerous.

His name was Michael "Butterball" Zane and he was the chairman of the Chicago Congress of Neighborhood Organizations. The title made the operation that Butterball represented sound like a civic-minded group. However, good government had nothing to do with CCNO. What it was in actuality was a coalition of street gangs whose territory covered a vast area of the Windy City.

The street gangs making up CCNO were mostly white with a few Hispanics and very few blacks thrown in. In the scheme of things, as far as street gang operations went, the individual groups, such as the Chicago Avenue Counts, TJO's, and Montrose Monarchs were small fry compared to the Gangster Disciples, the Latin Lords, and the El Rukns. But with the money to be made from street corner drug sales, the small gangs got involved. This led to conflicts with the larger gangs, which were able to easily smash their smaller rivals. Then, as they were on the verge of extinction, an overweight graduate history student named Mike "Butterball" Zane came forward with a proposal. In order to survive, the white street gangs at the beginning of the twenty-first century would have to do the same thing that the Irish and Jewish gangs had done to survive against Al Capone in the 1930s. Consolidate.

Because Zane was fat and odd looking, it took some doing for the obese man, who had been saddled with the nickname "Butterball" all of his life, to convince the gangs to join CCNO. But, finally, they had no choice. The impact was slow in coming, but as had been the case during Prohibition, the force of numbers began to make itself felt and CCNO became a criminal element to be reckoned with.

Mike Zane did not run the Chicago Congress of Neighborhood Organizations by force; he did not have the authority to do so. However, he was respected, because he had not only kept the white ethnic gangs from vanishing, but had also set up a system by which they controlled a vast narcotics operation. He was considered the brains of CCNO and was held in high esteem. So it was to the man nicknamed Butterball that the invitation containing the five-thousand-dollar cash payment had gone.

Butterball made his way across the main lobby of DeWitt Plaza drawing a number of curious and amused stares. The only items he carried in the pockets of his denim suit were a pocket computer, a wallet containing twenty dollars and a Visa credit card, a cell phone, and a set of keys to his apartment, which also served as his business office. He was not armed.

He was forced to wait for an elevator, that he could board alone, at the south end of the Plaza lobby. When he did step into the car, he felt it lurch under his weight. With a finger as large as a twenty-five-dollar cigar, he punched the button for the twenty-third floor. When the elevator arrived, he waddled off, breathing heavily from the exertion of lugging his four-hundred-plus-pounds across the city. He had taken public transportation from the northwest side, where his apartment was located a short distance from O'Hare airport, down to the Magnificent Mile of North Michigan Avenue. He arrived at the entrance to the McCall Room marked with the letter "C" seven minutes after Homicide Miller had entered through the door marked "A" and Vampire Campos had entered through the one marked by the letter "B."

Seeing the refreshment table, Butterball Zane went to it, moving more quickly than he had during his laborious journey to this place, and helped himself to the snack tray and soft drinks. The chairman of CCNO did not drink alcohol.

The final member invited to the meeting in the McCall Room on December 9 was Monica Talise. The only woman, she did not follow the preset time or route to reach the McCall Room entrance marked with the letter "D," because she had arrived twenty-four hours before the appointed time and checked into the DeWitt Plaza Hotel. Then she went to reconnoiter the McCall Room.

Monica Talise was a dark-haired, exotically beautiful woman of Sicilian ancestry. She was nicely built with prominent breasts, a slender waist, and legs that drew admiring stares wherever she went. Despite her heritage, she was not born into the mob; however, at an early age she had decided on two things. One was that she was going to make a fortune before she was thirty and the other was that she planned to make this money on the wrong side of the law.

Right out of high school in Teaneck, New Jersey, Monica had apprenticed herself to a high-class New York madam. The young woman did not take a position as a call girl, but instead took care of the administrative tasks that came with any business endeavor, whether it be legal or illegal. While keeping the books, Monica attended night school and in three years obtained a degree in business administration. Then she went to Fordham Law School. By the time she passed the New York State Bar exam, the call girl operation was under investigation by the NYPD. So it was time for Monica Talise to move on to greener and more lucrative endeavors. She headed west.

In the Windy City Monica used the connections she had made while in the employ of the New York City call girl operation and her Sicilian heritage to obtain a trusted position as a legal advisor and accountant with the Mattioli crime family. At this post she learned a great deal about the inner workings of a criminal empire that ranged from the boardrooms of Madison Avenue, to the casinos of Las Vegas, and the movie studios of Hollywood. From a front row seat she watched vast amounts of money change hands in illegal enterprises. She studied the intricacies of the organized criminal apparatus and was aware of its strengths as well as its weaknesses. Then, months before the actual event occurred, Monica Talise became aware of a dangerous power shift in the Mafia underworld. She realized that it was time for her to get out. She did so just in time, because Victor Mattioli, the reigning mob boss, was shot to death in his home by an unknown assassin.

After severing her ties with the Chicago Mafia, Monica put her skills on the market as a criminal consultant. She advised her clients, who ranged from narcotics traffickers to gamblers, pimps and loan sharks, on methods of improving their cash flow and collections. She recommended secure investments as tax shelters, methods to improve operations, and preventive measures they could employ to avoid arrests. Employing the sanctity of attorney/client privilege, Monica Talise made a very good living. Then the mysterious invitation containing the five thousand dollars, cash inducement arrived.

Monica's hotel room was on the twelfth floor of the fifty-story DeWitt Plaza building on North Michigan Avenue. Dressed in a dark blue business suit and carrying a smart black leather Mont Blanc portfolio under her arm, she took an elevator up to the twenty-third floor. She exited into a deserted corridor outside of the entrance to the McCall Room, which was marked with the letter "D." This was where her invitation stated that she was to go tomorrow at three o'clock in the afternoon. Now she wanted to get the lay of the land, so to speak, and possibly find out what was going on.

She went to the door under the D and tried to get in. It was locked. She walked around the exterior of the McCall Room and checked the doors to entrances A, B, and C. They were also locked.

She proceeded to the DeWitt Plaza Hotel lobby, which was

on the seventh floor of the building. At the information station she asked to speak to a catering representative. When the perky blond young woman in the blue and gray hotel uniform came out to greet her, Monica presented her business card and said, "I represent the Richardson and Gimble Investment Consortium, which will be sponsoring a formal dinner party for five hundred investors sometime next spring. My clients are interested in acquiring the McCall Room for this function."

"Of course, Ms. Talise," the young woman said, flashing a toothpaste ad smile. "Right this way."

In a business office located off the main lobby, the hotel representative quoted the catering and rental costs for the McCall Room. "That will be quite satisfactory." Monica said. "We will be forwarding a deposit with a given date for the affair. Now I would like to inspect the room."

The representative's perpetual smile remained in place, as she said a contrite, "Oh, I'm sorry, Ms. Talise, but the room is currently occupied."

"But I only need to take a quick look."

"We've been given strict instructions that the room is not to be disturbed without the permission of the leasing party."

"And who might that party be, dear?"

Just the slightest hint of suspicion dented the hotel rep's professional façade. "That information is confidential, ma'am."

Maintaining a calm outward demeanor, Monica returned to her twelfth-floor room and ordered a lunch of chicken salad and iced tea. While she waited, she contemplated her next move. She wanted to find out what was going on inside the McCall Room and she would do whatever she had to do to accomplish this.

When her food arrived, Monica enjoyed a nice, leisurely

lunch. When she was finished, she removed a cellular phone from her leather portfolio and dialed a local number. When the connection was made, she said, "This is Monica Talise. Let me speak to Irving."

Irving Bettis was a professional burglar who sought Monica's help when he had some difficulties fencing a cache of stolen jewels taken from a Wabash Avenue jeweler. The best offer he had been able to get from local fences was ten cents on the dollar for the merchandise. Monica had contacted a source she knew in the Netherlands who had upped the price to twenty-five cents on the dollar. Satisfied with the price, the burglar had paid the attorney's 30 percent finder's fee. Now it was Monica Talise who needed Irving Bettis's services.

The burglar did not look like a second story man, but instead an aging butcher or maybe a tailor. He stood five feet six inches tall and weighed 140 pounds. He was bald with a few wispy strands of silver hair sticking out above ears that protruded from the sides of his head like wings. He was in his late forties, but looked seventy. Dressed in a green work uniform and worn parka, he carried a scarred metal case as he entered the rear service entrance of DeWitt Plaza. Irving walked past the uniformed security guard stationed there and said, "When are they going to get the plumbing fixed in this joint?"

The guard, who had worked at the Plaza for six months, laughed. "That will be the day." Then he quickly forgot the nonthreatening little man.

Irving rode up to the twenty-third floor in a service elevator with a maid, who grumbled about having to work overtime. The burglar commiserated briefly with her before he stepped off the car into the twenty-third floor service corridor.

As he had been instructed to do by Monica Talise, he was to gain entry to the McCall Room, make a visual inspection of what was going on inside, and then call her on the cell phone so that she could come and take a look for herself. They had decided on a five-hundred-dollar fee for the job, which Monica had balked at paying. But there was no one around who could do the job any better than Irving Bettis. At least not anyone that Monica Talise trusted.

After checking all of the corridors around the McCall Room and the doors labeled A through D, he discovered that the twenty-third floor was deserted. All of the doors were secured with a keyless, electronic locking system, which was supposed to be burglar proof. But they weren't Irving Bettis proof.

He went to the D entrance, which Monica had told him she was specifically interested in. Opening his worn case, he removed a strip of clear plastic attached to a computer cable, which in turn led to a laptop computer terminal. After turning the computer on, he inserted the plastic into the terminal. It took twenty-two seconds for the computer to decipher the locking mechanism's code and open the door.

Disconnecting the computer, Irving Bettis entered the McCall Room through the D entrance.

Monica Talise waited all night in her room on the twelfth floor of the DeWitt Plaza Hotel for word from Irving Bettis. When, in her estimation, he'd had sufficient time to get into the entrance D door of the McCall Room, she called the contact number she had for the burglar. But they hadn't heard from him since he left for DeWitt Plaza.

During the night, she called back three times, but the response was the same. At midnight she took a ride back up to the twenty-third floor. When the doors opened on the deserted corridor outside entrance D, she was overcome by a sense of foreboding the likes of which she had never experienced before. She returned to her room and would have checked out of the hotel that night, but something stopped her.

Going to the mini bar in her room, she opened a bottle of champagne, poured herself a glass, and took a seat on the side of the bed. The five thousand dollars she had received was more than enough to cover her expenses so far, but there was the promise of a great deal more money if she liked what she heard tomorrow afternoon in the McCall Room. Now she was aware that whoever she was dealing with was not only very serious, but also equally dangerous.

Finishing her champagne, she took a long soak in the whirlpool bath in her room. Then she got into bed and watched commercial television until she dozed off. Her last waking thought and the first one she had upon awakening the next morning was: what had become of her hired burglar Irving Bettis?

The burglar's body was found in a trash Dumpster in the alley behind DeWitt Plaza at dawn the next morning. He had been shot in the chest with a large bore, semiautomatic pistol and the computer cable from the device he had used to break into the McCall Room was draped around his neck. His death was placed in the "unsolved" category by the Detective Division.

At the appointed time on the afternoon of December 9, Monica Talise, dressed in a bright red suit that enhanced her figure, went to the McCall Room on the twenty-third floor. She carried

her Mont Blanc leather portfolio with her, which concealed a
.45 caliber Smith and Wesson semiautomatic pistol containing
eight rounds. And she knew how to use this gun although, as
a rule, she abhorred violence.

When she tried the door to the "D" entrance she found it
unlocked. Taking a deep breath and clutching her portfolio
tightly against her side, she entered.

The hall had been rented and the audience was in attendance
waiting with varying degrees of anticipation for the performance to begin. Each of the four who had been invited had
been secretly observed since entering their designated section
of the McCall Room. Carey "Homicide" Miller remained in his
chair, sitting as immobile as a bronze statue. Adolpho "Vampire" Campos paced back and forth like a caged animal. Mike
"Butterball" Zane was occupied with consuming as much food
and drink from the refreshment table as he could. Monica Talise
sat in the lone chair with her shapely legs crossed. The only
indication of any possible stress she was under was the nervous
tapping of her foot on the carpeted floor.

The McCall Room served many functions for the rich patrons of DeWitt Plaza. It could be a ballroom, a banquet hall,
or, as it was being utilized today, a meeting room. As such, a
number of doors led from the main room into rear service areas,
through which food and drink could be delivered. Behind the
doors off of area C, where Butterball Zane was engaged in a
feeding frenzy, the hosts of this meeting watched their guests
on a laptop computer screen.

Each of the television monitors their guests were seated in
front of contained hidden transmitters, which broadcast the im-

ages in the McCall Room back to the computer. The pictures were displayed in a four-way, split-screen mode. Solomon Randolph and Joe Donegan studied these select members of the criminal element.

"The black guy will listen to what you've got to say," Donegan said. "But I don't see him making a commitment without you coming completely out in the open. Then he'll want to be made a full partner. The fat white boy looks like a complete waste of time. If anything, the broad will be the one to go for the proposition. Of course, she has the most to gain and the least to lose in the long run. She's probably also the smartest of the lot. You've got to admire that stunt she pulled last night with the burglar."

Dressed impeccably in a blue double-breasted, pin-striped suit, white shirt, and red "power" tie, Solomon Randolph didn't agree completely with the crooked cop. The larcenous entrepreneur did admit that there was some merit in Donegan's observations. "What about 'Vampire' Campos?"

The cop sneered. "I'm going to have to get rid of him just like the burglar that Talise woman sent last night. I bet he won't even let you get through the opening spiel before he walks out. On top of that, Matteo 'Pancake' Rodriguez, the leader of the Latin Lords, was the one invited; not this psycho."

As glacially cool in outward appearance as he was internally, Solomon Randolph said, "We'll just have to wait and see. Now it's show time."

At exactly 3:05 on the afternoon of December 9, the monitors in each of the four areas of the McCall Room came to life and the electronically masked face of Solomon Randolph appeared.

"Good afternoon, and thank you for responding to my invitation. I have a proposal for you that I'm quite sure you will find not only interesting, but also quite lucrative."

Randolph was seated in front of a television camera that was being operated by Joe Donegan. The cop was keeping one eye on the camera and the other on the four-way computer screen. As he had anticipated, the Hispanic was getting antsy even before Randolph got the introduction out. The big black guy and the woman were listening intensely. The fat white boy was still eating.

Donegan kept a close eye on Vampire Campos. If he posed a threat in any way, the Latin Lords' war chieftain would have to be dealt with. Campos was the weak link, but if he didn't let his machismo get in the way, what Solomon Randolph was proposing was indeed a slick, lucrative deal. In fact, it was the most brilliant the crooked cop had ever heard of. If the four people present went along with it, Randolph's plan would elevate the criminal element in Chicago to a corporate level on a par with such behemoths as General Motors, IBM, and Microsoft.

The audience heard the electronically masked man on the monitor say, "At one time in the modern industrialized world, La Cosa Nostra was the most powerful criminal organization in existence. They not only operated all major criminal enterprises, but also effectively controlled governmental interference in their affairs at the local, state, and national levels. This was accomplished not only because they were ruthless and prepared to do whatever was required to succeed, but also because they were organized along the lines of a successful legitimate busi-

ness corporation. What I am proposing is that we form our own
corporation with a similar objective in mind."

In Donegan's estimation, the presentation was going well. Although Vampire Campos had not taken a seat, he was now
listening. The Talise woman had removed a Steno pad from her
portfolio and was making notes. The white boy was still eating,
as he stood at the refreshment table, but he was looking at the
monitor. Carey "Homicide" Miller hadn't moved a muscle in
the past fifteen minutes. Donegan studied the immobile black
man and could detect a pronounced menace emanating from
him. Suddenly, the idea of being involved with this particular
man was not something that the crooked cop relished. Donegan
made a mental note to mention this to Randolph later.

Solomon Randolph's presentation took eighteen minutes.
Not one of the foursome left and even the impatient Vampire
Campos finally took a seat. What had been proposed to this
group was the formation of a criminal organization that would
control all non-Mafia-dominated activities in the Windy City.
Actually, under the stewardship of the current Mafia boss, Jake
Romano, a great deal of the mob's influence had waned creating
a vacuum in the control of citywide narcotics trafficking, prostitution, and gambling rackets. However, Randolph also proposed setting up organized arms brokering for the various street
gangs as well as an oversight commission to control all gang-
related activities. A very efficient, lucrative proposal, if they
went for it.

They did lock, stock, and barrel.

The conference was concluded with the still electronically
masked Solomon Randolph promising his audience that he
would be in touch with additional details of his proposal. They

were charged with going back to their own organizations and discussing the details with their associates. That is if that was necessary.

After shutting off the camera that had broadcast Randolph's image to the monitors in the McCall Room, Donegan watched the career criminals file out. Now came the tricky part. Utilizing the CPD Intelligence Unit computers and surveillance equipment, he would monitor their movements. Then, after a decent interval had elapsed, they would proceed to Phase II of Randolph's plan. This was Solomon Randolph and Joe Donegan's "fail-safe" position.

Donegan could see that Solomon Randolph was quite pleased over the outcome of this opening move in his plan to become the leader of a criminal empire. The young man was actually beaming over the triumph. But the crooked cop had learned to be a great deal more cautious when he was dealing with individuals like the ones who had just left. In fact, Donegan was careful in his dealings with everyone, including his sister Megan.

"What do you think?" Randolph said, obviously fishing for a compliment.

Joe Donegan was not the type who gave compliments. "Let's wait and see how they react before we start pinning medals on our chests. If they all do come in, we'll be in business." He made sure to place an emphasis on the "we."

If Solomon Randolph was displeased that Donegan did not share his sense of elation, he refused to show it. "Keep them under surveillance until we obtain their response to our proposal." He placed an equal emphasis on the "our."

"Don't worry, Mister Randolph, I've got everything covered."

25

It began as a routine narcotics raid, if entering a gang-infested, multi-storied public housing development that was constructed like a fortress could be considered routine. A squad consisting of one sergeant and eight police officers in casual dress—consisting of blue jeans and various types of sport shirts—under dark blue jackets with "Chicago Police Department—Narcotics Section" emblazoned in bold yellow letters across their backs, rushed toward the building at 4120 South Prairie Avenue.

The squad double-timed it from the alley into a rear entrance, which was on the opposite side of the building from the fenced-in galleries. This made it more difficult for the lookouts to spot them. Maintaining the same pace and rigid intervals, the squad ran up the dark, foul-smelling south staircase to the fifth floor. Before they rushed out onto the gallery, they stopped and once more went over the plan for this operation. Then, with the sergeant leading the way, they burst through the stair-well door and ran toward Apartment 506.

Everyone on the team, from the gray-haired, thin-faced sergeant to the newest officer, was in excellent physical condition. Two of them, who were the broadest across the shoulders, carried sledgehammers in case it became necessary to violently force the steel doors of the drug den. One of the three female officers present was in possession of a search warrant speci-fying the contraband they were to seize as ". . . a quantity of controlled substances, to wit: heroin, cocaine, and marijuana, and any paraphernalia related to the packaging, processing, or purveyance of said substances."

The officers had all engaged in this type of operation be-fore. Some more often than others. Serving search warrants against an organized street drug operation was one of the most dangerous jobs any law enforcement officer anywhere in the United States could undertake. In the past, the officers of this particular narcotics team had encountered problems. On a search warrant they had served back in October, they had been forced to kill two armed drug dealers. But despite the danger and complications, these cops kept coming back for more, be-cause it was exciting and, after all, they were the good guys.

They came out of the stairwell and were moving at a good clip toward the apartment designated in the warrant, when a tall, thin, dark-skinned black man wearing an Oakland Raiders starter jacket appeared at the opposite end of the gallery. The sergeant in the lead could only suspect that this man had come out of one of the apartments on that end or from the north stairwell. The other team members also saw the man, as they continued their sprint toward Apartment 506.

Winter darkness had settled over the city and the artificial lighting on the fifth floor was poor, which made it difficult for them to clearly see the man facing them. Because he was an unexpected variable in this operation, the narcotics team was forced to react to his presence. Two of the eight cops would keep going past the door to 506 and corral the man in the Oakland Raiders jacket and ensure that he would not only not pose a threat to the mission, but also not get in the way. This could prove to be a disaster for both them and him.

This alternation in their operational plan was dealt with without the need for any form of verbal communication. At this point everything was going as well as could be expected. Then the black man raised a .45 caliber Thompson submachine gun, which he had been holding down at his side.

The first to recognize this threat were the two officers—a male and a female—who had rushed past 506. The sergeant also saw the gun, but by then it was too late for all of them.

The black man fired the Thompson on full automatic. Each of the Narcotics officers had weapons drawn—the only firearms they carried other than handguns were two twelve-gauge pump shotguns—but they were late in returning the overwhelmingly superior fire. The rounds the cops did manage to get off had no effect on their attacker. Instantly, the sergeant and three of the cops were killed. The remaining five officers suffered wounds ranging in degrees of severity, but they managed to retreat back into the dark stairwell from which they had come.

The man in the Raiders' jacket emptied the fifty-round drum. Spent shell casings littered the fifth floor gallery accompanying the dead bodies of the sergeant and three police officers. Then, as quickly as the killer had appeared out of the shadows, he vanished.

The response to the shooting was quite pronounced. The initial wave consisted of uniformed police officers assigned to the Second Police District. These officers responded to calls from the surviving Narcotics officers of a "Ten-One," which is the code for a "Police Officer Needs Help." The first units to arrive at 4120 South Prairie escalated the emergency with the following exchange:

"Beat Two . . . Twenty-Two, emergency!"

"Go ahead, Twenty-Two," the dispatcher responded.

The cop's voice trembled close to the breaking point, as he managed to say, "We've got nine, I repeat nine, police officers severely wounded or dead at this location. We need . . . Send as much . . . Get me some ambulances here on the double, dammit!"

The next response wave brought every available uniformed and plainclothes officer from each of the four adjoining districts. This reaction was excessive, because there were now simply too many officers at the scene. Too many people were standing around as stunned spectators, actually getting in the way instead of serving any useful purpose.

The ranking officer at the scene was the Second District watch commander, Lieutenant Gary Rohrman, a thin, nervous man who possessed an extensive background in burglary investigation, but had no idea how to run a field operation of this magnitude. A large crowd of spectators had gathered and the news media had arrived, yet the numerous, uncoordinated officers at the scene weren't making any attempt to establish a secure perimeter. Confusion was the general state of affairs when Larry Cole and Blackie Silvestri showed up.

"Would you look at this mess?" Blackie said, as they followed a CFD ambulance, which was attempting to forge a path through the combined sea of cop/civilian spectators.

"I think we'd better locate whoever is in charge and establish some order," Cole responded, raising his handheld telephone/radio and requesting Lieutenant Rohrman's location.

It took time, but finally the confusion began to subside. Then the true horror of what had occurred at 4120 South Prairie Avenue on this winter evening became glaringly apparent.

The first thing that Cole instructed Lieutenant Rohrman to do was expedite the removal of the injured officers. It was quite apparent from the outset there was nothing that could be done for the sergeant and three officers who had been trapped on the fifth-floor gallery by the shooter. Of the six wounded cops, one expired before she could be removed from the scene and another died en route to University Hospital. The remaining survivors were treated at the trauma center and admitted in critical condition. The shooting at 4120 South Prairie was turning into the most horrific incident to befall the Chicago police department since the Haymarket Square bombing in 1886 in which eight officers were killed by an anarchist's bomb.

With the dead and wounded taken care of, Cole and Blackie, with the acquiescence of the Second District watch commander, dispatched every officer, who did not have a specific assignment, back to regular duty. An outer perimeter was established with yellow barrier tape to which all unauthorized civilian personnel were restricted. Then an inner perimeter was also put in place for those who had a legitimate professional reason to be at the scene, such as noninvestigative police support personnel, public housing officials, and the news media. Once the area was sanitized, Cole directed a "controlled" search of the high-rise building.

The chief of detectives knew that with six dead cops, emotions would be running high among the officers assigned to the search for the killer. There would also be a great deal of danger involved, because the suspect was armed with a submachine gun. These factors could result in the police officers doing the searching becoming trigger-happy. It was a strict requirement for everyone involved to walk a very narrow path between maintaining an appropriate safety factor and remaining mindful of the innocent high-rise-building residents they would encounter during the search.

Apartment 506 was empty, but there was substantial drug residue found. Access to this area was restricted and the ghetto apartment, along with the entire fifth floor, was evacuated until the crime lab could process the scene.

Then they went floor by floor and apartment by apartment looking for the gunman. A search warrant had been hastily obtained to enable the police to search occupied residences. No one was allowed into or out of the building while the search was in progress. And despite some extremely tense moments, the search was concluded without any major problems developing. However, they failed to find the shooter wearing the Oakland Raiders jacket or the Thompson submachine gun he had used on the Narcotics team.

After the last apartment on the sixteenth floor was searched, Cole and Blackie stood on the windswept gallery and looked down at the crowd of onlookers still occupying the inner and outer perimeters far below.

"He got out before we arrived, Blackie," Cole said. "But the raid was on a GD dope house, so our man with the machine gun was obviously protecting it."

Blackie lit up a fresh Parodi cigar with a disposable lighter that flamed brightly in the stiff wind. "We're going to have to put pressure on the gang until we come up with a lead on the shooter."

"Let's get started," Cole said, turning to walk rapidly to the elevator.

When they reached the ground, members of the press were clustered at the center of the outer perimeter. As Cole and

Blackie got closer, they saw that Alderman Skip Murphy was being interviewed.

"Now we have lost six dedicated police officers to the curse of illegal drugs," Murphy was saying, his breath forming vapor clouds in the frigid air with each word. "This is another graphic example, ladies and gentlemen, of what I've been talking about. We must decriminalize narcotics. We will then simultaneously take the police and the gangs out of the drug business."

As the media erupted with questions, Blackie snarled, "This guy is really starting to get on my nerves."

"Forget Murphy," Cole said. "We've got a hot case to solve."

Still at the center of the media gathering, Murphy looked over at the two cops, but did not acknowledge their presence.

They were headed for Cole's car when the chief's telephone rang. Removing the instrument from his inner coat pocket, he answered.

The voice on the other end was exceptionally deep and the speech pattern belonged to a man who had come off of the street. "I've got a deal for you, Mister Chicago Police Chief of Detectives. I will give you the shooter of the Narcs before midnight, but I want something in return."

With the compact radio/telephone pressed against his ear, Cole came to a dead halt in front of the massive high-rise building where the shooting had occurred. The lieutenant proceeded ten feet before he realized the chief was not with him. When Blackie turned around and took one look at his old friend's face, he knew that something bizarre was going down. He retraced his steps back to Cole's side in time to hear him say, "Give me the when and the where."

"I need some guarantees from you, Cole," the caller was saying.

"You keep your end of the deal and then we'll talk again." There was a long pause. "Okay, I'll get back to you at midnight. I also have something to sweeten the deal. Something that you won't be able to resist." The connection was broken.

"Who was that?" Blackie asked.

Cole slowly returned the communications instrument to his pocket. Then he looked at Blackie and said, "He didn't identify himself by name, but I'd know that voice anywhere. It was Carey Miller, the leader of the GDs. He goes by the street moniker 'Homicide.' "

Skip Murphy continued to address the news media concerning drug decriminalization.

When the final minicam strobe light was turned off and the reporters in front of 4120 South Prairie Avenue left to file their stories, Skip Murphy returned to his black Jaguar XJ9 sedan. He had parked this expensive vehicle between two police cars while the press was interviewing him. The recently waxed car was still there sitting untouched in its luxurious splendor. This would certainly not have been the case on this ghetto street if the cops hadn't been present in such large numbers. The alderman slid across the leather upholstery behind the wheel and a short time later was driving north on Lake Shore Drive back to his Central Station townhouse.

Sherman Ellison Edwards had alerted him to the shooting of the Narcotics Unit cops. Murphy's campaign, which he had launched a week ago at City Hall, was now gaining momentum. And the alderman had selected an issue, which was at once controversial and quite unique.

The initial publicity Murphy had received following the City Hall press conference was decidedly negative. This attitude did not improve in replays of his presentation, which showed periodic close-ups of the faces of a noncommittal Larry Cole and an obviously disapproving Blackie Silvestri. After the press conference, Cole's repeated "no comment" to the reporters' questions had also not provided Murphy with a boost in his personal popularity. In fact, as Murphy and Edwards had discussed after the press conference, the cop's silence was actually an asset, up to a point.

The proposal that Skip Murphy had made concerning the decriminalization of illegal narcotics brought initial howls of protest from coast to coast. The current United States drug czar, who was a political presidential appointee with no real law enforcement responsibilities, condemned the idea as ". . . imbecilic, ill-advised, and irresponsible." One of the local TV stations interviewed officers coming off duty on the day shifts in the Third, Eighteenth, and Twenty-fourth Districts. Some of the cops angrily disagreed with the proposal, others laughed at the idea, and a few uttered terse "no comments," but not one of them stated that drug decriminalization had the slightest merit.

On the floor of the Chicago City Council, the concept was viciously ridiculed by a number of Murphy's fellow aldermen, who were allied along a right-wing, law-and-order agenda. Then, as was the case with any other new and controversial idea, a small group began to emerge who were at least willing to give Murphy's proposal a hearing.

The first supporters were a North Side group of former hippies, who were now in their sixties. Calling themselves "The Flower Children for World Peace," they had petitioned every State of Illinois governor in the last thirty years to introduce a bill that would legalize marijuana. There were only seven members of the group and they were not viewed as being representative of mainstream Americana.

On the Saturday following Murphy's City Hall press conference, an early-morning talk show host raised the decriminalization issue on his radio program. A former city councilman himself, who had been convicted of bribery and served a stretch in prison, the host expected the callers voicing their opinions on the show to be decidedly against the issue. He was wrong.

There were comments against decriminalization following the same pattern of those that had already been stated. However, now there were a number of comments in favor of the issue.

"Whenever you make anything illegal," said a male caller, who spoke in the tones of a hell and brimstone preacher, "you will automatically make it more attractive, because the sweetest fruit always comes from the forbidden tree."

A female caller stated, "Forty years ago, we didn't have a drug problem in this country. Now our children can buy drugs on any street corner easier than they can get bubble gum. But you send one of them youngsters into a liquor store to buy a quart of beer or a package of cigarettes and they'll be carded so fast their little heads will spin. That's because the liquor store owners are afraid of losing their licenses. The same thing can be done with drugs."

"So I assume that you are for Alderman Murphy's proposal, ma'am," the talk-show host interrupted.

"You're darn right I am. Legalize it, tax it, and take it off our streets."

The next caller said, "Prohibition didn't work, as far as stopping the flow of booze into this country, but it sure made the Mafia powerful. The same thing is going on with drugs today. I agree with the last caller and Alderman Murphy. We should tax the stuff and put that money to work solving some of the real problems in our society."

From that point on a groundswell of support for decriminalization began to build.

The argument over the issue of narcotics decriminalization suddenly became the "in" thing to talk about and it spread beyond the talk shows, political gatherings, and cocktail parties of the Windy City, to the board rooms and lobbying caucuses of New York City and Washington, D.C. The national media picked up on the issue and ample coverage was provided of this newest and most controversial topic. Two items formed the centerpiece of each story: the text of Larry Cole's interview on the *Eye of the Public* television program and Alderman Skip Murphy's City Hall press conference. For Murphy, the desired effect had been accomplished; he had become a household word.

But at this point, as Christmas decorations were going up all across the Windy City, Murphy was no more than a minor, local politician championing a controversial issue. And although what had occurred tonight at 4120 South Prairie Avenue with the murders of the six Narcotics Unit officers kept the controversy alive, Murphy needed to escalate the issue to the next level. Then he would be in a perfect position to run for Congress.

Pulling into the private Central Station townhouse complex, the politician's dreams had suffused him with a warm glow. Parking in the garage behind his unit, he studied his reflection in the rearview mirror, smoothed his neatly trimmed beard, and struck a statesmanlike pose. "Congressman Murphy," he said, out loud. "Then someday, Ambassador Murphy."

Getting out of the car, he entered the townhouse. He had enough time to catch his interview on one of the local stations. He was still watching it when the telephone rang. Sherman Ellison Edwards was calling.

From the sound of his voice, Alderman Foghorn Leghorn had consumed a few cocktails, which made the cartoon character he was nicknamed after sound like Sir Laurence Olivier. "They carried your interview down at that there project building on CNN. My sources in the media are telling me that Ted Koppel, Larry King, and even Oprah are looking to interview you. You're on your way, son. Definitely on your way. Just don't forget your homeboy back in Chicago when you get to Washington."

"You'll always be my main man, Sherm," Murphy said easily, although he didn't relish holding conversations about his future with drunks on unsecured telephone lines. "I'm a little tied up right now. Let me get back to you later."

Edwards's slurred voice dropped to a conspiratorial purr. "Bet you got a fine woman with you."

"You know me, Sherm," Murphy lied.

"Bye."

Actually, there hadn't been a woman in his Central Station townhouse in over a month. Murphy had simply been too busy with politics. The thought made him smile. How times do change.

But he needed more than just his own political connections and a hot issue to keep his name in front of the public until the next election. To put him over the top as a strong candidate for the U.S. House of Representatives, he would need more than the help of Alderman Foghorn Leghorn. What he would need was Larry Cole on his side.

The news had concluded. Shutting off the television set and the lights in his living room, Murphy sat in the dark. He looked through the ground floor windows of his townhouse out at the headlights of cars traveling in front of the Field Museum of Natural History on South Lake Shore Drive. Since that summer day, ten years ago, when the two cops had confronted him about the disappearance of Sophie Novak, Cole and Silvestri had haunted him. It wasn't that they followed him around or made periodic intrusive entries into his life. But in his own mind they were always there waiting to pounce on him for that long-ago indiscretion with the Lake Shore Tap barmaid.

Murphy knew that Cole would never help him. At least not voluntarily. And the cop was not the type who made deals with politicians. His run-ins with Tommy Kingsley and E. G. Luckett, two former mayoral appointed directors of public safety, verified that. But Skip Murphy had indeed learned from the past.

Remaining in the darkness, the politician continued to plot his rise to fame and power. He finally came to the decision that if he couldn't enlist Cole's aid voluntarily, he would be forced to use coercion. To this end Murphy was quietly looking into the relationship the divorced chief of detectives had once had with a woman named Eurydice Vaughn.

26

The Chicago police headquarters building was quiet. The facility was closed to the public after 6:00 P.M. and most of the offices inside went dark from that time until 7:00 A.M. the next day. The offices of the superintendent and five bureau deputy superintendents were located in this building. All of the administrative functions for the CPD, such as personnel, finance, and the Internal Affairs Division were located within the headquarters complex at Thirty-fifth Street and South Michigan Avenue. The offices of the chiefs of the three operational department divisions—patrol, organized crime, and detectives—were also there.

As a rule, none of these offices remained open past 8:00 P.M., as all of the twenty-four-hour, seven-days-a-week field operations were administered from the five police area centers (Area Six had been abolished in the mid-1990s) and twenty-five police districts spread out across the city. Late into the night of December 9 and into the early morning hours of December 10, the lights continued to burn in the office of the chief of detectives.

Judy Daniels and Manny Sherlock were in their respective cubicles. Judy was working on a computer program listing the M.O.s of all of the known gang enforcers for the Gangster Disciples street gang. Eliminating any gang members who were dead or in prison left her with a list of thirty-one names. She was surprised that the number was so high. The list had been compiled from police case reports, arrest records, and Illinois Department of Corrections sentencing reports by the Intelligence Unit. A frown creased Judy's features when she realized that the information in the gang program had been put together by Sergeant Joe Donegan. And if the analysis was correct, the GDs had an army of killers out on the streets of the Windy City. But right now she was only interested in one particular Gangster Disciple shooter.

After printing out the list, she called out, "Manny."

He was in the adjoining cubicle and, although they had an intercom, she usually just yelled out his name. He would either respond right away in varying degrees from coming at a dead run, if he thought it was important, or yelling back, "What do you want?" Now she was met with silence.

Getting up from her work station, Judy walked around to his cubicle. She saw instantly why he hadn't answered. Manfred Wolfgang Sherlock was sound asleep. He was leaning back in his desk chair with his mouth open and he was snoring softly. She started to wake him up, but then decided to let him sleep. There was nothing he could do right now anyway. They were all waiting for a phone call.

Judy removed Manny's trench coat from the rack inside the cubicle entrance and covered him with it. He stayed asleep. Going back to her own cubicle, she removed the pages containing the list from her printer with the names of gang shooters and headed for Cole's office.

Larry Cole was seated behind the desk in his private office. He was staring at his compact radio/telephone unit. He didn't know how long he'd been doing this, but he planned to stay right here until Carey "Homicide" Miller called him back.

It was becoming another very long day for Cole. He remembered his promise to Stella Novak about taking it easier and getting more sleep. It was a nice, healthy idea, but there was no way that he could go home and sleep tonight with six police officers having been killed today. And the loss of a cop never got any easier despite Cole having spent twenty-five years on the force.

He remembered the first officer's death he experienced when he was a rookie in the Nineteenth District. In fact, Tactical Officer Hugh Cummings had been Blackie's partner before Cole. Cummings had been shot to death when he accidentally knocked on the Lincoln Avenue stick-up man's front door. Cole remembered attending the funeral on a cold, snowy day in December. With a heavy sigh, he realized that the funerals of the officers killed today would also be held on a cold, wintry day.

Sudden death was something that all police officers were forced to live with every second of their careers. It went with the territory. If there was any consolation to what had occurred today, it was that the shooter wearing the Oakland Raiders jacket would soon be in custody. At least that was what Homicide Miller had promised.

On cue, the telephone rang. Cole let it do so twice before he answered, "Hello."

It was Homicide. "You can find the shooter and his gun in the garage behind the house at 3736 South Michigan."

"What's the shooter's name?"

"Billy Ross. He's got a sheet, which you probably already have. Oh, and Cole, Billy's alone and won't give you or your cops any trouble, so there's no need for him to be killed."

"If he surrenders peacefully, he won't be. I give you my word on that. You said that you have something else for me."

"There is someone forming a criminal organization in this town that's going to make the Mafia and the street gangs look like small potatoes. The guy I heard from has real brains and I don't think it will take much effort on his part to run circles around you cops."

"And you want to give him up?"

The gang leader's voice developed a hard edge. "Yeah, I'm gonna give him up. I've been on the street raising hell since I was seven years old. I killed my stepdaddy with a butcher knife for beating up on my mother when I was eleven. I celebrated my sixteenth birthday in the state reformatory and my twenty-first birthday in Stateville. I've spent most of my life behind bars." Suddenly, Homicide Miller's voice changed. Now it sounded weary to the point of sadness. "Now I'm fifty-one years old and I'm tired. I want to go someplace where no one has ever heard of Carey 'Homicide' Miller or the damn Gangster Disciples street gang."

Cole couldn't help but feel a certain degree of pity for this man, even though he was a cold-blooded killer. "So in exchange for the information about this new criminal conspiracy that is being set up, you want me to get you into the Federal Witness Protection Program?"

A degree of Homicide Miller's defiance returned. "That's the general idea, Cole. Go pick up Billy Ross and we'll talk again later today. Take it easy, baby." The connection was broken.

Slowly, Cole returned the telephone to the surface of his desk. He recognized the irony of a killer as vicious as Miller suddenly wanting out of the street gang that he had been a member of all of his life. But if the information he was going to reveal was as important as he suggested, then putting him in the Witness Protection Program would be a small price to pay.

Cole got to his feet and began putting on his suit jacket. There was a knock on his office door.

"Come," he called out, pulling his Beretta and checking the load in the magazine and in his extra clips.

Judy came in. He noticed that she was dressed in one of her more conservative disguises consisting of a dark pageboy wig and black horn-rimmed glasses. The dark blue pants suit and the papers she was carrying made her look like an ordinary secretary instead of the CPD's infamous Mistress of Disguise/ High Priestess of Mayhem.

Seeing Cole checking his gun, she said, "Are we going to war, boss?"

Returning the weapon to his shoulder holster, he said, "I hope not. Go get Blackie and Manny."

The garage in the alley at 3736 South Michigan was a fifty-year-old brick structure that was fairly well maintained. It was off a paved, well-lighted alley between Michigan and Indiana Avenues. The CPD Special Weapons and Tactical Squad, under the operational command of Chief of Detectives Larry Cole, approached the structure from each of the eight points of the compass. There were twelve black-clad officers wearing helmets and body armor engaged in the operation. Each was also equipped with night goggles and high-powered compact special assault weapons that could fire at a rate seven hundred rounds a minute.

Cole, Blackie, Manny, and Judy remained in two unmarked

police cars parked at the corner of thirty-seventh and Indiana Avenue. They were monitoring the SWAT operation on their individual radios. Everyone was tense, because of this Billy Ross being in possession of a Thompson submachine gun.

William James Ross was on the list of GD gang shooters that Judy had compiled back at headquarters. He was twenty-six years old, had been born and raised in the Ida B. Wells public housing development, and had a record of twenty-six arrests; one for each year of his life. On his police record there were seven convictions for violent crimes ranging from gang intimidation to the attempted murder of a police officer. When Blackie saw the attempted-cop-killing arrest, his eyes filled with tears.

"If they'd kept that crazy bastard in the joint, those Narcotics cops would still be alive."

There was nothing that Cole, Judy, or Manny could say. The lieutenant was absolutely right.

The operation commenced at six minutes past 1:00 A.M. on December 10. The streets in the area were deserted, quiet, and cold, due to a temperature that had dropped below zero. The ground was covered with a four-inch accumulation of snow and a house across the street from where the police cars were parked displayed a flashing Santa Claus in a first floor window. The Christmas decoration and the snow gave the area a festive look. However, the cops waiting for word from the SWAT team were not in much of a Yuletide frame of mind.

The operation was four minutes and thirty-two seconds old when Cole's radio came to life. "SWAT One to Car Fifty."

Quickly, Cole responded, "This is Car Fifty."

"We've entered the garage and have the suspect in custody. Could you respond to this location?"

They were there within seconds.

The SWAT team members had secured the garage and were standing around the raised overhead door when Cole and his crew got out of their cars. The team leader motioned toward the interior of the garage. Going inside they found Billy Ross tied to a chair with thick rope at the center of a cluttered area that had apparently been used to repair or strip cars. The killer was still wearing the Oakland Raiders jacket and the machine gun, minus its drum magazine, was on the floor at his feet. The GD shooter had been severely beaten. Obviously, Ross had not given up voluntarily, which required his fellow gang members, at the direction of Homicide Miller, to use force. From the appearance of the shooter's face, his attackers had gotten carried away, because his eyes were swollen shut and blood flowed freely from his smashed mouth. But he was alive.

"Judy," Cole said, "I want an ambulance and an evidence technician here on the double. I want the tech to not only process that gun, but also take photographs of our suspect in case there are allegations that we were responsible for his injuries."

Despite his condition, Billy Ross managed to snarl an obscenity at Cole.

They walked back into the alley. "Manny," Cole continued, "did you complete the trace on my phone?"

"Yes, sir," the sleepy sergeant said. "I've got it right here." He handed Cole a slip of paper.

"What's that, boss?" Blackie asked.

"Manny placed a computerized trace on my phone that identified the location Miller called from. He's been known to move around frequently."

"Are we going to check it out tonight?" asked Blackie, who looked more exhausted than Manny.

"No," Cole responded. "We're all tired and Miller has held up his end of the deal. I want you, Manny, and Judy to take the rest of today off. Homicide can wait."

At that moment an ambulance, with its lights and siren going, pulled into the alley and sped toward the knot of cops standing outside the garage. The evidence technician's marked police car was right behind it.

Homicide Miller moved around because he was obsessively paranoid. He had been known to change residences from week to week. On occasion, when gang wars raged, he moved every day. He always kept suitcases containing toiletries and a change of clothing in the trunk of his car, which he had also been known to replace frequently. He kept wardrobes at a number of places in the city and suburbs, to include girlfriends' apartments and gang hangouts. Homicide would appear at these locations at odd hours of the day or night to grab a few items and then vanish like a ghostly apparition.

Along with the two nickel-plated Uzis he carried, Miller always had a great deal of cash on him. It was not unheard of for Homicide to have ten thousand dollars stuffed in a money belt strapped to his waist. These elaborate precautions had kept him alive for a long time, but the constant fear he lived with had finally taken its toll.

Although his decision to get out of the gang and vanish into the Witness Protection Program had been coming for a long time, he hadn't been able to decide on a firm course of action. Two things finally made him come to a decision. One was the electronically masked man who had made the proposal at DeWitt Plaza that afternoon. Although Homicide Miller would be on the ground floor of a lucrative criminal enterprise, it would also succeed in getting him more deeply mired in the criminal underworld. And if he took another felony arrest, he would spend the rest of his natural life in prison.

The other reason that he wanted out right now was because Billy Ross killed those six cops today.

Homicide Miller's life on the wrong side of the law had imbued him with a tremendous respect, as well as hatred, for police officers. An investigation led by Detectives Lou Bronson and Manny Sherlock of Area One had resulted in Carey Miller receiving his second conviction for murder and a life sentence. He actually did seven years. So when he learned that Billy Ross had used a machine gun on the raiding party in that project building on Prairie, Homicide knew that the cops wouldn't stop until they brought the shooter to justice. They would turn the Gangster Disciples street gang and him inside out until this was accomplished. That kind of heat the gang leader didn't relish.

The night before the meeting at DeWitt Plaza, he had stayed at a Holiday Inn in a southwestern suburb, paying cash for the room. Tonight he would be sleeping in a townhouse that the gang owned on South Jeffrey Boulevard. The two-unit brick building had recently been remodeled, iron bars covered all of the windows, and the entrances were secured with wrought iron steel doors. Both apartments were vacant even though the property was in demand. Homicide Miller kept it this way so that he could use it as a hideout.

He had parked his Mercedes in the alley behind the townhouse and, after making sure there was no one lurking in the shadows, entered through a rear door. There was a working stove and refrigerator in the kitchen, and the utilities were on. But there was no furniture in the house and the sleeping accommodations consisted of a bare mattress and a couple of thick, olive drab Army blankets on the living room floor.

When he walked in, Homicide carried one of his nickel-plated Uzis in one hand and a shopping bag containing cold cuts, condiments, French bread, and beer in the other. He carefully checked out both units of the townhouse before returning to his car for one of his numerous overnight bags. At midnight, he called Larry Cole on his cell phone.

Earlier, Billy Ross balked about giving himself up to the cops. Homicide could understand the shooter's position, because he was facing the death penalty. However, the GD gang leader had made a deal with Cole and he planned to uphold his end. It became necessary for Homicide and a couple of muscular GD enforcers to physically convince Ross. Then they tied him to that chair and left him in the Michigan Avenue garage.

After making the call to Cole, Homicide had taken a long, hot shower, made himself a large sandwich with ham, provolone cheese, lettuce, tomatoes, pickles, onions, and mayo, and curled up with a beer on the barren mattress. There were newspapers taped over the windows and the gang leader used a minimum amount of artificial light to maintain the security of his hideout. Tomorrow he would find another place to sleep.

While he ate, he casually examined his surroundings. With some furniture, a few paintings and maybe a plant or two, the place wouldn't be half-bad. The neighborhood was nice and for a moment the convicted killer unfocused and engaged in a brief fantasy. He could see himself mowing the front lawn and engaging in idle chitchat about the weather with a mythical next door neighbor. Then he would be just another citizen complaining about taxes, crabgrass, and depreciating property values.

Homicide Miller opened another beer and took a long pull. For the first time, he was starting to actually believe that he could indeed make it into the Witness Protection Program. By now Billy Ross, a bit worse for wear, would be in custody and Larry Cole was known as a man of his word. Once more Homicide looked around the empty townhouse. Soon he would no longer have to live like a fugitive.

He was starting to feel pretty good about himself when he smelled something burning. Whatever it was couldn't be coming from inside the townhouse, he rationalized, because he hadn't turned the stove on. He started to ignore the odor, but it became stronger and the air was suddenly filled with a smoky haze. Homicide Miller's hiding place was on fire.

The FBI had developed the computerized technology that Manny Sherlock used to track the location of the cell phone Homicide Miller operated to contact Cole. Joe Donegan and Solomon Randolph had employed the same technology through a computer terminal in the basement of Randy's Roost. Since the conclusion of the meeting on the afternoon of December 9, the masterminds of the new criminal element initiative had not only kept tabs on the locations of Homicide Miller, Vampire Campos, Butterball Zane, and Monica Talise, but had also been able to monitor their conversations. This was of course illegal.

"I didn't think that Miller would be the one to betray us," Randolph said, as Donegan replayed the recording made from the cell phone call between the gang leader and the chief of detectives.

"He'll have to be disposed of before he talks to Cole again," the cop said, switching off the tape.

Solomon Randolph frowned. "Do you think that will be necessary? I mean, what can he actually tell Cole about us?"

Donegan gave a noncommittal shrug, but his eyes bore intensely into those of his partner in crime. "Miller can tell Cole that he met with the anonymous crime figure down at DeWitt Plaza. Of course, Cole will either send someone or go himself to check out the McCall Room. If he's curious enough and smart enough, he'll manage to trace the rental of the ballroom back to that law firm you used as a front. The shysters will claim attorney/client privilege, but Cole is extraordinarily tenacious and he might find a way to coerce or cajole them into identifying you. Now if that doesn't work, Cole will then go back to DeWitt Plaza. He'll undoubtedly have all of the surveillance camera tapes checked out for the time that Miller tells him that he was in the McCall Room. That will probably yield photos of Vampire Campos and Butterball Zane. Knowing Cole, he won't stop there. He'll undoubtedly look into every crime committed in and around DeWitt Plaza for . . . " Donegan paused to do some silent figuring, " . . . I would say at least a week."

"Why would he do that?" Randolph questioned.

Donegan came close to losing his patience with this organizational genius, who was still a naive, fledgling criminal. "Because he's Larry Cole, Mr. Randolph! Who in the hell do you think we're dealing with? And when he finds out that the second-story man was found in a Dumpster behind DeWitt Plaza, he will proceed in very short order to form a connection between our dead burglar and Monica Talise. Then, Mister Randolph, your entire game will be blown sky high before it even gets started."

Solomon Randolph did not like the way that Donegan was talking to him, but he was forced to agree that he was absolutely right. Homicide Miller would have to die.

*   *   *

Donegan pulled his car into the alley behind the South Jeffrey
Boulevard townhouse and drove past Homicide Miller's Mercedes Benz. He parked at the end of the alley, removed a metal
case from the trunk, and returned to the rear of the townhouse.
The case contained military issue Thermite grenades, which
when detonated emitted flames capable of reaching temperatures of five thousand degrees. He figured that two of the grenades would do the trick; one in the front of the building and
one in the rear. Thermite initially burned slowly, taking up to
five minutes to reach its flash point. Then the flames would be
hot enough to melt steel.

In his examination of the building, Donegan noticed the
iron bars and the wrought iron storm doors. The evil cop
grinned. Homicide Miller had barricaded himself inside a ver-
itable fortress. A fortress from which there could be no escape.
Detonating the Thermite grenades, Donegan hurried back to his
car.

Inside the townhouse, Homicide Miller snatched on his pants,
but in a rising panic ignored his shirt, coat, and shoes. He
grabbed both of his Uzis and raced toward the back door. He
could see the glare from a wall of flames shining through the
storm door's barred window. He grabbed the door handle and
screamed when the skin was burned off his palm.

Frantically, he retreated from the kitchen toward the front
of the house only to find that the walls and ceiling were on
fire. The heat and smoke were becoming unbearable as he ran
into one of the bedrooms. The fire followed him like a living
predator.

He didn't touch any of the window surfaces. Instead he

fired both of his guns on full automatic. The glass exploded outward, but he was unable to escape that way because of the iron security bars. Then he screamed as the flames enveloped him. The last thing that Carey "Homicide" Miller saw in life were the bars of his fortress beginning to glow a bright orange.

27

DECEMBER 23, 2003
2:25 P.M.

The command officers' luncheon concluded at the Chicago Yacht Club located at Randolph Street and South Lake Shore Drive. Each of the 105 Chicago Police Department command officers attended a function that had become known as the survivors' luncheon. Chief Larry Cole, his three deputy chiefs, and five area commanders were in attendance in full uniform. After the affair concluded, the participants were leaving the yacht club to return to police headquarters when one of the superintendent's aides caught up with Cole.

"Chief, the boss was wondering if you could ride back to headquarters with him?" Although phrased as a request, it was obvious that Cole didn't have a choice in the matter.

After instructing Manny Sherlock, who had been pressed into service as his driver, to return to headquarters, Cole walked over to the top cop's black Lincoln and got in the backseat.

The headquarters building was buzzing about Cole having been offered a ride in the superintendent's car when he returned.

Blackie was waiting impatiently in the chief of detectives' office when Cole walked in. However, the chief did not mirror the lieutenant's high level of anxiety. Private audiences with the CPD's chief executive had been known to lead to disaster in the past. In fact, much to Blackie's consternation, Cole appeared amused.

With barely controlled exasperation, Blackie asked, "So what happened?"

Removing his cap and full-length dress uniform overcoat, and hanging them on the coat rack, Cole said, "We had a choice between roast turkey and smoked salmon as an entrée. There was tossed salad with a house dressing or tomatoes and onions with vinaigrette. . . ."

"C'mon, Larry," Blackie moaned. "You know what I'm talking about. What did you and the superintendent discuss on your way back to headquarters?"

Wearing his uniform blouse with the silver stars of a division chief on the epaulets, Cole sat down behind his desk. "Take it easy, Blackie. Everything is just fine. The boss simply wanted to talk to me about Alderman Murphy."

Sinking down into one of the desk chairs with obvious relief, Blackie said, "Did you tell him that Skip Murphy is an idiot?"

"I think that anyone who is in the know in Chicago knows Murphy's reputation, but apparently this drug decriminalization concept has gained a great deal of momentum. In the last ten days, the president and the governor have mentioned it in speeches and a rally is being planned for March first at McCormick Place. Fifty thousand people are expected to attend."

Blackie's jaw dropped. "You're joking?"

Cole chuckled. "No, I'm not. A Washington-based group called Citizens for the Legalization of Drugs has gotten behind Murphy and formed a national organization with him as the chairman. And, according to the superintendent, this Citizens for the Legalization of Drugs is growing every day."

"Is that all that the superintendent wanted to talk to you about?"

Cole shook his head in the negative. "Actually, he wanted to know what my position on decriminalization was, since Murphy claims that he got the idea from me."

Cole's intercom buzzed. As he reached for it, Blackie said, "And what is your position?"

"Hold on a minute." It was Judy calling and whatever she said froze Cole's face in a frown. When he hung up he appeared dazed.

"Something wrong, Larry?" Blackie asked.

It took him a moment to respond. "Just an old case. I'll deal with it later."

"So what did you tell the superintendent about decriminalization?"

Cole seemed preoccupied as he answered, "I told him we need to study the issue a great deal more before we either support it or condemn it." Blackie was about to ask another question when Cole said, "Excuse me, Blackie, but I've got something to do. I'll be on the radio."

Surprised at Cole being so abrupt, the lieutenant got quickly to his feet. At the door he stopped and gave his old friend a look of concern.

Blackie was on his way to his office, which was down the corridor. The sign on the lieutenant's door read, "Executive

Aide—D.D.H.Q." Before he could get inside, Judy intercepted him. He frowned when he saw her. "Did you dye your hair green?"

"It's a wig," she responded. He noticed that she was also wearing a pair of Christmas ornament earrings and a Christmas sweater adorned with similar ornaments flashing red, green, and yellow lights on and off. Blackie realized that she was disguised as a walking Christmas tree. He would have laughed, but he was worried about Larry Cole. From the look on her face, Judy was too.

"Is the boss okay?" she asked.

"Why shouldn't he be?"

She lowered her voice. "He just got a message from an old friend of his."

"Yeah, he said something about an old case." The lieutenant could sense disaster coming.

"An old case at the National Science and Space Museum that almost got him killed," she said. "That call was from Eurydice Vaughn, the museum's former curator. She left a message with me asking the boss to meet her in the Transportation of Yesteryear exhibit on the lower level of the museum."

"When?" Blackie asked.

"As soon as possible."

Cole changed out of his uniform into a white turtleneck, brown slacks, a beige camel-hair sport coat, brown loafers, and a tan overcoat before he left the headquarters building. He drove his car south on Michigan Avenue to Garfield Boulevard and turned east into Washington Park. He drove past the stately buildings of the University of Chicago campus and into Jackson Park. A few minutes later he pulled up in front of the National

Science and Space Museum. For a moment he sat behind the wheel of his car and studied the impressive gray stone edifice. Larry Cole had quite a history with this place. A history that at times he found difficult to believe himself.

He forced himself to get out of the car and walk toward the front entrance. A sharp wind blew off the lake making his eyes tear, but he was able to see the white Constellation space shuttle on display at the northeast edge of the museum grounds. As twilight approached, floodlights had been turned on to il-luminate the spacecraft. Cole could also see that the land to the north of the museum had been excavated and a multi-tiered underground parking garage constructed there. He knew that the parking garage was right next to the Transportation of Yes-teryear exhibit, which was his destination on this winter after-noon. An exhibit that was originally constructed in the eighteenth century as a fully functional train station. An exhibit that had remained a secret for nearly a hundred years. An ex-hibit in which Cole had nearly been killed.

He entered the museum and purchased an admission ticket. He didn't want to display his badge and identify himself as a cop. He wasn't here on official business anyway.

Walking through the main rotunda of the museum brought back a number of memories for Larry Cole. Because it was close to Christmas, there were few visitors present. He entered the deserted Heroes Past and Present exhibit hall. He could hear the clicking of his heels on the marble floor. His sense of alone-ness in this place was so complete as to be nearly oppressive. Then he heard what sounded like a footfall behind him. Spin-ning around, he reached inside his jacket and grasped the han-dle of his gun. The emptiness of the gallery yawned back at him. For an instant the image of a deformed seven-foot-tall giant named Homer, wearing a Death costume, flashed through Cole's mind. Pulling himself together, he continued on to the Transportation of Yesteryear exhibit.

To access the train station, museum visitors had to ride an escalator seventy-five feet below street level. As he descended, Cole recalled the area he was in now being flooded by lake water flowing from a rupture high up in the wall of this immense chamber. He could still feel the grip of the icy current attempting to drag him below the surface on that night years ago. He mumbled, "There are too many ghosts in this place. Far too many ghosts."

He reached the bottom of the escalator and stepped off onto the floor of the Transportation of Yesteryear exhibit. For a moment he stood there looking around. Then she stepped from the shadow of a gigantic locomotive. And she was no ghost.

As she came into the light, Cole was able to see her clearly. She was wearing a snug-fitting black dress that extended from the nape of her neck to mid-thigh and a pair of black high-heel shoes. Her hair was cut short in a boyish style and parted on the left. Her jewelry consisted of a diamond bracelet that reflected light as if it had its own power source. She wore a pair of heart-shaped diamond earrings, which he had given her. The final item of adornment was a jeweled Teddy bear–shaped brooch pinned over her left breast. The sight of this particular piece was what definitely identified the approaching woman. She was Josie Gray, the sister of former Chicago Police Sergeant Edna Gray. But it was obvious from the message she had left for him with Judy Daniels that she wished to once more be known by the name she had used when she was the curator of this museum: Eurydice Vaughn.

*   *   *

Joe Donegan drove his dirty Oldsmobile Cutlass into the underground parking garage of the National Science and Space Museum. He cursed under his breath at having to pay the five-dollar parking and museum admission fee, as he drove to the third sub-level. Shoving a metal case the size of a paperback novel into the pocket of his worn overcoat, the crooked cop headed for the Transportation of Yesteryear exhibit.

In the wake of the death of Carey "Homicide" Miller, Donegan had kept a very close electronic eye on Cole and his people. From computers located in the basement of Randy's Roost and the Intelligence Unit computer room, he recorded all of the communications on their cellular telephones, as well as their movements around the city. And much to Solomon Randolph's amazement, what was discovered proved that Joe Donegan had been 100 percent right about the investigative ability of Larry Cole.

The execution of Homicide Miller should have been looked upon by the law enforcement community as little more than the violent death of a man who had led a very violent life. And to most cops, it was. Of course Cole, Silvestri, Daniels, and Sherlock were not most cops. Especially since the leader of the Gangster Disciples had promised to turn over information to them concerning a major criminal conspiracy. So, after the Bomb and Arson investigators and local homicide detectives finished their investigation at the scene of the burned-out South Jeffrey Boulevard two-unit townhouse, Cole and his crew had quietly begun looking into Homicide Miller's death.

Randolph and Donegan monitored the course of the investigation with grudging admiration. Cole backtracked Homicide's activities prior to his death, just as Donegan had anticipated. However, without a specific location and time, there was a great deal of ground for the cops to cover. Also, the dead man had been extraordinarily secretive, making him little more than a shadow. Despite this, they managed to trace him to DeWitt Plaza on December 9.

"I told you that he was good," Donegan said to Solomon Randolph, as the partners in crime read a report they had intercepted from Judy Daniels's computer.

"Do you think he will be able to trace Miller to our meeting in the McCall Room?" Randolph asked with anxiety in his voice.

Donegan grinned at his partner's distress. "It's possible, but not likely. Cole will probably have his people take a stab at viewing the videotapes at DeWitt Plaza, but whoever does it will have to be damn good at picking needles out of haystacks to connect Homicide Miller to us."

"Suppose they spot Campos, Zane, or Talise?"

"Unless they can track them to the McCall Room, eyeballing them won't mean much, Mr. Randolph. It's Christmastime and DeWitt Plaza was filled with holiday-shopping suckers looking to buy some overpriced junk for their kids. As far as our unholy trio being on the wrong side of the law, you've got to remember that the swank North Michigan Avenue building where we convened our meeting is named after two of the most notorious serial killers in history—Neil and Margo DeWitt."

Solomon Randolph appeared far from convinced. "What if Cole does manage to put it all together, Sergeant Donegan?"

"Then, Mr. Randolph, in the parlance of the street, our inventive criminal enterprise will be busted."

Randolph glared at the cop. "I don't want that to happen."

"It won't. Just leave it to me. I'll take care of everything."

*　　*　　*

Donegan stopped at the glass doors leading from the underground parking garage into the lower level of the National Science and Space Museum. He could see Larry Cole descending the escalator and a woman standing concealed behind a mid–nineteenth century locomotive. Donegan waited until Cole reached the center of the old exhibit and the woman stepped out of the shadows to approach him, before the crooked cop made his move.

As fast as he could, Donegan climbed to the next level and exited from the parking garage onto the train station gallery. Before he went through the connecting glass doors, he was forced to stop and catch his breath. The stair climb had left him badly winded. He briefly considered taking Dr. Stella Novak's advice and starting an exercise program. After his heart rate slowed to a more normal pace, he quietly opened the door and stepped into the Transportation of Yesteryear exhibit.

Display cases lined the balcony, which completely encircled the area below. Inside these cases were photos and the original blueprints of classical train station architecture from around the world, old train tickets, and the original uniforms of turn-of-the-century conductors and engineers. The displays momentarily distracted Donegan, because he possessed an affinity for old things. Finally, he forced himself to concentrate on the job at hand. After all, Larry Cole was something of an obsession for Joe Donegan.

A four-and-a-half-foot tall ornate iron railing encircled the upper level of the Transportation of Yesteryear exhibit. Keeping out of sight from anyone standing down on the lower level, he removed the metal case from his pocket. Opening it, he revealed what appeared to be a portable radio with a pair of earphones attached. What this device was, in fact, was a high-tech listening and recording instrument developed for police operations by Motorola. Putting on the earphones and adjusting the control knobs, Donegan settled in to eavesdrop on Larry Cole and Eurydice Vaughn.

"I appreciate you coming so promptly, Larry," she said. "It has been a long time."

Cole noticed her educated speech patterns, as each word was enunciated precisely. She had learned to talk this way from the woman who had kidnapped her at the age of four and held her captive in this very place until she reached adulthood.

"How have you been, Eurydice?" Cole said, formally.

She tilted her head slightly to one side and a slight frown crossed her beautiful features. "You don't sound very glad to see me."

"You could say that I have less than fond memories of our relationship. Or should I say the relationship between you, me, and your sister Edna."

"Do you still hate us for what we did to you?"

"I wouldn't use the word 'hate,' Eurydice," he said with an angry edge in his voice. "But when you take advantage of someone who cares a great deal for you, a certain degree of animosity is bound to develop."

Maintaining a matter-of-fact tone, she said, "I didn't know how to initiate a relationship with you without making you believe that I was Edna Gray. Perhaps up to that point I was suffering from a severe psychological trauma. But keeping me locked up in a mental institution was not going to help me." Her voice dropped to a whisper. "I needed you, Larry."

Cole's anger flared and he barely kept himself under control. "Now that makes everything all right, doesn't it?"

* * *

From his gallery perch, Donegan could hear every word that passed between Cole and the woman named Eurydice. The crooked cop found it quite illuminating that the great Larry Cole was having woman problems. Donegan had discovered through the department rumor mill that Cole was divorced and had a kid who lived in Detroit. But everything else about his private life was shrouded in mystery. There had been some talk awhile back about Cole being involved with a policewoman, but at the time Donegan had been too busy using his badge to engage in illegal scams to pay much attention.

Now Cole was having a lover's spat with this woman here in the National Science and Space Museum. This could be turned to Donegan's advantage. But the crooked cop needed to find out more about this woman.

"Larry," Eurydice was saying, "you and I had a very intense personal relationship. We have done things together that couples who have been married for years won't do." Unconsciously, she reached up and touched the jeweled pin over her left breast. It had once contained a mind-altering aphrodisiac, which she had used on Cole in the past.

As her fingers caressed the pin, he said a harsh, "Don't."

Returning her hand to her side, she said, contritely, "I haven't had to use this in a very long time, Larry. Everything that happened between us was natural."

Cole laughed. "Now that was what I would call a gross exaggeration."

Eurydice turned as cold as a block of ice. "You don't play the wronged lover very well, Chief Cole. It detracts from that macho image you're so proud of."

Cole turned equally hard. "Why don't we put a stop to this walk down memory lane and get to the reason why you asked me to meet you here?"

Her manner did not change. "I asked you to come because I wanted to see you. I am completely recovered from the emotional trauma caused by Katherine Rotheimer kidnapping and brainwashing me. In fact, I used my former experience as the curator to get a job arranging exhibits here at the museum. I started last month."

Cole managed to say a sincere, "Congratulations."

"Thank you." She softened a bit. "It sounded like you really meant it."

"I did."

After a momentary pause, she said haltingly, "I was thinking that since I have become a more or less normal person . . ." Her voice broke and she turned away from him.

As he had once been in love with this woman, compassion swept over him and he stepped forward to take her gently in his arms. She slumped back against him. Then, just as quickly, she stood up straight again, shrugged out of his grasp, and brushed her hand across her face, wiping away tears. Turning once more to face him, she said, "I was hoping that we could see each other from time to time just like a normal, everyday American couple."

When Cole didn't comment right away, she quickly followed up with, "Why don't you take some time to at least consider it?"

She handed him a card she'd concealed in the palm of her hand. Taking it, Cole read, "Eurydice Vaughn—Exhibits Manager—National Science and Space Museum."

She continued, "After the holidays we could have lunch or a cup of coffee and discuss it some more."

With her card in his hand, Cole asked, pointedly, "Where is your sister?"

"She lives in Kentucky now and promised me she would never return to Chicago. That will give us a chance to see if we can make it without standing in her shadow. Please don't make a decision right now, Larry. Take some time and think it over."

Cole stared at her for a moment before finally looking at his watch and saying, "Look, I've got to go. I'll give you a call after the first of the year." Shoving her business card in his pocket, he turned to leave.

Remaining where she was, Eurydice called to him, "Larry?" He stopped and turned around. "Merry Christmas."

"Merry Christmas to you."

Donegan watched Cole cross the lower level of the exhibit and board the escalator. The crooked cop remained on the upper level gallery until the chief of detectives was out of sight. He was about to abandon the location from which he had spied on Cole when he noticed that the woman hadn't moved. He decided to wait and see what she did.

Still standing on the lower level of the Transportation of Yesteryear exhibit, Eurydice Vaughn removed a small cell phone from her pocket. The eavesdropping equipment he was using displayed the number she called on an LED readout. Then he heard the ringing at the other end.

"Hello," said a voice that Donegan recognized instantly.

"Larry Cole just left," she said. "He's fighting it, but I think that he'll eventually come around."

"Excellent, Miss Vaughn," Alderman Skip Murphy said. "I doubt if he will be able to resist your charms."

"I'm sure he won't."

After shutting off the cell phone, Eurydice Vaughn walked rapidly over to the escalator and ascended to the upper level as Cole had done moments before.

After waiting a decent interval, Joe Donegan returned to his car in the parking garage. Driving back across the city to the Intelligence Unit, there was a broad smile etched on his face.

28

DECEMBER 27, 2003

9:35 A.M.

Solomon Randolph arrived at Randy's Roost early for a meeting with Joe Donegan. The young businessman unlocked the jazz club and turned on the interior lights. The place smelled strongly of Pine Sol disinfectant due to Solomon continuing the practice started by his father of having the floors mopped after closing time each night. Leaving the door unlocked for Donegan, Solomon went up to his office and powered up one of the computers.

This morning they would be planning another conference with their criminal consortium. This time they would convene in a small private room at the Hancock Center down the street from DeWitt Plaza. Solomon's identity would remain unknown to them, but eventually he planned to come out in the open, although, not until he was certain that he could trust each of them implicitly. Also, before the next meeting, he planned to select a replacement for Homicide Miller.

Dollar Bill had taught Solomon to be very careful when dealing with other members of the criminal element. It had served him in good stead this time, because the Gangster Disciple's leader's treachery could have proven to be disastrous.

Sergeant Donegan had taken care of everything quite well in disposing of Homicide Miller. The local newspapers had reported no more than that the man had died in a mysterious fire. The Thermite grenades had burned so hot that no traces of them were found in the charred remains of the house where the gang leader had been trapped. Thorough. Very thorough indeed.

As the computer program he had set up for this enterprise appeared on the computer screen, Solomon considered his relationship with the crooked cop. The young man was educated enough to recognize the numerous psychological problems affecting Donegan. He was a sociopath, amoral, homicidally paranoid, and extremely violent. If Solomon could keep Donegan on a long enough leash everything would be fine. Of course, continued contact with the cop would be like leading a three-hundred-pound alligator around by a rope and hoping that it wouldn't turn on him.

Eventually it would be necessary to eliminate Donegan, but not until he had served his purpose.

Dollar Bill Randolph had installed a system that caused a buzzer to go off each time the front door opened. Now this buzzer sounded. Solomon was expecting either the day bartender, who started at ten, or Sergeant Donegan. Switching on the closed circuit security monitor, he saw that two men had

entered Randy's Roost and that neither of them were the bartender or Joe Donegan. It was Lieutenant Blackie Silvestri and
Sergeant Manny Sherlock.

Solomon Randolph had an unusual reaction to the appearance of the two cops. Of course he was startled, but he was not
frightened. In fact, he was so amused by this totally unexpected
development that he laughed. His amusement ran so deep that
he became convulsed with hysterics. He laughed so hard that
his sides began aching and tears flowed freely down his face.

Finally, he managed to pull himself together. With a clean
handkerchief he wiped the moisture from his face. Then he
went to greet his guests.

Blackie and Manny stood in the center of the main barroom of
Randy's Roost and looked around.

"Nice place," Manny said.

Maintaining a stony demeanor, Blackie quipped, "If you
like gin mills."

Solomon Randolph entered from the rear of the establishment. There was a broad smile etched on his face. "I'm sorry,
boys, but we're not open yet."

In tandem, the two cops flashed their badges. "We're not
here on that type of business." Blackie said, unable to figure
out what this guy found so funny.

Opening his eyes wide with exaggerated shock, Randolph
said a sarcastic, "Is it time for my contribution to the policeman's widows and orphans' fund or do you want to check my
business licenses?"

Now it was the cops's turn to become amused. However,
their grim smiles sobered Solomon Randolph a bit. "Actually,"
Blackie said, "we're here on another matter, but, if you insist,

we will have a peek at those licenses. After all, they are required by law."

"Right this way, gentlemen," Randolph said, stepping behind the bar and taking a framed glass display off the wall. Still grinning, he handed the licenses, taped beneath the glass, over to the cops. "I think you'll find everything in order."

"I forgot my spectacles back at headquarters, Manny," Blackie said. "You'll have to do the honors."

Manny began examining the licenses, recording the numbers and expiration dates in a pocket notebook. While the sergeant worked, Blackie looked around and said, "Nice place you've got here."

"If you like gin mills," Randolph countered.

"Who is Sharon P. Randolph?" Manny asked.

"That's my mother. I run the bar for her."

"Your entertainment license will expire on the thirty-first," Manny said. "You need to get it renewed."

"I'll take care of it today. Now if there's nothing else?"

"Just one more thing," Blackie said, placing his elbows on the bar and leaning toward Solomon. "We're investigating the murder of a professional burglar named Irving Bettis. He was found in a garbage Dumpster behind DeWitt Plaza on Michigan Avenue a few weeks ago. The exact date was December ninth."

Randolph affixed Blackie with a blank stare, but did not respond.

"We're interviewing everyone who we can verify was at DeWitt Plaza that day," Blackie added.

"I don't see what that's got to do with me," Randolph said. "I wasn't there on the ninth."

"Maybe you weren't, but your car certainly was," Blackie said.

Manny flipped through the notebook in which he had recorded the licenses. He read from it, "You are the owner of a 2002 BMW coupe bearing Illinois license PS-nine-four-three-two?"

All the humor drained out of Solomon Randolph. He nodded an acknowledgement of his vehicle ownership.

Now Blackie's manner hardened. "You've got to watch where you park your car, Solomon. The meter maid, who patrols the block DeWitt Plaza is located on, hung two tickets on your illegally parked car a short distance from the south entrance. One on the eighth for parking in violation of posted signs and another on the ninth for parking by a fireplug. You're lucky that nice BMW wasn't towed."

Solomon Randolph remained silent.

"Now, all of this is fairly routine," Blackie continued. "But there are two ways we can handle this little scenario; the easy way or the hard way. The easy way is that you tell us what you were doing at DeWitt Plaza earlier this month right here in the confines of your very own gin mill. The hard way is that you refuse to talk, which will make it necessary for us to place you under arrest for obstructing justice. Then we'll have to put handcuffs on you and take you down to police headquarters. I guarantee that it will not be the highlight of your holiday season."

Sergeant Joe Donegan arrived at Randy's Roost and parked his Cutlass behind a brand-new black four-door Ford. Before entering the tavern, he checked the Ford's license plate number on the official laptop computer he always carried in the front seat of his car. It came back as "Not yet in file." Although it looked like a police car, usually official registrations were placed into the State of Illinois system immediately. The black Ford could be an exception to this rule or it could simply be another civilian vehicle out on the street that looked like a cop car. Donegan had owned a couple of cars like that himself over the years.

But there was still something bothering the crooked policeman. He'd had this feeling all morning and no matter what he did was unable to shake it. He arrived at the Intelligence Unit computer lab before dawn and checked on every item of information that Cole and his people had placed in their computers in the last twenty-four hours. And there was a great deal of information, because the data on every major felony case in the city was routinely routed through the chief of detectives' office. To minimize having to go through each report, Donegan entered search words into the program such as "Monica Talise," "Butterball Zane," "Vampire Campos," and "Homicide Miller." He came up with a few hits on the quartet, but nothing that he considered to be of any consequence. However, Donegan failed to enter the words "DeWitt Plaza" or "Solomon Randolph." Had he done so he would have discovered that Manny Sherlock had run the license plate number of a late-model BMW, which received two parking tickets at DeWitt Plaza. Donegan would have been enraged by Randolph's stupidity, but even at that point he could have engaged in a certain degree of damage control. Perhaps come up with a plausible reason why the car had been there. He had no way of knowing that at this point it was too late.

Shutting off the computer, Donegan got out of his car and entered Randy's Roost. He was already through the rear door before he realized that Solomon Randolph was standing behind the bar talking to two men, whom even the most casual observer would recognize as being cops. Then the realization of who they were froze Donegan in place. Lieutenant Blackie Silvestri and Sergeant Manny Sherlock turned around and came face to face with the crooked cop.

Blackie Silvestri and Manny Sherlock were not only exceptional cops, but also smart and always prepared to face the unexpected. As such, when they entered Randy's Roost they had placed their back-up guns inside their overcoat pockets. During the entire time that they had been in the tavern, one of them had his hand on the handle of a gun. Blackie carried a two-inch barrel Colt Detective Special; Manny a .380 Smith and Wesson semiautomatic pistol. Also, during their interview of Solomon Randolph, each of them had maintained a continuous surveillance of their surroundings. They were constantly checking the entrance from the street and the passageways beside the bar through which their host had appeared when they came in.

Solomon Randolph was not necessarily a strong suspect in the death of Irving Bettis simply because they had so far been unable to discover a motive for the burglar's death. That was the reason why Blackie and Manny had decided to pay the young bar owner an unannounced visit. They had first gone to the mansion he still lived in with his mother. The butler, who identified himself as Jamison, had told them where "young Mister Randolph" could be found.

And with each passing second of the interview they were conducting at Randy's Roost, Solomon, who they knew to be the only son of the infamous, but now dead Dollar Bill Randolph, was becoming a stronger suspect. However, Blackie and Manny had separately decided that Solomon was not the type to shoot burglars and dump their bodies in garbage Dumpsters.

He was obviously hiding something directly connected to his car receiving the parking tickets at DeWitt Plaza. Blackie was about to apply pressure to discover what he was hiding when Joe Donegan of the CPD Intelligence Unit walked in.

There was a moment of stunned silence during which the four men stood stock-still. Donegan, wearing a seedy, too large, wrinkled overcoat, remained standing at the door, Randolph stayed behind the bar, and Blackie and Manny, their fingers on the triggers of their concealed guns, stood between them.

A moment of extreme tension passed between the four men standing in the barroom of Randy's Roost. Solomon Randolph stood frozen into a state of mannequin-like rigidity. Donegan remained just inside the front door and stared at Silvestri and Sherlock. He kept his hands down at his sides, but continuously clenched and unclenched his fists. He was attempting to make a decision as to how to deal with this unexpected development. Blackie and Manny simply waited, but were prepared to kill either one of these men if they made a wrong move. Finally, realizing that he would never be able to pull one of his guns before Silvestri and Sherlock cut him down, Donegan willed himself to relax.

"Lieutenant Silvestri and Sergeant Sherlock of the chief of detectives's office," Donegan said, affably. "I didn't recognize you at first. I thought someone was in here robbing Mister Randolph. I'm Sergeant Donegan from the Intelligence Unit."

"We know who you are, Donegan," Blackie said. "The question I have is, what are you doing here?"

Affixing the two cops with his chilling stare, Donegan responded, "The same thing that you are, lieutenant. I came in to check Mister Randolph's licenses." He nodded to the glass case resting on top of the bar.

"You do that a lot, Sergeant Donegan?" Manny said.

"We've all got to do our bit for the Windy City, Sergeant Sherlock."

Randolph found his voice. "Since I am the focus of so much official scrutiny this morning, I want to contact my attorney before I answer any more questions."

Without taking his eyes off Donegan, Blackie said, "Manny and I don't have anything else for you right now, Solomon. We have enough information for the time being. But you'll be hearing from us again real soon. Let's go, Manny."

With that they crossed to the entrance, stepped around Joe Donegan, and were gone.

"What was that you said about a needle in a haystack, Sergeant Donegan?" Randolph said.

Staring out the front window of Randy's Roost, the crooked cop watched Silvestri and Sherlock get into the new black Ford and drive away. Over his shoulder, Donegan said, "Do me a favor and shut up, Mister Randolph."

29

DECEMBER 27, 2003
11:45 A.M.

Skip Murphy was invited to lunch by Sherman Edwards at the Barristers' Club in the Chicago Loop. Foghorn Leghorn was not a member of the prestigious private institution, but had purloined an associate membership from a former member, who owed the alderman a favor. The Barristers' Club was famous for a number of things including good food, outstanding service, and, above all, the maintenance of strict privacy for its members, most of whom were attorneys and judges in the Cook County court system.

The two black city councilmen were known around the club, but were not considered among the upper echelon who frequented its posh environs. Politicians, with the exception of the governor and perhaps the mayor, were looked upon as a group of slightly unethical, minor government officials with little more social status than traffic cops or garbage workers. Edwards and Murphy came to the club occasionally. Actually, they only met there when they wished to discuss confidential matters in a secure place downtown. Sherman Edwards, dressed in a rumpled gray suit, was waiting in the lobby when Skip Murphy arrived. Murphy noticed that his old colleague was angry.

"What's the matter, Sherm?"

The alderman looked around the stately lobby, which was still decorated with Christmas ornaments. The lunch crowd was beginning to pick up as a number of well-known legal types hurryied to luncheon appointments on the upper levels of the club. "You know I've been standing here for fifteen minutes and not one of these people has said a single word to me. It's like I'm fucking invisible or something. Now I know what it was like to be black down South before the civil rights movement forced some changes in this country."

The depth of Edwards's fury surprised Murphy. "Let's go get something to eat, Sherm. It'll make you feel better."

They rode up to the fourth floor dining room on an elevator

with three young, white, male attorneys who were discussing a multimillion-dollar real estate deal. The lawyers paid no attention to the black men, which further infuriated Edwards. By the time they reached the table that Edwards had reserved for them in a corner alcove, Foghorn Leghorn appeared on the verge of throwing a full-blown fit.

"I'm ordering you a drink," Murphy said, motioning to the waiter to bring his luncheon companion and him a pitcher of vodka martinis, which were a specialty of the house.

After consuming half of his first drink in one long pull, Edwards calmed down a bit. However, he still snarled, "A black man don't mean nothing in this world, Skip, unless he's got money and power, and lots of both. That's what I wanted to talk to you about today."

"I've got plenty of money, Sherm. You know that."

"But you ain't got no power, man," he said, grabbing the martini pitcher and refilling his glass. "You and me ain't no more than a couple of jack-leg politicians leading a bunch of fools around, who don't have the good sense to elect officials who will really look after their best interests."

Skip Murphy didn't like the way Edwards was spouting off, because if he kept drinking he was going to either do or say something that would embarrass them both. "I think that we'd better order lunch. I've got some important business to take care of this afternoon."

Edwards remained quiet while they consumed a meal of thin-sliced leg of lamb served on a bed of mashed potatoes, tossed salad with house dressing, and a delicious split pea soup. When they finished, Alderman Foghorn Leghorn had sobered up.

"Too bad this joint is smoke-free, because I could sure use

a good cigar after consuming a meal like that." He punctuated his statement by emitting a belch.

Murphy glanced impatiently at his watch.

"Take it easy, Skip," Edwards said. "After we have dessert, you can be on your way."

Dessert was an apple tart topped with whipped cream. After they were served coffee, Edwards looked around to ensure that the tables closest to their alcove were deserted. Nevertheless, he lowered his voice and said, "Your drug decriminalization proposal has really taken off, Skip. I've been conducting a little unofficial poll among some of our city council colleagues and a few select members of the news media. If what I'm hearing is accurate, you've become damned near a household word in this town."

"The only poll that ever really amounts to anything is the one conducted on Election Day," Murphy said.

"So we need to schedule us an election."

Murphy had a mouthful of apple tart and took his time chewing. After swallowing, he said, "Schedule an election?"

Edwards leaned across the table and his voice dropped to a near whisper. "You want to become a United States congressman, right?"

Murphy nodded.

"The next election is nearly two years away, which isn't a very long time for your average idiot walking around out there on the street. But you're at the height of your popularity right now. You need to run for office while you're hot."

"The office of the U.S. Representative for the First Congressional District from the State of Illinois is currently occupied, Sherm," Murphy said.

"I know. But Walter Johnson is seventy-six years old and

in failing health. If something were to happen to him, the Board of Election commissioners would have to call a special election. And the odds are that you'll be the only candidate."

"What's wrong with Congressman Johnson?"

Edwards shrugged. "He had a bout with prostate cancer about ten years ago, which he more or less recovered from. I know he takes insulin injections and suffers from emphysema. He's not a well man, Skipper boy. Not a well man at all."

"But none of those ailments are life threatening in and of themselves," Murphy countered. "Hell, I had an uncle who had lung cancer and he lived for years."

Edwards dropped into his Foghorn Leghorn phony down-home drawl. "What we have here, in the parlance of an old movie, ' . . . is a failure to communicate.' "

"I'm still not following you, Sherm."

Edwards tossed his white linen napkin onto the table surface. "Think about it, Skip. You've been in this position before. You know what to do." With that, he got to his feet. "I've got to head back to City Hall for a meeting. You coming?"

Murphy shook his head. "I'm going to have another cup of coffee. I'll call you later."

Before leaving, Sherman Edwards said, "Think about what I just said, Skip. That House seat is yours for the taking."

After Edwards left, Murphy found himself alone in the Barristers' Club dining room, as all of the other midday diners had already left. The waiter poured him more coffee and left the bill. Edwards always stuck his rich colleague with the check. And although Murphy had pretended not to understand what his fellow alderman was talking about, he had actually caught on before Congressman Walter Johnson's ailments were catalogued.

Murphy realized that he would be taking a tremendous risk, but it was definitely worth it. In fact, he wouldn't have to take the chance personally and, if he played his cards right, he would be completely in the clear as had been the case when Reverend Harrison Jones, the last serious challenger for Murphy's aldermanic seat, had been disposed of years ago.

After paying the check, Murphy headed for his townhouse. It was time for him to again make contact with Joe Donegan.

Larry "Butch" Cole, Jr. had arrived in Chicago late on Christmas Eve night. He had been picked up by his father at Midway Airport and would remain in Chicago until January 3. The teenager lived with his mother, but came to Chicago as frequently as he could so he could be with the person whom he loved most in the world—his father. This was not to say that he didn't love his mother, because he did. But there was a bond between him and Larry Cole, Sr., that had been established at the instant that Butch came into this world. A bond that went beyond the physical to achieve a deeply spiritual level.

Every morning, weather permitting, when Butch was in Chicago, the two went for a run along the lakefront. When Butch was at home in Detroit, he always attempted to synchronize his run to coincide with his father's in Chicago. And the happiest times he experienced in his life were when he was hanging out with Cole, Blackie, Manny, and Judy, who was like a big sister to Butch. When he came of age, he planned to move back to the Windy City permanently.

After breakfast that morning the senior Cole had to go into his office at police headquarters for a couple of hours. Butch was supposed to meet him there at three o'clock and then they were going to see the most recent James Bond movie. Butch had been shocked when his father had informed him that Sean Connery, the actor who portrayed the Russian submarine captain in Butch's favorite movie, *The Hunt for Red October*, had been the first James Bond. His father had also said that Connery had been the best Bond. Butch, who was a big Pierce Brosnan fan, had doubted this until they rented all of the Connery Bond movies and spent a couple of nights watching them.

Brushing his teeth the night that they watched *From Russia, with Love*, Butch found himself leering in the bathroom mirror and saying with a fairly decent imitation of Connery, "Cole. Butch Cole, Jr." However, Pierce Brosnan remained his favorite Bond.

Butch was about to leave the apartment to catch a cab to police headquarters when the doorman rang up from the lobby. He went to answer the wall intercom. The condominium building that his father lived in was on Lake Shore Drive overlooking Grant Park. It had a reputation for being one of the safest and most secure in the city. After all, the Chicago Police Department chief of detectives resided there.

Pressing the "talk" button he started to answer, "Cole. Butch Cole," but reconsidered because he didn't think his father would approve of such an eccentricity. So he simply said, "Yes?"

"There's a woman with a delivery here for your father, Butch," Mr. Nash, the doorman, said.

Momentarily, Butch was puzzled. His father hadn't said anything to him about expecting a delivery. It was also possible that he'd simply forgotten it. "Okay, Mr. Nash, send her up."

A moment later Butch opened the door to find a stunningly beautiful woman wearing a full-length beige leather trench coat standing out in the hall. She was definitely not your everyday delivery person.

"Hello, Butch," she said with alarming familiarity. "My name is Eurydice Vaughn."

She walked past him into the apartment carrying a four-foot-long oblong cardboard box under her arm. She opened the leather coat, which revealed a stunning figure sheathed in a tight-fitting red dress. She exuded sensuality and intelligence, and the teenage male could only come up with one word to describe her: "Dynamite!"

Walking to the center of the living room, she looked around and said, "I see that your father purchased all new furniture when he moved here from your house on the South Side. This is so much more masculine. Much more Larry Cole." She turned to look at Butch. "Don't you think so?"

This Eurydice Vaughn apparently knew a great deal about his father, which was okay by Butch. He was old enough to not only understand, but also appreciate his father's interest in a looker like her.

In response to her question about the furnishings, he said, "I like it a lot."

She stared at him long enough to make him blush and look away. Then she said, "Of course you do. Well, I can see that you're on the way out, so I won't keep you." She placed the cardboard box down on the floor next to the leather sofa. "This is a belated Christmas present from me to your father."

Butch followed her out into the hall and locked the apartment door behind them. They rode down in the elevator together. She stood close enough for him to notice that her perfume had a pleasant, decidedly sexy fragrance. There was

no way that he could muster up the nerve to ask her what brand
it was.

As they crossed the lobby, she asked, "Are you going far?"

"Just to police headquarters to meet my dad."

"Why don't you let me give you a lift? My car is right out
front."

Butch Cole would have probably accepted the offer of a
ride from this beautiful woman anyway, but when he saw the
red Miata roadster she was driving, his mind was immediately
made up.

After making sure that he was securely buckled in, she
rocketed away from the front of the lakefront condo building.

Monica Talise maintained a business office in a strip mall storefront on West Taylor Street. The five-year-old mall was less
than a quarter of a mile from the Dan Ryan Expressway and
was located on a commercial strip that featured mom and pop
businesses that sold everything from refurbished business
equipment to Italian ice. Mama Mancini's Pizzeria, which was
Blackie Silvestri's favorite restaurant, was two blocks away
from the former mob attorney's office.

The business office bore the name "Consolidated Enterprises" emblazoned in large black letters across the front plate-
glass window. There were no telephone numbers or times of
operation listed and the establishment was never open for business "off the street." Actually, no one knew what kind of business Consolidated Enterprises engaged in. Periodically, people
were seen going in or leaving the premises. There were a couple
of mob types in suits and ties, and some maintenance personnel
observed, but most of the time the place was locked

up and the vertical blinds covering the windows remained closed.

Consolidated Enterprises was where Monica Talise received her mail, phone calls, and maintained a business address for tax purposes. The unlisted telephone number, which she seldom gave out, was monitored by an answering service. The interior of the storefront office was sparsely furnished with only a desk, a few chairs, a telephone console, and a coat rack. There was a small washroom equipped with a shower and a kitchen containing an empty refrigerator. The back door led into a clean, paved alley. There was a city-issued trash container there, which was brand new and seldom used.

The other businesses in the mall consisted of a Subway submarine-sandwich shop, a Baskin Robbins ice cream store, and a mystery bookstore called Dark and Stormy. Each of these businesses were equipped with state-of-the art alarm systems; however, Consolidated Enterprises was not. The Taylor Street area had a reputation for having mob connections. Part of this reputation was justified; most of it was not. Consolidated Enterprises did enjoy certain mob type benefits, which made electronic antitheft devices unnecessary. Actually, there was nothing inside the office worth stealing.

Since the strange meeting she had attended at DeWitt Plaza earlier this month and the murder of the burglar she had hired, Monica Talise had been keeping a low profile. In fact, after checking out of the DeWitt Plaza Hotel on the evening of the ninth of December, she proceeded directly to O'Hare International Airport and caught the first available flight to Fort Myers, Florida. From the plane, she called ahead and a chauffeur-driven Lincoln Town Car was waiting to whisk her to Marco

Island. There she maintained an oceanside villa surrounded by palm trees. She spent the next seventeen days lounging around her private pool, sunning herself and going over the proposal and the events surrounding that proposal that had been presented to her back in Chicago.

She had celebrated Christmas with some neighbors and opened the presents she had purchased for herself under a palm tree decorated with Christmas lights and tinsel. On the night of the twenty-sixth of December, Monica returned to Chicago without having made up her mind about this new enterprise. On the afternoon of the twenty-seventh, she bundled herself against the cold in a mink hat and matching coat, and went down to her Taylor street office to check her mail and telephone messages.

The attractive former mob attorney drove a new silver-gray Cadillac Seville. She parked in the strip mall lot in the space reserved for Consolidated Enterprises, got out, and was about to enter her office when two official-looking types got out of a white Ford, which was parked in front of the Dark and Stormy bookstore. Monica noticed them when she drove in, but was not concerned about their presence, because she had nothing to fear from the police. She was at the door to Consolidated Enterprises when one of the cops called to her.

"Excuse me, Ms. Talise."

She turned around and eyed the approaching men with a stare as chilling as the below-freezing Windy City temperatures. She did not respond.

They were both men—one thin and white; the other thinner and black. Another of her stereotypes was dashed, because she always thought that all cops were fat.

The black one held up a badge and said, "I'm Detective

Davis and this is Detective Nakoff. We're from Area One Detectives. I wonder if we could have a moment of your time."

"Not unless you have a warrant," she said, starting to turn
and unlock the door to her office.

Detective Davis's next words stopped her. "We have the
warrant right here, ma'am. You're under arrest."

It had indeed been like looking for a needle in a haystack,
which made the task difficult, but not impossible. The first thing
that Cole ordered his staff to do was reduce the size of the
haystack. Based on the information that Homicide Miller had
given him, Cole began looking for other participants in this
reputed "criminal conspiracy."

Homicide Miller's activities on the day that he died were
shrouded in the same secrecy with which he had led his life.
Nevertheless the Chicago Police Department Detective Division
was able to put together a fairly coherent time line of his activities on December 9. He had checked out of the Holiday Inn
on West Ninety-fifth Street in Oak Lawn, Illinois, southwest of
Chicago, at 11:30 A.M. On the registration form his car was
listed as a brown Lincoln Mark X, which he exchanged for the
silver Mercedes at a GD-owned private garage in Woodlawn
prior to his arrival at DeWitt Plaza. What Homicide Miller did
between noon and approximately 3:00 P.M. was a mystery. At
2:51 P.M. the security cameras at DeWitt Plaza showed Miller
driving into the parking garage. At 2:54 P.M. he was recorded
entering the plaza rotunda and proceeding to the elevator banks
servicing the nineteenth through twenty-seventh floors. He was
next observed at 3:46 P.M. reentering the parking garage to
retrieve his car. The detectives were covering a span of fifty-
five minutes. Cole had them expand the time period to ninety

minutes. If it became necessary, he would increase it to two hours.

For the expenditure of the manpower necessary to engage in this investigation, Cole used the follow-up of the murder of professional burglar Irving Bettis, whose body was found in the alley behind DeWitt Plaza on the morning of December 9. Then slowly the pieces of the puzzle began falling into place.

Irving Bettis had been known to hang out at a Sixty-third Street tavern called Carl's. It was your standard bucket-of-blood ghetto bar with a neon Budweiser sign flashing through a dirty front window. When Cole and Judy walked in early in the evening of December 26, the interior reeked of cigarette smoke and stale beer. He wore a trench coat over a dark gray tailored suit. She also had on a trench coat, but underneath it she was wearing a black SWAT uniform complete with combat boots and a six-inch barrel .44 Magnum revolver in a shoulder holster. Although concealed, the weapon was quite noticeable.

The smattering of drinkers at the bar and the bartender recognized the newcomers as cops without being forced to engage in any great mental feat of deduction. After issuing some well-phrased threats to the on-duty bartender about the problems Carl's could experience from the Board of Health, Fire Department safety inspectors, and the local district vice cops, Cole and Judy obtained the address and telephone number of Irving Bettis's contact man. Within less than twenty-four hours, the detectives had formed a connection between Bettis and former mob attorney Monica Talise.

By mid-afternoon on December 27, the investigation had taken on a life of its own with new leads coming in on a nearly continuous basis. Because of Monica Talise's organized crime background, Cole knew that she would not talk voluntarily to the police. But Bettis's contact man had provided confidential information to the police that the burglar had been engaged in an operation for the former female mob lawyer when he was killed. Based on this, Cole ordered Area One Detectives Davis and Nakoff to obtain a warrant for her arrest and pick her up. The charge was burglary, which Cole knew would never stick. But it would give him some leverage to use against the woman.

But she was not the only member of the criminal element that had been discovered at DeWitt Plaza between 2:30 and 4:00 P.M. on December 9. The others caught on the surveillance cameras were Michael "Butterball" Zane, Dominico "Vampire" Campos, Timothy "Preacher" Hill, and Cathy Schneider.

Preacher Hill, a gaunt, balding, white man, and Cathy Schneider, a short, rotund, white woman, were professional boosters, who had elevated shoplifting to the level of fine art. Preacher's street moniker came from his adoption of various forms of clerical garb—that of priests, rabbis, or Greek Orthodox ministers—he would wear while creating a diversion for his larcenous assistant. While the diversion was going on, Cathy Schneider would lift high-ticket items. During the targeted time period of December 9 the booster team went after the Mont Blanc custom pen shop on the main floor of DeWitt Plaza. Dressed as a rabbi, Preacher Hill had faked a heart attack outside the shop entrance. When the two female clerks rushed to provide aid, Cathy Schneider, who was already in the shop posing as a customer, stole ten thousand dollars in custom fountain pens, watches, and Mont Blanc signature jewelry. CPD detectives, who Cole sent out to nab the boosters, recovered all of the merchandise.

Cole was fairly certain that Preacher Hill and Cathy Schneider had nothing to do with any type of major criminal conspiracy. In the hierarchy of the criminal element, they were considered little more than petty thieves. But an examination of the backgrounds of the other criminals who were at DeWitt Plaza on the ninth—Zane, Campos, and Talise—revealed that each of them was a perfect candidate for recruitment into the type of operation that Homicide Miller had talked about before his death.

Then there was Dollar Bill Randolph's son, who wanted to be known by the name Solomon Randolph. A brilliant, young, college-educated man, who Blackie and Manny had found out had a connection to none other than Sergeant Joe Donegan.

Blackie and Manny were seated in Cole's office briefing him on the events that had occurred earlier at Randy's Roost. "For just a second there, boss," the lieutenant was saying, "I thought we were going to have to blow Donegan away. It was obvious he wasn't expecting to see us when he walked into the bar."

"And he didn't just stop by to check Randolph's business licenses, as he claimed," Manny added. "The Lone Stranger was up to something. From what Judy and I found out about him, he doesn't drink. Solomon Randolph's father was one of the slickest operators on the South Side before his death and I bet Donegan's engaged in some kind of illegal business with him now."

For a moment, Cole remained seated behind his desk staring at the far wall. Then he said, "Did the crime lab do the comparison on the bullet the M.E. took out of the burglar at DeWitt Plaza?"

Blackie nodded. "I think I know where you're going with that one. It's my understanding that Donegan carries a couple of large-bore firearms at all times. But do you think, if he was there, that he used one of his own pieces to kill the burglar?"

"He's too smart for that, Blackie," Cole said. "But if we do come up with the murder weapon, it might lead us right back to Sergeant Joe Donegan." Cole got to his feet. "Now let's see how our other guests react."

Dominico "Vampire" Campos had been spending the night at one of his girlfriends' apartments on North Avenue. The Latin Lords' "war chieftain" was known to slap his women around from time to time. The one he was with had often considered cutting his throat with his own razor while he slept because of the abuse. But she discovered a much better way of getting even with her violent lover. When she learned that a couple of Area Four Homicide detectives were looking for him, she decided to give him up.

Vampire was lying on his stomach, snoring noisily when he was awakened by the barrel of a semiautomatic pistol pressed against the back of his head. Initially, he thought that one of his enemies had gotten the drop on him and he only had seconds to live. But when he discovered the two men standing in the shadows of the darkened apartment were cops, he decided to resist arrest. His rationale: he was unarmed and the cops wouldn't shoot him down in cold blood. For engaging in such rebellious activity, he ended up with a bruised forehead, split lips, and chipped front teeth.

Following a trip to a local hospital, Vampire Campos was transported to police headquarters and booked on possession of narcotics and unlawful use of weapons charges, due to the ounce of cocaine the arresting officers found in his shoe and the illegal firearm under his pillow. To keep the woman who had turned him in from gang reprisals, the cops booked her on a minor narcotics charge and released her on an I bond. The state's attorney's office suspended the case before it reached court.

Vampire spent the rest of the night in a barren cell and shortly after noon of the following day, he was taken to Detective Division headquarters. Now he sat on a metal bench and was handcuffed to an iron ring embedded in the wall of a large, white cinder-block interview room.

Michael "Butterball" Zane came into police headquarters voluntarily after being notified by Area Three Detectives that he was wanted for questioning. He was accompanied by his attorney, Milton Levy, and had a bail bond service standing by in case the cops arrested him. Butterball was fairly certain that he had not been linked directly to any crime, but he had managed to survive as the head of CCNO because he always conducted all of his business affairs, both legal and illegal, in a very careful manner.

The obese man and his lawyer were escorted into a spacious interview room, which, although fairly modern—in keeping with the rest of the new headquarters complex—still possessed an oppressive atmosphere. Attorney Levy was prepared to defend his client's rights against police harassment even though he was aware that Michael Zane represented a formidable criminal organization. A criminal organization that paid Milton Levy a substantial fee.

There was one other occupant of the interview room. He was a thin Hispanic with a cadaverous face sporting noticeable bruises. He was handcuffed to the wall on the far side of the room and he glared evilly at the fat white man and his nattily dressed attorney when they entered. They kept as far away from him as they could.

Less than five minutes after Zane and Levy arrived, two women came in. One was expensively attired and classy looking; the other was a uniformed police sergeant with the name "Daniels" on the name tag pinned to her right breast. The classy one was wearing a very unflattering pair of Smith and Wesson handcuffs binding her wrists in front of her. The police officer and the prisoner took seats on a bench opposite Butterball Zane and his attorney. From the far end of the room, Vampire Campos grabbed his crotch with his free hand and made a loud sucking noise. The women ignored him.

"I demand to know why my client is here," Milton Levy demanded of the sergeant.

Affixing him with the noncommittal stare of the unemotional, detached public servant, she said, "I have no idea why your client is here, sir. My job is to guard this young lady."

An exasperated Milton Levy rolled his eyes.

High up in the corner of the fifty-foot by thirty-foot interview room was a closed-circuit television camera. Its unblinking lens took in the five occupants seated below and transmitted their images back to a monitor in the chief of detectives' office. Cole, Blackie, and Manny were studying the screen.

"Either they're damn good actors," Cole said, "or they've never met each other before."

"I think I've got that figured out, Chief," Manny said.

Cole and Blackie turned to look at the sergeant.

"We know that the three of them were at DeWitt Plaza on the ninth of December and that they probably met with the same person or people that Homicide Miller did. Now we know that Miller boarded an elevator that accessed only the nineteenth through the twenty-seventh floors. The only location we have been unable to come up with any information about on that day is the McCall Room."

Blackie snorted. "Yeah, kid, but that's a five-thousand-square-foot ballroom. You could put an army in there."

"You're right, Blackie," the young sergeant countered. "But it has four separate entrances and was partitioned off into four areas." He held up his hand and counted off, "One for Homicide Miller, one for Vampire Campos, one for Butterball Zane, and the last for Monica Talise."

Cole and Blackie first looked at each other then back at the closed-circuit monitor. They said as one, "So none of them has ever seen any of the others or Homicide Miller."

"And I'd be willing to bet," Manny added, "that they never saw their host either."

"What do we do now?" Blackie said.

"Book Campos on the narcotics and gun charges," Cole responded, "and let Zane go. Maybe we can make a deal with Ms. Talise."

A short time later, sans handcuffs, Monica Talise was seated in the chief of detectives' office across from Cole. Judy Daniels, still wearing her uniform as an effective disguise, was also present.

"Yes, I admit I was invited to the McCall Room of DeWitt Plaza on December ninth," she said. "At that time a business proposal was made to me. The details of it were somewhat sketchy, but the male host of the proceeding said he would be getting back in touch with me to schedule another meeting."

"Could you describe this 'host'?" Cole asked.

"Not really," the Talise woman said, crossing her legs and gracing Cole with a flirtatious smile. "He appeared on a closed-circuit monitor and his face and voice were electronically masked. Now, Chief Cole, you're really not planning to charge me with anything, are you?"

Cole returned her smile. "That depends entirely on you, Ms. Talise. What else have you got to tell me?"

This day had been a disaster for both Joe Donegan and Solomon Randolph. A few minutes after Silvestri and Sherlock's departure from Randy's Roost, the commander of the Intelligence Unit had beeped Donegan. He was ordered back to the office immediately. The uneasy feeling that had held him in its grip all morning intensified as he drove back across the city. The commander had never summoned him like this before, which meant that something unusual had occurred and Joe Donegan hated surprises.

"You've been transferred, Joe," the commander said.

Standing in the commander's office, Donegan responded, "I didn't request a transfer, sir."

"You're a Chicago Police Department supervisor, Joe. You go where you are needed."

"So where am I needed?"

"The Internal Affairs Division."

It was all that the crooked cop could do to keep himself from exploding in anger. He had been around long enough to know what was going on. He was being placed under a form of house arrest by the department. When he arrived at his new unit, he would be assigned to a desk job in an obscure corner. The numerous "finks" assigned to the IAD would carefully monitor all of his on-duty activities. And, although he was upset by this unexpected development, he had always lived with the possibility that someday this would eventually happen.

Other rogue officers had been singled out for such onerous reassignments in the past. However, this usually only occurred after a wealth of incriminating evidence had been gathered about them. Now Donegan would have to be concerned about what they actually had on him.

He had been so distracted by his thoughts that he didn't hear what the commander had just said. Now he replayed the words in his mind.

"The IAD commander wants their computer system upgraded and has been looking around for the right person to do it. Apparently your name came up."

It sounded innocent enough, but . . . "Who recommended me, Commander?"

"I heard that it was someone in Detective Division headquarters."

"Could you be more specific," Donegan pressed.

The Intelligence Unit commander began shuffling papers around on his desk as a signal to the sergeant that the interview was over. In a matter-of-fact tone, he responded, "I think it was that female disguise artist on Chief Cole's personal staff."

It all became very clear to Sergeant Joe Donegan. Being transferred to the Internal Affairs Division wasn't necessarily the disaster that he had originally thought it to be. Now his home computer system and the one he had installed in the basement of Randy's Roost were as sophisticated as anything that the Chicago Police Department possessed. Also, if he needed anything from official databanks nationwide, it would be simple enough for him to hack his way into the system.

Donegan turned to leave the Intelligence Unit C.O.'s office, but the commander stopped him. "It's been nice working with you, Joe."

"Sure," was the only response.

"There's just one more thing. I need your access codes. They'll have to be changed for security reasons."

Later Randolph and Donegan commiserated over the separate problems they had experienced this day. In addition to Donegan's career setback, Solomon Randolph's criminal mastermind enterprise was in shambles due to Larry Cole.

Randolph had appropriated a bottle of Remy Martin cognac from the bar and was making a concerted effort to single-handedly consume it. A grim-faced Joe Donegan sat across from him.

"I've got to give it to you, Sergeant Donegan," Randolph said, displaying amazing sobriety for a man who had just drunk half a fifth of booze. "You had Cole pegged right. He is definitely one helluva cop." To emphasize his words, he refilled the brandy snifter.

"You can always resurrect your operation, Mister Randolph," Donegan said. "We'll simply have to wait awhile and come up with a new team. Campos, Zane, and the Talise woman have been compromised by Cole."

"How long is 'awhile,' Sergeant Donegan?"

"A year. Maybe two."

Randolph laughed. "So what do we do in the meantime; go back to selling phony I.D.s?"

"That is a lucrative endeavor, Mister Randolph, but if you now find it distasteful . . ."

"I didn't say that," Randolph snapped. "I just wanted to do something on my own."

"To get out of your father's shadow, so to speak."

Randolph's jaw muscles rippled and he started to issue an

angry retort, but thought better of it and took another swig of booze.

They sat in silence for a time before Donegan said, "There is something we could turn our attention to. Something that could be quite profitable if we play it right."

Solomon Randolph was beginning to show a few tell-tale signs of inebriation. Spilling some of the cognac on his desk blotter, he asked, "Something like what?"

"Political intrigue."

Larry and Butch Cole returned to the lakefront condo after seeing the new James Bond movie. They had a friendly argument going about the stunts in the film.

"Butch, there wasn't one single thing James Bond did in that movie that a normal human being could accomplish and survive without serious injury."

"But that's what makes it so cool, Dad."

Cole laughed and was crossing the living room when he noticed the oblong cardboard box on the floor next to the sofa. "What is this?"

"Oh, that," Butch said. "The woman who gave me a lift down to headquarters dropped it off earlier." The teenager was surprised that he'd forgotten the good-looking woman with the jazzy sports car. But when he arrived at headquarters, he'd become engrossed in the investigation that his father, Blackie, Manny, and Judy were conducting.

"What woman, Butch?" There was an edge in the elder Cole's voice.

"Eurydice Vaughn. She had a really neat car, Dad. It was a . . ."

Cole grabbed the box and ripped it open. Inside there was a sheathed steel sword wrapped in velvet cloth.

"Wow!" Butch said. "That's a real sword."

Cole unsheathed the blade. The edge was smooth, but the point razor sharp. This was an exact replica of the sword Cole had wielded during a wild Halloween Party at the National Science and Space Museum some years ago. At the time Cole had been wearing a Zorro costume.

"Could I see it?" Butch asked.

He turned to his son. "Yes, but do me a favor, Butch. Before you go accepting rides from strange women, would you please give me a call?"

Butch frowned in obvious confusion. "Did I do something wrong? Eurydice did say that she was an old friend of yours."

Cole smiled. "She is, but I still want you to be careful."

Excited at the touch and feel of the ancient steel weapon, he responded, "I'm just like you and Uncle Blackie when it comes to danger, Dad. I'm always careful."

PART 3

"I will endure no more."
—Dr. Stella Novak

30

D r. Stella Novak was in love. Since she had emigrated from Poland, as a teenager, she had never dated anyone on a regular basis. Actually, if she were totally honest with herself, she would be forced to admit that she'd never been on a real date at all while she was living in America. When she graduated from medical school, she celebrated the occasion by going out for pizza and beer at Mama Mancini's Pizzeria with Larry Cole, Blackie Silvestri, Judy Daniels, Manny Sherlock, and Manny's wife, Lauren. Stella made her work her life, which was something that she periodically criticized her patients, especially Larry Cole, for doing. Periodically, when she was forced into social situations, such as weddings, baptisms, or professional gatherings, she felt painfully alone as a single female. But somehow she managed to survive without too many lingering pangs of loneliness. Then she met Allen Rollins.

It was by way of her relationship with Larry Cole that she was invited to give a talk at the monthly meeting of the Midwest chapter of Mystery Writers of America. The topic was forensic pathology, which she was forced to bone up on for the presentation.

Her audience consisted of twenty-five mystery writers gathered in a fourth floor, book-lined dining room of the venerable Chicago Athletic Club on Michigan Avenue. She was so nervous that she had been unable to eat the gourmet meal served prior to the formal meeting. But Cole, who had extended the invitation to Stella on behalf of mystery writers Barbara Zorin and Jamal Garth, was in attendance. His presence gave her some degree of moral support. The field of forensic pathology was not totally foreign to her, as she had taken a number of courses and attended seminars at such prestigious institutions as the FBI Academy at Quantico, Virginia and the Harvard Medical School. Perhaps someday, if she ever tired of her medical practice, she would become a forensic pathologist. Until then she planned to keep up on new developments in the field.

Despite Stella's anxiety, the talk went extremely well. She was able to answer all of the writers' questions and some queries were of a fairly complex nature. Especially those of a thin, scholarly young man wearing wire-frame glasses, who came up to her after the meeting and introduced himself as Allen Rollins. To her, he seemed pleasant enough in a shy, understated manner, but nothing in the least bit extraordinary. He had made a half-hearted attempt to get Stella's phone number and she responded by giving him one of her business cards.

Larry Cole gave her a lift home after the meeting. "So what did you think of the writers?" he asked.

"I have read a number of their books," Stella said. "Especially those of Mrs. Zorin and Mr. Garth. But my favorite author is still the adventure novelist Seth Champion."

"I saw you talking to him after the meeting."

Stella was confused. "I don't understand what you mean,

Commander," she said, continuing to use his official title from the days when she was his physical therapist.

"You were talking to Seth Champion right before we left, Stella," Cole said. "I thought that the two of you were getting along quite well."

"Commander, the only person I talked to after the meeting, other than you, Barbara, and Jamal, was that fellow Allen Rollins."

Cole smiled. "Who goes by the pen name of adventure novelist Seth Champion, Dr. Novak."

Allen Rollins called her office the next day.

"Why didn't you tell me that you are Seth Champion?" she demanded.

"I didn't have a chance. Seth and I are actually two separate people in a great many ways. Seth is more of the alter ego for the super spies and soldiers of fortune I write about. Allen Rollins is just an underpaid college writing instructor. However, both Seth and Allen would like to take you to dinner."

She agreed to go out with him.

Their relationship began in mid-November with that first date. She discovered that he was a widower with one child, a girl of seven named Stephanie, who was totally devoted to her father. Stella had been apprehensive about meeting the child, but her fears were groundless. The little girl, who had the same jet-black hair and gray eyes as her father, wanted to become a doctor someday. When she discovered Stella's occupation, the two instantly became fast friends.

In early December, Stella was Allen's guest at a writing

conference at Columbia College in downtown Chicago. He was one of the keynote presenters during the daylong program. That's when she got her first glimpse into the personality of the man who was her favorite fiction author. Standing at a podium next to a table on which the ten novels he had published were displayed, the shy, soft-spoken man she had met at the mystery writers' meeting became adventure-novelist Seth Champion. The dynamic storyteller, whose work had enthralled millions of readers, now revealed himself through the spoken word.

Initially, the practical-minded, near-stoic physician stayed within herself and did not let her feelings for the author get out of hand. However, he was never far from her thoughts. And she had learned that the man behind the words authored under the pseudonym Seth Champion was as complex and mysterious as any character in reality or fiction that she had ever encountered.

Stella noticed that at times there was a heavy sadness behind the shy face that Allen Rollins presented to the world. Then, bit by bit, she discovered the details of the life that the author drew from to create his adventure tales.

They had taken Stephanie to an indoor carnival at Navy Pier on a frigid December day. While the little girl was riding the merry-go-round, Stella and Allen stood behind a metal fence and watched her. A short distance away a group of teenagers were roughhousing. One of them blew up a paper bag and smashed it. The popping noise made by the explosion of compressed air was as loud as a small caliber pistol shot and startled a number of carnival visitors. The relative innocence of the prank gave way to relief for most and even humor for a few. This was not the case with Allen Rollins.

The initial sound caused him to spin around with a glare of such fury that he appeared to be a stranger to Stella. A terrifying stranger possessing the gaze of a man who was not only capable of killing, but who had also killed in the past. When he became aware that there was no real threat, he recovered quickly. However, he was still badly shaken.

Later they took Stephanie for an ice cream sundae at an old-fashioned soda fountain on the pier. The little girl was too engrossed in shoving ice cream, whipped cream, and nuts into her mouth to pay any attention to what the adults were saying. Stella noticed that Allen had become unusually quiet since the bag-popping incident. Then the man, who made his living with words, explained to her who and what he had been.

"I enlisted in the United States Army when I was sixteen years old. The Vietnam War was in its final stages, but there was still a great deal of killing going on. I was cross-trained as a sniper and a demolition expert in the Special Forces. My team engaged in a number of long-range patrols and I developed the ability to accurately hit a human target at a distance of from seven hundred and fifty to a thousand yards. I had eighty-seven confirmed kills. When the war ended, I completed my enlistment and became a freelance mercenary. I used the skills I had acquired in the Special Forces in brushfire wars in Africa, Afghanistan, Croatia, and South America. By the time I was twenty-five I had developed into a very efficient killing machine." He paused to look at his daughter, who was still busy with her ice cream. Although Allen maintained his composure, Stella could detect the deep sadness lying just beneath the surface. "One day I looked in the mirror and didn't like what I saw. So I retired from the mercenary business, returned to the States and used the G.I. Bill to get an education. I met Stephanie's mother while I was still in college. After we were married, I sat down to write my first novel as Seth Champion."

"Why didn't you write under your own name?" Stella asked.

He smiled, displaying more sadness than mirth. "Adopting the pen name was a way to insulate Allen Rollins from the memories that Seth Champion used to create the books."

Their relationship progressed to the point that they saw each other at least three times a week and spoke on the telephone at least once a day. Stella began taking a greater interest in her appearance and had the gray rinse removed that she used on her hair to make her look older in favor of reverting back to the original blond color. Accompanied by Judy Daniels, the doctor went shopping and purchased all new clothes. The false horn-rimmed glasses went into the back of a desk drawer in her office never to be worn again. But the transformation she experienced went beyond the physical. For the first time in her life she was becoming "comfortable" with someone who was not a relative. In fact, she hadn't been as close to anyone as she was with Allen and his little Stephanie since Sophie's disappearance. Yet Stella and Allen had yet to take their relationship beyond the "kiss on the doorstep at the end of the evening" level. Perhaps, Stella thought, they weren't supposed to.

Years ago Stella had come to the realization on her own that she was decidedly old-fashioned. She had strongly disapproved of Sophie's promiscuous lifestyle. Stella had always felt that intimacy was something to be restricted to the marital bed. Her relationship with Allen so far indicated that he felt the same way, although marriage had not been discussed. But eventually, she was sure that it would come up. In the brief time they had been together, they had become just that attached to each other.

On this February evening it was snowing in Chicago, but a significant accumulation was not expected. Allen was picking her up for a late supper at Gibson's Steak House on Rush Street. Dinner had been his idea, because Stella had been in the office since 7:30 that morning. She had seen patients all day and when the clinic closed at 6:00 P.M., she was forced to remain behind to review the records of her new patients. She had consumed a salad and a can of iced tea at her desk for lunch, but other than that she'd had nothing to eat since breakfast. Dr. Novak was definitely looking forward to the Rush Street late supper.

She was examining the medical file of Congressman Walter Johnson, who had been referred to her by Dr. Mark Kirchner, who had recently retired and turned all of his patients over to Stella. The congressman was an elderly man, who'd had a number of severe medical problems in the past. However, he also had the constitution of an ox. At the age of seventy-seven, he didn't move very fast anymore, but he had a cheerful attitude and a positive outlook on life.

The congressman was on a number of medications for everything from high blood pressure to diabetes. Other than that he was healthy and, from all indications in the medical file that Dr. Kirchner had compiled over the years, he maintained a hectic schedule of official duties in Washington and Chicago. Stella saw that the congressman hadn't had a complete physical in awhile, so this would be the first treatment she planned for him. It would also be a good way for her to get acquainted with her new patient, whom Dr. Kirchner had told her was cantankerous, but always good-natured.

Her telephone rang. "Hello."

"I'm sitting out in front of the building waiting for you,

Dr. Novak," Allen Rollins said. "The front door is locked."

She should have remembered that the front doors were secured at 6:30. "I'm sorry, Allen. I'll close up and be right with
you."

A few minutes later, Dr. Stella Novak got into the front seat
of the author's late-model Toyota Camry. They exchanged a
perfunctory kiss before he put the car in gear and drove away.
A half block south of the entrance to the medical center, Joe
Donegan sat behind the wheel of his now ragged, dirty Oldsmobile Cutlass. He had considered it a touch of extreme good
fortune when he discovered, via an illegal computer link, that
Walter Johnson was now a patient of his personal physician.
That would make it easier for Donegan to get to the congressman.

Donegan planned to make an appointment to see Stella in
the next day or so. Then he would make a decision on how to
proceed from that point.

The crooked cop's visit to the medical complex on this
night was purely accidental. He had simply been in the vicinity
and decided to drive by. When he saw her office lights on, he
considered paying her an unannounced visit. He knew how distasteful his presence was to her, so his late night visit would
be a decent form of sadistic entertainment for him. Since Donegan's assignment to the Internal Affairs Division, the sergeant
had found little to amuse him.

She came out before he could go inside, but the night was
not a total waste, because he saw her kiss the male driver of
the car parked in front of the medical center. "Well, hello, Doctor Novak!" he cried out loud at witnessing the intimacy. "What
do we have here?"

From the first time he laid eyes on her, Donegan had always considered the intense young Polish woman an emotional iceberg. Now she apparently had a boyfriend. This he would have to check out.

As he had done with her sister Sophie and Alderman Skip Murphy years ago, Sergeant Joe Donegan followed the Toyota Camry in which Dr. Stella Novak was riding.

Larry Cole and Eurydice Vaughn were also having a late supper on this frigid night. Besides being one of the most popular eating establishments in Chicago, which was frequented by celebrities ranging from movie stars to sports figures, Gibson's Steak House on Rush Street was a restaurant that had been one of Eurydice's favorites prior to her commitment to an institution for the criminally insane. It had also been a place where Cole and Eurydice's sister Edna had gone for romantic dinners. Eurydice had selected Gibson's for tonight's meal. This was not a good idea.

Since their meeting at the National Science and Space Museum in late December, this was the first date that Cole and his former lover had managed to arrange. As usual, Cole had been busy with police work and Eurydice involved with her own professional pursuits at the museum. However, their jobs were not the primary reason for their inability to get together. Cole had been avoiding her.

It was all he could do to contain his anger after the unannounced visit she had made to his apartment after Christmas. Not wanting to reveal the depth of emotion that Eurydice was capable of engendering in him, Cole didn't say anything else about her to Butch. By the time that his son returned to Detroit in early January, Cole had calmed down and was now capable of logically examining her reentry into his life. On the surface, it appeared to be fairly innocent, but he still felt that something wasn't right.

Eurydice called his office just about every day after the New Year. On most of those occasions, Cole had been occupied with his law enforcement responsibilities and not available. A few times he could have come to the phone, but had told whoever answered the call to take a message. The reason was that he simply didn't want to talk to Eurydice Vaughn.

Larry Cole was not a coward and didn't relish avoiding this woman indefinitely, so finally, a week before their dinner engagement, he had taken a call from her.

"I was just about to pay another visit to your apartment, since I was unable to get in touch with you by phone, Larry," she said in a tone of lighthearted humor.

Cole was not in much of a lighthearted mood. "I'm been very busy, Eurydice, and in the future I would appreciate it if you would get in touch with me before coming to my apartment."

There was a long pause from her end. Then, "I'm sorry if I offended you. I just wanted to deliver your Christmas present. I also got a chance to meet your son."

"I sent you a 'thank you' card," he responded. Cole realized that he was coming on much too hard. She didn't deserve this kind of treatment from him no matter what had occurred between them in the past. Managing to soften his tone, he said, "My son was impressed by both you and the sword."

"Did you tell him the story behind the weapon?"

"Perhaps I will someday."

Now they were getting along like a couple of old friends. Apparently, this was what she wanted. "We were supposed to be getting together after the first of the year to renew old acquaintances."

Something deep inside of him wanted to tell her that a date was out of the question and that he, in fact, never wanted to see her again. But at this moment he simply couldn't bring himself to say the words.

They decided on dinner at Gibson's.

A short time later, after he hung up the phone, Blackie came into the office.

"For Chrissakes, boss, you look like you're about to walk the plank."

"No," Cole said, glumly. "I've been invited out to dinner at Gibson's Steak House on Rush Street."

"Now that is a catastrophe," Blackie quipped.

Cole and Eurydice were seated at a table set for four in the glass-enclosed dining area, which provided a view to the north of the bright lights of Chicago's main night club district. She had called ahead to order an appetizer of boiled shrimp with cocktail sauce and a bottle of Brut extra dry champagne. As soon as they were seated, the waiter served them. This proved to be a mistake, as all that the appetizer and champagne did was remind Cole of the deception that she and her sister had knowingly perpetrated on him in and out of his bed.

Following a moment of protracted silence, during which Cole refused to touch either the appetizer or his wine glass, Eurydice sensed that her plan was not going well. "Would you like another appetizer?"

"No," he said, taking a sip of water. "Why don't we order the main entrée?"

"Whatever you say, Larry."

*   *   *

It began as a tingling sensation at the base of Allen Rollins's skull, which was a feeling he had not experienced since his days in the jungles of Southeast Asia in the early 1970s. His squad had been on a long-range patrol and was about to walk into a Viet Cong ambush. Staff Sergeant Rollins had stopped the Green Berets just in time. But that was in the jungle during a nearly forgotten war; now he was out on a date on the snow-covered streets of the Windy City. He began constantly checking his mirrors and the streets they were traveling for any signs of trouble. His nervousness prompted Stella to ask, "Is there something wrong?"

He managed a weak smile. "Everything is just fine."

Then he spotted the dirty car that had been behind them since they left the medical center. The former Green Beret NCO began planning to deal with this perceived threat just as he'd dealt with the ones he encountered in Vietnam. Chicago Police Sergeant Joe Donegan was unaware that what amounted to the cross hairs of a high-powered sniper's rifle had just been placed on the center of his forehead.

"You know, Larry," Eurydice was saying as they waited to be served, "you haven't changed since the moment I first laid eyes on you. I know that you work out and keep yourself in good shape, but that doesn't explain it completely. I was looking through one of your old photo albums when I visited your house some years ago. There was this picture of you and Blackie Silvestri . . ."

Cole could tell that she was trying to please him and he really couldn't fault her for that. In a way, he was flattered. But she was not the same calculating Eurydice Vaughn who always presented an icy front to the world while concealing a smoldering, white-hot passion underneath. This change in personality could have been the result of the therapy she received, which he had been an unknowing part of. She had also been under federal scrutiny for a time, because the government was interested in the bizarre research conducted by Katherine Rotheimer, the woman who had kidnapped Eurydice when she was a child. She had yet to mention anything concerning her relationship with the NSA and, in fact, Cole could actually do without hearing about his old friends, covert operatives Reggie Stanton and Ernest Steiger.

"Have you ever thought about having more children, Larry?"

The question refocused his attention on her. "So far," he said, feeling a trifle bit uneasy, "Butch has proven to be quite enough for me to handle."

"But one should never say never," she said, reaching across the table and taking his hand. "I think that a little girl would be the apple of your eye."

He really didn't like the way that this conversation was going and he was about to change the subject when another alternative presented itself. "Why, there's Stella and Allen."

Eurydice turned to see who he was talking about, as Cole got to his feet and motioned for them to come over. The maitre'd, who knew Larry Cole was the chief of detectives, led the couple to the table.

"Well, isn't this a coincidence," Cole said, attempting badly to conceal his relief. "Doctor Stella Novak, who by the way is my personal physician, and Mister Allen Rollins, who is also known as the famous mystery/adventure novelist Seth Champion, this is Ms. Eurydice Vaughn."

No sooner were the greetings exchanged than Cole said, much to Eurydice's consternation and surprise, "Won't the two of you join us?"

"We wouldn't want to intrude," Stella said.

"Thanks, Larry," Allen said, quickly pulling out the chair next to Cole's date for Stella.

For a moment, Eurydice appeared dumbfounded by this development; however, she recovered quickly. Leaving the foursome, the maitre'd returned to his station.

Joe Donegan was forced to park his car in a private lot a block from Gibson's Steak House. He considered the ten dollar fee he was forced to pay a form of highway robbery. On top of that, the young carhop had looked at Donegan's filthy, dilapidated car and said, "They got this new thing called a car wash, man. You should try it sometime."

Ignoring him, Donegan walked back to Gibson's. He entered the restaurant to find a long line waiting for tables. Donegan wasn't about to get in this line, because he would never pay the high prices they charged for food in this joint. Instead, he entered the bar, which was perpendicular to the entrance. It was also packed, but Donegan was able to squeeze through the throng into a corner. From this position he could see into the restaurant proper, where Stella Novak and her date were seated at a table with another couple. The demonic entity that guided Donegan in the conduct of his nefarious activities had once more smiled on him, as the doctor was sitting with Larry Cole and the woman Donegan had seen him with at the National Science and Space Museum. Ignoring the crowd surrounding him, Donegan settled in to spy on them.

* * *

What had originally appeared to be a setback, Eurydice Vaughn was turning to her advantage. She had seldom come in contact with any of Cole's friends, but she did know of them. And they were all cops. Now she had met his personal physician and one of the mystery writers she had heard him mention in the past. This situation could definitely be worked to her advantage. Perhaps she could even forge this into her and Larry Cole being considered a "couple."

"How long has Larry been your patient, Doctor Novak?" Eurydice asked.

"For over ten years. Actually, I was his physical therapist before I became his doctor," she responded. "And please call me Stella, Eurydice. That is such a beautiful name."

"The woman who raised me possessed something of a sense of the exotic." Eurydice looked across at Cole. "Didn't she, Larry?"

Without emotion, he said, "If you say so, Eurydice. After all, you knew her better than I did."

"I've got to go to the lady's room," she said, getting to her feet. When Dr. Novak remained seated, Eurydice said, "This is kind of a boy/girl thing, Stella. The women go to the powder room together, so that we can catch up on girl talk, while they talk about sports or guns or whatever."

A slight frown dented Stella's forehead. She didn't like being considered a "girl." After a brief hesitation, she also stood up saying, "Lead the way, Eurydice."

When they were gone, Allen said, "That woman is gorgeous, Larry."

Without displaying a great deal of enthusiasm, Cole responded, "She has her points, Allen, both good and bad."

"I'm kind of glad that they left together, because there's something I'd like to discuss with you without alarming Stella. Tonight we were followed from her office."

"Are you sure?"

"Certain. In fact, he's inside the bar right now. Since we sat down, he hasn't taken his eyes off of this table."

Cole didn't look up right away, but used his peripheral vision to first locate the man that Allen was talking about. Then he saw Sergeant Joe Donegan standing in the bar.

Donegan watched the women leave the table. The foursome was obviously going to be here for a while and, as he couldn't hear what they were talking about, sticking around for another couple of hours would simply be a waste of time. He had Stella's boyfriend's license plate number, which he would run later. Then Donegan would open a computer file on him and fill it with interesting items such as his credit rating, military record, police record, bank balance, and tax returns for the past five years. This would simply be a side pursuit or hobby for the crooked cop, as he was once more engaged in an illegal pursuit. An illegal pursuit that would result in the biggest payday of his career. A payday he would earn by murdering a United States congressman.

Skip Murphy had again contacted Donegan. The alderman had asked for a face-to-face meeting with Donegan for the first time in years. And this meeting was shrouded in as much secrecy as any clandestine espionage operation in history.

Donegan was instructed by Murphy to go to the Soldier Field parking lot on Lake Shore Drive at 3:00 A.M. The crooked cop had balked at the time and the place, but the alderman promised him that it would be well worth his while.

Because Donegan was always very cautious, he arrived an hour early and thoroughly checked the exterior of the football stadium and the area surrounding the huge parking lot. Then he parked next to a fence in a spot that effectively concealed his car in the shadows of a refreshment stand that was closed for the winter. With his engine off to prevent exhaust fumes from giving his location away, he settled in to wait in the cold.

At 2:45 A.M. a dark figure on foot entered the south end of the lot. Donegan pulled his .44 Magnum and placed it on the front seat beside him. He watched the newcomer proceed to the center of the immense parking lot. There he stopped and began bouncing from foot to foot in an attempt to stay warm.

Donegan continued to watch whoever was out there until the appointed time. Then he started the engine and, keeping the .44 handy and his headlights extinguished, cruised slowly to the center of the lot. Coming up on the dark figure, Donegan discovered that it was none other than a half-frozen Alderman Skip Murphy, who was bundled in a knit cap, scarf, navy pea coat, and gloves. The crooked cop let the alderman into his car.

"How long have you been here?" Murphy asked, blowing on his hands to restore circulation.

"Long enough," Donegan replied. "So what's so important that you call for a meeting in sub-zero weather in the wee small hours of the morning?"

"Do you remember the job you did for me back in ninety-two?"

"Alderman, why don't we dispense with the crap? If you want me to kill somebody for you, just come out and say so. Then I'll quote you a price. And this time my fee is not negotiable."

Murphy pulled off his cap and said, bluntly, "I'll pay you

two hundred and fifty thousand dollars to eliminate Congressman Walter Johnson and I want his death to appear to be of
natural causes."

Standing in a corner of the crowded bar of Gibson's Steak
House on Rush Street, Joe Donegan recalled that he had agreed
immediately to take on the job. The money Murphy was of-
fering would be more than enough, but there were a couple of
things that the alderman was unaware of. One was that Donegan knew of Murphy's secret relationship with the woman that
Chief Larry Cole was dating. The other was that Joe Donegan
now had a business partner in Solomon Randolph, which would
place an entirely different spin on any deals he made with Murphy.

For some minutes now, traffic in the bar had become so
heavy that Donegan had been unable to see Cole's table. Actually that didn't matter at this point, because Donegan was
ready to leave. He was turning to do just that when he found
his path blocked by Cole and Stella Novak's boyfriend.

"Hello, Joe," the chief of detectives said, looming over the
small disheveled man. "I didn't know you frequented Gibson's."

The rogue cop looked warily from Cole to the boyfriend.
And it was in the gaze of the other guy that Donegan recognized something that frightened him to the very marrow of his
larcenous being. As a killer, Donegan saw instantly that this
man was also capable of killing without reservation or com-
punction.

"It's a public place, Chief," Donegan managed to state with
more confidence than he felt. "I have the right to come in here

just like anyone else. Now if you will excuse me, I was just leaving."

"Give me a moment, Joe," Cole said, refusing to move.

Donegan again glanced at Stella Novak's friend and came to the decision that it would be best under the circumstances to do what he was told.

Cole stepped closer to Donegan and lowered his voice to a menacing whisper. "This is Allen Rollins, whom I understand that you followed from Doctor Novak's office."

"I don't know what you're talking about."

"Shut up and listen to me, Joe," Cole snapped. "Now unauthorized surveillances are a violation of First Amendment rights guaranteed by the Constitution. As a command officer of the Chicago Police Department, it is my responsibility to investigate any such violations, which, if discovered, could carry not only a suspension, but also jail time for the offending officer."

Donegan looked directly into Cole's eyes. "Are you threatening me, Chief?"

Cole graced the crooked cop with a chilly smile. "I wouldn't think of doing such a thing, Sergeant Donegan, but let me make one thing quite clear. I don't ever again want to look over my shoulder and see you lurking behind me." Pausing a moment to make sure that his words had soaked in, Cole stepped back and said, "Good night, Joe."

Donegan walked between the two men and out the front door into the cold Chicago night.

31

Dinner and dessert went well for Cole, Eurydice, Stella, and Allen. A genuine rapport had developed between them and they all got along in an exceptional fashion. When Eurydice confessed that she had never read a Seth Champion novel, Allen promised to give her an autographed copy of his latest book, which he retrieved from the trunk of his car when they left the restaurant. After coffee they parted in front of Gibson's with Cole and Eurydice getting into his police car and Stella and Allen driving off in the Camry.

"That was so very nice of Allen," Eurydice was saying, as she examined the hardcover book the author had given her. She read the text on the flyleaf of the dust jacket, "Seth Champion weaves sex, danger, intrigue, and mayhem into his tales with the pronounced skill of the master storyteller." She turned to look at Cole and said, " 'Sex, danger, intrigue, and mayhem' is kind of our thing, isn't it, Larry?"

He didn't answer her.

When they reached her apartment building on the northern edge of Jackson Park overlooking the National Science and Space Museum, he parked his car and escorted her to her eleventh floor apartment with the intention of saying a quick good night. In the deserted corridor, he was about to do just that when she flung herself at him.

In an instant her lips were clamped over his and she had her arms wrapped tightly around his neck as she pressed her pelvis against him. This was the Eurydice Vaughn style of foreplay, which Cole had experienced in the past. And her lovemaking was so violent that it could easily be compared to a form of physical combat. But this time, Cole resisted. Extricating himself forcibly from her grasp, he held her at arm's length. He could feel her body trembling beneath his touch.

For a long time he stared at her, as memories of the passion they had shared came back to him.

"Come inside, Larry," she said in a hoarse voice. "Please come inside."

Every ounce of his being screamed for him to turn around and walk away. But Larry Cole was also a human being. "I'll go inside with you, Eurydice, but you've got to promise me that you'll calm down if I do."

She lowered her eyes and said, "I promise."

He released her and she fumbled the keys out of her purse. The interior of the apartment was totally dark and he was unable to see his hand in front of his face when they stepped across the threshold. He could hear her moving around in the dark and then she switched on a table lamp on the other side of her sunken living room. The illumination from the lamp was dim, but Cole could easily see that she had taken off her shoes and dress. Before he could remove his trench coat, she had stripped off her bra, panties, and panty hose to stand nude in the center of the room. Her body was as enticing as ever.

Slowly, he removed his sports jacket, tie, and gun. Then he walked toward her. "Now we're going to do this nice and slow for a change, Eurydice. Nice and slow."

* * *

Joe Donegan arrived home shortly before midnight. As usual, he found his sister Megan planted in front of the TV set, where she could be found every day from morning until night. He ignored her as he unlocked the door to the study that he had turned into his private computer lab. After he disappeared inside and locked the door behind him, Megan looked up briefly displaying a vacant, emotionless gaze. Then she returned to the late night talk show she'd been watching.

Donegan had converted the room where his father had once consumed beer by the case into a smaller version of the Chicago Police Department's Intelligence Unit computer room. In fact, the rogue cop had a number of artificial intelligence applications that were beyond anything possessed by any law enforcement agency in the country with perhaps the exception of the FBI. And all of his computers were protected from any attempt to hack into them from outside. He didn't want anyone to do to him what he did to others on a regular basis.

Stella Novak's boyfriend's license number came back as issued to to Allen S. Rollins with a listed address in the exclusive, high-rent Lincoln Park area. Using the social security number listed on his driver's license, Donegan carried out a highly illegal, but deftly skillful computer hacking maneuver, which some computer experts would have bet their stock portfolios was totally impossible. But in a matter of seconds, Allen S. Rollins's most recent income tax return appeared on Joe Donegan's home computer screen.

The rogue cop whistled softly when he saw the amount of money that this guy Rollins made last year. Checking the occupation box, Donegan read, "college professor/author." He discovered the Seth Champion pen name on the itemized business loss statement. The adventure novelist's nom de plume meant nothing to Donegan, as he had never read a novel in his entire adult life, but this additional occupation did explain where most of his money came from. So Doctor Novak had a well-to-do boyfriend. But Joe Donegan could tell that there was a great deal more to this Allen Rollins than the "college professor/author" dual occupation listed on the income tax return.

For the next several hours, Donegan tracked Rollins through a number of databases until he had a complete dossier on the ex–Special Forces sniper. Perhaps this information would come in handy later when he made his move against Senator Walter Johnson. One thing that Donegan recognized following his confrontation with Cole and Rollins back at Gibson's Steak House, the next time the two of them came face to face, one of them would have to die.

Solomon Randolph had been spending his evenings at Randy's Roost. He often remained on the premises until closing time and had been known to mingle with a handful of regulars, who told him stories about his father. Stories that his mother had managed to conceal from him for most of Solomon's life.

To the background of soft jazz being played by the disc jockey, Solomon sipped whiskey and soda as he listened to legendary tales of the exploits of William S. "Dollar Bill" Randolph. On occasion, while the young man absorbed more of his father's lifelong involvement with the criminal element, he drank himself into a stupor.

Once, when he'd gotten himself in this state, he drove the mile-and-a-half distance in his red BMW from the Roost to the Jackson Park Highlands mansion where he lived with his mother and was attended by the ever-present butler Jamison. The next morning, or actually early afternoon, when he came downstairs in a badly hungover state, his mother was waiting for him in the dining room.

"I want to talk to you, Solomon," Sharon Powell Randolph said in her most "disapproving parent" tone.

"Maybe later," he mumbled, heading for the kitchen to have the cook prepare soft-scrambled eggs and dry wheat toast for him.

Standing up and adopting her most enraged posture, his mother said, "I will not be put off by a drunken manchild, who is ruining his life and embarrassing me with his antics!"

Solomon stopped and turned around to stare at his mother. The look that he gave her was of such murderous intensity that she was frightened into a pale, trembling state.

"Be careful how you address me, Mother," he said with measured menace, "because I am every ounce my father's son and will never let you control me as you did him. I'd rather see you dead first."

Leaving his stunned mother alone in the dining room, Solomon continued on to the kitchen. But he had caused a definite shift in the balance of power in the Randolph household.

Solomon did slow his drinking to an extent as the stories being related at Randy's Roost revealed that Dollar Bill was never out of control. At least not while he had an operation in progress. Now Solomon had such an operation of his own.

As the Randy's Roost night bartender announced last call on this February night, Solomon disengaged himself from the group of old-time drinkers he had been sitting with in a back booth. He had consumed enough liquor to make him decide to sleep on the cot in the office overnight and go home for a change of clothes in the morning. In that way he wouldn't be forced to creep around attempting to avoid his mother and Jamison. In fact, one of his longer-range plans was to eliminate the troublesome Sharon Powell Randolph and her constant shadow butler from his life.

Leaving closing-up chores to the bartender, Solomon climbed the stairs to the office with slow deliberation. Locking the door securely behind him, he slumped into a chair and turned on the desktop PC. A moment later a profile of Alderman Phillip "Skip" Murphy appeared on the screen. The biography was less than a page long, as the city councilman had hired a public relations firm to obscure some of the more sordid episodes of his public life, while Murphy pursued his drug decriminalization program.

Solomon was aware that Skip Murphy also had another agenda, which went far beyond the current controversial issue he was championing. An agenda that involved murder. Joe Donegan had disclosed the details of the assassination plot Murphy had laid out in the dark, cold Soldier Field parking lot. There was little that Solomon would be able to do to help the crooked cop carry out the deed, but later, with Randolph's assistance, Donegan was going to squeeze a great deal of cash out of the aspiring congressman. And the price of blackmail would not be based solely on the conspiracy surrounding Walter Johnson's death, but also the death of a barmaid named Sophia Novak years ago. A crime that Solomon's father had told him about, in which Joe Donegan was an accomplice along with Skip Murphy.

Solomon Randolph continued to stare at the alderman's image on the computer screen. The bearded politician had assumed a statesmanlike pose and now cut quite an impressive figure. With the right backing and the requisite funding, Murphy would be a shoo-in for the vacated congressman's seat, once Walter Johnson met his demise. However, Solomon saw Skip Murphy as representing a far more lucrative proposition than that of a simple blackmail victim. In a frantically heated race for the murdered congressman's seat, Skip Murphy would undoubtedly be the front-runner, because of all the recent publicity he'd been receiving. But Solomon could anticipate the field of candidates becoming quite extensive. And for the right price from the next in line for the congressional post, Randolph and Donegan were prepared to betray Murphy and his checkered past. But only, the still tipsy Solomon Randolph thought, for the right price.

Eurydice Vaughn screamed, and to keep her from alarming the neighbors, Cole covered her mouth with his own. Her exquisitely shaped legs were wrapped tightly around his waist and he continuously thrust himself inside her with slow, intense strokes that had already succeeded in making her climax three times. Despite Cole forcing her to slow the pace of her usual frantic lovemaking, she had attempted to speed up and even take control. This he would not allow, making it necessary for him to dominate her.

Had there been a voyeur with a stopwatch timing them, one hour and seventeen minutes had passed before they reached the final point of mutual sexual release and he pulled himself out of her. Rolling over on his back beside her in the pitch-black bedroom, Cole listened to the rhythm of her breathing return to normal. He was aware that the passion that they had just shared with such intensity was quite satisfying. But there had been no affection present. In fact, he felt a lingering animosity toward this woman.

"Larry," she said in the dark, "will you stay with me tonight?"

"No, Eurydice. I have an early day tomorrow, so I'll have to be going. Would you turn the light on?"

She made no immediate move to grant his request, but remained silent and motionless in the dark. Then there was a sharp click and the table lamp on her side of the bed snapped on.

She wore a sheer negligee when she walked him to her apartment door a short time later. Despite the intimacy they had shared only a short time ago, there was a marked formality about their parting. Before leaving, he took her in his arms and kissed her gently on the lips.

"I'll call you," were his parting words before he walked off down the corridor.

Eurydice closed her apartment door and once more shut off the lights, plunging the room back into pitch-blackness. From the darkness, she said, "I'm certain you will, Mister Larry Cole, Senior."

32

FEBRUARY 6, 2004
10:18 A.M.

Eurydice was in her office at the National Science and Space Museum when the call from Alderman Skip Murphy came in. This current office was smaller and a great deal more austere than had been the case with her previous accommodations when she had been the curator seven years ago. But it was quite comfortable with wall-to-wall carpeting, new furniture, and vintage photographs of the museum lining the walls. One such black-and-white picture was of the museum's founder Ezra Rotheimer and his entire family, which was taken circa 1901. Everyone in the photo was white with the exception of a muscular black man at the end of the last row. Although this picture had been taken over one hundred years ago, the resemblance between the black man, posing with the Rotheimers, and Larry Cole was extraordinary.

She was staring at this photo when her cell phone rang.

"Good morning, Ms. Vaughn," Murphy said, expansively. "And how are you today?"

Resorting to her cold outward professional manner, she responded, "I am quite well, Alderman Murphy."

When she didn't say anything more, he said, "So how are things going between you and Chief Cole?"

"Is my personal life a topic for discussion on an open line?"

"I can assure you that this line is quite secure. I had an expert in such matters take care of it."

"Someone from the Chicago Police Department?"

Murphy didn't answer her question. "Actually, I wasn't asking for details about your private life, as it pertains to Larry Cole, Eurydice. I simply wanted to know if you've been able to discover his thoughts on my drug decriminalization proposal."

Eurydice's icy façade dropped a degree or two. "As soon as the opportunity presents itself I will surreptitiously raise the issue with him. However, I think we should get a couple of things straight about my relationship with you and Larry Cole. First, although you are compensating me for the information you want me to provide, I am not what you would refer to as a 'hired hand.' Second, when I obtain that information I will contact you, but I will not be rushed."

"I wouldn't dream of rushing you, but I would like to know Cole's stance on the issue as soon as possible."

"That will be done, Alderman Murphy," she said, acidly. "As soon as I deem it possible. Good-bye."

Skip Murphy was currently the chairman of the Chicago City Council Commerce Committee. As such, he had an office and a staff of six, which was charged with council oversight on matters concerning the issuance or revocation of city licenses. By municipal ordinance this oversight was arbitrary, because Murphy's committee could exercise discretion in selecting which licenses it wished to examine or investigate. This meant that the Commerce Committee could do as little or as much work as it wanted to do. Since Murphy had been appointed chairman, the committee had handled a fair share of marginally important matters. Of course, Murphy only selected high profile cases referred for action from the police department. Such cases brought with them a degree of patented newsworthiness. After all, Skip Murphy was running for office, even though at this point he was doing so unofficially.

The alderman leaned back in the desk chair of the glass-enclosed "chairman's" cubicle in the offices of the Commerce Committee. He had set everything in motion and now it was time to reap the benefits. He would have to make sure that he had an airtight alibi for the time Congressman Walter Johnson met his unexpected death. The memory of Cole and Silvestri confronting him at City Hall over a decade ago, after the disappearance of Sophie Novak, still haunted Murphy.

The congressional aspirant would also have to be prepared to step in, after an appropriate period of mourning, and convince the electorate that he was the right candidate for the vacated seat.

Murphy had no reservations about engaging in murder in order to further his political career. Although he had only done it once before, when he was challenged by the Reverend Harrison Jones, he was now quite comfortable with the concept of assassination. In fact, Murphy had come to the realization, during the long years of his career, that death, as long as it wasn't your own, could be quite helpful in opening up opportunities for advancement up the political ladder.

Yes, Murphy thought, politics and murder went hand in hand. But first the deed would have to be done. The alderman glanced at the wall clock. It was almost 11:00 A.M.

The taxicab pulled up in front of the North State Parkway Medical Center and Congressman Walter Johnson paid the driver before getting out. It took him some time to extricate his aged arthritic frame from the backseat and he vehemently discouraged the assistance offered by the taxi driver. Finally, leaning heavily on an ebony cane, the congressman stood on the windswept street and looked at the modernistic gray stone and glass structure in which his new physician's offices were located.

Walter Johnson was seventy-seven years old and had lived a life as interesting as any six people who had managed to achieve octogenarian status. He was born in a small town outside of Jackson, Mississippi in 1927 and had spent his first sixteen years of life in a below-poverty-level existence. His

father was a sharecropper, who sired sixteen children primarily
to use as a work force to help him eke out a living on a cotton
plantation. Then the Second World War came along and swept
Walt Johnson out of the cotton fields and onto the battlefields
of Europe.

The future United States congressman fought in France,
Belgium, and finally Germany. He returned to the United States
in 1945 wearing a second lieutenant's bar after receiving a bat-
tlefield commission during the Battle of the Bulge. However,
he had made up his mind never to return to the South. In 1946,
although he had barely reached his nineteenth birthday, he had
already set a number of goals for himself.

The first thing Lieutenant Walter Johnson realized that he
had to do was establish a professional work history. The only
background that he possessed up to that point was that of an
itinerant farmer and a soldier. All that the United States Army
had taught him to do was kill people. But he had achieved a
certain degree of status in the military by nature of the battle-
field commission he had received. He also realized that his
options for advancement were limited due to the post-war
American society being severely segregated. After carefully examining all of his options, Walter Johnson opted to remain in
the army.

In 1948 President Harry S. Truman desegregated the United
States military, which made life marginally better for then First
Lieutenant Johnson. At the time he was assigned as a mess
officer at Fort Benning, Georgia, where he was denied admittance to the officers' club even after Truman's edict went into
effect. But despite his duties encompassing little more than
overseeing the activities of a few cooks, Johnson was still mak-

ing plans for a successful future. To that end he enrolled at a local "colored" college and began studying for a degree in political science.

By the time the Korean War broke out, the future United States congressman had been promoted to captain and assigned to a combat artillery unit. Before the war ended in 1953, Johnson attained the rank of major. For the next fifteen years, Walter Johnson remained at the same rank, as he was shuffled from duty station to duty station around the world. A couple of times during his unspectacular career, he received substandard evaluations from superior officers, who judged him primarily on the color of his skin as opposed to his professional competence. Finally, he was promoted to lieutenant colonel by a somewhat dismayed promotion board, which remarked in writing that an officer of Walter Johnson's qualifications should have been promoted years ago. This was true, because this particular lieutenant colonel of African-American descent had earned a Ph.D. in political science from Georgetown University and a law degree from the University of Washington.

Colonel Johnson's final duty assignment was as the military liaison officer to the Senate Armed Services Committee. He impressed a number of influential committee members, because he was not only smart but also had learned during a lifetime of enduring oppression to be politically savvy. As the Vietnam War escalated, Walter Johnson moved on to the next phase of his plan for a successful life. Retiring from the army after twenty-four years of service, he took a position as a senior aide with the same Armed Services Committee for which he had been the military liaison. Things progressed very fast for him after that.

During the next thirty-five years, Walter Johnson not only learned to play the game of politics American style, but also became one of its most skilled practitioners. But he was very unlike men like Phillip "Skip" Murphy or Sherman Ellison Edwards. And although the senior congressman from the State of Illinois was said to be capable of charming Saint Peter or cheating the devil, never once did he cause intentional harm to anyone or personally profit from any deal.

Along the way Johnson married and sired two offspring. His wife died when his children—a boy and a girl—were six and four years of age, respectively. Being a father was the only failure that Walter Johnson had ever experienced in his life. Perhaps the congressman spent too much time playing the political game or didn't possess the basic skills to be a single parent in the last half of the twentieth century, because both of his children turned out badly.

His son, Rodney James Johnson, began getting into minor scrapes with the law at an early age and, two weeks following his seventeenth birthday, was arrested for possession of a loaded handgun and three ounces of heroin. The congressman had interceded on his son's behalf, but Rodney was far from grateful. One arrest followed another until a broken-hearted Walter Johnson stood in a courtroom and watched his son be sentenced to twenty years in prison for armed robbery.

Although his daughter, Yolanda Marie Johnson, did not become a criminal, the way that she led her life was just as embarrassing to the congressman as his son's had been. She became pregnant in her sophomore year of high school and, following a legal abortion, she was again with child less than six months later. She never did obtain a high school diploma and currently had four children, all of which had been born out of wedlock. She was currently living in a ghetto apartment with a man who was not the father of any of her children. The congressman gave her money from time to time and visited his grandkids as often as possible. But it was obvious that his progeny had taken nothing from the life of sacrifice and achievement that he had lived in order to reach his current station.

However, if Walter Johnson did not have much of a family, he did have his political career. A career to which he planned to devote every available ounce of his energy as long as he lived.

The congressman reached the door of Doctor Novak's office in the North State Parkway Medical Center. He paused before entering. He hated doctors. When he joined the army back in '44, he had come close to fainting the first time he saw a hypodermic needle. His bouts with cancer, diabetes, and emphysema had forced him to spend long periods in hospitals, where he was punctured, poked, and prodded by a number of physicians. Then, when the congressman finally found a pill pusher he was comfortable with, Dr. Mark Kirchner had retired.

It had taken some doing for Walter Johnson to be convinced to entrust his health and his life to this Dr. Stella Novak. Despite his high elective office, the congressman was fairly old-fashioned in some of his beliefs, which made it difficult for him to accept a female physician. Particularly one who was not a native-born American. But Dr. Kirchner had been quite convincing, so here Johnson was at Dr. Novak's office for his first appointment. He reached out with the hand opposite the cane and opened the door.

The young woman behind the reception desk was a perky young thing in a clinging white sweater, which accentuated all of her curves. Congressman Johnson was indeed old and a bit infirm, but he wasn't dead yet.

"Good morning, young lady. I have an eleven o'clock appointment with Doctor Stella Novak."

The receptionist smiled. "Yes, Congressman Johnson. She's expecting you."

Johnson smiled back. "That sounds ominous."

"Doctor Novak will be right with you, sir. Please have a seat."

Johnson was turning to cross the reception area when the outer door opened and a disheveled, mean-looking white man came in. The congressman initially thought that the new arrival was a homeless person, but he didn't appear to have been living out on the street. Then a lifetime of evaluating people and coming to an instant determination as to whether they were friend or foe revealed to Congressman Walter Johnson that this unkempt man was a cop.

Before going to the reception station, the cop stopped and stared at Johnson. The congressman unflinchingly returned his gaze. When the cop turned away, Johnson sat down.

He heard the cop say, "I need to see Doctor Novak right away."

"But you don't have an appointment, Sergeant Donegan," the receptionist said.

"This is an emergency. Now call her and tell her I'm here." The last came out in harsh tones bordering on a threat and the young receptionist became visibly uncomfortable.

"Please take a seat and I'll let the doctor know you're here."

"You do just that, sweetheart," he said, turning away and once more making eye contact with Walter Johnson. Then he took a seat on the far end of a row of chairs opposite the congressman. As the receptionist picked up her telephone, the two men settled in to wait.

Stella Novak checked the congressman's blood pressure, heart rate, lung function, eyes, ears, and throat. She wasn't happy with a number of things that she found, but there was nothing unexpected. All of her new patient's ailments had been discovered and previously treated by Dr. Kirchner.

"I need to have some lab work done, Congressman Johnson," Stella said, as she made notes on the new medical file she had opened on him.

She noticed his shoulders sag at the prospects of what was in store. Stepping forward, she placed her hand on his arm. "I'm going to make sure that this goes as easy for you as is medically possible, Congressman. I promise that you will experience a minimal amount of discomfort."

Johnson looked at his new doctor. Something changed in his face, which she could only characterize as the beginnings of trust. His manner toward her softened, as he said, "I appreciate your concern, Doctor, and please call me Walter."

Stella started to refuse the first-name familiarity, but quickly reconsidered. This elderly man with the stately bearing needed a doctor he could not only trust, but also be comfortable with. Actually, he reminded her of her grandfather, who had fought in World War II. So for once she relaxed her rigid standards and said, "Very well, Walter it is. And you may call me Stella."

She escorted him to the lab on the floor above the suite of offices she occupied with Dr. Ramone. Once there, she personally extracted six ccs of blood before turning him over to lab personnel for other tests. As she was leaving, he said, "That was the most painless bloodletting that I've ever experienced, Stella."

She smiled at him and responded, "Thank you, Walter."

But once she exited the lab and was on the way back to her office, all of her humor drained away. Entering her waiting room and failing to find Sergeant Donegan there, she snapped at the receptionist, "Where is he?"

"I put him in examining room C."

With long purposeful strides, Stella walked rapidly to the examining room and flung open the door. The room was equipped with an examining table, locked medical supply cabinet, sink, desk, computer terminal, and desk chair. There were charts adorning the walls displaying the anatomy of the human body and the negative effects of untreated diabetes and high blood pressure. The small area was windowless and it was now also empty. Sergeant Joe Donegan was not there.

Stella returned to the reception area.

"You did say he was in C, didn't you?" There was an angry edge in the doctor's voice.

The receptionist looked anxiously at her boss and said a contrite, "I escorted him there myself, Doctor."

Stella forced herself to calm down. It wasn't this young woman's fault that the strange policeman had shown up without

an appointment and demanded to see her. Stella had reserved
all of the time until two o'clock that afternoon for the congressman. If Donegan had some form of nonemergency medical
problem, then he would just have to make an appointment to
see her just like everyone else. However, if he had an immediate emergency she would have to make time for him, because
Dr. Ramone was on vacation.

"Okay," she said to the receptionist, "I'm going back to my
office. If you see him wandering around, call me immediately."

A short time later, the doctor was going through some routine correspondence. She was unable to force Joe Donegan out
of her mind. Getting up, she returned to examining room C. It
was still empty. She was about to return to her office when
another thought occurred to her. She went to cubicle A, where
she had examined Congressman Johnson earlier. While he was
having his lab work done, he'd left his overcoat, hat, and suit
jacket on the coat rack in the examining room. Opening the
door, she found everything was apparently the same as it had
been when they left. She was about to leave when she noticed
a minor discrepancy. Walter Johnson's medical file was lying
open on the desk and Stella was almost certain that she had
closed it. She did realize that at the time she'd been more concerned about the welfare of her patient than the notes that she
was making for his treatment.

Crossing the examining area, she looked down at the open
file. She closed it and then opened it again attempting to remember if it had indeed been shut. The answer eluded her.
Then she came to the damning realization that someone had
been in examining room A since she left to escort Congressman
Johnson to the lab. This was because the medical computer on

top the desk had been shut off. This was something that she and her associate Dr. Ramone never did, except at the end of the day. So someone had indeed been in here and Stella Novak had a pretty good idea who it was.

33

FEBRUARY 6, 2004
1:39 P.M.

Chief Larry Cole left his office at police headquarters and descended two levels. After traversing a carpeted corridor on the east side of the building, he entered through a set of double glass doors bearing the black printed legend, "Internal Affairs Division." There was a plainclothes detective at the front desk and Cole requested to see the assistant deputy superintendent in charge.

Recognizing Cole, the IAD cop said, "Right away, Chief." The cop made a call on a police auxiliary phone and within less than a minute, Cole entered a corner office with windows overlooking the DeLaSalle Institute on Thirty-fifth Street.

Mary Anne Percy was the head of the internal investigating arm of the CPD. A light-complexioned black woman with short curly hair, Assistant Deputy Superintendent Percy was a few years older than Cole, but had a couple of years less seniority. She possessed advanced degrees in public administration and ethics and had spent a short time as a college professor at the University of Illinois at Chicago campus. She had not set out to become a law enforcement officer, but was aware very early on in her college teaching career that she wanted more from life than the world of academia had to offer. She took the Chicago Police Department entrance exam on a dare, but the moment she entered her first police car and switched on the emergency lights and siren, she knew that she had found her true profession.

Mary Anne Percy and Larry Cole had worked together in the past. In fact, she had been a detective on Cole's staff when he was the commander of Area One. She'd been slightly injured on the night Steven Zalkin blew up the Area One Police Center in April 1990. The now-dead millionaire had detonated a number of explosive devices inside the police station in retaliation for Cole and Blackie Silvestri's attempts to arrest him in the past. Mary Anne Percy had not requested the Internal Affairs post, but the superintendent at the time considered her the perfect candidate for the job. This was because she was smart, well educated, and held herself and all of her professional colleagues to the highest standards of conduct.

Assignment to the Internal Affairs Division was not something that most police officers desired. IAD investigators were usually viewed by their fellow cops with some degree of disdain. But the unit performed a very necessary function and had kept the Chicago Police Department virtually corruption free with a few rare exceptions.

Cole had come to Assistant Deputy Superintendent Mary Anne Percy's office to discuss one of those exceptions.

After exchanging a few short pleasantries, they got down to cases.

"Sergeant Donegan has been assigned to our computerized records section," Percy was saying. "However, he doesn't have access to any of our current cases that are under investigation."

"Watch him carefully, Mary," Cole said. "He's a real wizard with computers."

"Donegan's being closely monitored, Larry. We have him in what we call File thirteen status."

"File thirteen?" Cole said. "Isn't that the circular file where we dispose of all unnecessary reports?"

Affixing the chief of detectives with a knowing gaze, she responded, "And that is what Sergeant Donegan is doing. Under the direct supervision of a lieutenant and while continuously flanked by two investigators, whom I trust implicitly, Donegan has been assigned to purge old files from our central computer system. Needless to say, we have enough work to keep him busy for quite awhile."

"How has be behaved since coming to work here?"

The ADS shrugged. "He is as strange in person as the rumors are about him that preceded his arrival. He dresses like a bum and Jack Hardy, his section lieutenant, was forced to have a little talk with him about his personal hygiene. Other than that, he is prompt and does what he is told. We don't allow him into the office prior to his regular duty hours, nor can he remain after the tour concludes. He's sullen and doesn't say much, but he hasn't caused any problems. Of course, Donegan walking around the office with all those guns strapped on makes him look odd enough as it is."

"Is he working today?" Cole asked.

"I'm pretty sure that I saw him earlier," she said, reaching for the telephone on her desk and punching a single digit on the keypad. "Wanda, have Lieutenant Hardy step in here if he's not too busy."

A few minutes later there was a knock on the door and a

tall cop with extremely broad shoulders came into the office. "How's it going, Chief?" he said to Cole.

"Good, Jack," Cole responded. "How's your knee?"

"When it gets cold it gives me fits, but it also reminds me to thank God that the bullet didn't hit me in the head." Twelve years ago Cole had investigated the attempted murder of Jack Hardy and his partner during a domestic incident. A demented husband had taken his wife and children hostage in a South Side apartment building. Armed with a German luger pistol, the man fired a shot at his wife as she escaped out the front door, while a hostage negotiator attempted to keep him occupied. Hardy rushed into the house and caught a bullet in his left kneecap before he and his partner were forced to kill the gun-wielding spouse.

"Is Sergeant Donegan on duty?" the ADS asked the lieutenant.

"He worked this morning, boss," Hardy responded. "But he requested the afternoon off, so he could see his doctor."

"Is there something wrong with Donegan?" Cole asked.

Hardy grinned. "There's a bunch of stuff wrong with the Lone Stranger, Chief. But it's all up here." He tapped the side of his head.

Cole and Percy smiled. When Lieutenant Hardy was gone, Cole said, "I'm here to make a formal request, Mary."

"Anything that you need, Larry."

"I want to open a Confidential Investigation on Donegan." Confidential Investigations were conducted when malfeasance or corruption involving Chicago police officers was suspected. Official approval had to be given to conduct such investigations by the Assistant Deputy Superintendent of the IAD and they were carried out in a covert fashion using wiretaps and covert surveillance.

"You'll have to have solid grounds."

"I do," Cole said. "He's involved with the son of the late Dollar Bill Randolph, who was a notorious South Side gambler and all-around crook. The kid is named Solomon and there have been rumors out on the street that he's into a number of illegal operations, which he runs out of a tavern called Randy's Roost. Blackie Silvestri and Manny Sherlock from my staff went to the tavern to talk to Randolph and while they were there Donegan showed up.

"Now the reason Blackie and Manny wanted to interview Randolph was because his car was given a couple of traffic citations near the location of a homicide down on the Magnificent Mile. There's a lot more to Randolph and Donegan's relationship than meets the eye. We managed to get Donegan out of the Intelligence Unit computer room, but until we can investigate him officially there's no way that the department will ever be rid of him."

Cole didn't see the need to tell Mary Anne Percy about Donegan following Stella Novak and Allen Rollins to Gibson's Steak House.

She asked, "Who will conduct the investigation?"

"My staff. Actually, we've been after Donegan for a long time. If things fall right, this time we'll nail him."

"I'll get the paperwork started and you'll have written authorization before the end of the day."

The red-and-yellow taxi pulled up in front of the North State Parkway Medical Center. The driver was a Nigerian-born imigrant, who drove a taxi full-time along with working in a bakery three nights a week. He was putting himself through vocational school to become a master tailor. His plan was to someday open up a tailor shop in the economically burgeoning South Loop area. He had six months to go before he could qualify for an apprentice license. Then he would go to work for an established tailor who had come from his village in Africa. Until then he would continue to drive a hack and bake bread rolls in the wee small hours of the morning.

The Nigerian was waiting for a pick-up who wanted to be taken to the New Brownsville Homes on South Wabash. This made the taxi driver nervous, despite the area having been miraculously transformed from a gang-infested, high-rise-project jungle into an upper-middle-class, mixed-race enclave in the past five years. In the driver's estimation, the neighborhood was still unsafe and, if the city's taxi ordinance had not forbidden him from refusing the fare, he would never venture into the New Brownsville area at all.

The door to the medical center opened and an elderly black man, who walked slowly with the aid of a cane, and a slender blond woman wearing a white lab coat, came out. Seated in the relative warmth of his taxi, the Nigerian remarked to himself that the white woman was going to catch her death of cold. Then the cab driver recognized who the black man was. It was Walter Johnson, the congressman.

Jumping out of the taxi, he rushed around to help the couple over to his cab.

Walter Johnson was one of the first residents to move into the New Brownsville Homes. The modern, but somewhat austere, brick townhouses were the centerpiece in the revitalization of a neighborhood, which had been victimized by racism, poverty, and governmental neglect for decades. It was Congressman Johnson himself who had spearheaded the rejuvenation, beginning with the demolition of the monstrous sixteen-story housing developments along the State Street corridor. Developments that were the breeding grounds for gang crime and drugs.

Although Brownsville had changed remarkably, it was still far from being the slice of urban, middle-class suburbia that its developers had planned. It was indeed new and modern, but a couple of units in each of the six cul-de-sac complexes were boarded up due to a fire in one case and vandalism following a burglary in another. Charges had been made that the contractor on the initial construction project had used substandard materials and shoddy workmanship. Also, signs of urban blight were evident with derelict cars, broken glass, and excessive garbage in evidence.

But the tenants, led by their congressman, were combating these problems head on and planned to force the contractor to correct any problems with the construction, have undesirable tenants evicted, and demand that the city keep the area clean. And the congressman usually did more than his fair share for his constituents, but this would not be the case today.

Dr. Novak had done all that she could to ease the burden of the congressman's physical; however, it had still taken a toll on the seventy-seven-year-old man. Despite the talkative Nigerian cab driver's attempts to engage the political celebrity in conversation, Johnson had fallen asleep soon after he'd gotten settled in the backseat. When they arrived at the New Brownsville Homes complex, the Nigerian cab driver found it difficult waking the congressman up. Then, unlike what had been the case when Johnson had arrived at the North State Parkway

Medical Center, he permitted the driver to help him into his townhouse.

In the vestibule, the congressman paid the driver, gave him a generous tip, and thanked him for the assistance. Returning to his cab, the Nigerian took a look around the area. Despite the relative newness of all of the buildings, it was not the type of place he would choose to live. He looked at the cars parked near the congressman's residence. There were a couple of mid-sized late-model vehicles, a filthy blue piece of junk, and an abandoned fifteen-year-old Cadillac. Diversity was one thing, the driver mused, but this was ridiculous. The Nigerian vowed that when he obtained his master tailor's license, he would move as close to the Magnificent Mile of North Michigan Avenue as he could afford.

The dirty blue car the Nigerian cab driver had observed belonged to Joe Donegan. He had been waiting for the congressman to return from Stella's office. The manner in which he planned to dispose of Johnson came to him when he slipped into the cubicle where Johnson's clothes were hanging after Stella escorted her prize patient to the lab. The crooked cop knew of these overpriced ghetto dumps called the New Brownsville Homes. When he checked Johnson's wallet and discovered his address, Donegan had been surprised. But delightedly so.

Now that the driver of the red-and-yellow taxi had dropped the congressman off, it was time for Donegan to go to work. Opening a silver case on the front seat beside him, he removed a single Thermite grenade and placed it in his overcoat pocket. Then he got out of the dirty blue car and walked toward Congressman Johnson's townhouse.

34

It was one of those days when the endless meetings, tons of paperwork, and constant decision making that came with being the chief of detectives became a bit too much for Larry Cole to take in stride. Noticing that his desk's in basket was still full, he decided that he'd had enough work for today. Shutting off the lights and locking the door, he stopped by Blackie's office on his way out of the building.

"I'm out of here, Blackie," Cole said. "You're in charge."

Blackie checked the time on his desk clock. "It's kind of early for you to be going home, boss."

"I'm not going home. Kate Ford is singing at Sandy's Jazz Club tonight. I plan to catch her first set. See you tomorrow."

Eurydice Vaughn pulled her red Miata roadster over in front of the Michigan Avenue entrance of police headquarters. It was snowing heavily and a four- to six-inch accumulation was expected. She stared through the windshield at the front of the building. She was considering going inside and paying a visit to Larry Cole's office. She knew that he didn't like unannounced guests, but she was rapidly tiring of the game she was playing against him for Skip Murphy. Perhaps if she came right out and asked Cole how he felt about the drug decriminalization issue, he would tell her. Then she could put the subterfuge behind them and attempt to proceed normally with their relationship.

She drove around the block to a parking lot on the Wabash Avenue side of the building. There was a key-card operated gate across the entrance to the lot. This meant that she would have to find parking on the street. She was about to do just that when a black Mercury exited the lot onto Thirty-fifth Street. Eurydice only caught a glimpse of the driver's profile, but that was all she needed. It was Larry Cole. She wondered where he was going. With the falling snow acting as effective cover, she followed him.

The New Sandy's Jazz Club on Fifty-third Street in Hyde Park had been rebuilt from the rubble of the old club. That building had been destroyed by a criminally minded scientific genius named Jonathan Gault. Larry Cole had been responsible for Gault's final demise.

The new building was nearly a replica of the former structure and the interior was furnished along the lines of a Bourbon Street blues joint in New Orleans. There was a forty-foot-long, highly varnished hardwood bar, which stretched the complete length of one wall. The bar had been salvaged intact from the original club. The dining area consisted of tables set for four with marble tops and ornate wrought iron legs. The bill of fare at the New Sandy's consisted of mostly soul food ranging from spicy hot gumbo and chili to fried chicken and pork chops, which were so good a number of patrons came to the club for these dishes alone. However, the focus of everything in the New Sandy's Jazz Club was the stage.

Constructed at the back of the main room, the stage was

set four feet above floor level and was large enough to accommodate a twenty-piece orchestra. Generally, no more than a four- or five-piece band was playing and the club featured live entertainment every night of the week except Sunday when the club was closed.

The sole owner of the New Sandy's Jazz Club was Madam Sandra Devereaux, who was a very attractive, light-complexioned black woman of indeterminate age. Popular with her customers, Sandy, as she was called, was not only a gracious hostess, but also a talented singer in her own right. There was also something else about Madam Devereaux, which many of her patrons were aware of. She was a skilled Voodooienne, which was a practitioner of the religious art of voodoo. Some of her customers dismissed voodoo as no more than hackneyed superstition, but a greater number not only respected Sandy, but also feared her. This was because the jazz club owner had the reputed ability to help her friends, as well as fix her enemies.

The cocktail hour was in full swing when Madam Devereaux appeared on the balcony outside her office above the stage. She wore a full-length burgundy velvet dress and diamonds that sparkled brilliantly from her ears, throat, and wrists. She was a full-figured woman, who exuded sensuality with each graceful move. There was a slight hitch in her walk now, due to broken legs she had sustained when Jonathan Gault destroyed her former club. Now Sandy, like her new place, was nearly as good as new.

She came down the steps to the main floor and began mingling with the early-evening crowd. Most of the customers at both the bar and at the marble-topped tables knew the proprietress and her reputation as a bar owner and a high priestess of the dark arts. Nevertheless she was very popular. She covered the room with consummate skill greeting many and once telling the bartender to stop serving a Hyde Park optometrist, who'd had too much to drink. Then she instructed the maitre'd to call the eye doctor a taxi and pour him into it.

Sandy had just finished her rounds when her star vocalist of the evening arrived. Kate Ford was a nicely built, five-foot-two-inch blond woman, who had the pretty features of a mischievous pixie, the curious mind of a successful investigative journalist, and a voice that many who had heard her sing compared to Anita Baker, Chante' Moore, and Gloria Lynn.

"Katie, honey," Sandy said, embracing the smaller woman. "You going to sing pretty for us tonight?"

With a staged New Orleans' accent nearly as pronounced as Madam Devereaux's, Kate responded, "I'll have this dump rocking from the basement to the roof, Sandy."

"You'd better, girl. I reserved the table you wanted right down in front," Sandy said. "Who is your special guest?"

Kate looked away and her cheeks colored slightly. "Larry Cole."

Sandy's face split in a broad grin. "I'd say you got a thing for that big handsome policeman, Katie."

The vocalist shrugged. "We're just friends. At least for the time being."

"You'll work it out. Now you go on back and freshen up before your set. I'll greet Mister Cole when he comes in."

Back in her dressing room behind the stage, Kate Ford, who was dressed in a simple sleeveless black dress accented by a single strand of white pearls around her neck, began applying makeup. She felt the soft flutter of butterflies in her stomach.

She was not an entertainer by trade, but a Pulitzer Prize–winning investigative journalist. The written word was her life, but being able to exercise her talent as a jazz vocalist was as important to her as any of the scandals she had uncovered in the four well-received non-fiction books she had published.

After finishing with her face, she opened a bottle of Evian water and took a sip. She was looking forward to appearing on the jazz club stage and, in particular, singing for Larry Cole. Sandy had been quite right; Kate had a serious crush on the handsome cop. She even had a song that she planned to dedicate to him tonight, although she would not announce the dedication publicly. It was "Love Me or Let Me be Lonely." She wondered if Cole would get the point.

The object of Kate Ford's amorous intentions found a parking place on Fifty-third Street, a block from Sandy's, and trudged back through the accumulating snow. He was just about to enter the club when a red Miata roadster drove past. Cole paid no attention to this car, as it kept going farther down Fifty-third Street.

After an effusive greeting from Sandra Devereaux, which included a lusty hug that transmitted quite accurately to the cop that she had nothing on beneath that clinging velvet dress she was wearing, he was escorted to a table right in front of the stage. After he was served a whiskey and soda, Cole sat back to relax, forget about police work for a while, and enjoy the show.

Eurydice Vaughn easily found a parking place for her diminutive roadster on a side street and returned to the jazz club. She found a seat at the end of the bar and carefully scanned the interior for

Larry Cole. Due to the dense crowd in the bar, she was unable to locate Cole for a full five minutes. By the time that she did find him seated alone at a table in front of the stage, two men had offered to buy her drinks. She declined the offers with enough coldness to discourage further advances and ordered a wine spritzer from the bartender. Although a loud social commotion was going on around her, Eurydice possessed such a high degree of concentration that she was capable of easily eliminating the surrounding distractions. From her position she caught glimpses of Cole, and the thing that struck her as unusual was that he appeared to be totally relaxed.

From the instant that she first set eyes on him on that night some years ago when he ran across a bridge onto Haunted Island behind the National Science and Space Museum, Cole had always exuded a measure of controlled tension. Even when he was making passionate love to her, he held a part of himself back. It was as if he were always looking over his shoulder or around the next corner for some unexpected danger. Now, here in the jazz club, this was not the case and Eurydice was unable to fathom why.

She considered that part of the reason could be the ambience of this place. She was not much of an expert on such matters and had been in only a handful of bars in her life. With an analytical mind that had been developed by years of stressful study under extremely unusual conditions, she forced herself to explore additional options about her lover.

If it was not the place that was causing the alteration in Cole's manner, then it was either something or someone else. She noticed the drink on the table in front of him; however, he had barely touched it. A trio, consisting of a pianist, bass player, and drummer, took the stage and began warming up.

Before taking his seat, the middle-aged piano player walked to the edge of the stage and shook hands with the policeman. A short time later, the jazz trio began playing.

Eurydice had spied on Cole many times in the past. Occasionally, she had been quite fascinated by watching him from some remote location while he went about the daily activities of his life. But that was before she had been hospitalized in an institution for the criminally insane. Dr. Mitchell Vargas, her psychiatrist, made her see that such nefarious activities were not healthy. Now that she was supposedly "cured" and living a more or less normal life, she found that reverting to her former unhealthy habit enhanced her understanding. At least it did in regards to Larry Cole.

A young blond woman in a black dress came out from behind the stage and walked over to Cole's table. Eurydice watched Cole stand up and embrace her. The contact was innocent enough, but the former head curator at the National Science and Space Museum was an exceptional observer. This revealed quite accurately that the blonde was in love with Cole. A stab of jealousy knifed through Eurydice Vaughn. She had not experienced such a negative emotion since she had been forced to share Cole with her sister Edna.

It took her a moment to regain her composure. She had kept herself under complete control and displayed no outward signs of the internal stress she was under to any of the other patrons near her. The blond woman was a rival, which Eurydice would have to deal with. She resolved not to do so using tricks or subterfuge. That meant that Eurydice and Cole would have to start fresh without the shadow of the past or her relationship with Alderman Skip Murphy looming over them.

In the crowded, noisy bar of the New Sandy's Jazz Club

on East Fifty-third Street, Eurydice Vaughn removed her cell
phone from her purse and placed a call.

Skip Murphy was in his townhouse when the telephone rang.
Against the cold of this winter day, he was fixing himself a hot
rum toddy at the bar of his den. Picking up the wall extension
behind the bar, he answered, "Hello."

"You're almost there, Skipper Boy," Sherman Ellison Edwards said.

Maintaining a casual tone, Murphy responded, "I don't
know what you're talking about, Sherm."

"I'll give it to you just like I got it off the Channel Nine
News. Congressman Walter Johnson is currently hospitalized
in critical condition at University Hospital. He is suffering from
smoke inhalation and severe burns following a fire that consumed a number of units of the Brownsville housing development. Fire Department officials and Chicago police arson
detectives are on the scene conducting an investigation into the
circumstances surrounding the blaze."

"That's terrible, Sherm, but I heard that the Brownsville
development was constructed of sub-par materials. I might even
ask you to convene a special city council police and fire subcommittee hearing on the matter." Despite his easy manner,
Murphy had gone as taut as a violin string.

"We need to start making some plans now, Skip," Edwards
was saying.

"Let me get back to you, Sherm. I'm a little tied up right
now."

After hanging up, Murphy uncharacteristically slammed his
fist down on the bar. Walter Johnson wasn't dead and it was
no telling how long he'd linger. With the current advancements

in medical science there was the remote possibility that Johnson could even pull through.

The telephone rang again.

Murphy started to snatch the instrument off its cradle, but quickly composed himself. Now was not the time to panic. After taking a deep breath, he answered.

It was Eurydice Vaughn calling. He could barely hear her, because of the raucous background noise that made it quite evident that she was in a bar. However, what she said came through loud and clear. After hanging up, he hurried to dress for the street.

35

FEBRUARY 6, 2004
6:55 P.M.

Congressman Walter Johnson opened his eyes and stared up at the hospital room ceiling. There was an oxygen mask over his face and he felt as if he were tied down, because he was unable to move. He attempted to raise his head so he could see his lower body. Suddenly there was a woman wearing a nurse's cap looming over him. The nurse was black, had a mole on her chin and, in Johnson's estimation, was marginally attractive.

"You've got to remain still, Congressman Johnson," she said, pressing his shoulders back against the pillow. Once he was again settled, she added, "I'm going to get your doctor. Now I want you to lie quietly until I get back."

He didn't need much coaxing, because he was extremely weak. He once more closed his eyes, as the world spun around him. Then Dr. Stella Novak and the nurse returned.

Stella leaned down so that her face was only inches away from his. Her eyes were bright with a mixture of fear and concern for her patient. "Walter, you've been injured in a fire. You've got some severe burns, but they're not our main concern right now. Before the ambulance could get you to the hospital you went into cardiac arrest. You also sustained lung damage due to smoke inhalation."

He attempted to speak. The first time his lips moved but no sound came out. He tried again and Stella strained to hear a halting, "But I'm still alive."

She was forced to fight back tears, as she said, "Yes, you are, Walter, and I'm going to keep you that way."

The congressman lapsed back into unconsciousness.

Judy Daniels was dressed in her glamour girl disguise, which consisted of a Cleopatra wig, heavy makeup with long false lashes, and a form fitting "After Five" black dress. In deference to the falling snow, she wore a pair of leather knee-boots. When she arrived at the University Hospital emergency room and located the four arson investigators assigned to the Brownsville development blaze, she had been forced to endure a couple of lascivious stares and a wolf whistle before she flashed her sergeant's badge. The embarrassed expressions on their faces almost made the Mistress of Disguise/High Priestess of Mayhem smile. This was not because she was flattered by the male attention, but because their reaction told her that her disguise was effective. Maintaining a severe professional manner in keeping with her position with the chief of detectives' office, she said, "I need the details concerning the fire at Congressman Johnson's residence."

They were all so eager to assist her that they began talking at once, making it impossible for her to understand them. After calming the quartet of investigators down, Judy got the full story. And it was truly amazing.

Congressman Walter Johnson was still alive due to a combination of luck, divine intervention, and the efforts of an honest cab driver, who had aspirations of becoming a master tailor.

After helping the congressman into his townhouse, the Nigerian cab driver had quickly pocketed the fare and returned to his taxi. He had driven out of the housing complex onto Indiana Avenue. He traveled a few blocks before glancing at the money that Johnson had given him. Stopped for a red light, he removed the bills from his coat pocket. There was a twenty and two tens. The fare from the North State Parkway Medical Center to the New Brownsville apartment complex came to $18.75. A five-dollar tip would have been more than adequate. The Congressman had overtipped him, which seldom happened to the Nigerian. But Johnson had been ill and seemed disoriented. So the overtipping had been a mistake. The cab driver made a U-turn.

When he made it back to the Brownsville complex, smoke was visibly coming from the congressman's unit. Without any regard for his personal safety, the cab driver rushed to the front door and with some difficulty kicked it open. The interior was rapidly filling up with dense smoke and there were open flames visible coming from the rear. Flames that were spreading rapidly.

The cab driver found the congressman unconscious on the

living room floor. Johnson was heavier than the Nigerian and at first he found it impossible to get the unconscious man to his feet. Then the fire spread at an alarming rate turning the poorly constructed townhouse into a raging inferno. The Nigerian came close to abandoning the congressman and for his rescue efforts received severe third-degree burns on his legs and arms. But he managed to get Walter Johnson outside before the inferno completely enveloped the townhouse to finally engulf the entire complex. Miraculously, no one else was injured in the blaze.

The cab driver was hospitalized in the same wing of University Hospital as Walter Johnson, but Judy was unable to interview either of them. The arson investigators had been able to ascertain with a fair certainty that the fire had been intentionally set. The source of the flames was an intense accelerant ignited behind the congressman's townhouse. When asked for an unofficial opinion as to what that accelerant could be, one of the investigators had gone out on a limb and told Judy, "It had to be of military origin. I would guess it was an upgraded version of napalm called Thermite."

Judy remembered the fire in which Homicide Miller, the former leader of the Gangster Disciples street gang, had perished. Although no fire-starting residue had been discovered due to the previous fire's intensity, the point of origin and the estimated temperature was contained in the investigator's report. Thermite had also been suspected in the blaze that had killed the gang leader.

After finishing with the arson investigators, Judy went in search of the congressman's doctor. Stella Novak was in the hospital employees' lounge sipping a cup of coffee when the stylishly dressed woman walked in. The young physician was certain that she had never laid eyes on this woman before. That is until Judy said in a voice that sounded oddly familiar, "How's it going, Stella?"

"I'm sorry," the doctor said, "I don't think I've had the pleasure."

Then the police sergeant opened her badge case with the indistinct photo on the identification card. When Stella realized that it was Judy Daniels behind the glamorous disguise, she was initially dumbfounded. The doctor had heard stories about the Mistress of Disguise/High Priestess of Mayhem, but this was the first time that Stella had ever seen her in action.

With Stella continuing to stare at Judy with lingering shock, the cop said, "Someone attempted to assassinate the congressman today, Stella. When they find out that they failed, another attempt might be made. I'm going to have a guard placed on him, but I need your cooperation."

"I'll be glad to assist you in any way I can, Judy." Then the doctor frowned.

"Is there something wrong?"

Stella shook her head, as if she were attempting to wake herself from a bad dream. Judy could sense that there was something troubling the doctor.

"What is it, Stella?" she pressed.

"Congressman Johnson was in my office earlier today for a physical," she explained. "While he was there, something odd occurred."

Taking a seat across from the doctor, Judy said, "Something odd, like what?"

Exactly twenty-three minutes after he hung up the telephone in his Central Station townhouse, Alderman Skip Murphy, dressed in a white turtleneck and double-breasted blue pin-stripe suit, slid onto the barstool next to Eurydice Vaughn.

"This might not be a good idea, Ms. Vaughn," he said.

Exuding a pronounced degree of icy menace, she responded, "You wanted to know Larry Cole's position on drug decriminalization. Now is your chance to ask him yourself."

The bartender came over to take Murphy's order. "I'll have the same," he said, pointing at Eurydice's barely touched glass. When they were once more alone, Murphy said, "That wasn't exactly what I had in mind."

"Don't worry, Alderman," she said, sarcastically. "I'll be with you."

Kate Ford sang a medley of five songs during her opening set to include "Don't Go Chasing Waterfalls," "Downtown," "I Wish You love," which was done as a salute to Gloria Lynn, "Fly Me to the Moon," and, finally, a soulful rendition of "Love Me or Let Me be Lonely." As she sang the final song, she made frequent eye contact with Larry Cole. He was close enough for Kate to reach down and touch him had she so desired. When the set was over, the near capacity crowd erupted in thunderous applause. Sandra Devereaux joined her on the stage.

"That was beautiful, Katie," Sandy said. "Ladies and gentlemen, the New Sandy's Jazz Club's very own blues songbird, Ms. Kate Ford. Give her another round of applause."

Kate bowed and curtsied before leaving the stage to sit with Cole. Sandy made a few brief announcements about the next set, which was scheduled to begin in twenty minutes. Then she joined the singer at Cole's table.

"You're in good voice tonight, Kate," Cole said, saluting her with his drink. "I've never heard you sing better."

Motioning for a waiter to come over and take the singer's drink order, Sandy said, "Maybe it was who was sitting out in the club tonight that made my Katie sing so good, Larry."

Cole suspected the bar owner's hidden meaning, but concealed this suspicion behind a polite smile.

When the waiter arrived, Kate ordered a glass of white wine, which Cole instructed was to go on his tab. The cop also offered to buy Sandy a drink, but she declined, explaining that she didn't plan to consume anything alcoholic until after the club closed at 2 A.M.

They made small talk for a time before the waiter returned. However, instead of a glass of white wine for the vocalist, he carried a tray on which was an ice bucket containing a bottle of champagne.

"What is this?" Sandy questioned.

The slender white man, who was wearing the red vest, black trousers, black bow tie, white shirt, and white apron of all Sandy's Jazz Club service personnel, responded, "One of Kate's fans purchased this for her, Madam Devereaux. There's a note accompanying the order."

Kate exchanged an amused look with Cole. "I'm jealous," he said, as the waiter set the tray down revealing that the wine was a very expensive magnum of Dom Perignon. "All I offered to buy you was a single glass of wine."

Then both Kate and Cole noticed that something about Sandra Devereaux had changed. In the blink of an eye the bar owner had become silent and withdrawn. When the waiter began uncorking the iced champagne, Sandy said, "What does the message say?"

Kate picked up the folded sheet of white "Sandy's" stationery from the tray. She read aloud, "Dear Ms. Ford, my companion and I enjoyed your singing immensely. Please accept this libation for you and your party as a token of our esteem. If it wouldn't be too much of an imposition, we would be honored if we could join you." Kate looked up at Cole and Sandy before staring off across the crowded room in search of this admiring fan. Unable to locate anyone familiar, she said, "How flattering."

The waiter poured Kate a few drops of the bubbly liquid. She sampled it and nodded her approval.

"Is the note signed?" Sandy asked.

"It's from an Alderman Skip Murphy," Kate said.

Larry Cole tensed. Noticing the changes in their attitudes, Kate said, "What's with you guys? You look as if I just swore in church."

Sandy leaned forward and patted the singer's hand. "Enjoy your champagne, Katie. You deserve it. But be careful, honey." With that she got up and left the table.

A bewildered Kate Ford turned to Cole. "You're not going to leave me too, are you?"

"I'm not going anywhere," he said with a smile.

"So should I invite Alderman Murphy and his date over to the table?"

"He bought you a bottle of champagne," Cole said with ease. "I don't see how it could do any harm."

"There's something that you're not telling me, Larry," she said.

"Not really. It's just that I've known the alderman for a long time."

Kate considered her decision for another moment before turning to the waiter and saying, "Please ask the gentlemen and his date to join us." When the waiter was gone, she said to

Cole, "I think that this is going to be a very interesting evening."

Since his confrontation with Blackie Silvestri and Manny Sherlock back in December, Joe Donegan was very careful before he entered Randy's Roost. He checked the street from all angles and then drove into the alley, where he parked his car next to the garage. Solomon Randolph had given him a key to the side door. Dollar Bill Randolph's Rolls Royce was still parked in the garage. It was now covered with a thick coating of dust. Solomon was apparently keeping the luxury car for sentimental reasons. If Donegan had anything to say about it, the Rolls would have been sold before old Dollar Bill was cold in his grave.

There was a back staircase off the garage, which led up to the office and down into the basement, where the counterfeiting equipment was stored. Donegan wasn't happy about this arrangement. They hadn't sold a phony I.D. since before Christmas and at the rate that Solomon Randolph was going, it would be a long time before they sold another one at all. From a purely business perspective, Donegan was concerned about his partner. Solomon was drinking too much, which made him not only unreliable, but also dangerous.

The cop found Solomon in the office above the bar. The young man was more or less sober, but he had been drinking. A bottle of cognac and a brandy snifter containing two inches of the dark liquid rested on the desk. Donegan knew that by closing time, the bottle would be empty. Right now Donegan needed Randolph sober.

"We need to make arrangements to collect our money from Murphy," the crooked cop said.

Solomon was glassy-eyed, as he responded, "Shouldn't we wait until Johnson expires?"

Donegan was quickly losing his patience. "The deed is done, Mister Randolph. The man is seventy-seven years old, sustained severe burns and suffered smoke inhalation, which will no doubt aggravate the emphysema he already suffers from. Playing around until Johnson is cold in his grave will give Murphy a chance to weasel out on us."

"What do you want me to do?"

Donegan remained standing. "We need to set up a meet to collect the money in cash as soon as possible. Preferably before Johnson does croak and gets classified as a murder victim. Then the heat will definitely be on and our friend Larry Cole will be looking at the congressman's death from every angle to include anyone who aspires to the vacant House seat. In fact, we need to meet with Murphy away from the city. He's got a cabin up in Union Pier, Michigan. That would be as good a place as any. But we've got to get this done soon."

"How soon?" Randolph said, reaching for the cognac bottle.

Donegan watched his partner refill the brandy snifter. "Right now."

After spending the majority of his life as a cop, Larry Cole had learned to take the unexpected in stride. But when he looked up and saw Eurydice Vaughn accompanying Skip Murphy, Cole was initially shocked beyond words. Then the pieces of the puzzle that was his renewed relationship with Eurydice began falling into place.

"Thank you so much for allowing us to come over, Ms. Ford," Murphy said, taking Kate's hand and bending to kiss it in a gallant manner. The politician spoke in such a loud tone of voice that his presence was noticed by a number of club patrons sitting nearby. This was by design, as Murphy was always running for office in one way or another. Then he turned to acknowledge Cole's presence. "Chief of Detectives Larry Cole. I didn't know that you were a blues fan."

Cole's smile was chilling. "You'd be surprised what some members of the Chicago Police Department are into, Alderman Murphy."

Murphy appeared momentarily uncomfortable, but he recovered quickly. "Ms. Ford, allow me to introduce Eurydice Vaughn, the curator at the National Science and Space Museum."

Cole noticed with no little degree of interest that the two women had been sizing each other up. This was carried out in a subdued, polite fashion, but it was nevertheless quite evident. Despite himself, Cole found the drama unfolding inside of Sandy's Jazz Club becoming quite entertaining.

When they sat down at the table, Eurydice said, "I'm actually the assistant curator at the museum, Ms. Ford. I've also read all of your books. You have quite a discerning eye for intrigue and cover-ups."

"I seem to have a knack for uncovering dishonesty, Ms. Vaughn," Kate responded.

"Please call me, Eurydice."

"And you can call me, Kate." The singer of the hour removed the champagne bottle from the ice bucket. "Won't the two of you join us?"

"We'd be delighted," Murphy said, effusively. The politician was obviously attempting to use his outgoing manner to offset the obvious tension at the table. After Kate poured, Murphy raised his glass. "In the words of the immortal Gloria Lynn, and the song that Kate sang so beautifully just a short time ago, 'I wish you love.' "

After the toast concluded a brief period of awkward silence ensued. This was amplified by the taped music being played over speakers during the intermission. Finally, Eurydice said to Cole, "Skip and I are only casual friends, Larry."

"Yes," Murphy quickly interjected. "Eurydice is one of the many supporters of my drug decriminalization proposal." When this statement failed to elicit a response from any of those present, Murphy deftly switched gears. "As you're an investigative journalist of no little reputation, Kate, I'm certain that you would be interested in drug decriminalization."

Kate responded, "I recall hearing something about the issue. Didn't you attend a press conference about it, Larry?"

"I was there," Cole said, flatly.

Murphy rushed on. "I believe that I've come up with some very sound arguments in favor of the proposal. I foresee a complete change in the criminal justice system in this country if my sweeping recommendations are implemented. It would even effect the Detective Division of the Chicago Police Department, Larry."

Cole refused to take the bait.

Eurydice spoke up. "What are your thoughts about the decriminalization of drugs, Larry?"

They all turned to look at Cole.

After leaving Cole's table, Sandra Devereaux went behind the stage to an area where the entrance to a private elevator was located. Using a key, she activated the car and boarded it for the short ride up to her office. She exited the elevator into a spacious, carpeted room dominated by a large antique desk at its center. There was indirect lighting, tasteful white leather furniture, and the painting of a stately black man wearing a fur-collared cape on the wall behind the desk. On the opposite wall from the portrait there was an altar covered with a lace cloth on which were arranged a picture of the Blessed Virgin Mary, a rosary, a crystal decanter of brandy, and two white wax candles in golden holders.

Sandy stopped briefly at the altar to light the candles before making the sign of the cross. She was unable to kneel in prayer because of the damage that had been done to her legs. She remained at the altar for a short time before turning to go behind the desk. At the altar she had invoked a certain form of magic; now she needed to call on the darker arts.

The frame of the oil portrait swung open on hinges to reveal a wall safe. Sandra Devereaux worked the combination. Inside the safe there was an ornate sterling silver box. Carefully, Sandy picked it up with both hands and carried it over to the desk. Before opening the box she glanced once more at the altar and mumbled a silent prayer. Then she reached out with trembling hands and opened the lid.

The interior was lined with coarse black cloth. At the center of this cloth was a silver ring fashioned in the form of a writhing serpent. The head of the snake was ornamented with green emeralds for the eyes and the mouth was open displaying golden fangs. She removed the ring from the case and placed it on the second finger of her left hand. It fit the Voodooienne perfectly, but within seconds of coming in contact with her skin the metal began to change. Sandra Devereaux was aware of the change and with it she dropped into a trance. The texture of the metal began to develop the characteristics of living tissue.

In her trance the serpent ring with the emerald eyes came to life.

The ancient piece of jewelry had been passed down from generation to generation for over two thousand years. To some it was a talisman of voodoo symbolizing the serpent that had given the initial gift of sight to Adam and Eve in the Garden of Eden. By itself, the ring was no more than a rather bizarre piece of ornate jewelry. In the hands of a Voodooienne it became an instrument of knowledge. Knowledge that could be extremely dangerous, as well as powerful.

Remaining in the trance, she became aware of the emerald-eyed serpent dominating her mind. It was at this point that the Voodooiene reached out, searching for answers about the four people seated at the table downstairs in her club.

"If drug decriminalization will help lower the crime rate, then I'm all for it," Cole said.

"Oh, it will do that, Larry. It will definitely do that," Skip Murphy said. "But the crime issue is only a small part of the overall program. There will also be increased health care benefits for recovering addicts, social and educational programs to help those afflicted by the scourge of controlled substances to become contributing members of society, and a windfall of tax dollars available for other aspects of the program. That will occur after we realign the budgets of every governmental agency involved in our current abortive war on drugs, which will, in effect, take the United States out of the illegal drug business."

Kate Ford spoke up. "That all sounds very impressive, Alderman Murphy, but isn't your theory a bit oversimplistic?"

A flicker of annoyance crossed the politician's face. His

pitch was being made to Cole and he didn't need any interference at this crucial juncture.

"Of course there are details that must be worked out," Murphy said, attempting to keep the testiness out of his voice. "But with the requisite support I am certain that we can carry the day." He addressed his next remarks exclusively to Cole. "I got the initial idea for the drug decriminalization proposal from you, Larry. In the past, you have proven yourself to be a law enforcement officer of extraordinary talent, bravery, and intellect. I'm certain that you can see the value of what I have in mind."

At that moment Cole's compact combination radio/telephone buzzed. The noise was fairly loud, as he had set the "ringer" on the emergency setting, which some CPD command officers had remarked in the past was capable of waking the dead. After removing the instrument from his inside pocket and turning the ringer off, he stood up. "I need to go someplace where I can take this call in private," he said to Kate.

"Why don't we go back to my dressing room?"

The singer and the cop left Skip Murphy and Eurydice Vaughn sitting alone.

The alderman was unable to conceal his frustration at having his target slip away. "Cole was almost ready to commit," he said, angrily. "I could feel it!"

Eurydice graced him with a mocking grin. "I wouldn't be so sure about that if I were you, Skip. But there is one thing certain."

"And that is?"

"Cole was definitely saved by the bell."

Murphy failed to see the humor in her comment.

They remained alone and in silence at the table in front of

the stage for several moments. Then Sandra Devereaux came down the stairs and walked over to them. Both Eurydice and Murphy were aware of the jazz club owner's identity; however, that was all that they knew about her. They were about to discover a great deal more.

Sandy pulled out the chair that Kate Ford had recently vacated and sat down. Eurydice and Skip Murphy noticed that Madam Devereaux either had a grimace of anger or one of pain on her face. It was actually both. They also could see that her hand had been recently bandaged and blood was visible soaking through the white gauze covering.

Once settled, the Voodooienne affixed them with a fierce glare and said, "I want to talk to both of you about my friend Larry Cole and I suggest that you listen to me very carefully."

Back in Kate Ford's dressing room, Cole took a call from Blackie Silvestri. The vaguely suspected involvement of Sergeant Joe Donegan in the attempted assassination of Congressman Walter Johnson made Cole's earlier relaxed attitude vanish.

"I'll meet you at headquarters in a few minutes, Blackie," Cole said, shutting off the communications device.

Kate Ford was waiting in the hall outside. She could easily detect the change in the policeman's manner. "Is everything okay, Larry?"

"Just the usual murder and mayhem on the streets of the Windy City, Kate," he said. "But I can't stay for your second set."

She was disappointed, but managed to conceal it. "Maybe next time."

Stepping forward, he kissed her on the forehead. Then they

went back out to the main room of Sandy's Jazz Club. Their table was empty.

"What happened to your guests?" Cole asked.

"If you ask me, good riddance," she responded.

She walked him to the entrance, watched as he put on his overcoat, and then head out into the snowy night. The part-time blues singer was still standing at the front of the club when Sandra Devereaux stepped up beside her. Kate also noticed her recently bandaged hand.

"Did you hurt yourself, Sandy?"

"Just a minor cut, Katie. Now don't you worry about Larry Cole," the Voodooienne said. "He now has some very powerful protection against his enemies."

Later that night, the two women would sip brandy after the club closed and Sandy would tell the investigative journalist/part-time blues singer about a place called Diggstown, Mississippi and the mythical she-devil entity that had protected it years ago.

36

FEBRUARY 7, 2004
DAWN

Sergeant Joe Donegan was preparing to face the new day. He felt exceptionally good due to the four hours of sleep he had gotten. He seldom slept in his own bedroom, but instead in the bungalow study, which he had turned into a computer lab. The old leather recliner that had once belonged to his father served as Donegan's bed. The surface of the chair was worn smooth with age and sagged in spots, but it was the one place where the crooked cop was able to rest. In slumber, he remained fully clothed and covered himself with a quilt that had been handmade by his mother.

Before he dozed off at 2 A.M., he glanced at the old cast-iron safe in the corner. The safe was now equipped with a computerized keypad combination and contained over three-quarters of a million dollars in cash. This money represented the proceeds from his illegal acts over the course of his police career. The fee for the assassination of Congressman Walter Johnson would put Donegan over the million-dollar mark. When he collected that money from Skip Murphy, he planned to retire from the Chicago Police Department. He wouldn't remain idle and was already preparing to obtain a private detective's license. Then he would continue his larcenous pursuits without having to be concerned about cops like Larry Cole or finks from the Internal Affairs Division. By then he would also be rid of his business partner Solomon Randolph.

After rising from the leather recliner, Donegan checked his computers, which were all running programs. Making sure that everything was operating within normal parameters, he let himself out of the study and locked the door behind him. His sister Megan would never dare enter his private domain and Donegan was not really concerned about her. But he was paranoid enough to sincerely believe that there were prying eyes everywhere.

By the time he showered and changed into a new sport coat and pair of wash-and-wear slacks that his sister had purchased for him at a JC Penney outlet, he was ready to began his countdown to retirement. Breakfast would be at a fast-food restaurant

drive-in. His IAD shift began at 8:00 A.M. and he was always
on time. Before leaving the house, he returned to the study.

The instant he stepped through the door, he saw that something was very wrong. All of his computer screens now flashed,
"Unable to Establish Satellite Link." Donegan went to one of
the units and attempted to bring his cable- and telephone-line
backup systems on-line. All requests to reestablish service were
denied. He was too much of a computer wizard to fail to understand what was happening. The only way that all of his
systems could fail at once was that he was being jammed from
the outside. And there was only one entity powerful enough to
carry out such an operation and that was the National Security
Agency. That meant Chief Larry Cole and his people were involved.

Returning to his bedroom he pulled a scarred suitcase from
the back of a closet. Back in the study, he opened the safe and
began shoving neat stacks of one-hundred-dollar and fifty-
dollar bills into the suitcase. He'd had the foresight over the
years to store all of his money in large bills in case the day
came when he would have to pack up and move very fast to
effect an escape. The money fit and he closed the case cursing,
because he didn't have a key. The battered suitcase had belonged to his dead parents.

Before leaving the study, he checked each of his guns and
made sure that he had plenty of extra ammunition. He didn't
believe that the jamming of his computers was an isolated act
and he would have to be prepared for anything that came up.

In the wake of last night's snowstorm, a warm front had
blown across the city. The hot air of the jet stream coming into
contact with the thick blanket of snow on the ground caused a
heavy fog to envelop the Windy City. The streets possessed an

East End of London "pea soup" eerieness and visibility was extremely poor. Carrying his suitcase and keeping his hand on the handle of a 9mm automatic pistol concealed in his overcoat pocket, Donegan stepped out onto the front porch of the Marquette Park bungalow. He was unable to see the twenty feet out to the curb where his dirty blue Cutlass was parked. This would make it difficult for him to detect any signs of a surveillance. It would also make it equally difficult for anyone to see him.

After locking the suitcase in the trunk, he got in his car and checked the laptop computer he kept concealed beneath the front seat. The same "Unable to Establish Satellite Link" blinked on and off the screen. This was not an unexpected development, but did succeed in increasing his anxiety level to the point that he began hyperventilating. After starting the engine, Donegan rolled the window down and took deep breaths of the foggy air, which left a metallic aftertaste in his mouth. He licked his dry lips and swore that he could taste cordite, as if a gun had been fired close by. He was forced to remark that the taste in his mouth could also be that of blood.

Flicking on his headlights, he guided the car out into traffic.

Over eight billion communications transmissions take place on the planet Earth each day. Via telephone lines, radio waves, and satellite uplinks, the world is alive with information. It would seem impossible for any one intelligence agency of even the most sophisticated superpower to monitor such a high volume of electronically transmitted data. However, the technology did exist for each of the daily transmissions to be monitored, the identity of the sender and the receiver noted, and the contents of the message recorded. That intelligence entity was the United States National Security Agency. And all such monitoring was done under the umbrella of being "in the interests of national security."

A veil of secrecy surrounded the NSA's activities and there were few in or out of the intelligence community who were aware of either their exact operations or the identity of their operatives. Chicago Police Chief of Detectives Larry Cole had had dealings with this agency in the past and knew two of its agents. These agents were Reggie Stanton, a former Chicago cop, and his half-brother Ernest Steiger. They used Chicago as their base of operations.

The brothers had a history of engaging in diabolical activities and lived in a remodeled brownstone on South Martin Luther King, Jr. Drive. Their residence, which had been originally constructed in the late nineteenth century, was in an economically rejuvenated area in the same section of town where the New Brownsville Homes were located. Had Reggie and Ernest been more social than secretive, their house would have been listed as one of the most significant historical landmark residences in the city. It was a beautiful three-story structure that many had admired from the outside, as few guests were ever invited inside. Those that did receive invitations were almost exclusively attractive young women, who were seldom permitted to remain on the premises overnight.

The most secure area of the fortresslike structure was a spacious L-shaped basement. To enter the basement one had to go through a six-inch-thick steel reinforced door, which could only be opened by a palm-sensing access device. The interior was furnished with modern furniture, wall-to-wall carpeting, and beige painted walls, which had been soundproofed. Along one leg of the "L" was a fully equipped weapons range on which the brothers maintained high proficiency with both fire-arms and the thrown dagger. The dagger was actually their weapon of choice and had been passed down from generation to generation in their family for centuries. There was also a workout area with free weights, a computerized exercise ma-chine, and a Stairmaster. A small office section was equipped with two utilitarian desks, two government-issue style desk chairs, and two state-of-the-art computers with attached printers.

Utilizing these computers, they could monitor any of the eight billion communications taking place worldwide via a sat-ellite uplink. They could also jam these communications, whether they be telephonic or computerized.

Seated side by side at their separate computers, the brothers were at work. Reggie Stanton was the elder by three years. He was a light-complexioned, extremely well built black man with curly light brown hair and startling gray/blue eyes. His brother Ernest Steiger was a blond, slender white man with pretty rather than handsome features. Due to injuries he'd received in their particularly hazardous line of work, Ernest was now forced to walk with a cane. Despite the racial disparity, they were broth-ers in every sense of the word. Occasionally, like now, they were not in total agreement.

"I don't see why we're extending ourselves again for Larry Cole," Ernest argued. "If you ask me, that particular cop is bad news."

Reggie, who was rapidly punching keys at his computer, responded, "He's after a bad guy, Ernest, and we are all on the same side."

"I'm not so sure about that," Ernest muttered.

"Just make sure that this Sergeant Donegan's computer systems are completely locked out from access to any data bank in the world."

Ernest sighed. "That's done, big brother, but suppose he uses another computer?"

"He probably will try, but Donegan'll have to use his password to gain access to the data banks he normally enters and I've locked him out of those as well."

"I must say," Ernest said, leaning back in his chair and placing his hands behind his head, "we are very thorough. Your friend Larry Cole is fortunate to have men of our caliber on his side."

This remark succeeded in getting an unusual grin from the normally stoic Reggie Stanton. "Sometimes I wonder about you, little brother."

The dense fog slowed traffic to a crawl on the streets of the Windy City. The pavement was still slick from last night's snowfall and numerous auto accidents clogged the main thoroughfares and expressways. Making slow progress in the dirty Cutlass, Donegan's mind raced as he examined his situation. He initially thought about heading for Randy's Roost, but if they were on to him they would know about Solomon Randolph as well. He considered toughing it out by heading for police headquarters and walking right into the Internal Affairs Division as if nothing was wrong. Before he decided on a course of action, he needed to carefully assess his situation.

Donegan's home computers being jammed was an ominous sign, which indicated quite clearly that the NSA didn't want him to transmit or receive information. The only motivation there could be for such a move was that he had been implicated in the attempted assassination of Congressman Walter Johnson.

But having been a cop for so many years forced Donegan to
doubt this supposition. If he were suspected in the Brownsville
Homes arson, he would already be in custody.

Through the dense fog, Donegan saw a McDonald's restaurant up ahead. He pulled out of the slow-moving traffic and
into the drive thru. He ordered a sausage and egg biscuit sandwich and black coffee. He drove to a remote corner of the
restaurant lot and parked in such a manner that he could see
anyone approaching. The McDonald's was doing a brisk business and there was a great deal of activity, both foot and vehicular, in the general area. As he ate his breakfast, Donegan
watched everything that moved.

The last time that he had encountered any problems with
one of his criminal operations was on the day that he planned
to kill Larry Cole. Later that same night Sergeant Elaine Anderson and the pair of snooping cops with her gained illegal
entry to his computer lab. Despite the gunshot wound he had
sustained at the hands of the robbers Cole was chasing, he had
disposed of the three intruders to his domain in such an artful
fashion that Cole's attempts to pin the deaths on him were
totally frustrated.

Since then there had been only the inconsequential con-
frontation with Blackie Silvestri and Manny Sherlock at
Randy's Roost and he had taken his reassignment from the
Intelligence Unit to the IAD in stride.

Donegan balled up his breakfast sandwich wrapper and,
totally ignoring anti-littering signs, threw it out the window. He
remained parked in the lot sipping his coffee.

It all came back to Congressman Walter Johnson. Donegan
would have turned the car radio on and dialed a news station

to find out how the congressman was doing, but the radio didn't work. Once more he tried the laptop and the "Unable to Establish Satellite Uplink" continued to flash on the screen.

Perhaps, Donegan surmised, he was simply overreacting. He had been outsmarting the Chicago Police Department since the day he came on the job. The hit on Johnson had come off clean. Perhaps it wasn't the slickest operation he'd ever undertaken, but he was going to collect a lot of money for it from Skip Murphy, one way or another. Because information about the congressman's home address, telephone number, and other personal data were deleted from all computerized files for security reasons, it became necessary for Donegan to pay an unannounced visit to Dr. Stella Novak's office on the day of her new patient's scheduled visit. Everything had gone off without a hitch. After Stella's airhead receptionist escorted Donegan to examining room C, he had slipped out and found Johnson's clothing hanging in examining room A. A quick search of the congressman's suit jacket revealed a wallet with the Brownsville Homes address inside of it. The rest had been fairly "routine," as they always said on TV cop shows. Donegan had left no evidence in cubicle A except . . .

Two things occurred to Joe Donegan at the same time. One was that he had physically touched Walter Johnson's medical file. He had completely forgotten that he had turned off the computer in the cubicle, because he did this automatically with his own computers when he wasn't running a program. But he was primarily concerned that he had left his fingerprints on the medical file and that those fingerprints had been discovered. By itself this wouldn't mean a great deal as far as hard evidence went and if he was questioned, Donegan would admit being in the cubicle. The reason? He was simply curious about the congressman's ailments. After all, he was a cop. So sue him for being nosy.

The second thing that Joe Donegan realized, while parked in the McDonald's on this foggy morning, was that he was being followed by at least two undercover police cars. One was a beat up Chevy Caprice with tinted windows to enhance the vehicle's surveillance capability. The other vehicle was a white-and-blue United Cable Television Systems installer's van with a ladder rack on the roof. The evil cop couldn't see how many occupants were in the Chevy, which was by design, but there were two men visible in white coveralls in the United Cable van.

Both vehicles had entered the McDonald's at about the same time that he had arrived and they could also be having a fast-food breakfast just like him. But they had made a fundamental investigative mistake. Sergeant Joe Donegan had previously run the Chicago Police Department's Intelligence Unit computer room. While doing so he had kept tabs on certain department operations to make sure that no honest cop was on to him. This led to the crooked cop maintaining a list of all CPD covert vehicles and their license plate numbers. Donegan was also aware that there was no such business operation as the United Cable Television System and the old Chevy with the tinted windows had been exposed during an undercover operation when a uniformed patrol car stopped it because of the illegal windows.

"That is extremely sloppy work, boys," Donegan said, tossing his coffee cup out the window to land on the parking lot surface next to the sandwich wrapper. "Now we're going to play a little game called, 'Catch me if you can.' "

As Joe Donegan pulled slowly away from McDonald's, the United Cable Television Systems van and the battered Chevy with the tinted windows followed.

37

FEBRUARY 7, 2004
8:50 A.M.

Larry Cole was in his office monitoring the information coming in on the interdepartment confidential investigation that had officially begun on Sergeant Joe Donegan. Cole had used the Detective Division's Special Investigations Unit to begin the initial surveillance on the suspected crooked cop earlier that morning. As the day progressed, the four detectives assigned to the two surveillance vehicles tailing Donegan would be spelled by Judy Daniels, Manny Sherlock, and, possibly, even Cole and Blackie. Calling in a long-standing debt with covert NSA agent Reggie Stanton, Cole had arranged to have Donegan's computers jammed after the crooked cop arrived at his IAD assignment. The chief of detectives had no way of knowing that the NSA operative and his brother had jumped the gun. They had not only jammed all of Donegan's computers, but had also alerted him to the scrutiny.

Manny Sherlock came rushing into the office carrying a manila folder. "I think I've come up with something, boss," Manny said, pulling a sheet of paper from the folder and placing it on top of Cole's desk. The heading on the cover sheet bore the logo of the Department of the Army Criminal Investigations Division. The subject of the report, in response to a Chicago Police Department inquiry, was Thermite canisters.

The sergeant was too excited to wait for Cole to read the report. "In the past twenty-six months the army has reported two cases of Thermite canisters missing. Both of them were in the continental United States. There were eight canisters in each case and they were lost right here in Chicago at the M. J. Parker Research Lab at Forty-third and Pulaski. This lab had the contract to produce Thermite and was particularly careful about security. Each canister was scrupulously accounted for. That is until the fire."

Cole waited and Manny didn't let him down.

"At the time it appeared to be an arson, but a later investigation by Bomb and Arson detectives could only classify the blaze as being of undetermined origins." Manny produced another single page report from his folder and placed it on the desk beside the C.I.D. report. "The Chicago Fire Department responded quickly and the blaze was struck before too much damage was done." This last sheet was a Chicago Fire Department duty roster for a company stationed on the West Side of the city. Cole saw the name at the top of the list, "Lieutenant Robert M. Donegan."

Solomon Randolph awoke with a world-class hangover. It took him a moment to orient himself to his surroundings and he was surprised to find himself in his bedroom as opposed to lying on the cot in his Randy's Roost office. He couldn't recall driving home last night. In fact, he couldn't remember much at all after Donegan left. Randolph had placed a call to Skip Murphy at Donegan's behest, but he'd been forced to leave a message with the alderman's answering service. Solomon sat up in bed to notice that he was fully clothed including his expensive, but now wrinkled, suit. He had a dim remembrance of Murphy calling him back last night after Donegan left.

Solomon got out of bed and made his way into the washroom, which was still decorated with wallpaper bearing the cartoon images of Bugs Bunny and Daffy Duck from his childhood. He fought through the alcohol vise imprisoning his brain to remember what Murphy had said. He ran cold water into the face bowl and, while it filled, he drank directly from the tap. The cold water hitting his stomach almost made him sick, but he managed to keep the contents down.

He splashed water on his face, head, and neck. This action succeeded in not only soaking his clothing, but also the bathroom floor. Ignoring the mess, he returned to his bedroom and began to undress. Solomon's initial plan was to go back to bed and sleep for at least three more hours. He checked the titanium-encased Swiss Army watch that had been a gift from his father. It was actually the last thing that Dollar Bill had given his son. Solomon was shocked that it was so early in the morning, if 8 A.M. could be considered early. It was at this point that a bit more of what had transpired in connection with Skip Murphy came back to him.

Last night the alderman had spoken in angry tones, calling Donegan a fool, who had ". . . botched the job." Despite being drunk, Solomon had been cunning enough to not make any direct references to any individual or place over the telephone. He did state the necessity for him and his "associate," as he referred to Joe Donegan, and the alderman to meet at an isolated location outside of Chicago. He assumed that Murphy got the point; however, on the morning after, Solomon couldn't recall exactly why. Perhaps after he'd managed to get a few more hours sleep, he'd give the alderman another call and find out.

Stripping off his wet, wrinkled suit, Solomon was about to get back into bed when hunger overcame him. Donning a silk robe and house slippers, he left his bedroom and was about to descend the main staircase to the first floor when he heard his mother's voice. The sound came from behind the closed door of the master bedroom down the hall. He could tell that Sharon Powell Randolph was not talking, but actually moaning. Solomon first thought that she was in pain, but then there was something odd about the sound she was making.

The master bedroom was where the mistress of the house had once slept with her late, estranged husband. Solomon had been sired in the four-poster canopied bed that had been imported from Spain at no little cost. Before the Randolphs split up, Solomon's crib had occupied a space in the master bedroom. Since reaching adulthood, he seldom went in there. Now he was being inexorably drawn to it, because of his mother's moans of undeniable passion.

Before entering, he stopped in the hall and listened. Suddenly, he had a vivid recollection of his mother scolding him for eavesdropping on her at the Ladies' Altar and Rosary Society meeting some months ago. At this moment her words stung him and he angrily reached out and opened the unlocked door.

Sharon Powell Randolph and the butler Jamison were in the canopied bed. From Solomon's vantage-point at the entrance to the huge bedroom, he could see the back of Jamison's gray-haired head, his bare shoulders, and heaving buttocks. Solomon's mother was lying beneath him. Her face—eyes closed, mouth open, and usually immaculately coifed hairdo askew— was suffused with sexual ecstasy. With a voyeur's fascination, he watched them writhing on the bed so absorbed in screwing the daylights out of each other that they were unaware of his presence.

Like an awestruck child, he stood there watching them for nearly five minutes. Finally, he slowly turned and left the room, closing the door softly behind him. His head was pounding with a fierce headache as he descended the staircase to the main floor to cross the immense living room, the music room—dominated by the grand piano his mother had insisted that he learn to play at the age of seven—to his father's old study. This room was lined with books that Dollar Bill Randolph had actually read and was distinctively old-fashioned. Besides the books there was a lot of old, dark, heavy wooden furniture and a gun rack. The rack contained a number of shotguns and rifles that his father had used for hunting. Because Sharon Powell Randolph hated firearms, the glass door of the rack was always kept locked. She would have disposed of the guns a long time ago, but Solomon, who had inherited the contents of the rack from Dollar Bill, wouldn't hear of it.

Solomon Randolph didn't have the patience to retrieve the key from the combination-lock safe concealed inside the desk. Instead he removed the 936-page volume, *Freedom from Fear*, by David Kennedy from the bookcase and hurled it at the glass, which shattered. Solomon was not concerned about the aging lovers hearing him, because the house was huge and they were much too occupied with each other. He selected a Remington twelve-gauge shotgun and succeeded in slashing his hand on a shard of glass as he pulled the gun from the rack. Ignoring the blood pouring from the wound, he loaded the weapon and headed back upstairs.

Solomon Randolph was badly hungover and in a rage over this final, most damning insult to his dead father. Perhaps his mother's influence on him had been greater than he thought possible, because he considered her act of fornication with the butler in his father's bed to be the most grievous of mortal sins.

Seconds later, shotgun blasts ripped through the stately calm of the Jackson Park Highlands mansion.

Bracketed by the pair of Detective Division covert vehicles following him, Joe Donegan drove his old Cutlass northbound on the Dan Ryan Expressway. At Fifty-fifth Street he took the exit ramp, as opposed to staying on the expressway to the Thirty-fifth Street exit that would take him to headquarters. The Special Investigation Unit detectives working the Joe Donegan surveillance were notified of their assignment an hour before they arrived outside the Marquette Park bungalow. They didn't have the opportunity to obtain any high-tech surveillance equipment, because it was initially believed that Donegan was simply going to police headquarters.

Lieutenant Blackie Silvestri had given them the instructions. "We just want you to babysit this guy until we can do a little more background work on him. When he leaves his house, he should be on his way into headquarters. Once he arrives there give me a call and we'll do the rest from the chief's office."

Blackie hadn't told them what to do if Donegan didn't go to headquarters. Now, as the dirty Cutlass proceeded up the exit ramp, the surveillance teams were forced to come to a decision.

"Five-seven-oh-five to five-seven-oh-six," the United Cable Systems van called on the car-to-car frequency to the Chevy Caprice with the tinted windows.

"Five-seven-oh-six go."

"The subject is getting off the Ryan. How do you want to play it?"

"We'll follow him. You stay on the expressway and exit at Fifty-first Street. That way we'll have him between us."

"Do you think he's going to stop at Area One?"

The Area One Police Center was located on Fifty-first Street on the east side of the Dan Ryan Expressway.

"That's anybody's guess," the detective in the Caprice said. "But this job would be a lot easier if this fog would let up a bit."

Up on the Wentworth Avenue surface street above the expressway, the blue Cutlass proceeded across Garfield Boulevard and continued north. Donegan's car was unable to travel faster than twenty miles an hour due to the dense fog, and at times visibility was reduced to less than thirty feet. The surveillance vehicle was forced to hang back to prevent detection and the Caprice lost sight of the Cutlass as soon as it crossed the Garfield Boulevard and Wentworth Avenue intersection.

"Five-seven-oh-six to five-seven-oh-five."

"Go, 'oh-five."

"Are you still on the expressway?"

"Ten-four. We're entering the Fifty-first Street exit ramp right now."

"Pull over in front of Area One and see if you can spot the Cutlass when it passes you. We'll continue on Wentworth and see if we can pick him up."

"Ten-four," came the response from the white van.

The Caprice continued to creep through the fog, as the detectives attempted in vain to catch sight of the Cutlass. They passed the huge Area One Police Center parking lot, which was filled with cars. A moment later they pulled up beside the white surveillance van. The detective on the passenger side of the Chevy rolled the window down and said to the driver of the van, "Did the Cutlass pass you?"

"Haven't seen it."

"The only place he could have gone was into the parking lot," the Caprice's passenger said. "Let's go."

It took the pair of surveillance vehicles thirty minutes to locate the dirty Cutlass parked in the Area One Police Center parking lot. It was empty and Joe Donegan and his suitcase full of money were long gone.

38

FEBRUARY 7, 2004
9:04 A.M.

Skip Murphy and Eurydice Vaughn couldn't recall much of what Madam Devereaux had said to them last night at Sandy's Jazz Club. Both the alderman and the assistant curator at the National Science and Space Museum would agree that the attractive woman with the café au lait complexion had come on in a decidedly hostile manner. But no actual threat was made; instead a warning had been quite clearly conveyed. However, the next day they were unable to recall what they had been warned about.

Everything had slipped away from Murphy's and Eurydice's minds that had occurred after Larry Cole and Kate Ford left the table. The co-conspirators had obviously left the jazz club and gone home, because they were alone in their respective residences the next morning. In the opening hours of his day, the alderman had been more concerned about the condition of Congressman Walter Johnson than he was about the events that had occurred at Sandy's Jazz Club the previous night. Murphy was also somewhat preoccupied by what he was going to do about Joe Donegan. The fact that the crooked cop was now allied with the son of the late Dollar Bill Randolph made it doubly imperative that Murphy sever all contacts with both of them at the earliest possible opportunity.

When Murphy returned the telephone call from Solomon Randolph last night, the intoxicated man had muttered something about him and Donegan wanting to have a meeting outside of town. Randolph made a vague reference to Murphy's Union Pier cabin, which anyone listening in would have easily been able to identify. At this point none of that mattered to Murphy, because as long as Johnson was still alive, neither Randolph nor Donegan would get a dime out of him.

Skip Murphy was trimming his beard in the bathroom mirror when his thoughts turned to Larry Cole for the first time that day. He was attempting to gauge the cop's reaction to the pitch he had made for drug decriminalization when he felt something slither across his bare feet. He jumped, which caused the scissors to slip and open up a deep gash across his right cheek. Vermin of any type were unheard of in the expensive Central Station townhouse complex, but when Murphy looked down at the floor nothing was there. When he chanced to look back up into the mirror, he saw that he was bleeding profusely.

"Sonofabitch!" he swore, as he grabbed a towel and attempted to stop the bleeding. The terrycloth quickly turned red and he knew that he needed to obtain immediate medical assistance. Tossing the blood-soaked towel to the floor and snatching another from the rack, he went to call his medical doctor neighbor, who lived two doors away.

Eurydice Vaughn was equally as affected as Skip Murphy over thoughts about Larry Cole, but her experience had come in a dream.

Like Murphy, she recalled little that had occurred with Madam Devereaux or after they had left the jazz club. She had not been frightened by the Voodooienne and had instead simply thought of the woman as strange and unpleasant. Driving home had been more or less uneventful and she'd gone to bed without incident. In the pitch-black darkness of her apartment overlooking the National Science and Space Museum, sleep came easily.

Over the years she'd had many dreams about Larry Cole. A number of them had been erotic. The one on this night became a full-blown nightmare.

It had begun with her standing on the lower level of the museum train station, where she had met with Cole back in December. She saw him board the escalator on the upper level of the exhibit and begin to descend. She watched him approach, noticing that something about him was difficult to identify. But by the time he came up to her, she could see that it wasn't Larry Cole at all. What she saw in her dream was a monstrous half man/half snake creature. Terrified, she turned and fled across the train station. The monster pursued her.

Eurydice knew her dream setting better than any place else

on Earth and in a waking state could have eluded anyone or, for that matter, just about anything while she was in the museum. In the nightmare that was not to be. She found herself running through a dark, dank subterranean chamber that she didn't recognize. She was moving quickly, but could feel the monster gaining on her. She chanced a glance back. Now there was more than one of the snake creatures and, as she looked on in horror, they multiplied until there were hundreds of them chasing her. She tripped and fell. Before she could get to her feet, a strong hand reached down and helped her up. She looked into the face of a smiling Larry Cole and for a brief instant she felt a surge of relief. Then the cop was transformed into one of the snake creatures with the gigantic hissing head of a cobra.

Eurydice screamed herself awake. She sat up in the bed feeling the icy, sour sweat of fear making her nightgown cling to her body. She was breathing heavily, but relieved to find that the terrifying experience had only been a nightmare. Then something beside her in the bed shifted violently and when she reached out through the dark she touched a large scaly body that moved.

She again screamed and jumped out of the bed. As in her dream, she was again being pursued. In her mind, she could see the snake creature. She dashed across the living room, but tripped over a throw rug in the dark. She landed hard and scurried across the floor until she ran into a table. Reaching up, she switched on the light. With wide-eyed terror, she looked for her pursuer.

Eurydice Vaughn was alone. Curling herself into a fetal ball, she remained on the living room floor until dawn. She did not go back to sleep. She didn't go to work at the museum that day either.

*   *   *

Blackie Silvestri and Manny Sherlock parked behind a marked police vehicle on the residential street in Marquette Park where Lieutenant Robert M. Donegan lived. Getting out of their police car, they approached the plain brick two-story house in mid-block, which was encircled with yellow barrier tape bearing the admonition in black letters, "Crime Scene—Do Not Cross." A small crowd had gathered in this usually sedate residential neighborhood and two uniformed officers—an older heavyset white male and a young slender black female in a new uniform—were stationed in the front yard in case the curious gawkers decided to disregard the tape. Although Blackie and Manny were easily recognizable as cops, they flashed their badges at the uniforms.

"How's it going, Blackie?" the white cop said.

The lieutenant read the name tag and recognition dawned. "Jeez, it's Howie York. I haven't seen you in twenty years. Where have you been keeping yourself?"

"Out of trouble," York responded. "I'm a field training officer now." He nodded at the young woman in the crisp uniform. "I try to teach these kids some of what I've learned about this job in the last thirty-odd years."

"There's nobody around who can do it any better than you, Howie," Blackie said. "This is Sergeant Manny Sherlock. He works with me on Chief Cole's staff." In turn, York introduced his partner as Probationary Police Officer Eugenia Thurmond. The introductions out of the way, Blackie asked York, "What happened in there?"

"The area detectives are still putting it together, but it looks like this smoke-eater named Robert Donegan was the victim of a home invasion. He was divorced and lives alone." York cocked a thumb at the brick front of the house. "He apparently let somebody into the house that he knew and for his trouble caught a bullet in the back of the head from a large bore pistol. Damn near decapitated him. The house is a bit untidy." York was interrupted by Officer Thurmond's derisive snort. "Okay," he corrected, "the joint is a wreck, but it doesn't look like the offender searched the place for valuables. The dead guy had on a gold watch and his wallet was still in his back pocket. Whoever did him searched the garage and stole his late-model Ford station wagon."

The interior of the Marquette Park house that had belonged to Lieutenant Robert M. Donegan of the Chicago Fire Department was just as Probationary Officer Thurmond had indicated: a mess. Discarded clothing covered the furniture in every room and there were empty beer cans everywhere. The dead body was lying facedown on the filthy living room floor. In life, the deceased had been a pot-bellied man of average height. What that height was would now have to be estimated, because most of his head had been blown away.

Blackie and Manny only took a peek at the dead man before going around to the garage behind the house. The overhead door stood open and the crime lab was wrapping up their examination. The detective division supervisor in charge knew Blackie Silvestri and Manny Sherlock.

"You checking up on me, guys?" Sergeant Rick Stewart said with a grin. He was a dead ringer for former Chicago cop-turned-actor Dennis Farina.

"Naw, Rick," Blackie responded. "We came over here to talk to the dead guy about a case we're working."

"Would you be looking to question the dead fireman about his brother?" Stewart asked.

"You nailed that one," Manny said. "Was the brother here?"

"According to the next door neighbor, the brother, who the neighbor says she hasn't seen in years, arrived in a taxi about thirty minutes ago. He was lugging a battered suitcase with him and the neighbor said that she thought he was moving in. After the brother entered the house, the neighbor hears a single gunshot. By the time she called nine-one-one the brother was driving away in the fireman's station wagon."

Blackie and Manny turned to look at the garage. "Did you know that the fireman's brother's a cop?" Blackie asked Sergeant Stewart.

Stewart was shocked. "That's the first I heard of it, Blackie."

"Can you tell if anything is missing other than the station wagon?" Manny said.

Sergeant Stewart pointed to the back of the cluttered garage. "There's an old freezer back there that was operational, but has obviously been buried under some old boxes for a long time. The killer was apparently looking for whatever was in there."

"Mind if we take a look?" Blackie requested.

"Go right ahead."

The garage was as messy and cluttered as the dead man's house and there was just enough space allotted for the missing Ford station wagon to be parked. Blackie and Manny crossed the cracked cement floor.

"What do you think Joe Donegan was keeping in here, Blackie?" Manny asked.

"When we catch up with this Lone Stranger, kid," the lieutenant said with a scowl, as he stuffed one of his twisted black cigars in the corner of his mouth and lit it with a disposable lighter, "remind me to ask him."

A search of the garage failed to turn up any Thermite canisters.

39

Judy Daniels had donned her "Sweet Sixteen from the 1950s" disguise, which consisted of a blond ponytail wig, heavily made-up eyebrows and eyelashes, and a slash of carmine red lipstick on her lips. She wore a sweater that was a shade tight across her torso and a full skirt that extended to mid-calf. When she came into Cole's office, the chief initially didn't recognize her, because the disguise was just that effective. Silently, Cole wished that his son was here, because Butch could always instantly recognize Judy no matter how elaborate her disguise. No one, including Judy, had yet been able to discover Butch's secret.

"A report just came in from the Office of Emergency Communications that there's been a double homicide out in the Third District," the Mistress of Disguise/High Priestess of Mayhem said. "The beat officers, who responded to a call of Shots Fired in the Jackson Park Highlands area, have a suspect in custody. A suspect who goes by the name of Solomon Randolph."

Cole's interest was immediately heightened. "Who were the victims?"

"His mother and the family butler. Randolph caught them in bed together and flew into a rage. He used a twelve-gauge shotgun fired at close range. According to OEC, the bodies were literally blown to pieces."

Before Cole could comment, his intercom buzzed. It was the sergeant in charge of the Detective Division's Special Investigations Unit contritely reporting that his men had lost Joe Donegan. At that moment Cole didn't see this development as being critical; however, he was far from pleased. He was about to call the IAD, in case Donegan had reported for work, when the desk intercom sounded again. This time it was Blackie Silvestri calling.

As Judy looked on, Cole tensed while he listened to Blackie tell him what had been discovered at the home of Lieutenant Robert M. Donegan of the Chicago Fire Department. When Cole hung up, she waited for him to tell her what had occurred. "After eluding the surveillance, Donegan killed his brother, who Blackie and Manny went out to talk to about some stolen Thermite canisters. Donegan then removed something from an old freezer in the garage behind the fireman's house and took off in a stolen station wagon. Blackie's having the crime lab go over the freezer. This is no longer an internal department investigation, but a murder case. Blackie's put out a wanted message for Donegan and if he's still driving the stolen station wagon, we'll eventually nab him. But I want this nailed down real tight, Judy, because Donegan is a strong suspect in the attempted assassination of Congressman Johnson." Cole stood up. "Let's take a ride. There are a couple of people I want to talk to."

Before they left the office, Judy said, "There's just one more thing that I didn't get a chance to tell you. Eurydice Vaughn called a little while ago and asked to speak to you."

"I haven't got time for her right now," Cole said, heading for the door.

"I understand that, boss," she said, quickly, "but she was in a bad way."

Cole stopped. "What was wrong with her?"

Judy shrugged. "She sounded like she'd been frightened out of her wits."

Cole continued out the door. "She'll just have to wait for the time being."

The fog continued to hang over the city like a shroud. Both municipal airports were forced to close and an emergency plan was put into place to handle the high volume of traffic accidents. City Hall implemented a special operation that was usually only put into place for heavy snow or the occasional violent storm that could result in widespread power failures. This situation severely limited the search for suspected sibling killer and political assassin, Sergeant Joe Donegan.

Allen Rollins was working on a novel in his Lincoln Park apartment when he glanced up at the plate-glass window, which overlooked the eastern shore of Lake Michigan. Usually he looked out at an impressive view, but today all that he could see was a wall of impenetrable fog. It was as if someone had hung a white sheet over his front window.

The author returned to his computer and typed for a time before concentration deserted him. His gaze again shifted to the window. He couldn't recall the last time he had seen fog this thick in Chicago. He switched over to the Internet and checked the weather forecast. A "Dangerous Condition" warning was forecast for the entire western shore of Lake Michigan and the Northern Indiana area. Allen's daughter's school was only a block away and he walked little Stephanie there each day and picked her up in the afternoon. Then his thoughts went to Stella Novak.

Allen pressed a "speed dial" button on his telephone console and heard the ringing at the other end on his speakerphone.

"Dr. Novak," Stella answered.

"Hi. It's Allen."

"How is the great Seth Champion enjoying this lovely Chicago weather that we're having?"

"Champion never has problems with the weather," Allen said, "because he doesn't have to worry about getting kids to school and attractive young lady doctors roaming around in the fog. Did you have a difficult time getting to the office today?"

"The traffic was bad," she responded, "but I made it, which is more than I can say for my receptionist. In fact, the entire medical center seems deserted. All of my morning patients have cancelled their appointments. I have to go over to the hospital and check on Congressman Johnson this afternoon, but he was upgraded from critical to serious condition overnight. His prognosis for recovery is now excellent, but I'm still going to watch him closely."

Stella had told Allen about her suspicions concerning Joe Donegan's visit to her office yesterday.

"Have you heard from Cole about what they are going to do about that strange cop?" Allen asked.

"I haven't talked to Larry, but Judy Daniels told me that she would . . ." She paused abruptly. "Hold on a second, Allen. There's someone in the outer office."

Allen Rollins waited. He noticed that the fog outside his window was still thick, but the sun was fighting to break through and the sky had brightened noticeably in the past few minutes. Time passed and Stella still did not return to the phone. Finally, he heard her voice coming from a location some distance from the instrument. She was talking to someone. Allen then heard a second voice that was definitely that of a male. He managed to pick up parts of their conversation.

Stella was saying, "I don't understand how . . ." The rest was garbled.

"It's up to . . ." the man said. ". . . your sister . . . after all these years. . . ."

Allen couldn't accurately hear what Stella said next, but she sounded stressed. Then he was met with complete silence. The line remained open. After waiting a moment or so longer, he disconnected and redialed the office. After four rings, the medical center's automated answering service kicked in. He dialed the number twice more with the same result.

Grabbing his coat, Allen left the apartment. After retrieving his car from the parking garage in the building, he drove out into the dense fog still blanketing the city. He was headed for the North State Parkway Medical Center to personally check on Dr. Stella Novak.

Megan Donegan had never seen a black man inside of her house before. Once in a while, over the years, they'd had an occasional postman or deliveryman of color; however, her brother, Joe, and their father, Bob Sr., before him, had been adamant that none of "them" were to ever be allowed inside the house. Now their father was dead and it was obvious, because of all the cops streaming in and out of the house, that

Joe was finally in the type of awful trouble that Megan had seen coming for years.

The initial cops to arrive were white and had presented her with a search warrant for the Marquette Park bungalow. The race of the scowling lieutenant, whose name she had failed to catch, had been of little comfort to her. The other policeman was younger and even possessed a hint of boyish innocence. Then after she had been in Sergeant Sherlock's presence for a short time, Megan realized that he was all business and going about his duties with a cold efficiency. She sat in the living room with her hands folded on her lap and silently remarked to herself that the scowling lieutenant and Sergeant Sherlock were like her brother Joe in many ways. In other ways they were also very different. She did realize that despite her fear of the lieutenant and Sergeant Sherlock, she was actually more comfortable in their presence than she had ever been with Joe.

More policemen arrived and they approached the forced entry to Joe's locked den very carefully. Megan started to warn them that her brother wouldn't like them going in there without his permission. But it was quite obvious by their manner that they really didn't care how Joe felt about the intrusion.

Within a short period after the scowling lieutenant and Sergeant Sherlock arrived, there were seven, maybe as many as ten, police officers in the house. They were all white. Then the tall black man arrived. By the way that all of the others deferred to the newcomer, it was obvious that he was in charge. There was a white policewoman with the black man, who didn't look like a law enforcement official to Megan at all. The lady cop was wearing an I.D. card around her neck and there was a badge on the dated patent leather belt she wore. She took an instant dislike to the policewoman, because she reminded Megan of Darla O'Hara, who had been the prom queen in Megan's senior-year high school class. It was Darla O'Hara who had saddled Megan with the nickname "Dumbbell." The sole Donegan clan girl-child had been scarred by that insulting name all of her life.

The scowling lieutenant and the black man came over to where Megan was seated on the living room couch. Before she could catch herself, she began thinking that the black man was handsome. Darla O'Hara would have classified him as a real "hunk." Megan became so deeply ashamed of herself over this thought that she blushed crimson and lowered her eyes. She knew that if any of her brothers ever discovered that she had any attraction at all for a black man, they would have most certainly killed her.

"Ms. Donegan," the scowling lieutenant said, "this is Chief of Detectives Larry Cole. He wants to ask you some questions about your brother."

At the mention of the black man's name, Megan's head came up with a snap and her eyes widened, as she stared at the black man towering over her. Forgetting the ingrained prejudice that had been drilled into her all of her life, she studied the newcomer.

Absorbing her gaze, Cole said a polite, "Hello, Ms. Donegan."

She continued to stare at him. She was attempting to discover something by this scrutiny that would give her some clue as to why her brother was so afraid of this man of color. She had heard Cole's name spoken many times before in this house. Joe said it almost every night, but he didn't do so in conversations with Megan, because the brother and sister rarely talked at all. But Joe had been plagued with nightmares over the past ten or twelve years. Nightmares during which he yelled out loud in his sleep. Nightmares that Megan had been too frightened to wake him from. Nightmares during which he had yelled out, such words as "the barmaid," "Stella," "Skip," "Dollar Bill," and invariably a screamed, "Damn you, Larry Cole!"

"Ms. Donegan," Cole was saying. "I need to talk to you about your brothers."

Megan frowned and repeated, "My brothers?"

"Yes," Cole said. "Robert and Joe."

By his manner, Megan could tell that something terrible had happened. Something terrible that was going to affect her for the rest of her life. Now her lifelong racial prejudice indoctrination was forgotten and she said to her brother's nemesis, "Would you care for a cup of coffee, Chief Cole? I have a great deal to tell you."

40

Gradually the dense fog lifted; however, an eerie haze still remained over a major portion of the southern end of Lake Michigan. The strain on the traffic congestion in Chicago eased and life began returning to a more or less normal level. On South Stony Island Avenue, an opal blue Mercedes sedan approached the entrance to the Chicago Skyway at Seventy-seventh Street. Dr. Stella Novak was driving her car with Sergeant Joe Donegan seated beside her. The crazed cop held a 9mm Browning semiautomatic pistol on his lap, and was closely watching the doctor and her driving.

Stella Novak's hands clutched the steering wheel so tightly that her knuckles were bloodlessly white. Back at her office, Sergeant Donegan told her he had located her sister Sophie after all these years. Her first reaction was to doubt him, but he had produced an item from his pocket that had nearly sent Stella into shock. It was a golden, heart-shaped locket, which her father had given Sophie before she left Poland for America. The locket was a family heirloom containing a miniature portrait of their great grandmother, whose name had also been Sophia.

"Where did you get this?" Stella was so stunned by this development that she spoke in her native tongue.

"Talk American, doc," Donegan scolded. When she repeated her question in English, he said, "Sophie sent it to you by me so you'd come with me to see her."

Stella noticed that the glint of madness in his eyes was more pronounced than she had ever seen it before and there was also an evil, manic presence that was frightening. Despite the many years that she had spent searching in vain for her sister, she didn't want to go anywhere with this man.

They were standing at the door to Stella's private office. The telephone on her desk was still off the hook, because she had been talking to Allen. She turned to tell the author what was going on when Donegan pulled the Browning pistol and said, "You're wasting time, Stella. Sophie's waiting."

With that, he stepped past her into the office and snatched her coat, hat, and purse from the coat rack. "Now you and me are going to walk out of here nice and slow just like a regular couple. I'm even going to let you drive. We've got to stop and pick up a couple of things from my car before we get started."

Donegan kept Dr. Novak right beside him, as they left the North State Parkway Medical Center and retrieved her car from the outdoor parking lot across the street. Once she had driven into the fog, he forced her to stop and get out of the car with him. There was a station wagon parked at an odd angle in a bus stop a half-block from the medical center. Donegan made her stand close to him as he removed a battered suitcase and a thick canvas bag from the back of the station wagon, which he placed in the trunk of her Mercedes. The contents of these bags were a mystery, but Stella's deep sense of impending doom increased with each passing second.

Fear had placed Stella in a daze, as she followed his directions and drove east to Lake Shore Drive before proceeding south to Fifty-seventh Street. They entered Jackson Park, passing the National Science and Space Museum. A few miles later they were about to enter the Chicago Skyway.

Frustrated at the situation in which she found herself, she screamed, "Where are we going, Sergeant Donegan?!"

"Take it easy, Doc. Like I told you, we're going to see Sophie." As the Mercedes ascended the ramp onto the Skyway, he added, "She's just about an hour's drive down this road. Then we'll have a nice family reunion."

Solomon Randolph was handcuffed to an iron ring in an interrogation room in the Third District Police Station at Seventy-first Street and Cottage Grove Avenue. His injured hand was bandaged and he was racing furiously through the alternatives facing him to extricate himself from this predicament. He was not experiencing the slightest degree of remorse for the murders he had committed; one of which had been of his mother. His main concerns were first getting a good lawyer and then making a deal with the cops. And Solomon Randolph had a lot to deal with. As such, he had used his incarceration telephone call to contact J. Ellis Montgomery, who was one of the best criminal attorneys in the Midwest. Randolph had also sent a message through the officers who had arrested him, to Chief Larry Cole.

Solomon Randolph had been confined in the narrow, white cinder-block room for nearly an hour when the door opened and Cole entered, followed by Blackie Silvestri. The double-breasted blue pinstriped suit that the chief of detectives was wearing instantly impressed the prisoner. For a cop, Cole dressed pretty good. The suit had to be Georgio Armani and the polished black loafers were from Bally. This was Solomon Randolph's kind of guy. At least as far as Larry Cole dressed.

At this moment Cole didn't look to be in much of a mood to discuss male fashion trends. "You asked to see me?"

"I want to talk to you alone, Cole."

He nodded at Blackie, who gave Solomon Randolph a hard look before stepping back out into the corridor. When the door closed, Cole leaned against the wall, folded his arms, and waited.

Solomon was wearing a wrinkled blue cotton shirt, a pair of trousers that looked as if they had been caught in a trash compactor, and a pair of sandals that exposed his recently manicured toenails. His hair was uncombed, his injured hand bandaged, and he was obviously badly hungover. But Cole could easily detect the criminal cunning in his face.

"I've got a deal for you," Randolph said.

Cole affixed the handcuffed man with a riveting gaze. "You

just killed your mother, Solomon. What kind of leniency do you think you're going to get from me or anyone else, much less a judge and jury?"

"I've heard that the great Larry Cole can do anything."

Cole's gaze did not alter. "Why should I do anything for you?"

The prisoner looked down at the bland pattern in the tile floor. "Eleven years ago a barmaid named Sophia Novak mysteriously vanished. The last person she was seen with was Alderman Skip Murphy. You've been personally working the missing persons investigation since then, but you haven't turned up much."

"Weren't you a little young back then?"

"Yeah," Randolph responded without looking up. "But my father told me what went down. You see, Cole, that night when Murphy and the barmaid left the Lake Shore Tap they were followed by a crooked cop. A cop who was shaking the bar down for kickbacks to avoid a license revocation. The cop followed them to the South Michigan Avenue Motel. Murphy and the barmaid got into some type of scrap in the room and the alderman killed her. Then the cop not only helped Murphy dispose of the body, but he also burned the motel to the ground to destroy all of the evidence."

"Was your father there, Solomon?"

"No. When he was alive he was in a position to know things."

"I assume that your father told you that the cop you're talking about is Sergeant Joe Donegan, whom I hear is your current business partner," Cole said.

Randolph looked up. "That's right, Cole. But Donegan and Murphy have been in cahoots together for years."

"Who gave Dollar Bill the information about Donegan and Murphy with the barmaid?"

"My father got it right from Donegan's mouth."

Cole took one of the chairs in the small interview room, turned it around, and straddled it backwards. "You're going to have to come up with a great deal more than that, Solomon. All that you've given me so far is hearsay."

"I know that," Randolph said defiantly. "I've got more."

Cole waited in silence.

"Donegan was hired by Murphy to kill Congressman Walter Johnson last night. The alderman wants to use this drug decriminalization issue he's been blabbing about as a springboard into the Senate. But first he had to get rid of Johnson."

"How did Donegan try to assassinate the congressman?"

"It was all over the news, Cole. He set Johnson's townhouse on fire."

"With what?" Cole demanded. The manner in which the arson had been committed had not been released to the press.

Randolph went back to staring at the floor. "He used a substance called Thermite."

"You're doing very well, Solomon," Cole said. "But there are some things that you're not telling me."

Randolph didn't look up at the cop. "Like what?"

"What your involvement was in the Donegan/Murphy conspiracy to assassinate the congressman. Then I want you to tell me all about what you were setting up down at DeWitt Plaza that involved Homicide Miller, the former leader of the Gangster Disciples, and a burglar named Irving Bettis."

"And if I do, what do I get out of it?"

The cop shrugged. "You start talking and then I'll see what I can do."

There was a knock on the interview room door. Before getting up to answer it, Cole said, "Think about what I said, Solomon. But when your attorney gets here, all bets are off."

Blackie motioned Cole out into the hall. "Allen Rollins called headquarters in something of a panic. He says that somebody kidnapped Stella Novak. While you were in with Randolph, an Eighteenth District beat car found Donegan's murdered brother's station wagon parked in a bus stop half a block from the North State Parkway Medical Center. Allen says that her car is missing from the parking lot across the street. He was on the phone with Stella when someone entered her office. Allen was able to hear a male voice, that could have been our boy Joe Donegan, saying something about having found Stella's missing sister."

Cole let this sink in for a moment before Blackie noticed him visibly stiffen. "That crazy bastard," Cole said.

"What is it, boss?" Blackie said with dismay.

"I'm going to talk to Solomon again. I want you to send Manny and Judy to locate and stick with Alderman Skip Murphy. I also need emergency transportation for us as soon as I'm through with Randolph."

Before Cole reentered the interview room, Blackie said, "What kind of emergency transportation?"

"Preferably, a helicopter."

41

Greg King, the host of the *Eye of the Public* program, was in his dressing room in the John Hancock Building TV studio when his producer knocked on the door. The young man with the lank hair and bad complexion said, "We've got a problem."

They were preparing to tape a segment of the show that would air on the following Sunday evening. The program's guest was Chicago Alderman Skip Murphy; the topic was drug decriminalization.

"What is it?" King asked the producer. "Our guest stand us up?"

"I wish it was that simple. The alderman's here, but I don't see how we can put him on camera."

"I'm not following you."

Greg King accompanied the producer to the reception area. The instant King saw the controversial alderman, he understood exactly what his producer was talking about.

Murphy rose from the couch in the reception area and extended his hand to the talk show host. The greeting was cordial enough under the circumstances. The alderman was appropriately dressed in a tailored black suit, pastel gray shirt, and black-and-white stripped tie that wasn't too busy for the television camera. His hair was neat, his mustache and beard neatly trimmed. The only problem was that a white bandage covered the left side of his face from just beneath his eye down to the upper area of his jaw. To the *Eye of the Public* program people, the politician looked like he'd just been mugged.

Noticing the focus of their stares on his bandaged face, Murphy said, "I had a slight accident while I was trimming my beard this morning. The scissors slipped and it took six stitches to close the cut. I guess I was lucky, because my doctor said that the scar will be barely noticeable."

A future scar was not the problem facing Greg King and his producer. From their experience in the industry, they knew that the bandage would be the focus of viewer scrutiny and that a number of questions would be raised about their guest's injury. The bandage could not be covered with makeup, so Skip Murphy would just have to go on camera with it exposed.

After they escorted Murphy into the studio, King and the producer met in the control room.

"Maybe we should postpone the drug decriminalization segment to another time," the producer said.

King shook his head. "We've got a schedule to keep. A postponement will throw us off for weeks. Position the alderman so that the camera only picks him up in a three-quarter profile shot of his right side."

"The bandage will still be visible."

"We can't help that. In fact, as far as the interview goes, we're going to ignore the bandage completely. The issue the alderman will be talking about is so controversial the viewing audience will soon forget about the bandage."

The producer was not convinced, but King was the boss.

They seated Skip Murphy on the set so that he was positioned in a three-quarter right profile. The bandage was indeed visible, but only partially. In the control booth, the producer studied Murphy on one of the monitors, took a deep breath, and crossed his fingers. The taping began.

After the initial introductions, King commenced the interview. "It is my understanding that you actually got the drug decriminalization concept from a segment of this program, Alderman Murphy."

"That's correct, Greg," Murphy said, using his baritone voice to optimum effect. "You had Chicago Police Department Chief of Detectives Larry Cole as your guest a few weeks ago. In the field of law enforcement, Cole is a genuine legend."

"He was also a fascinating guest," King interjected.

"Well, it was during that interview, Greg, that the issue of the United States futile war on so-called illegal substances came up. Chief Cole was candid enough to mention a number of strategies that could be employed to stem the flow of drugs into our communities. Those strategies ranged from a no-holds-barred, military-style response to the opposite end of the spectrum, which would be drug decriminalization."

In the control booth, the producer stood behind a video technician. There were separate monitors receiving feeds from the three in-studio cameras recording the interview. So far the camera focusing on Murphy's three-quarter right profile shot had revealed little of the bandage on the left side of his face. A second camera was focused exclusively on Greg King and a third, situated at a slightly different angle, took in both the interviewer and the subject. The shot from this last camera exposed a great deal more of the alderman's face. If possible, no part of the footage from the third camera would be used at all.

However, now, as the producer and the video technician stared at the monitor, the white bandage on Murphy's face began to darken. Skip Murphy was bleeding.

The producer checked the first monitor. From that angle, the spreading red stain was not yet visible.

On the set, Greg King also noticed that his guest was bleeding. He didn't know how much of the spreading red stain was being picked up on camera. This was actually academic at this point, because he was going to have to stop the interview. Then enough blood accumulated beneath the bandage to begin dripping down onto Murphy's shirt collar. The alderman appeared oblivious to his rapidly worsening condition.

"We simply cannot continue to throw bad money at a situation that is simply unwinnable," Murphy continued. "Under my plan, we would begin at the national level by setting up a series of medical centers across the country . . ."

The flow of blood had become a virtual hemorrhage. "Excuse me, Alderman Murphy," the talk show host said.

The politician was annoyed at the interruption. "I think I should be able to finish my point before you ask a question, Greg."

"Stop the tape," King said into his mike.

"What in the hell is going on?" Murphy snarled.

"You're bleeding badly, sir," King said.

Murphy reached up and touched the side of his face. His hand came away covered with blood.

With all of the municipal airports closed due to weather conditions in Chicago, it became almost impossible for the police to obtain emergency transportation by helicopter. As the morn-

CRITICAL ELEMENT 463

ing progressed, the dense fog began to fade and there were even a few sporadic patches of sunlight visible. But there was nothing man-made flying over the city.

Cole was waiting in the Third District commander's office. The chief of detectives was attempting to come up with an alternative plan of action to pursue Joe Donegan and his hostage, Dr. Stella Novak, when Blackie rushed in.

The lieutenant was breathing heavily, as he had apparently run from wherever he had obtained the news he wanted to so urgently convey.

"Okay," Cole said, "calm down, Blackie, before you give yourself a coronary."

Blackie managed to take a couple of deep breaths before saying, "We caught a break on the helicopter, boss. One has managed to get airborne, but we're going to have to get over to the Area One heliport as soon as possible so that it can pick us up." Blackie paused for a moment to take another breath and swallow before adding, "The air traffic control liaison office at OEC asked for a destination for the flight."

"I'm playing a hunch, so we're going to Union Pier, Michigan. I've already talked to a state police supervisor, who will meet us when we touch down."

With that, they headed for the Area One heliport at Fifty-first and Wentworth.

It took Stella Novak and Joe Donegan nearly ninety minutes to travel the eighty miles from Chicago to Union Pier, Michigan. There were no extreme traffic tie-ups, but the lingering ground mist made highway travel slow.

At the New Buffalo exit, Donegan said, "Okay, Doc, this is it. At the bottom of this ramp make a left turn."

Stella was now so exhausted by the fear and frustration that this crazed man had visited upon her today that she was operating on a human form of automatic pilot. If there was any light shining through the veil of gloom in which she found herself trapped, it was that she would soon discover her long-missing sister's fate. Even though Stella was certain that Sergeant Joe Donegan was now totally insane, she possessed an odd faith that he was telling her the truth about Sophie.

"There's a side road coming up in about a mile," Donegan said. "You're going to make a right turn there."

When they reached the turnoff, she was forced to slow down. This gave her an opportunity to take her eyes off the road momentarily and glance down at the gun he was holding on her. Since the moment they drove away from the medical center back in Chicago, the weapon had not wavered a single centimeter. Stella Novak was forced to face her situation head on.

Despite Donegan telling her that Sophie had been found, forcing her here at gunpoint placed her in the most dangerous situation that she had ever been before in her life. There would now be people looking for her, but she was now miles away from Chicago and it was a very big world. So she would have to depend on her own resources to extricate herself from the clutches of a madman. One thing that Dr. Stella Novak knew to a certainty was that she was not a weak person.

"Pull over here," he ordered in a more urgent tone than she had heard him use before.

She drove the Mercedes onto the gravel shoulder of the paved two-lane road. The area was surrounded by leafless trees and there was still snow on the ground giving the landscape a bleak, near alien quality. There were a few houses visible, but they were set back off the road. Stella followed Donegan's gaze to a lone ranch-style house that was barely visible through the trees. A white commercial vehicle with the sign "Smith's Cleaning Service" in green lettering was parked in front of the house. Keeping the gun trained on her, Donegan said, "Now we wait, Stella. We just wait."

Cole and Blackie heard the Bell Ranger light observation helicopter coming in from the east. The aircraft with the narrow nose and white-and-silver fuselage swept in over the Area One Police Center before beginning a vertical descent onto the helicopter pad in the parking lot, where Joe Donegan had abandoned his dirty Cutlass earlier that morning. The cops braced themselves against the prop wash until the aircraft touched down. Then they ran for the starboard-side rear door.

The pilot had his back to Cole and Blackie when they boarded. He was wearing a leather jacket, aviator glasses, and a baseball cap. A pair of headphones were fastened to his head over the cap. Half turning in his seat, the pilot motioned for them to put on matching communications headgear lying on the rear seats and fasten their seat belts. The engine began to rev preparatory to takeoff, as the pilot said over the onboard intercom, "What is our destination, Larry?"

Cole recognized the voice instantly. Allen Rollins was flying the helicopter. Cole was less than pleased over this development. "Allen, what are you doing here?"

"What no other qualified, licensed helicopter pilot in Chicago or the collar counties is willing to do under these weather conditions and that is fly this aircraft."

The author had him there. "Okay, you're the pilot," Cole said, "but that's all you are. Do I make myself clear?"

"Aye aye, sir. Now where to?"

"Union Pier, Michigan."

42

For Manny Sherlock and Judy Daniels, the assignment Cole had given them to locate Alderman Skip Murphy proved to be much easier than they thought it would be. They were on their way to City Hall in Blackie's squad car. The radio was turned to an easy listening jazz station, which the lieutenant had given strict orders was never to be changed. The station provided hourly news updates and at eleven o'clock a report was broadcast that Murphy had been rushed by Chicago Fire Department ambulance from a television studio on the Magnificent Mile to University Hospital. The alderman's medical problem had not been released to the media.

At the emergency room, the cops located the ambulance attendants, who had brought Murphy in. Despite Manny and Judy wearing their police identification cards on their outer garments, the attendants eyed the Mistress of Disguise/High Priestess of Mayhem's Sweet Sixteen from the 1950's outfit with open skepticism. Once they were convinced that Judy was indeed a cop, they told them about Murphy.

"The alderman was taping the *Eye of the Public* TV show

when a cut on his cheek started bleeding. But it wasn't like anything that I've ever seen before," the short, moon-faced male paramedic said.

The pretty Asian female added, "He said that he cut himself shaving this morning. The wound itself was fairly minor and he was attended by a doctor, who closed it with six stitches. During the taping of the television show, he tore the stitches and the wound reopened."

"How did he do that?" Judy asked.

The male attendant shrugged and the female shook her head. She said, "Beats me, but he lost so much blood before we got him here that the emergency room personnel are giving him a transfusion."

Manny and Judy exchanged glances punctuated by raised eyebrows. It was obvious that Alderman Skip Murphy wouldn't be going anywhere for a while.

The housekeeping crew completed their twice-monthly work at Skip Murphy's Union Pier, Michigan, home. Donegan waited until the truck left the driveway and disappeared down the access road. Then he said to Stella, "Let's go, Doc. Drive around in back of the cabin."

Obediently, she did as he instructed. With the Mercedes out of sight, Donegan ordered Stella to come out of the car behind him through the passenger side door. He retrieved the canvas bag from the trunk, leaving the battered suitcase. He forced Stella to leave her purse in the car and slipped the car keys into his coat pocket. He made his hostage walk in front of him onto the enclosed wooden porch. At the back door he motioned her to stand off to the side while he stepped back and kicked the door open.

The interior of Skip Murphy's cabin possessed a pleasantly fresh smell. The hardwood floors and all the furniture had been polished and wood was stacked in the fireplace waiting to be lit.

"Nice place, isn't it, Stella?" he said, dropping the canvas bag on the floor.

"Where is my sister, Sergeant Donegan?" she demanded.

"In due time, my dear Doctor Novak, but first things first."

He grabbed her roughly by the arm and forced her into Murphy's den. The wood-paneled room was tastefully furnished and equipped with a pool table, bar, and sophisticated television, video player, and stereo system console. There was also a computer and printer on a stand beside the desk. Donegan eyed the computer momentarily before spotting something that was of greater interest to him.

"Right this way, Doc."

He forced Stella over to a door in a corner of the room adjacent to Murphy's desk. Opening this door revealed a bathroom without windows. He made her stand over by the shower stall, while he checked the medicine cabinet, which was empty, and a storage area beneath the sink where cleaning supplies were stored. Satisfied that there was nothing that she could use as a weapon against him, Donegan said, "Take a little time and freshen yourself up, Doc, so you'll look pretty for your sister."

He then backed out of the room and secured the door from the outside with a straight-back wooden chair. Then Donegan went to work.

The Bell Ranger helicopter flew across the southern end of Lake Michigan en route to Union Pier. Allen Rollins, who had learned to fly during the period of his life that he had spent as a soldier of fortune, was pushing the helicopter to the point that the aircraft began vibrating. Blackie was not pleased with this development.

Cole, keeping an eye on the tops of the low-level clouds beneath them, brought Allen and Blackie up-to-date on the investigation he had begun back in 1993.

"I've always suspected that someone else was involved with Skip Murphy in the mysterious disappearance of Stella's sister. Then the South Michigan Avenue Motel was burned to the ground, and the bartender and a barmaid that worked with Sophia Novak at the Lake Shore Tap were both killed. My theory that Murphy was involved was valid, but there was no way that I could convince anyone, much less myself, that he carried this off alone. Now we know that Joe Donegan was involved right from the start."

"But what does he want with Stella?" Allen Rollins asked over the onboard intercom.

"I'm still working on that," Cole said. "Joe's brother, Lieutenant Robert M. Donegan, Jr. of the Chicago Fire Department, had something of a larcenous streak in him. He'd been suspected of stealing from fire scenes for years. His superiors were never able to prove anything and Bob Donegan actually received a number of awards for bravery. However, their sister Megan shed some light on Bob Jr.'s alleged valor. Her older brother rushed into burning buildings and hazardous situations so he would be the first to see if there was anything there worth stealing. Because of the suspicions about him at the fire department, he had been passed over twice for promotion. Megan told me that Joe fenced Bob Jr.'s contraband to include a couple of cases of Thermite grenades. The Donegan brothers split the profits right down the middle, but a few years ago they had a falling out."

"Why did the Lone Stranger kill him?" Blackie asked.

"Joe Donegan's psychotic, Blackie. According to Solomon Randolph, he was responsible for the explosion that killed Harrison Jones, who was the last serious challenger for Skip Murphy's aldermanic seat."

"But we can't use what Randolph said in court," Blackie said.

"Not without strong corroboration, but we've got a lot more on Sergeant Joe Donegan than a decade-old murder," Cole responded.

"You still haven't told me what he wants with Stella and why we're going to Union Pier." Allen said.

Cole sighed. "I'm playing a hunch. Donegan told Randolph that he wanted to arrange a meeting at Murphy's cabin to collect the fee for the congressman's assassination. I believe he's on his way there now and kidnapped Stella for a reason."

Allen was forced to fly the helicopter on computerized instrumentation as they descended through the fog. "And that reason is?" he questioned.

Cole answered. "Stella is bait for a trap."

Joe Donegan busied himself around the interior of Skip Murphy's Union Pier cabin. He was wiring the place to explode and then burn to the ground. He had begun planning this massive conflagration using three highly flammable Thermite grenades since the moment he accepted the contract to assassinate Congressman Johnson. The trap was originally planned for Skip

Murphy and Solomon Randolph. Now it would accommodate none other than Chief of Detectives Larry Cole.

Donegan knew that Cole was hot on his trail. All of the signs were there from his computers being jammed to the amateurish attempt to tail him earlier. Then, as he fled through the fog, the crooked cop had decided to make this a game. "Catch me if you can," was what he called it when he first detected the surveillance at the McDonald's restaurant back in Chicago. Now the game was in progress and getting more interesting with each passing second.

With the money in the trunk of Stella's car and the head start he had, Donegan could have vanished and been halfway across the country by now. But that wouldn't stop Cole. The cop would keep coming, which would force Donegan to constantly look back over his shoulder for the rest of his life. Of course, no matter what happened to Cole, Donegan knew that he would remain a wanted man. Cole's death would send major repercussions through the international law enforcement community. That would make them come after him with everything that they had. This would only succeed in making the game that much more interesting. Especially with him still being in possession of a lot more Thermite grenades.

Donegan's psychosis did not allow him to experience any remorse or guilt over the murder of his own brother. They had been at odds since Joe decided that his split would be seventy-thirty from the sale of the items Bob Jr. pilfered from fire scenes. After all, being the fence, the cop was taking all of the chances. Actually Bob Jr.'s death had been a good thing, because it provided another clue for the great Larry Cole to follow. Then there was Dr. Stella Novak.

He once more checked the wiring of the Thermite canisters.

The cop had learned everything that he knew about starting fires from his father and his brothers. In order to effectively fight a fire, smoke eaters had to know how they started.

Satisfied that all of his preparations for Cole's fiery trap were in place, Donegan was about to spring the special surprise on Stella. He was crossing Murphy's den when he heard a helicopter flying overhead. The aircraft was at such a low altitude that the walls of the cabin shook.

Donegan grinned. Stella would soon have company.

He retrieved the final item from the canvas bag in which he had carried the Thermite. He placed it on the desk in Murphy's study between two lamps. He was looking forward to Stella's reunion with Sophie. A reunion that would eventually include Larry Cole. A reunion that would be permanent for all parties concerned.

When everything was in readiness, Donegan went to get Stella out of the bathroom. He removed the chair propped against the knob and opened the door.

Three blue-and-maize-colored Michigan State Police cars, their Mars lights flashing, were waiting in the vacant parking lot behind the Sports Challenge Bar in Union Pier. Allen set the helicopter down gently and he and his passengers deplaned. A state police sergeant, sporting the name tag "Januczyk" on his uniform jacket, stood just beyond the backwash from the propeller blades. He was forced to hold onto his drill sergeant–style hat to keep it from being blown off.

When Cole approached, the sergeant saluted and said, "We got your message from our headquarters, Chief Cole. We're here to escort you to wherever you want to go and assist you in whatever you need to do."

Before Cole could brief Januszyk, he spied Allen Rollins standing close by. "Excuse me a second, Sarge."

He took Allen off to the side out of earshot of the state cops. "You should stay here, Allen."

"No way, Larry," he argued. "If it hadn't been for me, you and Blackie wouldn't be here now. I've got to find out if Stella is okay."

Cole didn't like it, but at this moment he really had no choice, "Okay, come along but remember what I told you back in Chicago about staying out of the way."

Seconds later, the three police cars—with their emergency equipment off—sped toward Skip Murphy's cabin.

Stella's grandmother had told her stories about the atrocities the Polish people had suffered during and after World War II. First there had been the Nazis with their SS extermination squads. The Germans had killed three million Poles in concentration camps and made slave laborers out of millions more. Then the Russians came and the lot of the Polish people remained just about the same. For centuries the natives of Stella Novak's homeland had been disenfranchised and oppressed by stronger nations. This had imbued them with a sense of national nobility in the face of adversity and a strong survival instinct. Stella now called on these qualities in her place of imprisonment in the bathroom of Skip Murphy's Michigan cabin.

In the moments of solitude she had experienced since Sergeant Donegan locked her in, Stella recalled one of her grandmother's stories from postwar Poland.

There had been a Russian colonel, who periodically came to their village outside of Lodz. Backed up by a squad of soldiers armed with automatic weapons, the Russian selected any woman in the village that he wanted and forced her to submit to him sexually. It didn't matter how old or young the Polish female was or if she was married or not. The Russian had the power of life or death over the Poles and from time to time, along with the rapes, he would exercise that right by indiscriminately having villagers killed.

Finally, one of his victims decided that something had to be done about the Russian officer. When he selected her for sex, she went with him. After submitting to his advances in a hotel room, she waited for the Russian to fall asleep. Then she killed him with his own pistol. Knowing that she could never escape after what she had done, the Polish woman committed suicide. Before she pulled the trigger on herself, she used the Russian's blood to leave a message on the wall of the hotel room where she had been violated. It read, "Ja wiecej tego nie zcierpie," in Polish. Translated, "I will endure no more."

Although Sergeant Donegan had made no sexual advances toward Stella, he had nevertheless violated her as viciously as the Russian officer had done the Polish woman. And the young physician had forced herself to come to the terrible realization that he had not brought her here for a reunion with her sister. At least not with Sophie still being alive. Then he had held Stella at gunpoint and wouldn't let her tell Allen where they were going. She was certain that after he played out this bizarre charade, he was going to kill her.

"Ja wiecej tego nie zcierpie," she said into the clean emptiness of the cabin bathroom. "I will endure no more."

Stella had taken a seat on the side of the bathtub. She wasn't in the bathroom more than two minutes when she came to a decision. Rising, she crossed the tile floor and opened the cabinet beneath the sink. When Sergeant Donegan opened it, she had seen the cleaning supplies. Perhaps he had not noticed or didn't see the threat posed by the bottle of Liquid Plumber behind the containers of Pine Sol and Comet, and the scrub brushes and rags. She knew that Liquid Plumber was a highly toxic substance used to open clogged drains, and would make a very formidable weapon. Removing the bottle from the cabinet, she found that it was nearly full. Unscrewing the cap, she moved to stand a foot from the door. Clutching the bottle tightly in her right hand, she waited. Joe Donegan opened the door three minutes and seventeen seconds later.

"Okay, Doc, Sophie . . ." he managed to say before she threw nine ounces from the thirty-two ounce bottle of Liquid Plumber into his face. The substance splashed from his head to his throat and before he could blink his eyes shut, he was blinded. Clutching at his burning face, Donegan let out a blood-curdling scream and stumbled back into the den.

The three Michigan State Police cars stopped on the paved road running in front of Skip Murphy's cabin. Cole, Blackie, and Allen Rollins, accompanied by Sergeant Januszyk and four troopers, exited their vehicles. They all waited for the Chicago police chief of detectives to give them instructions as to what they were to do next.

"Sarge, send two of your people to cover the rear of the cabin. We'll give them a couple of minutes to get into place, then we'll go in from the front."

After Sergeant Januszyk dispatched two of the troopers, Blackie asked Cole, "How are we going to play it from this end, boss?"

"I'm working on it, Blackie," Cole said, staring off through the trees at the ranch-style house. "I'm working on it."

Then the sounds of gunshots carried through the woods to their position. Gunshots that had come from inside the cabin.

The Liquid Plumber that Stella Novak had thrown in his face blinded Joe Donegan. The tremendous pain caused by his seared flesh that was beginning to melt off his face complicated this blindness. From being a psychotic homicidal maniac, Donegan had deteriorated to the level of a predatory beast. A wounded, dangerous predatory beast.

The initial shock of the attack by the woman, whom he had initially thought to have no more guts than a frightened mouse, had so disoriented him that he collapsed to his knees and then pitched forward to lie facedown on the floor. He clawed at his chemically scalded face, tearing away flesh in an attempt to rid himself of the unbelievable pain. And in those initial seconds of hellish agony, he was aware of a deafening noise surrounding him. The pain did not ease, but began reaching a bearable level, if an injury as horrible as the one inflicted on him could ever be tolerated. It was then that he realized that the horrendous sound was that of his own screams.

He got up on all fours and attempted to open his eyes. His vision was nothing but a red blur. His screams had become a series of groans. Then Donegan formed a dedicated resolve in his mind. Gritting his teeth, he crawled forward. He crashed head-on into a wall, but his facial burns negated any pain from the collision.

With some difficulty, he got to his feet. Leaning back against the wall gave him some degree of orientation in his blinded state. He was standing against the east wall facing the interior of Murphy's den. The bathroom, in which he had imprisoned Stella Novak, was somewhere along this wall. However, this was of no importance to him at this moment. Joe Donegan's entire being became focused on killing the woman who had blinded him. He realized that this would be the last act of his life.

He pulled his .44 Magnum revolver and 9mm pistol and held them out in front of him at arm's length. Then he tried to speak, but the only sound that came out of his mouth was a muffled grunt. He was attempting to call out to Stella, but his mouth wouldn't work. This was because his lips, chin, and most of the flesh on both of his cheeks had been so severely burned that his teeth were exposed. Standing against the wood-paneled wall with his guns pointed, Joe Donegan looked like a ghoul that had just climbed from an ancient grave.

After successfully attacking her captor, Stella Novak intended to get out of this house in the woods as quickly as she could. Donegan was lying on the floor outside of the bathroom. He was writhing in pain and screaming. Under different circumstances, she would have rushed to attend him. Now she couldn't risk going near him even if he did have her car keys in his coat pocket.

After throwing the caustic liquid in the policeman's face, Stella retreated back into the bathroom and watched Donegan fall to the floor. Satisfied that her captor was sufficiently incapacitated, she moved forward carefully. Stepping out of the bathroom, she inched around his prone form until he was between her and her former prison cell. Then she turned to flee.

Stella was crossing the study when she noticed a pair of lamps on the desk. She would have paid them no attention except that there was something extremely odd resting on the desk between them. It was a human skull.

Despite being in a panic, which brought her close to hysterics, Stella stopped to look at the fire-blackened object. Then she realized why Joe Donegan had brought her here.

The skeleton's head was Sophie's. All of the remaining teeth were visible and Stella was able to recall enough about her sister's dental work to identify what was there. Slowly, she sank down on her knees in front of the desk. She reached out her hand to touch what was left of her long-dead sister and tears filled her eyes. She was not aware of Joe Donegan rising from the floor on the other side of the room.

Stella made the sign of the cross, lowered her head, and began crying softly.

Although blind, Donegan homed in on the sound of her sobs and opened fire. He hit her twice.

Cole and the officers outside surrounded the cabin. They were aware that the shots they had heard came from inside the house and had not been directed at them. They had the cabin covered from every angle and were preparing to advance when flames became visible spreading rapidly throughout the structure.

Allen Rollins charged toward the front door, but Blackie quickly tackled him and held him down. The author struggled to free himself, but the lieutenant held him fast.

As Cole looked on, the fire began spreading and it was apparent that a Thermite grenade had been detonated inside. There was nothing that anyone outside could do.

Stella sustained a superficial graze gunshot wound across her back and a more serious wound to the back of her right thigh. When Donegan opened fire, he discharged four rounds from each weapon in the general direction of Stella's sobs. Of the remaining six rounds, five became embedded harmlessly in cabin walls. But the sixth struck one of the Thermite canisters that Donegan had rigged inside. It had been his original plan to handcuff Stella to a chair in front of Sophie's skull. Then he'd leave her there while he made his way out the back door. The Thermite canisters would totally destroy the doctor, her dead sister's remains, Murphy's cabin, and everything else from two to as far away as five miles. The artistic part of Donegan's plan was that the initial detonation would only occur when someone, whom he expected would be Larry Cole, opened the front door.

Now the blaze had been prematurely ignited. Donegan remained with his back against the east wall and felt the heat spreading rapidly through the cabin. It would soon be over for him, but he wasn't about to surrender to the element he'd used against so many others in the past. Donegan began shooting into the wall of flame approaching him. By the time the fire consumed him, his guns were empty.

State Police Sergeant Januszyk was tied up on his walkie-talkie for some minutes requesting fire-fighting equipment to respond to this area of Union Pier. At Chief Cole's direction, the state police supervisor had instructed his dispatcher to request the nearest military facility to rush a flame-retardant chemical capable of extinguishing Thermite. Almost immediately a Huey H41L tanker helicopter was dispatched from the Glenview Naval Air Station in Illinois. It had an ETA at the Union Pier fire site of eleven minutes. By that time the intensity of the blaze had already forced the cops, who had rushed to rescue Stella Novak, back to the access road.

The troopers, assigned by Sergeant Januszyk to cover the

rear of the cabin, were forced to take a long detour through the woods to escape the rapidly spreading fire. When they reappeared, walking up the access road from the west, they were not alone. The troopers were carrying a bleeding, soot-blackened Dr. Stella Novak.

Cole and Allen Rollins rushed to help them. The two male troopers explained that they had found the injured woman in a daze wandering through the woods after the cabin caught fire. Allen demanded to be allowed to carry Stella to one of the police cars at the scene, which was going to take her to the hospital. Before they departed, Cole asked Stella, "Where's Donegan?"

She managed to weakly point toward the expanding wall of flame. "He's still in there with Sophie."

After the police car departed with lights flashing and siren blaring, the Huey tanker helicopter arrived to begin spraying a flame-retardant substance on the blaze. Cole and Blackie stood on the access road watching the fire die.

"What did Stella mean about Donegan being in the cabin with Sophie, boss?" Blackie asked.

Cole stared through the remains of the charred woodland at the pile of smoldering debris that had once been Skip Murphy's resort cabin. "Back at the Third District Station, Solomon Randolph told me that Donegan had proof that Murphy was involved in Sophie Novak's disappearance and death. When I asked Randolph what kind of proof, our would-be young criminal genius said that the evidence could be identified with a scientific certainty."

Blackie chuckled. "Don't tell me that Donegan's been carrying around parts of Sophie's body for the past ten years?"

"No," Cole responded. "He didn't carry them around, but

he probably did store them in that freezer in the garage behind his brother's house."

"Why?" Blackie asked with dismay.

"It was his insurance policy to be used against Murphy if the Alderman ever crossed him. If that happened, Donegan would stash whatever was left of Stella's sister's body up here somewhere and then give us an anonymous call as to where we could find the remains."

"Then we'd pinch Skip Murphy and charge him with murder."

Cole shook his head. "We would have done some investigating, Blackie, but I think it would be necessary to have Donegan testify against the alderman for us to get a conviction. Of course that would have worked both ways."

"Now that Donegan's dead it doesn't look like we're going to recover much evidence from what's left of that cabin." The Huey helicopter had succeeded in completely extinguishing the Thermite blaze. By some miracle, none of the other cabins in the area were damaged. "So what are we going to do about Murphy?" Blackie said.

Cole continued to stare at the blackened forest. He responded simply, "Nothing."

43

Stella Novak was hospitalized for two days for smoke in-halation and treatment of the gunshot wounds Joe Donegan had inflicted on her. Luckily, if being shot can be construed as being lucky in any form, she had not been hit by the crooked cop's powerful .44 magnum revolver. The first of two 9mm rounds seared the flesh of her back leaving a six-inch gash an eighth of an inch deep. The second pierced her thigh and lodged in a muscle. The bullet was removed without complications and the scar would be barely noticeable. Actually, the only person, other than her own physician, who would ever see the scar, would be her husband.

Congressman Walter Johnson was released from University Hospital a week after Stella Novak returned to Chicago from Michigan. The young doctor, although weakened by her ordeal at the hands of a madman, attended her recovering patient daily in a hospice, which was close to the North State Parkway Medical Center. By March 1, Walter Johnson was strong enough to attend the rally for Skip Murphy's drug decriminalization proposal that was being held at McCormick Place.

Contrary to expectations, the rally only drew about a third of the anticipated fifty thousand supporters that Murphy had projected. In fact, all of the attendees were not backers of the controversial issue, as one thousand vocal demonstrators opposing the issue picketed in front of the convention center. The police were called in for crowd control because of a violent scuffle that broke out between pro- and anti-drug decriminalization factions. Twenty-nine people were arrested in the melee.

Congressman Johnson was accompanied to the rally by his doctor, Stella Novak; the doctor's fiancé, Allen Rollins, aka adventure-novelist Seth Champion; and a slightly built young woman, who wore her short dark hair plastered to her skull with pomade and a pair of tortoise-shell glasses. This woman, who was paid scant attention by anyone at the rally who observed her, appeared to be a member of the congressman's staff. She was actually there in a more official capacity, as an observer for the Chicago police department. It was none other than Judy Daniels, the Mistress of Disguise/High Priestess of Mayhem.

An usher, who was active in Skip Murphy's aldermanic ward organization, escorted the congressman and his entourage to the VIP section in the front row of the Arie Crown Theater. Of the fifty-member Chicago City Council, only four of Murphy's fellow aldermen put in an appearance. Of course, Alderman Foghorn Leghorn was there.

Skip Murphy's supporters saw Walter Johnson's appearance at the rally as a boost for the drug decriminalization issue. This was not necessarily true. The congressman, who had so recently come face-to-face with death, did see a degree of merit in some of the things Murphy had so far proposed, but he also saw a number of serious flaws. He was here tonight to address those flaws.

A few minutes before the rally was scheduled to begin, Murphy sent word to Johnson by one of his ushers requesting that the congressman say a few words to the assemblage, if he

was up to it. It was anticipated that Johnson would be brief due
to his very serious medical problems. The congressman accepted the invitation, which succeeded in lifting Alderman
Murphy's flagging spirits.

Skip Murphy was resting in a lounge behind the stage of the
bowl-shaped theater. The past month had been the worst of his
life. In fact, he was forced to admit that what he had just been
through was worse than the ordeal he had experienced on the
morning Sophia Novak died. The events of February 6 and 7
had taken Murphy from the heights of an anticipated political
triumph to the depths of criminal desperation. In a period of
less than twenty-four hours, he had seen his plot to capture the
much-coveted congressional seat come crashing down. Against
all odds, Walter Johnson had not only miraculously survived,
but made a complete recovery. Then Solomon Randolph had
been arrested for killing his own mother and Joe Donegan was
trapped in Murphy's Michigan cabin, where the crooked cop
had been burned to death in a fire. The news that day had come
in ever worsening waves. Some of the events were reported by
the Chicago media; however, Murphy learned most of them
from someone who had immediate access to internal department information; the chairman of the Police and Fire Committee, Alderman Sherman Ellison Edwards (aka Foghorn
Leghorn).

Murphy was still in the emergency treatment area of University Hospital when Edwards arrived. The cut on Murphy's
cheek had stopped bleeding, but the attending physician told
him that all of the stitches had been mysteriously ripped open.
The doctor questioned Murphy's activities that morning looking for an explanation for what had occurred, but the patient

was unable to come up with any answers. Murphy was hooked to an IV in an attempt to replenish the blood he had lost and there was even talk of admitting him to the hospital for overnight observation. Then there was a commotion outside the curtained cubicle followed by Sherman Edwards forcing his way inside over the vociferous objections of a nurse.

"We've got to get you out of here right now, Skipper boy," Edwards said with such urgency that the heart monitor Murphy was attached to began beeping wildly. "A couple of Cole's people are sitting outside in the waiting room and they're not paying you a condolence call. Now get your butt up and let's go."

Murphy summoned the doctor and forced him to remove the IV. With his wounded cheek re-stitched, the alderman left the hospital on wobbly legs through a rear exit. Edwards had a car waiting and they sped away believing that they had eluded the cops. But after traveling only a couple of blocks, the black Ford sedan driven by Manny Sherlock caught up with them.

Over the next few days Skip Murphy didn't find a great deal to worry about as far as Larry Cole and the Chicago police department were concerned. Yes, cops followed him around, but only periodically. In the morning, Murphy would open the drapes in the living room of his Central Station townhouse and see an unmarked police car parked on the street. However, by the time Murphy left for City Hall, the police car would be gone. At night, it was the same thing. Sometimes there was a cop car there; sometimes there wasn't.

During the ensuing weeks, following the Union Pier conflagration in which the diabolical Joe Donegan had finally met his flaming demise, Murphy drove his Jaguar around Chicago and would spot one of the drab, late-model American-made sedans filling the reflection in his rearview mirror. Then, as with the surveillance outside his townhouse, the cars suddenly vanished.

Finally, he tired of this game of cat and mouse. With the support of Sherman Ellison Edwards, Murphy demanded that Cole come to City Hall for a face-to-face meeting, which Murphy intended to turn into a confrontation. He planned to charge the chief of detectives with unwarranted harassment and to that end had a small contingent of media types standing by. But Cole failed to show. The arrogant cop sent a message back that he was much too busy engaged in the hunt for a dangerous serial killer who had been preying on school children in the Windy City. Again, on the advice of Alderman Foghorn Leghorn, Murphy did not press the issue. Before he could decide on an alternate course of action, the woman for whom the alderman had bought a magnum of champagne at Sandy's Jazz Club on a wintry night, called his office and made an appointment to see him. Murphy's enormous ego was still functioning despite his bandaged face and he agreed to meet with investigative journalist Kate Ford.

On the afternoon of her scheduled appointment, the alderman put his best foot forward. He donned a new light green, tailored suit, which had been delivered by his tailor just the day before. He selected his accessories with exquisite care and when he arrived at City Hall, despite the bandage still adorning his cheek, he received a number of compliments on his ensemble.

Waiting in his Commerce Committee offices for the part-time jazz singer to arrive, Skip Murphy's old playboy instincts began acting up. Kate Ford was a sexy young woman with a good pedigree. In fact, being seen with her socially could become something of a feather in his cap. And despite the reversals Murphy had suffered, he realized that Congressman Walter Johnson couldn't live forever.

At the appointed time, the journalist arrived and was promptly ushered into his office by the committee secretary. As Kate came through the door, Murphy stood to greet her and extended his hand. Her grip was a shade masculine for the alderman's tastes, but that translated to him that she would not be a timid lover.

They settled in for the interview. He had only seen this woman once before and that was under the stage lights of Sandy's Jazz Club. There she had looked soft, very feminine, and even a tad vulnerable. Sitting across from him now, he noticed that she was quite different. She was still attractive in a wholesome, girl-next-door fashion, but there was also something hard-edged to the point of cynicism about her. Murphy suddenly had the decidedly disorientating thought that she came on like a cop. Then his injured cheek began tingling. Subconsciously, he reached up and touched the bandage. Much to his relief, his fingertips came away dry.

"Do you mind if I tape the interview?" she asked, removing a compact Sony recorder from the leather shoulder bag she carried.

"Be my guest," he responded, leaning forward to steeple his hands in front of his face and look over the tops of his fingertips at her with a gaze that he thought was seductive.

She began with, "Alderman Murphy, you have been the center of a great deal of controversy these past few weeks."

He slid easily into his role as champion of drug decriminalization by saying, "Please call me Skip, Kate. When anyone comes up with a new idea, which challenges long-standing, firmly held beliefs, there is bound to be vocal opposition. I give you such examples from history as Copernicus, Galileo, Doctor Martin Luther King, Jr. and . . ."

"Actually," she interrupted, "I wasn't talking about drug decriminalization. It has been rumored that you were involved in a conspiracy with a corrupt police officer to assassinate Congressman Walter Johnson."

Any degree of sexual interest Skip Murphy had in this woman vanished. With a tight voice, he said, "Where did you get such a ridiculous accusation?"

"A young man named Solomon Randolph will soon go on trial charged with two counts of first degree murder. His attorney of record is J. Ellis Montgomery of whom you have no doubt heard. I have it on good information that Mr. Montgomery plans to subpoena you as a witness."

Murphy laughed. "I assure you, Ms. Ford, I had nothing to do with the murders that Solomon Randolph is accused of committing."

"That is probably true, but Montgomery has hinted to a select few, including me, that he has evidence, through his client, that you were not only involved with the assassination attempt, but also the murder of a woman named Sophia Novak some years ago."

Murphy thought that he handled the shock of this unexpected development well. Without losing his composure, he said, "Please shut off your tape recorder, Ms. Ford."

She complied, but left the instrument on his desk.

"Everything that you just alluded to is no more than groundless rumor, which has no basis in fact, much less any evidentiary value in a court of law. Now if you want to talk about drug decriminalization, I'm your man. As far as your line of questioning goes up to this point, I would have to warn you that you are coming very close to slander."

"Do you have any comment at all about Solomon Randolph's allegations?" she pressed.

"Nothing more than my belief that J. Ellis Montgomery is grasping at straws in an attempt to mount an insanity plea for his client. I had nothing to do with Solomon Randolph or the deceased Sergeant Joe Donegan and you can quote me on that."

Returning her tape recorder to her shoulder bag, Kate stood up.

"Is the interview over so soon?" Murphy actually sounded disappointed.

"I know when I'm wasting my time, Alderman." She turned for the door, but stopped before grasping the knob. "Could I ask you one more question?"

"Sure."

"How did you know that the crooked cop I was talking about was Sergeant Joe Donegan?"

Before he could explode from the mixture of frustration and outrage warring within him, she pointed at his face and said, "You're bleeding again, Skip. Madame Devereaux, the owner of Sandy's Jazz Club in Hyde Park where we met, recommends a combination of Mercurochrome and witch hazel applied in the shape of tiny crosses to close difficult to heal cuts like yours. A bit of holy water thrown in wouldn't hurt. I suggest that you give her remedy a try as soon as possible." With that she let herself out.

With Kate Ford's damning, but unverifiable allegations echoing through his head, Skip Murphy went home early that day, after a visit to a Catholic Church in his ward, and tried the odd nightclub owner's remedy. To his amazement, the cut showed definite signs of improvement the next day and did not reopen again.

Now on the night of March 1, as he sat in the lounge behind the Arie Crown Theater, Skip Murphy reviewed the disaster that the last few weeks of his life had been. Despite the problems, he was forced to admit that it could have been a great deal worse. Had Joe Donegan survived and been forced by Larry Cole to testify against him, Murphy could be looking forward to spending the next twenty years of his life in prison. Rising from his chair to preside over the rally for drug decriminalization, he had no way of knowing that he was far from being out of the woods as far as his political career was concerned.

After the rally, Sherman Ellison Edwards offered to buy Murphy a drink. This wasn't a purely social invitation, because Murphy needed the dubious medicinal properties of distilled spirits to prevent him from having a nervous breakdown. To say that Skip Murphy was badly shaken after the drug decriminalization rally would have been an understatement. What he had originally anticipated as being a night of triumph ended up being one of total disaster.

Murphy was reeling from the impact of the brief remarks that Congressman Walter Johnson had made. Johnson had not only destroyed the alderman's initial decriminalization proposal, but had come up with the outline for an alternative program, which made the issue that Murphy had been championing all these weeks sound as if the congressman had come up with the initial concept on his own. Such was the nature of politics Chicago style.

Sherman Edwards picked Murphy up from the loading dock below the Arie Crown Theater at McCormick Place. The area was isolated from the media and the crowd that had attended the rally. Skip Murphy was in something of a daze when he slid into the front passenger seat of Edwards's Cadillac. Murphy was aware that Edwards was talking as they drove onto Lake Shore Drive and sped north, but the former champion of drug decriminalization in America was unable to focus on what Foghorn Leghorn was saying.

Edwards selected a bar that was dark to the point of being subterranean. When they sat down in a booth in the back, Murphy found the place to be oddly familiar. It wasn't until an overweight cocktail waitress, whose fat body was stuffed into a bunny costume, came over to the table did the realization dawn on him as to where they were. It was the Lake Shore Tap. The shock brought Murphy out of his daze.

Edwards had not stopped talking. "We can turn this to our advantage, Skipper boy. We're not dead with this drug decriminalization thing yet." He looked up at the obese waitress. "Bring us a couple of double vodka martinis, sweetheart, and tell Don, the bartender, that Alderman Sherm Edwards is in the house with a guest."

"Pardon, sir," she said with a thick Eastern European accent. The look of confusion on her face indicated that she hadn't understood a word that he said.

"Excuse me a second, Skip," Edwards said, leaving the booth and brushing past the cocktail waitress. He went over to the bar to place the order himself. The bewildered woman followed him.

Being alone in this bar was the last thing in the world that Murphy wanted. There were two many ghosts present. Then there was someone standing over him. Murphy looked up at Larry Cole.

"Rough night, Alderman?" the cop said, flashing a mocking grin.

"Are you also going to start following me around, Cole?" Murphy said, looking anxiously in the direction of the bar, where Edwards was busy talking to the bartender.

"No," Cole responded. "The Chicago Police Department has no further interest in you, Skip. You've beaten the system, which doesn't happen often, but does indeed occur from time-to-time."

Murphy scowled. "I'm not in the mood right now, Cole."

The cop's mocking manner did not change, nor did he move. "I heard that Congressman Johnson wasn't very complimentary about your drug decriminalization plans at the rally tonight."

"He found one or two problems," Murphy admitted.

In fact, Walter Johnson had called Murphy's proposal not only foolhardy, but also ill-conceived and flawed to the point of criminal negligence. Johnson had used those exact words during the brief remarks he had made during the rally.

Murphy said to Cole, "But the congressman did say that he was going to recommend the formation of a House subcommittee to study drug decriminalization."

"Why do I get the impression that you're not happy about tonight's developments?" Cole said.

"It worked out, Cole," Murphy snapped. "Now maybe you can answer a question for me."

"Go ahead, Alderman. Ask away."

"What have you got against me?"

"Nothing at all, Skip. In fact, drug decriminalization, at

least the concept that Congressman Johnson has proposed, will someday be put in place in America."

Cole's revelation surprised Murphy. "Then why didn't you come out in support of me?"

"Because you're not interested in public safety," Cole said, with a hard edge in his voice. "Your only concern is advancing your political career."

"And what's wrong with that?" Murphy said with open disbelief.

At that moment, Sherman Edwards returned to the table followed closely by the plump waitress, who was carrying a tray containing a pair of large martinis garnished with four olives each.

"Well, well, well," Foghorn Leghorn boomed, "the great Larry Cole. I didn't think a guy like you would be caught dead in a dive like this."

"I go where the job demands, Alderman," Cole said.

Edwards returned to his seat, while the waitress busied herself serving them. She flashed Murphy a flirtatious smile, which revealed a gap between her front teeth. He slid further into the booth to put some distance between them.

Seeing that Cole had not moved, Edwards said, "Won't you join us?"

"I was just leaving. I'm sure I'll be seeing the two of you again." With that Cole turned and walked out of the Lake Shore Tap.

"What was that all about?" Edwards asked, picking up his martini and taking a healthy pull.

"Nothing," Murphy said. "Absolutely nothing."

The two elected officials consumed five rounds of double vodka martinis after Cole departed. Murphy unwound suffi-

ciently to begin viewing the fat waitress in a more complimentary light.

"I think I've reached my limit," Murphy said, chewing on
the last olive of his fifth martini. Despite the amount of alcohol
he'd consumed, Murphy appeared stone-cold sober. Edwards
was a different story. In a word, Foghorn Leghorn was blitzed.

"Let's have another one, Skipper boy." His phony down
home accent was slurred so badly it was nearly incomprehen-
sible.

"You've had enough, Sherm," Murphy scolded. "I'm going
to drive you to my place. You can spend the night if you like or
I'll put you in a cab, but you're not getting behind the wheel."

"That's bullshit, Skip." But Edwards was too drunk to
mount much of an argument.

The crack addict was in a bad way. He began using the cheap,
instantly addicting crystalline rocks when he was twelve years
old. He was now seventeen. He was underweight, had ulcera-
tions inside both nasal passages, and was going slowly blind
due to a poisonous additive that was being employed by a local
pusher to cook the drug.

As junkies go, this one was unremarkable in most aspects.
He had been born in a single-parent household in the depressed
Englewood neighborhood of Chicago. He possessed the equivalent of a third-grade education and had virtually no medical
care during the early years of his life, which led to him experiencing numerous physical problems. He stood five-foot-
seven-inches tall and had been victimized all of his life by
family members, gangbangers, and fellow addicts. He had been
sexually assaulted, beaten into a coma, and stabbed four times.
Then he bought a gun.

The weapon was a .25 caliber Browning blue steel semi-automatic pistol that could easily be mistaken for a toy. It carried a seven-round magazine and could be quite deadly at close range. The gun was the addict's most prized possession, because it was his principal source of income.

The crack addict had committed twenty-three armed robberies since obtaining the weapon. During the commission of these crimes, he shot nine people with six of them dying. Nineteen of his robberies were committed in Englewood, where he was known. The police had papered the area with wanted posters containing the junkie's most recent mugshot. This had forced him to flee the neighborhood, as every cop on the southwest side of the city was looking for him.

Escape was fairly easy, as all the addict had to do was hop an elevated train and travel into the more densely populated downtown area. There he roamed the streets mingling with the crowds ranging along the Magnificent Mile of North Michigan Avenue, State Street, and Lake Shore Drive. The pickings were better than they were in the depressed area he had run from. Within a period of nine hours he robbed a single-clerk jewelry store, a flower delivery van driver, a businessman on his lunch break in Olive Park, and a woman who was out walking her dog. Luckily there were no fatalities and all of the crimes were committed in the Eighteenth Police District. It soon became apparent that the same sickly looking male of small stature was responsible for this string of robberies. By nightfall every cop on the North Side was looking for him.

The addict made a connection with a street-corner pusher near the old Cabrini Green housing development. If a couple of gangbanger types hadn't been nearby serving as security for the dealer, the addict would have robbed the pusher.

After obtaining his fix, the addict wandered aimlessly in a drugged daze managing to avoid the police dragnet that had been cast for him. His robberies yielded over five hundred dollars, but the money didn't mean anything to him. Cash was simply a means to obtain drugs. The only food he had consumed that day was a hot dog purchased from a curbside vendor in front of the Water Tower on Michigan Avenue. As the night progressed, he snorted another crack rock from a soda can he heated with a disposable cigarette lighter in an alley. When he emerged from the alley, he saw two men come out of a bar and begin walking toward a Cadillac. One of the men was staggering and the other was holding him up. Reaching into his coat pocket the addict grasped the handle of his gun and went after them.

After leaving the Lake Shore Tap, Larry Cole met with Blackie Silvestri and Judy Daniels at the Area Three Police Center located at Belmont and Western. Judy, who had left Congressman Johnson and Stella Novak after the drug decriminalization rally concluded, had spent the day gathering information for Blackie about the serial killer that had been preying on school children in the Windy City. The CPD Detective Division was coordinating the efforts that had turned up four strong suspects in the ten slayings to date. These suspects consisted of a school principal, a grammar school math teacher, and two building custodians. In the past year, each of these men had been assigned to schools the murdered children had attended.

They met with the Area Three Detective Division watch commander in a second floor office. Cole and Blackie had not been in this facility since the day Cole had requested former Commander Richard Shelby to assign a detective to look into the disappearance of Stella Novak's sister. Recent events brought decade-old memories back to them. Judy, who was still clad in her disguise with the pomaded hair and tortoise-shell glasses, briefed the chief and her lieutenant on what had been uncovered about the serial killer to date.

"Each of the victims disappeared at a different time of day and from various locations to include their schools, nearby playgrounds, and while they were either en route to school or on their way home after school. Their bodies were always found in an isolated wooded area. We'll continue to keep an eye on all of the suspects until we can narrow the list down."

Cole looked to Blackie and the Area Three watch commander to see if they had anything to add. When they did not, he said, "Okay, stay on top of this until we get a break. Hopefully, it will be before any more children are killed."

Judy and Blackie left the police center with Cole. The Mistress of Disguise/High Priestess of Mayhem made an observation to her chief. "You seem a little preoccupied tonight, boss."

At the front door they stopped. With a sigh and a resigned shrug of his shoulders, Cole said, "I have to remember, Judy, that in this business we can't win them all."

With that the three cops headed home.

Skip Murphy didn't realize how drunk Sherman Edwards was. He was barely able to walk when they left the bar and exposure to the chilly fresh air of the March night only succeeded in worsening his condition. Murphy managed to get his city council colleague into the front seat of his Cadillac and belt him in with some difficulty before Edwards passed out.

Murphy closed the door and was about to go around and get in behind the wheel when he came face to face with the armed seventeen-year-old crack addict. The alderman looked from the young man's emaciated face and bloodshot eyes to the small rusty weapon in his hand. Perhaps it was the alcohol he had consumed or the political setbacks he'd recently suffered that made him fail to see the imminent danger he was in. Instead he viewed the junkie as representing an opportunity to resurrect his flagging drug decriminalization program. Murphy might yet be able to gain a strategic advantage over Congressman Walter Johnson.

Slowly, the alderman raised his hands and, keeping his voice low said, "You're in need of help. You have to get a fix. Your life is out of control and you don't know where to turn. At times you feel totally alone in the world. I can understand your predicament and I want to help you."

The addict stared quizzically at the well-dressed man, but didn't say anything. Taking this as a good sign, Murphy kept talking. "Our society has made you a victim and everyone, including your family and friends, has turned their backs on you."

A single tear escaped the addict's right eye and rolled down his cheek.

"If it's money that you want," Murphy said, "then it is money that I will give you. But I am prepared to do a great deal more. A great deal more indeed."

The Lake Shore Tap waitress who had served Murphy and Edwards martinis, happened to walk by the bar's front door. She looked outside and could see Murphy with his hands raised. She couldn't see the addict's weapon, but it was obvious that something was wrong. She ran to tell the bartender what was happening.

Cole was on Lake Shore Drive approaching North Avenue when the call of a robbery in progress outside the Lake Shore

Tap came over the police radio. He accelerated toward the location of the call.

"I don't know if you've ever heard of me," Murphy was saying, "but I'm the elected official who recommended that this country stop victimizing people like you by legalizing drugs and providing proper health care and training so that you can better your lot in life."

Now not only were tears streaming from both the addict's eyes, but his nose was running freely.

"I can see how emotional you have become, so if you'll just let me . . ." Murphy lowered his left hand and extended it to the addict.

The junkie pulled the trigger of the .25 caliber automatic. The small caliber bullet tore into Skip Murphy's abdomen.

When Larry Cole arrived back at the Lake Shore Tap, there were already two marked Eighteenth District units on the scene. The officers had arrived within seconds of the shooting, arrested the addict, and confiscated his weapon without difficulty. They were handcuffing the shooter when Cole pulled up next to Sherman Edwards's Cadillac. As the chief of detectives got out of his car, he saw Skip Murphy leaning against the side of the luxury car. One of the uniformed cops standing on the street informed Cole, "The alderman's been shot, boss. We've got a fire ambulance on the way with an ETA of three minutes."

"Where's the other alderman?"

The officer frowned. "There's a guy passed out drunk in the front seat of the Cadillac, but I didn't know that he was an alderman too. I recognized Murphy from all the publicity he's been getting about this crazy drug decriminalization thing he's been talking about."

"What was he shot with?" Cole asked.

The patrolman pulled the now unloaded, rusty .25 caliber automatic from his jacket pocket. Cole didn't touch the weapon, but noticed that the handle was chipped.

Then Cole went to check on Murphy.

The wounded man was leaning against the side of the car with an almost nonchalant attitude. His hands were crossed in front of his abdomen and Cole noticed a small amount of blood seeping from between his fingers. Other than that, Skip Murphy didn't appear to be injured at all.

"We've got an ambulance on the way for you, Alderman," Cole said. "Are you sure you don't want to sit down until it arrives?"

Murphy managed a weak laugh. "Nobody wants to listen to my drug decriminalization spiel anymore, Cole. I really thought I was getting through to that junkie who shot me. Hell, he would have benefited from what I've been trying to sell the people of this country."

Off in the distance the wail of an approaching siren became audible.

"You'll be at the hospital in a few minutes, Skip," Cole said.

"Yeah," Murphy's voice became raspy. "The news people are going to have a field day at my expense with this."

"But your being wounded will show how much we are all affected by drug-related violence," Cole said.

Murphy's expression brightened. "I never thought about it that way." With that the alderman collapsed onto the sidewalk. By the time the ambulance arrived on the street outside the Lake Shore Tap, Skip Murphy was dead.

EPILOGUE

10:02 A.M.

Alderman Phillip "Skip" Murphy, Jr. was given a state funeral, which was one of the grandest to ever take place in the Windy City. The funeral mass was celebrated at Holy Name Cathedral and the procession to the cemetery stretched for over two miles. Streets were blocked off and thousands of curious onlookers lined the route. Despite the perceived solemnity of the occasion, the atmosphere was festive for most of the participants as well as the spectators. The former champion of drug decriminalization's burial qualified as one of the social events of the year.

Murphy was eulogized by the mayor and Alderman Sherman Ellison Edwards, who became so emotional during the presentation that he couldn't finish his remarks. Although in attendance, Congressman Walter Johnson did not speak. A number of police officials, including the superintendent, were in attendance. Chief of Detectives Larry Cole was not.

As the funeral cortege wound south through the Chicago streets en route to Holy Sepulchre Cemetery, Cole entered the National Science and Space Museum at 5700 South Lake Shore Drive. After making inquiries at the lobby information desk, Cole proceeded to the assistant curator's office on the second floor. From there he was directed to the Heroes Past and Present exhibit, where Eurydice Vaughn was working.

It had been years since Cole had been in this particular section of the museum and, as was the case with the rest of this place, the policeman had less than fond memories of it. Eurydice was working in one of the display cases, which contained replicas of awards ranging from the batons of Roman generals to Super Bowl trophies. Her back was to Cole as he approached and she was unaware of his presence until he was standing within arm's length of her.

"Eurydice," he said, softly. He was shocked by her reaction.

The assistant curator was rearranging the items inside the exhibit case. She was replacing the replica of the Stanley Cup in its original place in the hockey section when Cole said her name. At the sound off his voice, she jumped and spun around so violently that she lost her balance and fell backwards into the display case. Her fall resulted in a chain reaction, which knocked over exhibit items from one end of the case to the other. She stared up at him with eyes gone bright with fear. When he extended his hand to help her up, she flinched and cringed away from him. Confused, he stepped back and watched her get to her feet on her own. She stepped out of the display case and once out on the gallery floor she averted her eyes. For just a brief moment he thought she was going to run. Although she did not attempt to flee, she did place more distance between them. He detected the fear causing her body to tremble from head to toe.

"What's the matter with you?" Cole demanded.

"There's nothing wrong with me," she snapped, still refusing to make eye contact with him. "You startled me, that's all."

They stood that way for another moment before he said, "The last time you called the office, Judy said that you sounded frightened."

Now Eurydice looked at him. "I called you over a week ago."

"And I've been busy," he said without contrition.

"Well, I'm just fine now so, if you don't mind, I've got a lot of work to do."

Cole stared at her a bit longer before turning around and saying over his shoulder as he walked away, "I'll see you around, Eurydice."

She did not take her eyes off him until he was out of sight.

JUNE 3, 2004
3:15 P.M.

Saint Stanislaus Catholic Church was in the Lake View area, where Stella Novak had lived for the entire time that she had been in the United States. On this sunny afternoon it was decorated for a wedding.

The interior of the church was designed in a decidedly European style. There were gold frescoes lining the walls and the altar was dominated by a life-sized statue of the crucified Christ.

For the occasion the parishioners had decorated the church with fresh flowers, crepe paper bunting and a red carpet in the center aisle. When the pastor, who had been born in Warsaw, saw how his church had been transformed, he muttered in awe, "Welcome to Heaven."

By the time the mid-afternoon wedding was scheduled to begin, the church was filled with guests attending the wedding of Dr. Stella Novak and Mr. Allen Rollins. The best man was mystery novelist Jamal Garth, the maid of honor was Chicago Police Sergeant Judy Daniels, and Chief of Detectives Larry Cole gave the bride away. Manny and Lauren Sherlock, Blackie and Maria Silvestri, and Barbara Zorin and her husband Anthony made up the rest of the wedding party.

After the ceremony a reception was held in the glass-enclosed hall adjacent to the church. It was a bright, sunny day with temperatures in the mid-eighties. As the champagne flowed, wedding cake was consumed and the bridal bouquet tossed to the single women in attendance, the sun cast an odd shadow through the west windows of the reception hall. Stella and Allen were posing for a picture with Larry Cole, Butch Cole, Kate Ford, and Judy Daniels in front of these windows. The professional photographer, whom Stella had hired to record the events on videotape and with still photos, noticed an odd refraction of light coming through the windows causing the bride's veil to cast a reflection that made it appear as if someone was standing behind her. Squinting through his lens, the photographer could have sworn there was a blond woman behind Stella Rollins. He adjusted his equipment, but the strange image remained. He would have reposed the shot, but that would be too much trouble. So he snapped the picture.

Two weeks later, after Stella and Allen returned from their honeymoon in Paris, the newlyweds examined the wedding pictures. When they came to the photo with the odd reflection, Allen heard his wife gasp.

"What is it, honey?" he asked, noticing tears beginning to flood her eyes.

She pointed at the photograph. Taking the eight-by-ten glossy, Allen was confused, as he could see nothing unusual there. Then he saw what appeared to be a blond woman standing behind Stella. Initially, he thought this to be no more than a double exposure. Then Stella said, "That's Sophie."

Allen looked back at the picture and it dawned on him that the image captured at their wedding bore an uncanny resemblance to earlier photos he had seen of his wife's dead sister. He suspected that there was some type of logical explanation for what they were seeing; however, the man who published adventure novels under the pseudonym Seth Champion doubted it. Cradling his wife in his arms, he continued to stare at the wedding photograph for a long time.

JUNE 5, 2004
9:15 A.M.

Represented by the flamboyant J. Ellis Montgomery, Solomon Randolph attended a preliminary hearing on the two counts of first-degree murder that he was charged with. The defendant appeared to be adapting well to the concrete and-steel zoo atmosphere of the Cook County Jail. Randolph's father had many contacts within the criminal element of the Windy City and while housed in the jail, Solomon had been protected. In fact, he had made a number of contacts on his own. Contacts that would serve him well on the day he was released from prison.

Standing at the defendant's table in the dated courtroom in the Criminal Courts building at Twenty-sixth and California in Chicago, Solomon Randolph was confident that the day would come when he would indeed get out of jail. This was due to J. Ellis Montgomery being just that good an attorney, which his enormous retainer attested to. And the distinguished African-American lawyer, with the penchant for wearing custom-tailored suits, matching pastel-colored shoes and socks, and natty straw hats, was pulling out all of the stops to get his client acquitted of the charges.

From the extensive psychological tests Solomon had been forced to take, all the way to making a series of motions to suppress all of the evidence collected by the police, Montgomery had not missed a legal trick. But his machinations went beyond the realm of the strictly legal. He was also secretly shopping for the right judge, who would be sympathetic to the plight of his reputedly psychologically impaired client. Such sympathy would of course come with a price tag, but then, "It ain't on the legit."

Solomon Randolph's formal trial would begin in mid-September and by then he would have the basic structure for a new master criminal plan in place. Larry Cole and the Chicago Police Department had not heard the last of him.

JUNE 10, 2004

3:14 P.M.

The slightly built, gray-haired custodian arranged all of the recently washed trash containers against the rear wall of the junior high school building. Removing a red-and-white patterned handkerchief from his back pocket, he mopped his forehead. He was through with all of his official duties for the day and he was efficient enough to have set up all of his cleaning equipment for tomorrow's workday. Retrieving a pair of hedge clippers from his workroom in the basement, he wandered around in front of the school.

The school day was ending and young students rushed out of the front entrance, down the stone steps and off down the street. The vast majority of these students ignored the nondescript little man in the gray work uniform. However, he was watching each of them very closely.

The initial rush ebbed in a matter of minutes with only the occasional straggler still in evidence. Now the custodian became more alert and actually assumed the instincts and heightened physical faculties of a wild beast. He was certain that his senses of smell, hearing, and sight had become enhanced, and he could feel blood pounding through his body with each heartbeat.

The custodian ambled slowly in front of the building, clipping an errant branch from hedges surrounding the structure. The hunt he was engaged in was a random operation, which at times yielded prey. On most such predatory outings, he came up empty. That was acceptable, because the act of locating and tracking his victims was as enjoyable as the capture and what followed that capture.

The last students, three young boys, trotted off down the street toward a nearby commercial area, where a video arcade, pizzeria, hot dog stand, and McDonald's was located. This area would be teeming with potential victims, but it would be too dangerous for him to go hunting there because there would also be a great many potential witnesses present. He was about to give up for today when the girl came out of the front entrance.

She was dressed in a red plaid jumper, blue short-sleeved blouse, white anklet socks, and black-and-white saddle shoes.

Her dark hair was swept back into a braid that hung to her shoulders; she wore wire-frame glasses, and carried a book bag adorned with the Spice Girls logo. Her bare legs were muscular and the outline of her breasts was visible, indicating that she was maturing early. He estimated that she could be anywhere from eleven to fourteen years of age; however, he had been wrong before. The custodian had estimated the age of his last victim at twelve. After her body was discovered, the news reports had stated that she had been nine.

The custodian did not look directly at the girl, but watched her out of the corner of his eye as she bounced past him. His senses had now become so acute that he could detect the mixed aroma of talcum powder and bubble gum emanating from her. His nostrils flared and his eyes bulged from their sockets. This one he had to have.

He became intensely excited when she turned in the opposite direction from the commercial area, where most of the other students had gone. She was headed toward the park located a block away from the school. He had never attacked any of his victims there, which made it virgin territory for him. Unable to control himself, he tossed the gardening shears behind a hedge, checked to make sure there were no prying eyes to observe him, and followed the girl.

She moved along at a jaunty pace, but did not rush. There were people along the route, but they were some distance away from the custodian and his intended victim. This would make later positive identification of predator and prey impossible. The custodian had also learned to cover his physical tracks from forensic evidence gatherers. Before he sexually assaulted his victims, he covered his hands, head, and genitals with cellophane. Then he carefully scrubbed and hosed down the bodies before wrapping the corpses in canvas tarpaulin and then dumping them at an isolated location. There had been no detectable physical evidence left behind in any of the previous crimes to lead the police back to him. The custodian realized that the only way they would ever get him was to catch him in the act and he sincerely believed he was too smart for that to happen.

The girl reached the park and turned to enter the walkway that would take her into a densely wooded area, which had become overgrown with untended weeds and bushes. This was perfect.

Despite his relatively small stature, years of physical labor had made him exceptionally strong. He also had a great deal of experience and this girl would be his fifty-eighth victim. As they advanced further into the park, he planned his attack. He would rush her, wrap his left forearm around her throat, and squeeze hard enough to cut off any screams. Before pulling her into the bushes, he would hit her over the head. The handle of the hammer he carried in a tool-kit holster on his belt would do the job. It would be over quickly. Then he would stash the bound body while he went back for his 1987 four-door Chevy. The trunk of his car was lined with a plastic drop cloth that he would dispose of at a separate location from the girl's body. He was now ready to go on the attack.

Then something began bothering him. This was too easy. Where was she going? There was nothing out in the park but dense trees and there were no activities anywhere nearby. He slowed his pace and his intended victim began putting some distance between them.

The wind shifted and he again caught her scent, which wiped out any vestiges of logical thought from his mind. She

HUGH HOLTON

was no more than a stupid little bitch, who was in the wrong
place at the wrong time and for that he was going to make her
suffer. Grasping the handle of his hammer, the custodian quick-
ened his pace.

He closed to within three feet and was raising his hammer
to strike her in the back of the head when she spun around to
face him. He froze in his tracks and all of the color drained
from his face making his usually pale complexion take on a
chalk-white hue. The girl he intended to kidnap, rape, and kill
was pointing a two-inch barrel, nickel-plated, .38 caliber Colt
Detective Special at him. In a microsecond of denial, the custodian attempted to rationalize that the shiny gun wasn't real.
But he was close enough to see the deadly openings of the
steel-jacketed bullets in the revolver's chamber. Then he attempted to convince himself that his young intended victim
would never pull the trigger. However, she held the gun dead
steady and, as if she was reading his mind, said, "If you so
much as twitch, I'll blow your head off." To punctuate her
statement, she cocked the gun.

With the desperate sinking feeling of the trapped animal,
the serial-killing school custodian realized at once that he was
in a great deal of trouble and that his intended victim was not
a child.

"I've got him, boss," Judy Daniels said into the miniature microphone concealed in the inexpensive-appearing ballpoint pen
in the pocket of her red jumper.

Within a matter of seconds eight cops, five in uniform and
three in civilian dress, came running down the isolated patch
in the park where the school custodian had planned to claim
another in his long list of victims. Blackie Silvestri and Manny

Sherlock frisked the custodian before snapping handcuffs on his wrists. Then he was spun around to face Larry Cole, whose cold gaze made the serial killer flinch.

"Dwight Frazier," the chief of detectives said, "you are under arrest for murder."

Despite his predicament, the serial killer managed a smile and replied defiantly, "What took you so long to catch me, Cole?"

Then the cops led the killer away, experiencing the grim satisfaction that they had removed another member of the criminal element from the streets of Chicago.